The Four Horsemen of the Apocalypse

by

Vicente Blasco Ibanez

The Echo Library 2006

Published by

The Echo Library

Echo Library
131 High St.
Teddington
Middlesex TW11 8HH

www.echo-library.com

Please report serious faults in the text to complaints@echo-library.com

ISBN 1-84702-700-8

THE FOUR HORSEMEN OF THE APOCALYPSE

(Los Cuatro Jinettes del Apocalipsis)

by Vicente Blasco Ibanez

Translated by Charlotte Brewster Jordan

4

CONTENTS

PART I

PART II

PART III

PART I

CHAPTER I

THE TRYST

(In the Garden of the Chapelle Expiatoire)

They were to have met in the garden of the Chapelle Expiatoire at five o'clock in the afternoon, but Julio Desnoyers with the impatience of a lover who hopes to advance the moment of meeting by presenting himself before the appointed time, arrived an half hour earlier. The change of the seasons was at this time greatly confused in his mind, and evidently demanded some readjustment.

Five months had passed since their last interview in this square had afforded the wandering lovers the refuge of a damp, depressing calmness near a boulevard of continual movement close to a great railroad station. The hour of the appointment was always five and Julio was accustomed to see his beloved approaching by the reflection of the recently lit street lamps, her figure enveloped in furs, and holding her muff before her face as if it were a half-mask. Her sweet voice, greeting him, had breathed forth a cloud of vapor, white and tenuous, congealed by the cold. After various hesitating interviews, they had abandoned the garden. Their love had acquired the majestic importance of acknowledged fact, and from five to seven had taken refuge in the fifth floor of the rue de la Pompe where Julio had an artist's studio. The curtains well drawn over the double glass windows, the cosy hearth-fire sending forth its ruddy flame as the only light of the room, the monotonous song of the samovar bubbling near the cups of tea—all the seclusion of life isolated by an idolizing love—had dulled their perceptions to the fact that the afternoons were growing longer, that outside the sun was shining later and later into the pearl-covered depths of the clouds, and that a timid and pallid Spring was beginning to show its green finger tips in the buds of the branches suffering the last nips of Winter—that wild, black boar who so often turned on his tracks.

Then Julio had made his trip to Buenos Aires, encountering in the other hemisphere the last smile of Autumn and the first icy winds from the pampas. And just as his mind was becoming reconciled to the fact that for him Winter was an eternal season—since it always came to meet him in his change of domicile from one extreme of the planet to the other—lo, Summer was unexpectedly confronting him in this dreary garden!

A swarm of children was racing and screaming through the short avenues around the monument. On entering the place, the first thing that Julio encountered was a hoop which came rolling toward his legs, trundled by a childish hand. Then he stumbled over a ball. Around the chestnut trees was gathering the usual warm-weather crowd, seeking the blue shade perforated with points of light. Many nurse-maids from the neighboring houses were working and chattering here, following with indifferent glances the rough games of the children confided to their care. Near them were the men who had brought their papers down into the garden under the impression that they could read them in the midst of peaceful groves. All of the benches were full. A few women were occupying camp stools with that feeling of superiority which ownership always confers. The iron chairs, "pay-seats," were serving as resting places for various suburban dames, loaded down with packages, who were waiting for straggling members of their families in order to take the train in the Gare Saint Lazare. . . .

And Julio, in his special delivery letter, had proposed meeting in this place, supposing that it would be as little frequented as in former times. She, too, with the same thoughtlessness, had in her reply, set the usual hour of five o'clock, believing that after passing a few minutes in the Printemps or the Galeries on the pretext of shopping, she would be able to slip over to the unfrequented garden without risk of being seen by any of her numerous acquaintances.

Desnoyers was enjoying an almost forgotten sensation, that of strolling through vast spaces, crushing as he walked the grains of sand under his feet. For the past twenty days his rovings had been upon planks, following with the automatic precision of a riding school the oval promenade on the deck of a ship. His feet accustomed to insecure ground, still were keeping on terra firma a certain sensation of elastic unsteadiness. His goings and comings were not awakening the curiosity of the people seated in the open, for a common preoccupation seemed to be monopolizing all the men and women. The groups were exchanging impressions. Those who happened to have a paper in their hands, saw their neighbors approaching them with a smile of interrogation. There had suddenly disappeared that distrust and suspicion which impels the inhabitants of large cities mutually to ignore one another, taking each other's measure at a glance as though they were enemies.

"They are talking about the war," said Desnoyers to himself. "At this time, all Paris speaks of nothing but the possibility of war."

Outside of the garden he could see also the same anxiety which was making those around him so fraternal and sociable. The venders of newspapers were passing through the boulevard crying the evening editions, their furious speed repeatedly slackened by the eager hands of the passers-by contending for the papers. Every reader was instantly surrounded by a group begging for news or trying to decipher over his shoulder the great headlines at the top of the sheet. In the rue des Mathurins, on the other side of the square, a circle of workmen under the awning of a tavern were listening to the comments of a friend who accompanied his words with oratorical gestures and wavings of the paper. The traffic in the streets, the general bustle of the city was the same as in other days, but it seemed to Julio that the vehicles were whirling past more rapidly, that there was a feverish agitation in the air and that people were speaking and smiling in a different way. The women of the garden were looking even at him as if they had seen him in former days. He was able to approach them and begin a conversation without experiencing the slightest strangeness.

"They are talking of the war," he said again but with the commiseration of a superior intelligence which foresees the future and feels above the impressions of the vulgar crowd.

He knew exactly what course he was going to follow. He had disembarked at ten o'clock the night before, and as it was not yet twenty-four hours since he had touched land, his mentality was still that of a man who comes from afar, across oceanic immensities, from boundless horizons, and is surprised at finding himself in touch with the preoccupations which govern human communities. After disembarking he had spent two hours in a cafe in Boulogne, listlessly watching the middle-class families who passed their time in the monotonous placidity of a life without dangers. Then the special train for the passengers from South America had brought him to Paris, leaving him at four in the morning on a platform of the Gare du Nord in the embrace of Pepe Argensola, the young Spaniard whom he sometimes called "my secretary" or "my valet" because it was difficult to define exactly the relationship between them. In reality, he was a mixture of friend and parasite, the poor comrade, complacent and capable in his companionship with a rich youth on bad terms with his family, sharing with him the ups and downs of fortune, picking up the crumbs of prosperous days, or inventing expedients to keep up appearances in the hours of poverty.

"What about the war?" Argensola had asked him before inquiring about the result of his trip. "You have come a long ways and should know much."

Soon he was sound asleep in his dear old bed while his "secretary" was pacing up and down the studio talking of Servia, Russia and the Kaiser. This youth, too, skeptical as he generally was about everything not connected with his own interests, appeared infected by the general excitement.

When Desnoyers awoke he found her note awaiting him, setting their meeting at five that afternoon and also containing a few words about the threatened danger which was claiming the attention of all Paris. Upon going out in search of lunch the concierge, on the pretext of welcoming him back, had asked him the war news. And in the restaurant, the cafe and the street, always war . . . the possibility of war with Germany. . . .

Julio was an optimist. What did all this restlessness signify to a man who had just been living more than twenty days among Germans, crossing the Atlantic under the flag of the Empire?

He had sailed from Buenos Aires in a steamer of the Hamburg line, the Koenig Frederic August. The world was in blessed tranquillity when the boat left port. Only the whites and half-breeds of Mexico were exterminating each other in conflicts in order that nobody might believe that man is an animal degenerated by peace. On the rest of the planet, the people were displaying unusual prudence. Even aboard the transatlantic liner, the little world of passengers of most diverse nationalities appeared a fragment of future society implanted by way of experiment in modern times—a sketch of the hereafter, without frontiers or race antagonisms.

One morning the ship band which every Sunday had sounded the Choral of Luther, awoke those sleeping in the first-class cabins with the most unheard-of serenade. Desnoyers rubbed his eyes believing himself under the hallucinations of a dream. The German horns were playing the Marseillaise through the corridors and decks. The steward, smiling at his astonishment, said, "The fourteenth of July!" On the German steamers they celebrate as their own the great festivals of all the nations represented by their cargo and passengers. Their captains are careful to observe scrupulously the rites of this religion of the flag and its historic commemoration. The most insignificant republic saw the ship decked in its honor, affording one more diversion to help combat the monotony of the voyage and further the lofty ends of the Germanic propaganda. For the first time the great festival of France was being celebrated on a German vessel, and whilst the musicians continued escorting a racy Marseillaise in double quick time through the different floors, the morning groups were commenting on the event.

"What finesse!" exclaimed the South American ladies. "These Germans are not so phlegmatic as they seem. It is an attention . . . something very distinguished. . . . And is it possible that some still believe that they and the French might come to blows?"

The very few Frenchmen who were travelling on the steamer found themselves admired as though they had increased immeasurably in public esteem. There were only three;—an old jeweller who had been visiting his branch shops in America, and two demi-mondaines from the rue de la Paix, the most timid and well-behaved persons aboard, vestals with bright eyes and disdainful noses who held themselves stiffly aloof in this uncongenial atmosphere.

At night there was a gala banquet in the dining room at the end of which the French flag and that of the Empire formed a flaunting, conspicuous drapery. All the German passengers were in dress suits, and their wives were wearing low-necked gowns. The uniforms of the attendants were as resplendent as on a day of a grand review.

During dessert the tapping of a knife upon a glass reduced the table to sudden silence. The Commandant was going to speak. And this brave mariner who united to his nautical functions the obligation of making harangues at banquets and opening the dance with the lady of most importance, began unrolling a string of words like the noise of clappers between long intervals of silence. Desnoyers knew a little German as a souvenir of a visit to some relatives in Berlin, and so was able to catch a few words. The Commandant was repeating every few minutes "peace" and "friends." A table neighbor, a commercial commissioner, offered his services as interpreter to Julio, with that obsequiousness which lives on advertisement.

"The Commandant asks God to maintain peace between Germany and France and hopes that the two peoples will become increasingly friendly."

Another orator arose at the same table. He was the most influential of the German passengers, a rich manufacturer from Dusseldorf who had just been visiting his agents in America. He was never mentioned by name. He bore the title of Commercial Counsellor, and among his countrymen was always Herr

Comerzienrath and his wife was entitled Frau Rath. The Counsellor's Lady, much younger than her important husband, had from the first attracted the attention of Desnoyers. She, too, had made an exception in favor of this young Argentinian, abdicating her title from their first conversation. "Call me Bertha," she said as condescendingly as a duchess of Versailles might have spoken to a handsome abbot seated at her feet. Her husband, also protested upon hearing Desnoyers call him "Counsellor," like his compatriots.

"My friends," he said, "call me 'Captain.' I command a company of the Landsturm." And the air with which the manufacturer accompanied these words, revealed the melancholy of an unappreciated man scorning the honors he has in order to think only of those he does not possess.

While he was delivering his discourse, Julio was examining his small head and thick neck which gave him a certain resemblance to a bull dog. In imagination he saw the high and oppressive collar of a uniform making a double roll of fat above its stiff edge. The waxed, upright moustaches were bristling aggressively. His voice was sharp and dry as though he were shaking out his words. . . . Thus the Emperor would utter his harangues, so the martial burgher, with instinctive imitation, was contracting his left arm, supporting his hand upon the hilt of an invisible sword.

In spite of his fierce and oratorical gesture of command, all the listening Germans laughed uproariously at his first words, like men who knew how to appreciate the sacrifice of a Herr Comerzienrath when he deigns to divert a festivity.

"He is saying very witty things about the French," volunteered the interpreter in a low voice, "but they are not offensive."

Julio had guessed as much upon hearing repeatedly the word Franzosen. He almost understood what the orator was saying—"Franzosen—great children, light-hearted, amusing, improvident. The things that they might do together if they would only forget past grudges!" The attentive Germans were no longer laughing. The Counsellor was laying aside his irony, that grandiloquent, crushing irony, weighing many tons, as enormous as a ship. Then he began unrolling the serious part of his harangue, so that he himself, was also greatly affected.

"He says, sir," reported Julio's neighbor, "that he wishes France to become a very great nation so that some day we may march together against other enemies . . . against OTHERS!"

And he winked one eye, smiling maliciously with that smile of common intelligence which this allusion to the mysterious enemy always awakened.

Finally the Captain-Counsellor raised his glass in a toast to France. "Hoch!" he yelled as though he were commanding an evolution of his soldierly Reserves. Three times he sounded the cry and all the German contingent springing to their feet, responded with a lusty Hoch while the band in the corridor blared forth the Marseillaise.

Desnoyers was greatly moved. Thrills of enthusiasm were coursing up and down his spine. His eyes became so moist that, when drinking his champagne, he almost believed that he had swallowed some tears. He bore a French name.

He had French blood in his veins, and this that the gringoes were doing—although generally they seemed to him ridiculous and ordinary—was really worth acknowledging. The subjects of the Kaiser celebrating the great date of the Revolution! He believed that he was witnessing a great historic event.

"Very well done!" he said to the other South Americans at the near tables. "We must admit that they have done the handsome thing."

Then with the vehemence of his twenty-seven years, he accosted the jeweller in the passage way, reproaching him for his silence. He was the only French citizen aboard. He should have made a few words of acknowledgment. The fiesta was ending awkwardly through his fault.

"And why have you not spoken as a son of France?" retorted the jeweller.

"I am an Argentinian citizen," replied Julio.

And he left the older man believing that he ought to have spoken and making explanations to those around him. It was a very dangerous thing, he protested, to meddle in diplomatic affairs. Furthermore, he had not instructions from his government. And for a few hours he believed that he had been on the point of playing a great role in history.

Desnoyers passed the rest of the evening in the smoking room attracted thither by the presence of the Counsellor's Lady. The Captain of the Landsturm, sticking a preposterous cigar between his moustachios, was playing poker with his countrymen ranking next to him in dignity and riches. His wife stayed beside him most of the time, watching the goings and comings of the stewards carrying great bocks, without daring to share in this tremendous consumption of beer. Her special preoccupation was to keep vacant near her a seat which Desnoyers might occupy. She considered him the most distinguished man on board because he was accustomed to taking champagne with all his meals. He was of medium height, a decided brunette, with a small foot, which obliged her to tuck hers under her skirts, and a triangular face under two masses of hair, straight, black and glossy as lacquer, the very opposite of the type of men about her. Besides, he was living in Paris, in the city which she had never seen after numerous trips in both hemispheres.

"Oh, Paris! Paris!" she sighed, opening her eyes and pursing her lips in order to express her admiration when she was speaking alone to the Argentinian. "How I should love to go there!"

And in order that he might feel free to tell her things about Paris, she permitted herself certain confidences about the pleasures of Berlin, but with a blushing modesty, admitting in advance that in the world there was more—much more—that she wished to become acquainted with.

While pacing around the Chapelle Expiatoire, Julio recalled with a certain remorse the wife of Counsellor Erckmann. He who had made the trip to America for a woman's sake, in order to collect money and marry her! Then he immediately began making excuses for his conduct. Nobody was going to know. Furthermore he did not pretend to be an ascetic, and Bertha Erckmann was certainly a tempting adventure in mid ocean. Upon recalling her, his imagination always saw a race horse—large, spare, roan colored, and with a long stride. She was an up-to-date German who admitted no defect in her country except the excessive weight of its women, combating in her person this national menace with every known system of dieting. For her every meal was a species of torment, and the procession of bocks in the smoking room a tantalizing agony. The slenderness achieved and maintained by will power only made more prominent the size of her frame, the powerful skeleton with heavy jaws and large teeth, strong and dazzling, which perhaps suggested Desnoyers' disrespectful comparison. "She is thin, but enormous, nevertheless!" was always his conclusion.

But then, he considered her, notwithstanding, the most distinguished woman on board—distinguished for the sea—elegant in the style of Munich, with clothes of indescribable colors that suggested Persian art and the vignettes of mediaeval manuscripts. The husband admired Bertha's elegance, lamenting her childlessness in secret, almost as though it were a crime of high treason. Germany was magnificent because of the fertility of its women. The Kaiser, with his artistic hyperbole, had proclaimed that the true German beauty should have a waist measure of at least a yard and a half.

When Desnoyers entered into the smoking room in order to take the seat which Bertha had reserved for him, her husband and his wealthy hangers-on had their pack of cards lying idle upon the green felt. Herr Rath was continuing his discourse and his listeners, taking their cigars from their mouths, were emitting grunts of approbation. The arrival of Julio provoked a general smile of amiability. Here was France coming to fraternize with them. They knew that his father was French, and that fact made him as welcome as though he came in direct line from the palace of the Quai d'Orsay, representing the highest diplomacy of the Republic. The craze for proselyting made them all promptly concede to him unlimited importance.

"We," continued the Counsellor looking fixedly at Desnoyers as if he were expecting a solemn declaration from him, "we wish to live on good terms with France."

The youth nodded his head so as not to appear inattentive. It appeared to him a very good thing that these peoples should not be enemies, and as far as he was concerned, they might affirm this relationship as often as they wished: the only thing that was interesting him just at that time was a certain knee that was seeking his under the table, transmitting its gentle warmth through a double curtain of silk.

"But France," complained the manufacturer, "is most unresponsive towards us. For many years past, our Emperor has been holding out his hand with noble loyalty, but she pretends not to see it. . . . That, you must admit, is not as it should be."

Just here Desnoyers believed that he ought to say something in order that the spokesman might not divine his more engrossing occupation.

"Perhaps you are not doing enough. If, first of all, you would return that which you took away from France!" . . .

Stupefied silence followed this remark, as if the alarm signal had sounded through the boat. Some of those who were about putting their cigars in their mouths, remained with hands immovable within two inches of their lips, their eyes almost popping out of their heads. But the Captain of the Landsturm was there to formulate their mute protest.

"Return!" he said in a voice almost extinguished by the sudden swelling of his neck. "We have nothing to return, for we have taken nothing. That which we possess, we acquire by our heroism."

The hidden knee with its agreeable friction made itself more insinuating, as though counselling the youth to greater prudence.

"Do not say such things," breathed Bertha, "thus only the republicans, corrupted by Paris, talk. A youth so distinguished who has been in Berlin, and has relatives in Germany!" . . .

But Desnoyers felt a hereditary impulse of aggressiveness before each of her husband's statements, enunciated in haughty tones, and responded coldly:—

"It is as if I should take your watch and then propose that we should be friends, forgetting the occurrence. Although you might forget, the first thing for me to do would be to return the watch."

Counsellor Erckmann wished to retort with so many things at once that he stuttered horribly, leaping from one idea to the other. To compare the reconquest of Alsace to a robbery. A German country! The race . . . the language . . . the history! . . .

"But when did they announce their wish to be German?" asked the youth without losing his calmness. "When have you consulted their opinion?"

The Counsellor hesitated, not knowing whether to argue with this insolent fellow or crush him with his scorn.

"Young man, you do not know what you are talking about," he finally blustered with withering contempt. "You are an Argentinian and do not understand the affairs of Europe."

And the others agreed, suddenly repudiating the citizenship which they had attributed to him a little while before. The Counsellor, with military rudeness, brusquely turned his back upon him, and taking up the pack, distributed the cards. The game was renewed. Desnoyers, seeing himself isolated by the scornful silence, felt greatly tempted to break up the playing by violence; but the hidden knee continued counselling self-control, and an invisible hand had sought his right, pressing it sweetly. That was enough to make him recover his serenity. The Counsellor's Lady seemed to be absorbed in the progress of the game. He also looked on, a malignant smile contracting slightly the lines of his mouth as he was mentally ejaculating by way of consolation, "Captain, Captain! . . . You little know what is awaiting you!"

On terra firma, he would never again have approached these men; but life on a transatlantic liner, with its inevitable promiscuousness, obliges forgetfulness. The following day the Counsellor and his friends came in search of him, flattering his sensibilities by erasing every irritating memory. He was a distinguished youth belonging to a wealthy family, and all of them had shops and business in his country. The only thing was that he should be careful not to mention his French origin. He was an Argentinian; and thereupon, the entire chorus interested itself in the grandeur of his country and all the nations of South America where they had agencies or investments—exaggerating its importance as though its petty republics were great powers, commenting with gravity upon the deeds and words of its political leaders and giving him to understand that in Germany there was no one who was not concerned about the future of South America, predicting for all its divisions most glorious prosperity—a reflex of the Empire, always, provided, of course, that they kept under Germanic influence.

In spite of these flatteries, Desnoyers was no longer presenting himself with his former assiduity at the hour of poker. The Counsellor's wife was retiring to her stateroom earlier than usual—their approach to the Equator inducing such an irresistible desire for sleep, that she had to abandon her husband to his card playing. Julio also had mysterious occupations which prevented his appearance on deck until after midnight. With the precipitation of a man who desires to be seen in order to avoid suspicion, he was accustomed to enter the smoking room talking loudly as he seated himself near the husband and his boon companions.

The game had ended, and an orgy of beer and fat cigars from Hamburg was celebrating the success of the winners. It was the hour of Teutonic expansion, of intimacy among men, of heavy, sluggish jokes, of off-color stories. The Counsellor was presiding with much majesty over the diableries of his chums, prudent business men from the Hanseatic ports who had big accounts in the Deutsche Bank or were shopkeepers installed in the republic of the La Plata, with an innumerable family. He was a warrior, a captain, and on applauding every heavy jest with a laugh that distended his fat neck, he fancied that he was among his comrades at arms.

In honor of the South Americans who, tired of pacing the deck, had dropped in to hear what the gringoes were saying, they were turning into Spanish the witticisms and licentious anecdotes awakened in the memory by a superabundance of beer. Julio was marvelling at the ready laugh of all these men. While the foreigners were remaining unmoved, they would break forth into loud horse-laughs throwing themselves back in their seats. And when the German audience was growing cold, the story-teller would resort to an infallible expedient to remedy his lack of success:—

"They told this yarn to the Kaiser, and when the Kaiser heard it he laughed heartily."

It was not necessary to say more. They all laughed then. Ha, ha, ha! with a spontaneous roar but a short one, a laugh in three blows, since to prolong it, might be interpreted as a lack of respect to His Majesty.

As they neared Europe, a batch of news came to meet the boat. The employees in the wireless telegraphy office were working incessantly. One night, on entering the smoking room, Desnoyers saw the German notables gesticulating with animated countenances. They were no longer drinking beer. They had had bottles of champagne uncorked, and the Counsellor's Lady, much impressed, had not retired to her stateroom. Captain Erckmann, spying the young Argentinian, offered him a glass.

"It is war," he shouted with enthusiasm. "War at last. . . . The hour has come!"

Desnoyers made a gesture of astonishment. War! . . . What war? . . . Like all the others, he had read on the news bulletin outside a radiogram stating that the Austrian government had just sent an ultimatum to Servia; but it made not the slightest impression on him, for he was not at all interested in the Balkan affairs. Those were but the quarrels of a miserable little nation monopolizing the attention of the world, distracting it from more worthwhile matters. How could this event concern the martial Counsellor? The two nations would soon come to an understanding. Diplomacy sometimes amounted to something.

"No," insisted the German ferociously. "It is war, blessed war. Russia will sustain Servia, and we will support our ally. . . . What will France do? Do you know what France will do?" . . .

Julio shrugged his shoulders testily as though asking to be left out of all international discussions.

"It is war," asserted the Counsellor, "the preventive war that we need. Russia is growing too fast, and is preparing to fight us. Four years more of peace and she will have finished her strategic railroads, and her military power, united to that of her allies, will be worth as much as ours. It is better to strike a powerful blow now. It is necessary to take advantage of this opportunity. . . . War. Preventive war!"

All his clan were listening in silence. Some did not appear to feel the contagion of his enthusiasm. War! . . . In imagination they saw their business paralyzed, their agencies bankrupt, the banks cutting down credit . . . a catastrophe more frightful to them than the slaughters of battles. But they applauded with nods and grunts all of Erckmann's ferocious demonstrations. He was a Herr Rath, and an officer besides. He must be in the secrets of the destiny of his country, and that was enough to make them drink silently to the success of the war.

Julio thought that the Counsellor and his admirers must be drunk. "Look here, Captain," he said in a conciliatory tone, "what you say lacks logic. How could war possibly be acceptable to industrial Germany? Every moment its business is increasing, every month it conquers a new market and every year its commercial balance soars upward in unheard of proportions. Sixty years ago, it had to man its boats with Berlin hack drivers arrested by the police. Now its commercial fleets and war vessels cross all oceans, and there is no port where the German merchant marine does not occupy the greatest part of the docks. It would only be necessary to continue living in this way, to put yourselves beyond the exigencies of war! Twenty years more of peace, and the Germans would be lords of the world's commerce, conquering England, the former mistress of the seas, in a bloodless struggle. And are they going to risk all this—like a gambler who stakes his entire fortune on a single card—in a struggle that might result unfavorably?" . . .

"No, war," insisted the Counsellor furiously, "preventive war. We live surrounded by our enemies, and this state of things cannot go on. It is best to end it at once. Either they or we! Germany feels herself strong enough to challenge the world. We've got to put an end to this Russian menace! And if France doesn't keep herself quiet, so much the worse for her! . . . And if anyone else . . . ANYONE dares to come in against us, so much the worse for him! When I set up a new machine in my shops, it is to make it produce unceasingly. We possess the finest army in the world, and it is necessary to give it exercise that it may not rust out."

He then continued with heavy emphasis, "They have put a band of iron around us in order to throttle us. But Germany has a strong chest and has only to expand in order to burst its bands. We must awake before they manacle us in our sleep. Woe to those who then oppose us! . . ."

Desnoyers felt obliged to reply to this arrogance. He had never seen the iron circle of which the Germans were complaining. The nations were merely unwilling to continue living, unsuspecting and inactive, before boundless German ambition. They were simply preparing to defend themselves against an almost certain attack. They wished to maintain their dignity, repeatedly violated under most absurd pretexts.

"I wonder if it is not the others," he concluded, "who are obliged to defend themselves because you represent a menace to the world!"

An invisible hand sought his under the table, as it had some nights before, to recommend prudence; but now he clasped it forcibly with the authority of a right acquired.

"Oh, sir!" sighed the sweet Bertha, "to talk like that, a youth so distinguished who has . . ."

She was not able to finish, for her husband interrupted. They were no longer in American waters, and the Counsellor expressed himself with the rudeness of a master of his house.

"I have the honor to inform you, young man," he said, imitating the cutting coldness of the diplomats, "that you are merely a South American and know nothing of the affairs of Europe."

He did not call him an "Indian," but Julio heard the implication as though he had used the word itself. Ah, if that hidden handclasp had not held him with its sentimental thrills! . . . But this contact kept him calm and even made him smile. "Thanks, Captain," he said to himself. "It is the least you can do to get even with me!"

Here his relations with the German and his clientele came to an end. The merchants, as they approached nearer and nearer to their native land, began casting off that servile desire of ingratiating themselves which they had assumed in all their trips to the new world. They now had more important things to occupy them. The telegraphic service was working without cessation. The Commandant of the vessel was conferring in his apartment with the Counsellor as his compatriot of most importance. His friends were hunting out the most obscure places in order to talk confidentially with one another. Even Bertha commenced to avoid Desnoyers. She was still smiling distantly at him, but that smile was more of a souvenir than a reality.

Between Lisbon and the coast of England, Julio spoke with her husband for the last time. Every morning was appearing on the bulletin board the alarming news transmitted by radiograph. The Empire was arming itself against its enemies. God would punish them, making all manner of troubles fall upon them. Desnoyers was motionless with astonishment before the last piece of news—"Three hundred thousand revolutionists are now besieging Paris. The suburbs are beginning to burn. The horrors of the Commune have broken out again."

"My, but these Germans have gone mad!" exclaimed the disgusted youth to the curious group surrounding the radio-sheet. "We are going to lose the little sense that we have left! . . . What revolutionists are they talking about? How could a revolution break out in Paris if the men of the government are not reactionary?"

A gruff voice sounded behind him, rude, authoritative, as if trying to banish the doubts of the audience. It was the Herr Comerzienrath who was speaking.

"Young man, these notices are sent us by the first agencies of Germany . . . and Germany never lies."

After this affirmation, he turned his back upon them and they saw him no more.

On the following morning, the last day of the voyage. Desnoyers' steward awoke him in great excitement. "Herr, come up on deck! a most beautiful spectacle!"

The sea was veiled by the fog, but behind its hazy curtains could be distinguished some silhouettes like islands with great towers and sharp, pointed minarets. The islands were advancing over the oily waters slowly and majestically, with impressive dignity. Julio counted eighteen. They appeared to fill the ocean. It was the Channel Fleet which had just left the English coast by Government order, sailing around simply to show its strength. Seeing this procession of dreadnoughts for the first time, Desnoyers was reminded of a flock of marine monsters, and gained a better idea of the British power. The German ship passed among them, shrinking, humiliated, quickening its speed. "One might suppose," mused the youth, "that she had an uneasy conscience and wished to scud to safety." A South American passenger near him was jesting with one of the Germans, "What if they have already declared war! . . . What if they should make us prisoners!"

After midday, they entered Southampton roads. The Frederic August hurried to get away as soon as possible, and transacted business with dizzying celerity. The cargo of passengers and baggage was enormous. Two launches approached the transatlantic and discharged an avalanche of Germans residents in England who invaded the decks with the joy of those who tread friendly soil, desiring to see Hamburg as soon as possible. Then the boat sailed through the Channel with a speed most unusual in these places.

The people, leaning on the railing, were commenting on the extraordinary encounters in this marine boulevard, usually frequented by ships of peace. Certain smoke lines on the horizon were from the French squadron carrying President Poincare who was returning from Russia. The European alarm had interrupted his trip. Then they saw more English vessels patrolling the coast line like aggressive and vigilant dogs. Two North American battleships could be distinguished by their mast-heads in the form of baskets. Then a Russian battleship, white and glistening, passed at full steam on its way to the Baltic. "Bad!" said the South American passengers regretfully. "Very bad! It looks this time as if it were going to be serious!" and they glanced uneasily at the neighboring coasts on both sides. Although they presented the usual appearance, behind them, perhaps, a new period of history was in the making.

The transatlantic was due at Boulogne at midnight where it was supposed to wait until daybreak to discharge its passengers comfortably. It arrived, nevertheless, at ten, dropped anchor outside the harbor, and the Commandant gave orders that the disembarkation should take place in less than an hour. For this reason they had quickened their speed, consuming a vast amount of extra coal. It was necessary to get away as soon as possible, seeking the refuge of Hamburg. The radiographic apparatus had evidently been working to some purpose.

By the glare of the bluish searchlights which were spreading a livid clearness over the sea, began the unloading of passengers and baggage for Paris, from the transatlantic into the tenders. "Hurry! Hurry!" The seamen were pushing forward the ladies of slow step who were recounting their valises, believing that they had lost some. The stewards loaded themselves up with babies as though they were bundles. The general precipitation dissipated the usual exaggerated and oily Teutonic amiability. "They are regular bootlickers," thought Desnoyers. "They believe that their hour of triumph has come, and do not think it necessary to pretend any longer." . . .

He was soon in a launch that was bobbing up and down on the waves near the black and immovable hulk of the great liner, dotted with many circles of light and filled with people waving handkerchiefs. Julio recognized Bertha who was waving her hand without seeing him, without knowing in which tender he was, but feeling obliged to show her gratefulness for the sweet memories that now were being lost in the mystery of the sea and the night. "Adieu, Frau Rath!"

The distance between the departing transatlantic and the lighters was widening. As though it had been awaiting this moment with impunity, a stentorian voice on the upper deck shouted with a noisy guffaw, "See you later! Soon we shall meet you in Paris!" And the marine band, the very same band that three days before had astonished Desnoyers with its unexpected Marseillaise, burst forth into a military march of the time of Frederick the Great—a march of grenadiers with an accompaniment of trumpets.

That had been the night before. Although twenty-four hours had not yet passed by, Desnoyers was already considering it as a distant event of shadowy reality. His thoughts, always disposed to take the opposite side, did not share in the general alarm. The insolence of the Counsellor now appeared to him but the boastings of a burgher turned into a soldier. The disquietude of the people of Paris, was but the nervous agitation of a city which lived placidly and became alarmed at the first hint of danger to its comfort. So many times they had spoken of an immediate war, always settling things peacefully at the last moment! . . . Furthermore he did not want war to come because it would upset all his plans for the future; and the man accepted as logical and reasonable everything that suited his selfishness, placing it above reality.

"No, there will not be war," he repeated as he continued pacing up and down the garden. "These people are beside themselves. How could a war possibly break out in these days?" . . .

And after disposing of his doubts, which certainly would in a short time come up again, he thought of the joy of the moment, consulting his watch. Five o'clock! She might come now at any minute! He thought that he recognized her afar off in a lady who was passing through the grating by the rue Pasquier. She seemed to him a little different, but it occurred to him that possibly the Summer fashions might have altered her appearance. But soon he saw that he had made a mistake. She was not alone, another lady was with her. They were perhaps English or North American women who worshipped the memory of Marie Antoinette and wished to visit the Chapelle Expiatoire, the old tomb of the executed queen. Julio watched them as they climbed the flights of steps and crossed the interior patio in which were interred the eight hundred Swiss soldiers killed in the attack of the Tenth of August, with other victims of revolutionary fury.

Disgusted at his error, he continued his tramp. His ill humor made the monument with which the Bourbon restoration had adorned the old cemetery of the Madeleine, appear uglier than ever to him. Time was passing, but she did not come. Every time that he turned, he looked hungrily at the entrances of the garden. And then it happened as in all their meetings. She suddenly appeared as if she had fallen from the sky or risen up from the ground, like an apparition. A cough, a slight rustling of footsteps, and as he turned, Julio almost collided with her.

"Marguerite! Oh, Marguerite!" . . .

It was she, and yet he was slow to recognize her. He felt a certain strangeness in seeing in full reality the countenance which had occupied his imagination for three months, each time more spirituelle and shadowy with the idealism of absence. But his doubts were of short duration. Then it seemed as though time and space were eliminated, that he had not made any voyage, and but a few hours had intervened since their last interview.

Marguerite divined the expansion which might follow Julio's exclamations, the vehement hand-clasp, perhaps something more, so she kept herself calm and serene.

"No; not here," she said with a grimace of repugnance. "What a ridiculous idea for us to have met here!"

They were about to seat themselves on the iron chairs, in the shadow of some shrubbery, when she rose suddenly. Those who were passing along the boulevard might see them by merely casting their eyes toward the garden. At this time, many of her friends might be passing through the neighborhood because of its proximity to the big shops. . . . They, therefore, sought refuge at a corner of the monument, placing themselves between it and the rue des Mathurins. Desnoyers brought two chairs near the hedge, so that when seated they were invisible to those passing on the other side of the railing. But this was not solitude. A few steps away, a fat, nearsighted man was reading his paper, and a group of women were chatting and embroidering. A woman with a red wig and two dogs—some housekeeper who had come down into the garden in order to give her pets an airing—passed several times near the amorous pair, smiling discreetly.

"How annoying!" groaned Marguerite. "Why did we ever come to this place!"

The two scrutinized each other carefully, wishing to see exactly what transformation Time had wrought.

"You are darker than ever," she said. "You look like a man of the sea."

Julio was finding her even lovelier than before, and felt sure that possessing her was well worth all the contrarieties which had brought about his trip to South America. She was taller than he, with an elegantly proportioned slenderness. "She has the musical step," Desnoyers had told himself, when seeing her in his imagination; and now, on beholding her again, the first thing that he admired was her rhythmic tread, light and graceful as she passed through the garden seeking another seat. Her features were not regular but they had a piquant fascination—a true Parisian face. Everything that had been invented for the embellishment of feminine charm was used about her person with the most exquisite fastidiousness. She had always lived for herself. Only a few months before had she abdicated a part of this sweet selfishness, sacrificing reunions, teas, and calls in order to give Desnoyers some of the afternoon hours.

Stylish and painted like a priceless doll, with no loftier ambition than to be a model, interpreting with personal elegance the latest confections of the modistes, she was at last experiencing the same preoccupations and joys as other women, creating for herself an inner life. The nucleus of this new life, hidden under her former frivolity, was Desnoyers. Just as she was imagining that she had reorganized her existence—adjusting the satisfactions of worldly elegance to the delights of love in intimate secrecy—a fulminating catastrophe (the intervention of her husband whose possible appearance she seemed to have overlooked) had disturbed her thoughtless happiness. She who was accustomed to think herself the centre of the universe, imagining that events ought to revolve around her desires and tastes, had suffered this cruel surprise with more astonishment than grief.

"And you, how do you think I look?" Marguerite queried.

"I must tell you that the fashion has changed. The sheath skirt has passed away. Now it is worn short and with more fullness."

Desnoyers had to interest himself in her apparel with the same devotion, mixing his appreciation of the latest freak of the fashion-monger with his eulogies of Marguerite's beauty.

"Have you thought much about me?" she continued. "You have not been unfaithful to me a single time? Not even once? . . . Tell me the truth; you know I can always tell when you are lying."

"I have always thought of you," he said putting his hand on his heart, as if he were swearing before a judge.

And he said it roundly, with an accent of truth, since in his infidelities—now completely forgotten—the memory of Marguerite had always been present.

"But let us talk about you!" added Julio. "What have you been doing all the time?"

He had brought his chair nearer to hers, and their knees touched. He took one of her hands, patting it and putting his finger in the glove opening. Oh, that accursed garden which would not permit greater intimacy and obliged them to speak in a low tone, after three months' absence! . . . In spite of his discretion, the man who was reading his paper raised his head and looked irritably at them over his spectacles as though a fly were distracting him with its buzzing. . . . The very idea of talking love-nonsense in a public garden when all Europe was threatened with calamity!

Repelling the audacious hand, Marguerite spoke tranquilly of her existence during the last months.

"I have passed my life the best I could, but I have been greatly bored. You know that I am now living with mama, and mama is a lady of the old regime who does not understand our tastes. I have been to the theatres with my brother. I have made many calls on the lawyer in order to learn the progress of my divorce and hurry it along . . . and nothing else."

"And your husband?"

"Don't let's talk about him. Do you want to? I pity the poor man! So good . . . so correct. The lawyer assures me that he agrees to everything and will not impose any obstacles. They tell me that he does not come to Paris, that he lives in his factory. Our old home is closed. There are times when I feel remorseful over the way I have treated him."

"And I?" queried Julio, withdrawing his hand.

"You are right," she returned smiling. "You are Life. It is cruel but it is human. We have to live our lives without taking others into consideration. It is necessary to be selfish in order to be happy."

The two remained silent. The remembrance of the husband had swept across them like a glacial blast. Julio was the first to brighten up.

"And you have not danced in all this time?"

"No, how could I? The very idea, a woman in divorce proceedings! . . . I have not been to a single chic party since you went away. I wanted to preserve a certain decorous mourning fiesta. How horrible it was! . . . It needed you, the Master!"

They had again clasped hands and were smiling. Memories of the previous months were passing before their eyes, visions of their life from five to seven in the afternoon, dancing in the hotels of the Champs Elysees where the tango had been inexorably associated with a cup of tea.

She appeared to tear herself away from these recollections, impelled by a tenacious obsession which had slipped from her mind in the first moments of their meeting.

"Do you know much about what's happening? Tell me all. People talk so much. . . . Do you really believe that there will be war? Don't you think that it will all end in some kind of settlement?"

Desnoyers comforted her with his optimism. He did not believe in the possibility of a war. That was ridiculous.

"I say so, too! Ours is not the epoch of savages. I have known some Germans, chic and well-educated persons who surely must think exactly as we do. An old professor who comes to the house was explaining yesterday to mama that wars are no longer possible in these progressive times. In two months' time, there would scarcely be any men left, in three, the world would find itself without money to continue the struggle. I do not recall exactly how it was, but he explained it all very clearly, in a manner most delightful to hear."

She reflected in silence, trying to co-ordinate her confused recollections, but dismayed by the effort required, added on her own account.

"Just imagine what war would mean—how horrible! Society life paralyzed. No more parties, nor clothes, nor theatres! Why, it is even possible that they might not design any more fashions! All the women in mourning. Can you imagine it? . . . And Paris deserted. . . . How beautiful it seemed as I came to meet you this afternoon! . . . No, no, it cannot be! Next month, you know, we go to Vichy. Mama needs the waters. Then to Biarritz. After that, I shall go to a castle on the Loire. And besides there are our affairs, my divorce, our marriage which may take place the next year. . . . And is war to hinder and cut short all this! No, no, it is not possible. My brother and others like him are foolish enough to dream of danger from Germany. I am sure that my husband, too, who is only interested in serious and bothersome matters, is among those who believe that war is imminent and prepare to take part in it. What nonsense! Tell me that it is all nonsense. I need to hear you say it."

Tranquilized by the affirmations of her lover, she then changed the trend of the conversation. The possibility of their approaching marriage brought to mind the object of the voyage which Desnoyers had just made. There had not been time for them to write to each other during their brief separation.

"Did you succeed in getting the money? The joy of seeing you made me forget all about such things. . . ."

Adopting the air of a business expert, he replied that he had brought back less than he expected, for he had found the country in the throes of one of its periodical panics; but still he had managed to get together about four hundred thousand francs. In his purse he had a check for that amount. Later on, they would send him further remittances. A ranchman in Argentina, a sort of relative, was looking after his affairs. Marguerite appeared satisfied, and in spite of her frivolity, adopted the air of a serious woman.

"Money, money!" she exclaimed sententiously. "And yet there is no happiness without it! With your four hundred thousand and what I have, we shall be able to get along. . . . I told you that my husband wishes to give me back my dowry. He has told my brother so. But the state of his business, and the increased size of his factory do not permit him to return it as quickly as he would like. I can't help but feel sorry for the poor man . . . so honorable and so upright in every way. If he only were not so commonplace! . . ."

Again Marguerite seemed to regret these tardy spontaneous eulogies which were chilling their interview. So again she changed the trend of her chatter.

"And your family? Have you seen them?" . . .

Desnoyers had been to his father's home before starting for the Chapelle Expiatoire. A stealthy entrance into the great house on the avenue Victor Hugo, and then up to the first floor like a tradesman. Then he had slipt into the kitchen like a soldier sweetheart of the maids. His mother had come there to embrace him, poor Dona Luisa, weeping and kissing him frantically as though she had feared to lose him forever. Close behind her mother had come Luisita, nicknamed Chichi, who always surveyed him with sympathetic curiosity as if she wished to know better a brother so bad and adorable who had led decent women from the paths of virtue, and committed all kinds of follies. Then Desnoyers had been greatly surprised to see entering the kitchen with the air of a tragedy queen, a noble mother of the drama, his Aunt Elena, the one who had married a German and was living in Berlin surrounded with innumerable children.

"She has been in Paris a month. She is going to make a little visit to our castle. And it appears that her eldest son—my cousin, 'The Sage,' whom I have not seen for years—is also coming here."

The home interview had several times been interrupted by fear. "Your father is at home, be careful," his mother had said to him each time that he had spoken above a whisper. And his Aunt Elena had stationed herself at the door with a dramatic air, like a stage heroine resolved to plunge a dagger into the tyrant who should dare to cross the threshold. The entire family was accustomed to submit to the rigid authority of Don Marcelo Desnoyers. "Oh, that old man!" exclaimed Julio, referring to his father. "He may live many years yet, but how he weighs upon us all!"

His mother, who had never wearied of looking at him, finally had to bring the interview to an end, frightened by certain approaching sounds. "Go, he might surprise us, and he would be furious." So Julio had fled the paternal home, caressed by the tears of the two ladies and the admiring glances of Chichi, by turns ashamed and proud of a brother who had caused such enthusiasm and scandal among her friends.

Marguerite also spoke of Senor Desnoyers. A terrible tyrant of the old school with whom they could never come to an understanding.

The two remained silent, looking fixedly at each other. Now that they had said the things of greatest urgency, present interests became more absorbing. More immediate things, unspoken, seemed to well up in their timid and vacillating eyes, before escaping in the form of words. They did not dare to talk like lovers here. Every minute the cloud of witnesses seemed increasing around them. The woman with the dogs and the red wig was passing with greater frequency, shortening her turns through the square in order to greet them with a smile of complicity. The reader of the daily paper was now exchanging views with a friend on a neighboring bench regarding the possibilities of war. The garden had become a thoroughfare. The modistes upon going out from their establishments, and the ladies returning from shopping, were crossing through the square in order to shorten their walk. The little avenue was a popular short-cut. All the pedestrians were casting curious glances at the elegant lady and her companion seated in the shadow of the shrubbery with the timid yet would-be natural look of those who desire to hide themselves, yet at the same time feign a casual air.

"How exasperating!" sighed Marguerite. "They are going to find us out!"

A girl looked at her so searchingly that she thought she recognized in her an employee of a celebrated modiste. Besides, some of her personal friends who had met her in the crowded shops but an hour ago might be returning home by way of the garden.

"Let us go," she said rising hurriedly. "If they should spy us here together, just think what they might say! . . . and just when they are becoming a little forgetful!"

Desnoyers protested crossly. Go away? . . . Paris had become a shrunken place for them nowadays because Marguerite refused to go to a single place where there was a possibility of their being surprised. In another square, in a restaurant, wherever they might go—they would run the same risk of being recognized. She would only consider meetings in public places, and yet at the same time, dreaded the curiosity of the people. If Marguerite would like to go to his studio of such sweet memories! . . .

"To your home? No! no indeed!" she replied emphatically "I cannot forget the last time I was there."

But Julio insisted, foreseeing a break in that firm negative. Where could they be more comfortable? Besides, weren't they going to marry as soon as possible? . . .

"I tell you no," she repeated. "Who knows but my husband may be watching me! What a complication for my divorce if he should surprise us in your house!"

Now it was he who eulogized the husband, insisting that such watchfulness was incompatible with his character. The engineer had accepted the facts, considering them irreparable and was now thinking only of reconstructing his life.

"No, it is better for us to separate," she continued. "Tomorrow we shall see each other again. You will hunt a more favorable place. Think it over, and you will find a solution for it all."

But he wished an immediate solution. They had abandoned their seats, going slowly toward the rue des Mathurins. Julio was speaking with a trembling and persuasive eloquence. To-morrow? No, now. They had only to call a taxicab. It would be only a matter of a few minutes, and then the isolation, the mystery, the return to a sweet past—to that intimacy in the studio where they had passed their happiest hours. They would believe that no time had elapsed since their first meetings.

"No," she faltered with a weakening accent, seeking a last resistance. "Besides, your secretary might be there, that Spaniard who lives with you. How ashamed I would be to meet him again!"

Julio laughed. . . . Argensola! How could that comrade who knew all about their past be an obstacle? If they should happen to meet him in the house, he would be sure to leave immediately. More than once, he had had to go out so as not to be in the way. His discretion was such that he had foreseen events. Probably he had already left, conjecturing that a near visit would be the most logical thing. His chum would simply go wandering through the streets in search of news.

Marguerite was silent, as though yielding on seeing her pretexts exhausted. Desnoyers was silent, too, construing her stillness as assent. They had left the garden and she was looking around uneasily, terrified to find herself in the open street beside her lover, and seeking a hiding-place. Suddenly she saw before her the little red door of an automobile, opened by the hand of her adorer.

"Get in," ordered Julio.

And she climbed in hastily, anxious to hide herself as soon as possible. The vehicle started at great speed. Marguerite immediately pulled down the shade of the window on her side, but, before she had finished and could turn her head, she felt a hungry mouth kissing the nape of her neck.

"No, not here," she said in a pleading tone. "Let us be sensible!"

And while he, rebellious at these exhortations, persisted in his advances, the voice of Marguerite again sounded above the noise of the rattling machinery of the automobile as it bounded over the pavement.

"Do you really believe that there will be no war? Do you believe that we will be able to marry? . . . Tell me again. I want you to encourage me . . . I need to hear it from your lips."

CHAPTER II

MADARIAGA, THE CENTAUR

In 1870 Marcelo Desnoyers was nineteen years old. He was born in the suburbs of Paris, an only child; his father, interested in little building speculations, maintained his family in modest comfort. The mason wished to make an architect of his son, and Marcelo was in the midst of his preparatory studies when his father suddenly died, leaving his affairs greatly involved. In a few months, he and his mother descended the slopes of ruin, and were obliged to give up their snug, middle-class quarters and live like laborers.

When the fourteen-year-old boy had to choose a trade, he learned wood carving. This craft was an art related to the tastes awakened in Marcelo by his abandoned studies. His mother retired to the country, living with some relatives while the lad advanced rapidly in the shops, aiding his master in all the important orders which he received from the provinces. The first news of the war with Prussia surprised him in Marseilles, working on the decorations of a theatre.

Marcelo was opposed to the Empire like all the youths of his generation. He was also much influenced by the older workmen who had taken part in the Republic of '48, and who still retained vivid recollections of the Coup d'Etat of the second of December.

One day he saw in the streets of Marseilles a popular manifestation in favor of peace which was practically a protest against the government. The old republicans in their implacable struggle with the Emperor, the companies of the International which had just been organized, and a great number of Italians and Spaniards who had fled their countries on account of recent insurrections, composed the procession. A long-haired, consumptive student was carrying the flag. "It is peace that we want—a peace which may unite all mankind," chanted the paraders. But on this earth, the noblest propositions are seldom heard, since Destiny amuses herself in perverting them and turning them aside.

Scarcely had the friends of peace entered the rue Cannebiere with their hymn and standard, when war came to meet them, obliging them to resort to fist and club. The day before, some battalions of Zouaves from Algiers had disembarked in order to reinforce the army on the frontier, and these veterans, accustomed to colonial existence and undiscriminating as to the cause of disturbances, seized the opportunity to intervene in this manifestation, some with bayonets and others with ungirded belts. "Hurrah for War!" and a rain of lashes and blows fell upon the unarmed singers. Marcelo saw the innocent student, the standard-bearer of peace, knocked down wrapped in his flag, by the merry kicks of the Zouaves. Then he knew no more, since he had received various blows with a leather strap, and a knife thrust in his shoulder; he had to run the same as the others.

That day developed for the first time, his fiery, stubborn character, irritable before contradiction, even to the point of adopting the most extreme resolution. "Down with War!" Since it was not possible for him to protest in any other way, he would leave the country. The Emperor might arrange his affairs as best he could. The struggle was going to be long and disastrous, according to the enemies of the Empire. If he stayed, he would in a few months be drawn for the soldiery. Desnoyers renounced the honor of serving the Emperor. He hesitated a little when he thought of his mother. But his country relatives would not turn her out, and he planned to work very hard and send her money. Who knew what riches might be waiting for him, on the other side of the sea! . . . Good-bye, France!

Thanks to his savings, a harbor official found it to his interest to offer him the choice of three boats. One was sailing to Egypt, another to Australia, another to Montevideo and Buenos Aires, which made the strongest appeal to him? . . . Desnoyers, remembering his readings, wished to consult the wind and follow the course that it indicated, as he had seen various heroes of novels do. But that day the wind blew from the sea toward France. He also wished to toss up a coin in order to test his fate. Finally he decided upon the vessel sailing first. Not until, with his scanty baggage, he was actually on the deck of the next boat to anchor, did he take any interest in its course—"For the Rio de la Plata." . . . And he accepted these words with a fatalistic shrug. "Very well, let it be South America!" The country was not distasteful to him, since he knew it by certain travel publications whose illustrations represented herds of cattle at liberty, half-naked, plumed Indians, and hairy cowboys whirling over their heads serpentine lassos tipped with balls.

The millionaire Desnoyers never forgot that trip to America—forty-three days navigating in a little worn-out steamer that rattled like a heap of old iron, groaned in all its joints at the slightest roughness of the sea, and had to stop four times for repairs, at the mercy of the winds and waves.

In Montevideo, he learned of the reverses suffered by his country and that the French Empire no longer existed. He felt a little ashamed when he heard that the nation was now self-governing, defending itself gallantly behind the walls of Paris. And he had fled! . . . Months afterwards, the events of the Commune consoled him for his flight. If he had remained, wrath at the national downfall, his relations with his co-laborers, the air in which he lived—everything would surely have dragged him along to revolt. In that case, he would have been shot or consigned to a colonial prison like so many of his former comrades.

So his determination crystallized, and he stopped thinking about the affairs of his mother-country. The necessities of existence in a foreign land whose language he was beginning to pick up made him think only of himself. The turbulent and adventurous life of these new nations compelled him to most absurd expedients and varied occupations. Yet he felt himself strong with an audacity and self-reliance which he never had in the old world. "I am equal to everything," he said, "if they only give me time to prove it!" Although he had fled from his country in order not to take up arms, he even led a soldier's life for a brief period in his adopted land, receiving a wound in one of the many hostilities between the whites and reds in the unsettled districts.

In Buenos Aires, he again worked as a woodcarver. The city was beginning to expand, breaking its shell as a large village. Desnoyers spent many years ornamenting salons and facades. It was a laborious existence, sedentary and remunerative. But one day he became tired of this slow saving which could only bring him a mediocre fortune after a long time. He had gone to the new world to become rich like so many others. And at twenty-seven, he started forth again, a full-fledged adventurer, avoiding the cities, wishing to snatch money from untapped, natural sources. He worked farms in the forests of the North, but the locusts obliterated his crops in a few hours. He was a cattle-driver, with the aid of only two peons, driving a herd of oxen and mules over the snowy solitudes of the Andes to Bolivia and Chile. In this life, making journeys of many months' duration, across interminable plains, he lost exact account of time and space. Just as he thought himself on the verge of winning a fortune, he lost it all by an unfortunate speculation. And in a moment of failure and despair, being now thirty years old, he became an employee of Julio Madariaga.

He knew of this rustic millionaire through his purchases of flocks—a Spaniard who had come to the country when very young, adapting himself very easily to its customs, and living like a cowboy after he had acquired enormous properties. The country folk, wishing to put a title of respect before his name, called him Don Madariaga.

"Comrade," he said to Desnoyers one day when he happened to be in a good humor—a very rare thing for him—"you must have passed through many ups and downs. Your lack of silver may be smelled a long ways off. Why lead such a dog's life? Trust in me, Frenchy, and remain here! I am growing old, and I need a man."

After the Frenchman had arranged to stay with Madariaga, every landed proprietor living within fifteen or twenty leagues of the ranch, stopped the new employee on the road to prophesy all sorts of misfortune.

"You will not stay long. Nobody can get along with Don Madariaga. We have lost count of his overseers. He is a man who must be killed or deserted. Soon you will go, too!"

Desnoyers did not doubt but that there was some truth in all this. Madariaga was an impossible character, but feeling a certain sympathy with the Frenchman, had tried not to annoy him with his irritability.

"He's a regular pearl, this Frenchy," said the plainsman as though trying to excuse himself for his considerate treatment of his latest acquisition. "I like him because he is very serious. . . . That is the way I like a man."

Desnoyers did not know exactly what this much-admired seriousness could be, but he felt a secret pride in seeing him aggressive with everybody else, even his family, whilst he took with him a tone of paternal bluffness.

The family consisted of his wife Misia Petrona (whom he always called the China) and two grown daughters who had gone to school in Buenos Aires, but on returning to the ranch had reverted somewhat to their original rusticity.

Madariaga's fortune was enormous. He had lived in the field since his arrival in America, when the white race had not dared to settle outside the towns for fear of the Indians. He had gained his first money as a fearless trader, taking merchandise in a cart from fort to fort. He had killed Indians, was twice wounded by them, and for a while had lived as a captive with an Indian chief whom he finally succeeded in making his staunch friend. With his earnings, he had bought land, much land, almost worthless because of its insecurity, devoting it to the raising of cattle that he had to defend, gun in hand, from the pirates of the plains.

Then he had married his China, a young half-breed who was running around barefoot, but owned many of her forefathers' fields. They had lived in an almost savage poverty on their property which would have taken many a day's journey to go around. Afterwards, when the government was pushing the Indians towards the frontiers, and offering the abandoned lands for sale, considering it a patriotic sacrifice on the part of any one wishing to acquire them, Madariaga bought and bought at the lowest figure and longest terms. To get possession of vast tracts and populate it with blooded stock became the mission of his life. At times, galloping with Desnoyers through his boundless fields, he was not able to repress his pride.

"Tell me something, Frenchy! They say that further up the country, there are some nations about the size of my ranches. Is that so?" . . .

The Frenchman agreed. . . . The lands of Madariaga were indeed greater than many principalities. This put the old plainsman in rare good humor and he exclaimed in the cowboy vernacular which had become second nature to him— "Then it wouldn't be absurd to proclaim myself king some day? Just imagine it, Frenchy;—Don Madariaga, the First. . . . The worst of it all is that I would also be the last, for the China will not give me a son. . . . She is a weak cow!"

The fame of his vast territories and his wealth in stock reached even to Buenos Aires. Every one knew of Madariaga by name, although very few had seen him. When he went to the Capital, he passed unnoticed because of his country aspect—the same leggings that he was used to wearing in the fields, his poncho wrapped around him like a muffler above which rose the aggressive points of a necktie, a tormenting ornament imposed by his daughters, who in vain arranged it with loving hands that he might look a little more respectable.

One day he entered the office of the richest merchant of the capital.

"Sir, I know that you need some young bulls for the European market, and I have come to sell you a few."

The man of affairs looked haughtily at the poor cowboy. He might explain his errand to one of the employees, he could not waste his time on such small matters. But the malicious grin on the rustic's face awoke his curiosity.

"And how many are you able to sell, my good man?"

"About thirty thousand, sir."

It was not necessary to hear more. The supercilious merchant sprang from his desk, and obsequiously offered him a seat.

"You can be no other than Don Madariaga."

"At the service of God and yourself, sir," he responded in the manner of a Spanish countryman.

That was the most glorious moment of his existence.

In the outer office of the Directors of the Bank, the clerks offered him a seat until the personage the other side of the door should deign to receive him. But scarcely was his name announced than that same director ran to admit him, and the employee was stupefied to hear the ranchman say, by way of greeting, "I have come to draw out three hundred thousand dollars. I have abundant pasturage, and I wish to buy a ranch or two in order to stock them."

His arbitrary and contradictory character weighed upon the inhabitants of his lands with both cruel and good-natured tyranny. No vagabond ever passed by the ranch without being rudely assailed by its owner from the outset.

"Don't tell me any of your hard-luck stories, friend," he would yell as if he were going to beat him. "Under the shed is a skinned beast; cut and eat as much as you wish and so help yourself to continue your journey. . . . But no more of your yarns!"

And he would turn his back upon the tramp, after giving him a few dollars.

One day he became infuriated because a peon was nailing the wire fencing too deliberately on the posts. Everybody was robbing him! The following day he spoke of a large sum of money that he would have to pay for having endorsed the note of an acquaintance, completely bankrupt. "Poor fellow! His luck is worse than mine!"

Upon finding in the road the skeleton of a recently killed sheep, he was beside himself with indignation. It was not because of the loss of the meat. "Hunger knows no law, and God has made meat for mankind to eat. But they might at least have left the skin!" . . . And he would rage against such wickedness, always repeating, "Lack of religion and good habits!" The next time, the bandits stripped the flesh off of three cows, leaving the skins in full view, and the ranchman said, smiling, "That is the way I like people, honorable and doing no wrong."

His vigor as a tireless centaur had helped him powerfully in his task of populating his lands. He was capricious, despotic and with the same paternal instincts as his compatriots who, centuries before when conquering the new world, had clarified its native blood. Like the Castilian conquistadors, he had a fancy for copper-colored beauty with oblique eyes and straight hair. When Desnoyers saw him going off on some sudden pretext, putting his horse at full gallop toward a neighboring ranch, he would say to himself, smilingly, "He is going in search of a new peon who will help work his land fifteen years from now."

The personnel of the ranch often used to comment on the resemblance of certain youths laboring here the same as the others, galloping from the first streak of dawn over the fields, attending to the various duties of pasturing. The overseer, Celedonio, a half-breed thirty years old, generally detested for his hard and avaricious character, also bore a distant resemblance to the patron.

Almost every year, some woman from a great distance, dirty and bad-faced, presented herself at the ranch, leading by the hand a little mongrel with eyes like live coals. She would ask to speak with the proprietor alone, and upon being confronted with her, he usually recalled a trip made ten or twelve years before in order to buy a herd of cattle.

"You remember, Patron, that you passed the night on my ranch because the river had risen?"

The Patron did not remember anything about it. But a vague instinct warned him that the woman was probably telling the truth. "Well, what of it?"

"Patron, here he is. . . . It is better for him to grow to manhood by your side than in any other place."

And she presented him with the little hybrid. One more, and offered with such simplicity! . . . "Lack of religion and good habits!" Then with sudden modesty, he doubted the woman's veracity. Why must it necessarily be his? . . . But his wavering was generally short-lived.

"If it's mine, put it with the others."

The mother went away tranquilly, seeing the youngster's future assured, because this man so lavish in violence was equally so in generosity. In time there would be a bit of land and a good flock of sheep for the urchin.

These adoptions at first aroused in Misia Petrona a little rebellion—the only ones of her life; but the centaur soon reduced her to terrified silence.

"And you dare to complain of me, you weak cow! . . . A woman who has only given me daughters. You ought to be ashamed of yourself."

The same hand that negligently extracted from his pocket a wad of bills rolled into a ball, giving them away capriciously without knowing just how much, also wore a lash hanging from the wrist. It was supposed to be for his horse, but it was used with equal facility when any of his peons incurred his wrath.

"I strike because I can," he would say to pacify himself.

One day, the man receiving the blow, took a step backward, hunting for the knife in his belt.

"You are not going to beat me, Patron. I was not born in these parts. . . . I come from Corrientes."

The Patron remained with upraised thong. "Is it true that you were not born here? . . . Then you are right; I cannot beat you. Here are five dollars for you."

When Desnoyers came on the place, Madariaga was beginning to lose count of those who were under his dominion in the old Latin sense, and could take his blows. There were so many that confusion often reigned.

The Frenchman admired the Patron's expert eye for his business. It was enough for him to contemplate for a few moments a herd of cattle, to know its exact number. He would go galloping along with an indifferent air, around an immense group of horned and stamping beasts, and then would suddenly begin to separate the different animals. He had discovered that they were sick. With a buyer like Madariaga, all the tricks and sharp practice of the drovers came to naught.

His serenity before trouble was also admirable. A drought suddenly strewed his plains with dead cattle, making the land seem like an abandoned battlefield. Everywhere great black hulks. In the air, great spirals of crows coming from leagues away. At other times, it was the cold; an unexpected drop in the thermometer would cover the ground with dead bodies. Ten thousand animals, fifteen thousand, perhaps more, all perished!

"WHAT a knock-out!" Madariaga would exclaim with resignation. "Without such troubles, this earth would be a paradise. . . . Now, the thing to do is to save the skins!"

And he would rail against the false pride of the emigrants, against the new customs among the poor which prevented his securing enough hands to strip the victims quickly, so that thousands of hides had to be lost. Their bones whitened the earth like heaps of snow. The peoncitos (little peons) went around putting the skulls of cows with crumpled horns on the posts of the wire fences—a rustic decoration which suggested a procession of Grecian lyres.

"It is lucky that the land is left, anyway!" added the ranchman.

He loved to race around his immense fields when they were beginning to turn green in the late rains. He had been among the first to convert these virgin wastes into rich meadow-lands, supplementing the natural pasturage with alfalfa. Where one beast had found sustenance before, he now had three. "The table is set," he would chuckle, "we must now go in search of the guests." And he kept on buying, at ridiculous prices, herds dying of hunger in others' uncultivated fields, constantly increasing his opulent lands and stock.

One morning Desnoyers saved his life. The old ranchman had raised his lash against a recently arrived peon who returned the attack, knife in hand. Madariaga was defending himself as best he could, convinced from one minute to another that he was going to receive the deadly knife-thrust—when Desnoyers arrived and, drawing his revolver, overcame and disarmed the adversary.

"Thanks, Frenchy," said the ranchman, much touched. "You are an all-round man, and I am going to reward you. From this day I shall speak to you as I do to my family."

Desnoyers did not know just what this familiar talk might amount to, for his employer was so peculiar. Certain personal favors, nevertheless, immediately began to improve his position. He was no longer allowed to eat in the administration building, the proprietor insisting imperiously that henceforth Desnoyers should sit at his own table, and thus he was admitted into the intimate life of the Madariaga family.

The wife was always silent when her husband was present. She was used to rising in the middle of the night in order to oversee the breakfasts of the peons, the distribution of biscuit, and the boiling of the great black kettles of coffee or shrub tea. She looked after the chattering and lazy maids who so easily managed to get lost in the nearby groves. In the kitchen, too, she made her authority felt like a regular house-mistress, but the minute that she heard her husband's voice she shrank into a respectful and timorous silence. Upon sitting down at table, the China would look at him with devoted submission, her great, round eyes fixed on him, like an owl's. Desnoyers felt that in this mute admiration was mingled great astonishment at the energy with which the ranchman, already over seventy, was continuing to bring new occupants to live on his demesne.

The two daughters, Luisa and Elena, accepted with enthusiasm the new arrival who came to enliven the monotonous conversations in the dining room, so often cut short by their father's wrathful outbursts. Besides, he was from Paris. "Paris!" sighed Elena, the younger one, rolling her eyes. And Desnoyers was henceforth consulted in all matters of style every time they ordered any "confections" from the shops of Buenos Aires.

The interior of the house reflected the different tastes of the two generations. The girls had a parlor with a few handsome pieces of furniture placed against the cracked walls, and some showy lamps that were never lighted. The father, with his boorishness, often invaded this room so cherished and admired by the two sisters, making the carpets look shabby and faded under his muddy boot-tracks. Upon the gilt centre-table, he loved to lay his lash. Samples of maize scattered its grains over a silk sofa which the young ladies tried to keep very choice, as though they feared it might break.

Near the entrance to the dining room was a weighing machine, and Madariaga became furious when his daughters asked him to remove it to the offices. He was not going to trouble himself to go outside every time that he wanted to know the weight of a leather skin! . . . A piano came into the ranch, and Elena passed the hours practising exercises with desperate good will. "Heavens and earth! She might at least play the Jota or the Perican, or some other lively Spanish dance!" And the irate father, at the hour of siesta, betook himself to the nearby eucalyptus trees, to sleep upon his poncho.

This younger daughter whom he dubbed La Romantica, was the special victim of his wrath and ridicule. Where had she picked up so many tastes which he and his good China never had had? Music books were piled on the piano. In a corner of the absurd parlor were some wooden boxes that had held preserves, which the ranch carpenter had been made to press into service as a bookcase.

"Look here, Frenchy," scoffed Madariaga. "All these are novels and poems! Pure lies! . . . Hot air!"

He had his private library, vastly more important and glorious, and occupying less space. In his desk, adorned with guns, thongs, and chaps studded with silver, was a little compartment containing deeds and various legal documents which the ranchman surveyed with great pride.

"Pay attention, now and hear marvellous things," announced the master to Desnoyers, as he took out one of his memorandum books.

This volume contained the pedigree of the famous animals which had improved his breeds of stock, the genealogical trees, the patents of nobility of his aristocratic beasts. He would have to read its contents to him since he did not permit even his family to touch these records. And with his spectacles on the end of his nose, he would spell out the credentials of each animal celebrity. "Diamond III, grandson of Diamond I, owned by the King of England, son of Diamond II, winner in the races." His Diamond had cost him many thousands, but the finest horses on the ranch, those which brought the most marvellous prices, were his descendants.

"That horse had more sense than most people. He only lacked the power to talk. He's the one that's stuffed, near the door of the parlor. The girls wanted him thrown out. . . . Just let them dare to touch him! I'd chuck them out first!"

Then he would continue reading the history of a dynasty of bulls with distinctive names and a succession of Roman numbers, the same as kings—animals acquired by the stubborn ranchman in the great cattle fairs of England. He had never been there, but he had used the cable in order to compete in pounds sterling with the British owners who wished to keep such valuable stock in their own country. Thanks to these blue-blooded sires that had crossed the ocean with all the luxury of millionaire passengers, he had been able to exhibit in the concourses of Buenos Aires animals which were veritable towers of meat, edible elephants with their sides as fit and sleek as a table.

"That book amounts to something! Don't you think so, Frenchy? It is worth more than all those pictures of moons, lakes, lovers and other gewgaws that my Romantica puts on the walls to catch the dust."

And he would point out, in contrast, the precious diplomas which were adorning his desk, the metal vases and other trophies won in the fairs by the descendants of his blooded stock.

Luisa, the elder daughter, called Chicha, in the South American fashion, was much more respected by her father. "She is my poor China right over again," he said, "the same good nature, and the same faculty for work, but more of a lady." Desnoyers entirely agreed with him, and yet the father's description seemed to him weak and incomplete. He could not admit that the pale, modest girl with the great black eyes and smile of childish mischief bore the slightest resemblance to the respectable matron who had brought her into existence.

The great fiesta for Chicha was the Sunday mass. It represented a journey of three leagues to the nearest village, a weekly contact with people unlike those of the ranch. A carriage drawn by four horses took the senora and the two senoritas in the latest suits and hats arrived, via Buenos Aires, from Europe. At the suggestion of Chicha, Desnoyers accompanied them in the capacity of driver.

The father remained at home, taking advantage of this opportunity to survey his fields in their Sunday solitude, thus keeping a closer oversight on the shiftlessness of his hands. He was very religious—"Religion and good manners, you know." But had he not given thousands of dollars toward building the neighboring church? A man of his fortune should not be submitted to the same obligations as ragamuffins!

During the Sunday lunch the young ladies were apt to make comments upon the persons and merits of the young men of the village and neighboring ranches, who had lingered at the church door in order to chat with them.

"Don't fool yourselves, girls!" observed the father shrewdly. "You believe that they want you for your elegance, don't you? . . . What those shameless fellows really want are the dollars of old Madariaga, and once they had them, they would probably give you a daily beating."

For a while the ranch received numerous visitors. Some were young men of the neighborhood who arrived on spirited steeds, performing all kinds of tricks of fancy horsemanship. They wanted to see Don Julio on the most absurd pretexts, and at the same time improved the opportunity to chat with Chicha and Luisa. At other times they were youths from Buenos Aires asking for a lodging at the ranch, as they were just passing by. Don Madariaga would growl—

"Another good-for-nothing scamp who comes in search of the Spanish ranchman! If he doesn't move on soon . . . I'll kick him out!"

But the suitor did not stand long on the order of his going, intimidated by the ominous silence of the Patron. This silence, of late, had persisted in an alarming manner, in spite of the fact that the ranch was no longer receiving visitors. Madariaga appeared abstracted, and all the family, including Desnoyers, respected and feared this taciturnity. He ate, scowling, with lowered head. Suddenly he would raise his eyes, looking at Chicha, then at Desnoyers, finally fixing them upon his wife as though asking her to give an account of things.

His Romantica simply did not exist for him. The only notice that he ever took of her was to give an ironical snort when he happened to see her leaning at sunset against the doorway, looking at the reddening glow—one elbow on the door frame and her cheek in her hand, in imitation of the posture of a certain white lady that she had seen in a chromo, awaiting the knight of her dreams.

Desnoyers had been five years in the house when one day he entered his master's private office with the brusque air of a timid person who has suddenly reached a decision.

"Don Julio, I am going to leave and I would like our accounts settled."

Madariaga looked at him slyly. "Going to leave, eh? . . . What for?" But in vain he repeated his questions. The Frenchman was floundering through a series of incoherent explanations—"I'm going; I've got to go."

"Ah, you thief, you false prophet!" shouted the ranchman in stentorian tones.

But Desnoyers did not quail before the insults. He had often heard his Patron use these same words when holding somebody up to ridicule, or haggling with certain cattle drovers.

"Ah, you thief, you false prophet! Do you suppose that I do not know why you are going? Do you suppose old Madariaga has not seen your languishing looks and those of my dead fly of a daughter, clasping each others' hands in the presence of poor China who is blinded in her judgment? . . . It's not such a bad stroke, Frenchy. By it, you would be able to get possession of half of the old Spaniard's dollars, and then say that you had made it in America."

And while he was storming, or rather howling, all this, he had grasped his lash and with the butt end kept poking his manager in the stomach with such insistence that it might be construed in an affectionate or hostile way.

"For this reason I have come to bid you good-bye," said Desnoyers haughtily. "I know that my love is absurd, and I wish to leave."

"The gentleman would go away," the ranchman continued spluttering. "The gentleman believes that here one can do what one pleases! No, siree! Here nobody commands but old Madariaga, and I order you to stay. . . . Ah, these women! They only serve to antagonize men. And yet we can't live without them!" . . .

He took several turns up and down the room, as though his last words were making him think of something very different from what he had just been saying. Desnoyers looked uneasily at the thong which was still hanging from his wrist. Suppose he should attempt to whip him as he did the peons? . . . He was still undecided whether to hold his own against a man who had always treated him with benevolence or, while his back was turned, to take refuge in discreet flight, when the ranchman planted himself before him.

"You really love her, really?" he asked. "Are you sure that she loves you? Be careful what you say, for love is blind and deceitful. I, too, when I married my China was crazy about her. Do you love her, honestly and truly? . . . Well then, take her, you devilish Frenchy. Somebody has to take her, and may she not turn out a weak cow like her mother! . . . Let us have the ranch full of grandchildren!"

In voicing this stock-raiser's wish, again appeared the great breeder of beasts and men. And as though he considered it necessary to explain his concession, he added—"I do all this because I like you; and I like you because you are serious."

Again the Frenchman was plunged in doubt, not knowing in just what this greatly appreciated seriousness consisted.

At his wedding, Desnoyers thought much of his mother. If only the poor old woman could witness this extraordinary stroke of good fortune! But she had died the year before, believing her son enormously rich because he had been sending her sixty dollars every month, taken from the wages that he had earned on the ranch.

Desnoyers' entrance into the family made his father-in-law pay less attention to business.

City life, with all its untried enchantments and snares, now attracted Madariaga, and he began to speak with contempt of country women, poorly groomed and inspiring him with disgust. He had given up his cowboy attire, and was displaying with childish satisfaction, the new suits in which a tailor of the Capital was trying to disguise him. When Elena wished to accompany him to Buenos Aires, he would wriggle out of it, trumping up some absorbing business. "No; you go with your mother."

The fate of his fields and flocks gave him no uneasiness. His fortune, managed by Desnoyers, was in good hands.

"He is very serious," again affirmed the old Spaniard to his family assembled in the dining roam—"as serious as I am. . . . Nobody can make a fool of him!"

And finally the Frenchman concluded that when his father-in-law spoke of seriousness he was referring to his strength of character. According to the spontaneous declaration of Madariaga, he had, from the very first day that he had dealings with Desnoyers, perceived in him a nature like his own, more hard and firm perhaps, but without splurges of eccentricities. On this account he had treated him with such extraordinary circumspection, foreseeing that a clash between the two could never be adjusted. Their only disagreements were about the expenses established by Madariaga during his regime. Since the son-in-law was managing the ranches, the work was costing less, and the people working more diligently;—and that, too, without yells, and without strong words and deeds, with only his presence and brief orders.

The old man was the only one defending the capricious system of a blow followed by a gift. He revolted against a minute and mechanical administration, always the same, without any arbitrary extravagance or good-natured tyranny. Very frequently some of the half-breed peons whom a malicious public supposed to be closely related to the ranchman, would present themselves before Desnoyers with, "Senor Manager, the old Patron say that you are to give me five dollars." The Senor Manager would refuse, and soon after Madariaga would rush in in a furious temper, but measuring his words, nevertheless, remembering that his son-in-law's disposition was as serious as his own.

"I like you very much, my son, but here no one overrules me. . . . Ah, Frenchy, you are like all the rest of your countrymen! Once you get your claws on a penny, it goes into your stocking, and nevermore sees the light of day, even though they crucify you. . . ! Did I say five dollars? Give him ten. I command it and that is enough."

The Frenchman paid, shrugging his shoulders, whilst his father-in-law, satisfied with his triumph, fled to Buenos Aires. It was a good thing to have it well understood that the ranch still belonged to Madariaga, the Spaniard.

From one of these trips, he returned with a companion, a young German who, according to him, knew everything and could do everything. His son-in-law was working too hard. This Karl Hartrott would assist him in the bookkeeping. Desnoyers accepted the situation, and in a few days felt increasing esteem for the new incumbent.

Although they belonged to two unfriendly nations, it didn't matter. There are good people everywhere, and this Karl was a subordinate worth considering. He kept his distance from his equals, and was hard and inflexible toward his inferiors. All his faculties seemed concentrated in service and admiration for those above him. Scarcely would Madariaga open his lips before the German's head began nodding in agreement, anticipating his words. If he said anything funny, his clerk's laugh would break forth in scandalous roars. With Desnoyers he appeared more taciturn, working without stopping for hours at a time. As soon as he saw the manager entering the office he would leap from his seat, holding himself erect with military precision. He was always ready to do anything whatever. Unasked, he spied on the workmen, reporting their carelessness and mistakes. This last service did not especially please his superior officer, but he appreciated it as a sign of interest in the establishment.

The old man bragged triumphantly of the new acquisition, urging his son-in-law also to rejoice.

"A very useful fellow, isn't he? . . . These gringoes from Germany work well, know a good many things and cost little. Then, too, so disciplined! so servile! . . .

I am sorry to praise him so to you because you are a Frenchy, and your nation has in them a very powerful enemy. His people are a hard-shelled race."

Desnoyers replied with a shrug of indifference. His country was far away, and so was Germany. Who knew if they would ever return! . . . They were both Argentinians now, and ought to interest themselves in present affairs and not bother about the past.

"And how little pride they have!" sneered Madariaga in an ironical tone. "Every one of these gringoes when he is a clerk at the Capital sweeps the shop, prepares the meals, keeps the books, sells to the customers, works the typewriter, translates four or five languages, and dances attendance on the proprietor's lady friend, as though she were a grand senora . . . all for twenty-five dollars a month. Who can compete with such people! You, Frenchy, you are like me, very serious, and would die of hunger before passing through certain things. But, mark my words, on this very account they are going to become a terrible people!"

After brief reflection, the ranchman added:

"Perhaps they are not so good as they seem. Just see how they treat those under them! It may be that they affect this simplicity without having it, and when they grin at receiving a kick, they are saying inside, 'Just wait till my turn comes, and I'll give you three!'"

Then he suddenly seemed to repent of his suspicions.

"At any rate, this Karl is a poor fellow, a mealy-mouthed simpleton who the minute I say anything opens his jaws like a fly-catcher. He insists that he comes of a great family, but who knows anything about these gringoes? . . . All of us, dead with hunger when we reach America, claim to be sons of princes."

Madariaga had placed himself on a familiar footing with his Teutonic treasure, not through gratitude as with Desnoyers, but in order to make him feel his inferiority. He had also introduced him on an equal footing in his home, but only that he might give piano lessons to his younger daughter. The Romantica was no longer framing herself in the doorway—in the gloaming watching the sunset reflections. When Karl had finished his work in the office, he was now coming to the house and seating himself beside Elena, who was tinkling away with a persistence worthy of a better fate. At the end of the hour the German, accompanying himself on the piano, would sing fragments from Wagner in such a way that it put Madariaga to sleep in his armchair with his great Paraguay cigar sticking out of his mouth.

Elena meanwhile was contemplating with increasing interest the singing gringo. He was not the knight of her dreams awaited by the fair lady. He was almost a servant, a blond immigrant with reddish hair, fat, heavy, and with bovine eyes that reflected an eternal fear of disagreeing with his chiefs. But day by day, she was finding in him something which rather modified these impressions—his feminine fairness, except where he was burned by the sun, the increasingly martial aspect of his moustachios, the agility with which he mounted his horse, his air of a troubadour, intoning with a rather weak tenor voluptuous romances whose words she did not understand.

One night, just before supper, the impressionable girl announced with a feverish excitement which she could no longer repress that she had made a grand discovery.

"Papa, Karl is of noble birth! He belongs to a great family."

The plainsman made a gesture of indifference. Other things were vexing him in those days. But during the evening, feeling the necessity of venting on somebody the wrath which had been gnawing at his vitals since his last trip to Buenos Aires, he interrupted the singer.

"See here, gringo, what is all this nonsense about nobility which you have been telling my girl?"

Karl left the piano that he might draw himself up to the approved military position before responding. Under the influence of his recent song, his pose suggested Lohengrin about to reveal the secret of his life. His father had been General von Hartrott, one of the commanders in the war of '70. The Emperor had rewarded his services by giving him a title. One of his uncles was an intimate councillor of the King of Prussia. His older brothers were conspicuous in the most select regiments. He had carried a sword as a lieutenant.

Bored with all this grandeur, Madariaga interrupted him. "Lies . . . nonsense . . . hot air!" The very idea of a gringo talking to him about nobility! . . . He had left Europe when very young in order to cast in his lot with the revolting democracies of America, and although nobility now seemed to him something out-of-date and incomprehensible, still he stoutly maintained that the only true nobility was that of his own country. He would yield first place to the gringoes for the invention of machinery and ships, and for breeding priceless animals, but all the Counts and Marquises of Gringo-land appeared to him to be fictitious characters.

"All tomfoolery!" he blustered. "There isn't any nobility in your country, nor have you five dollars all told to rub against each other. If you had, you wouldn't come over here to play the gallant to women who are . . . you know what they are as well as I do."

To the astonishment of Desnoyers, the German received this onslaught with much humility, nodding his head in agreement with the Patron's last words.

"If there's any truth in all this twaddle about titles," continued Madariaga implacably, "swords and uniforms, what did you come here for? What in the devil did you do in your own country that you had to leave it?"

Now Karl hung his head, confused and stuttering.

"Papa, papa," pleaded Elena. "The poor little fellow! How can you humiliate him so just because he is poor?"

And she felt a deep gratitude toward her brother-in-law when he broke through his usual reserve in order to come to the rescue of the German.

"Oh, yes, of course, he's a good-enough fellow," said Madariaga, excusing himself. "But he comes from a land that I detest."

When Desnoyers made a trip to Buenos Aires a few days afterward, the cause of the old man's wrath was explained. It appeared that for some months past Madariaga had been the financial guarantor and devoted swain of a German prima donna stranded in South America with an Italian opera company. It was she who had recommended Karl—an unfortunate countryman, who after wandering through many parts of the continent, was now living with her as a sort of gentlemanly singer. Madariaga had joyously expended upon this courtesan many thousands of dollars. A childish enthusiasm had accompanied him in this novel existence midst urban dissipations until he happened to discover that his Fraulein was leading another life during his absence, laughing at him with the parasites of her retinue; whereupon he arose in his wrath and bade her farewell to the accompaniment of blows and broken furniture.

The last adventure of his life! . . . Desnoyers suspected his abdication upon hearing him admit his age, for the first time. He did not intend to return to the capital. It was all false glitter. Existence in the country, surrounded by all his family and doing good to the poor was the only sure thing. And the terrible centaur expressed himself with the idyllic tenderness and firm virtue of seventy-five years, already insensible to temptation.

After his scene with Karl, he had increased the German's salary, trying as usual, to counteract the effects of his violent outbreaks with generosity. That which he could not forget was his dependent's nobility, constantly making it the subject of new jests. That glorious boast had brought to his mind the genealogical trees of the illustrious ancestry of his prize cattle. The German was a pedigreed fellow, and thenceforth he called him by that nickname.

Seated on summer nights under the awning, he surveyed his family around him with a sort of patriarchal ecstasy. In the evening hush could be heard the buzzing of insects and the croaking of the frogs. From the distant ranches floated the songs of the peons as they prepared their suppers. It was harvest time, and great bands of immigrants were encamped in the fields for the extra work.

Madariaga had known many of the hard old days of wars and violence. Upon his arrival in South America, he had witnessed the last years of the tyranny of Rosas. He loved to enumerate the different provincial and national revolutions in which he had taken part. But all this had disappeared and would never return. These were the times of peace, work and abundance.

"Just think of it, Frenchy," he said, driving away the mosquitoes with the puffs of his cigar. "I am Spanish, you French, Karl German, my daughters Argentinians, the cook Russian, his assistant Greek, the stable boy English, the kitchen servants Chinas (natives), Galicians or Italians, and among the peons there are many castes and laws. . . . And yet we all live in peace. In Europe, we would have probably been in a grand fight by this time, but here we are all friends."

He took much pleasure in listening to the music of the laborers—laments from Italian songs to the accompaniment of the accordion, Spanish guitars and Creole choruses, wild voices chanting of love and death.

"This is a regular Noah's ark," exulted the vainglorious patriarch.

"He means the tower of Babel," thought Desnoyers to himself, "but it's all the same thing to the old man."

"I believe," he rambled on, "that we live thus because in this part of the world there are no kings and a very small army—and mankind is thinking only of enjoying itself as much as possible, thanks to its work. But I also believe that we live so peacefully because there is such abundance that everyone gets his share. . . . How quickly we would spring to arms if the rations were less than the people!"

Again he fell into reflective silence, shortly after announcing the result of his meditations.

"Be that as it may be, we must recognize that here life is more tranquil than in the other world. Men are taken for what they are worth, and mingle together without thinking whether they came from one country or another. Over here, fellows do not come in droves to kill other fellows whom they do not know and whose only crime is that they were born in an unfriendly country. . . . Man is a bad beast everywhere, I know that; but here he eats, owns more land than he needs so that he can stretch himself, and he is good with the goodness of a well-fed dog. Over there, there are too many; they live in heaps getting in each other's way, and easily run amuck. Hurrah for Peace, Frenchy, and the simple life! Where a man can live comfortably and runs no danger of being killed for things he doesn't understand—there is his real homeland!"

And as though an echo of the rustic's reflections, Karl seated at the piano, began chanting in a low voice one of Beethoven's hymns—

"We sing the joy of life,
    We sing of liberty,
We'll ne'er betray our fellow-man,
    Though great the guerdon be."

Peace! . . . A few days afterward Desnoyers recalled bitterly the old man's illusion, for war—domestic war—broke loose in this idyllic stage-setting of ranch life.

"Run, Senor Manager, the old Patron has unsheathed his knife and is going to kill the German!" And Desnoyers had hurried from his office, warned by the peon's summons. Madariaga was chasing Karl, knife in hand, stumbling over everything that blocked his way. Only his son-in-law dared to stop him and disarm him.

"That shameless pedigreed fellow!" bellowed the livid old man as he writhed in Desnoyers' firm clutch. "Half famished, all he thinks he has to do is to come to my house and take away my daughters and dollars. . . . Let me go, I tell you! Let me loose that I may kill him."

And in order to free himself from Desnoyers, he tried further to explain the difficulty. He had accepted the Frenchman as a husband for his daughter because he was to his liking, modest, honest . . . and serious. But this singing Pedigreed Fellow, with all his airs! . . . He was a man that he had gotten from . . . well, he didn't wish to say just where! And the Frenchman, though knowing perfectly well what his introduction to Karl had been, pretended not to understand him.

As the German had, by this time, made good his escape, the ranchman consented to being pushed toward his house, talking all the time about giving a beating to the Romantica and another to the China for not having informed him of the courtship. He had surprised his daughter and the Gringo holding hands and exchanging kisses in a grove near the house.

"He's after my dollars," howled the irate father. "He wants America to enrich him quickly at the expense of the old Spaniard, and that is the reason for so much truckling, so much psalm-singing and so much nobility! Imposter! . . . Musician!"

And he repeated the word "musician" with contempt, as though it were the sum and substance of everything vile.

Very firmly and with few words, Desnoyers brought the wrangling to an end. While her brother-in-law protected her retreat, the Romantica, clinging to her mother, had taken refuge in the top of the house, sobbing and moaning, "Oh, the poor little fellow! Everybody against him!" Her sister meanwhile was exerting all the powers of a discreet daughter with the rampageous old man in the office, and Desnoyers had gone in search of Karl. Finding that he had not yet recovered from the shock of his terrible surprise, he gave him a horse, advising him to betake himself as quickly as possible to the nearest railway station.

Although the German was soon far from the ranch, he did not long remain alone. In a few days, the Romantica followed him. . . . Iseult of the white hands went in search of Tristan, the knight.

This event did not cause Madariaga's desperation to break out as violently as his son-in-law had expected. For the first time, he saw him weep. His gay and robust old age had suddenly fallen from him, the news having clapped ten years on to his four score. Like a child, whimpering and tremulous, he threw his arms around Desnoyers, moistening his neck with tears.

"He has taken her away! That son of a great flea . . . has taken her away!"

This time he did not lay all the blame on his China. He wept with her, and as if trying to console her by a public confession, kept saying over and over:

"It is my fault. . . . It has all been because of my very, very great sins."

Now began for Desnoyers a period of difficulties and conflicts. The fugitives, on one of his visits to the Capital, threw themselves on his mercy, imploring his protection. The Romantica wept, declaring that only her brother-in-law, "the most knightly man in the world," could save her. Karl gazed at him like a faithful hound trusting in his master. These trying interviews were repeated on all his trips. Then, on returning to the ranch, he would find the old man ill-humored, moody, looking fixedly ahead of him as though seeing invisible power and wailing, "It is my punishment—the punishment for my sins."

The memory of the discreditable circumstances under which he had made Karl's acquaintance, before bringing him into his home, tormented the old centaur with remorse. Some afternoons, he would have a horse saddled, going full gallop toward the neighboring village. But he was no longer hunting hospitable ranches. He needed to pass some time in the church, speaking alone with the images that were there only for him—since he had footed the bills for them. . . . "Through my sin, through my very great sin!"

But in spite of his self-reproach, Desnoyers had to work very hard to get any kind of a settlement out of the old penitent. Whenever he suggested legalizing the situation and making the necessary arrangements for their marriage, the old tyrant would not let him go on. "Do what you think best, but don't say anything to me about it."

Several months passed by. One day the Frenchman approached him with a certain air of mystery. "Elena has a son and has named him 'Julio' after you."

"And you, you great useless hulk," stormed the ranchman, "and that weak cow of a wife of yours, you dare to live tranquilly on without giving me a grandson! . . . Ah, Frenchy, that is why the Germans will finally overwhelm you. You see it, right here. That bandit has a son, while you, after four years of marriage . . . nothing. I want a grandson!—do you understand THAT?"

And in order to console himself for this lack of little ones around his own hearth, he betook himself to the ranch of his overseer, Celedonio, where a band of little half-breeds gathered tremblingly and hopefully about him.

Suddenly China died. The poor Misia Petrona passed away as discreetly as she had lived, trying even in her last hours to avoid all annoyance for her husband, asking his pardon with an imploring look for any trouble which her death might cause him. Elena came to the ranch in order to see her mother's body for the last time, and Desnoyers who for more than a year had been supporting them behind his father-in-law's back, took advantage of this occasion to overcome the old man's resentment.

"Well, I'll forgive her," said the ranchman finally. "I'll do it for the sake of my poor wife and for you. She may remain on the ranch, and that shameless gringo may come with her."

But he would have nothing to do with him. The German was to be an employee under Desnoyers, and they could live in the office building as though they did not belong to the family. He would never say a word to Karl.

But scarcely had the German returned before he began giving him orders rudely as though he were a perfect stranger. At other times he would pass by him as though he did not know him. Upon finding Elena in the house with his older daughter, he would go on without speaking to her.

In vain his Romantica transfigured by maternity, improved all opportunities for putting her child in his way, calling him loudly by name: "Julio . . . Julio!"

"They want that brat of a singing gringo, that carrot top with a face like a skinned kid to be my grandson? . . . I prefer Celedonio's."

And by way of emphasizing his protest, he entered the dwelling of his overseer, scattering among his dusky brood handfuls of dollars.

After seven years of marriage, the wife of Desnoyers found that she, too, was going to become a mother. Her sister already had three sons. But what were they worth to Madariaga compared to the grandson that was going to come? "It will be a boy," he announced positively, "because I need one so. It shall be named Julio, and I hope that it will look like my poor dead wife."

Since the death of his wife he no longer called her the China, feeling something of a posthumous love for the poor woman who in her lifetime had endured so much, so timidly and silently. Now "my poor dead wife" cropped out every other instant in the conversation of the remorseful ranchman.

His desires were fulfilled. Luisa gave birth to a boy who bore the name of Julio, and although he did not show in his somewhat sketchy features any striking resemblance to his grandmother, still he had the black hair and eyes and olive skin of a brunette. Welcome! . . . This WAS a grandson!

In the generosity of his joy, he even permitted the German to enter the house for the baptismal ceremony.

When Julio Desnoyers was two years old, his grandfather made the rounds of his estates, holding him on the saddle in front of him. He went from ranch to ranch in order to show him to the copper-colored populace, like an ancient monarch presenting his heir. Later on, when the child was able to say a few words, he entertained himself for hours at a time talking with the tot under the shade of the eucalyptus tree. A certain mental failing was beginning to be noticed in the old man. Although not exactly in his dotage, his aggressiveness was becoming very childish. Even in his most affectionate moments, he used to contradict everybody, and hunt up ways of annoying his relatives.

"Come here, you false prophet," he would say to Julio. "You are a Frenchy."

The grandchild protested as though he had been insulted. His mother had taught him that he was an Argentinian, and his father had suggested that she also add Spanish, in order to please the grandfather.

"Very well, then; if you are not a Frenchy, shout, 'Down with Napoleon!'"

And he looked around him to see if Desnoyers might be near, believing that this would displease him greatly. But his son-in-law pursued the even tenor of his way, shrugging his shoulders.

"Down with Napoleon!" repeated Julio.

And he instantly held out his hand while his grandfather went through his pockets.

Karl's sons, now four in number, used to circle around their grandparent like a humble chorus kept at a distance, and stare enviously at these gifts. In order to win his favor, they one day when they saw him alone, came boldly up to him, shouting in unison, "Down with Napoleon!"

"You insolent gringoes!" ranted the old man. "That's what that shameless father has taught you! If you say that again, I'll chase you with a cat-o-nine-tails. . . . The very idea of insulting a great man in that way!"

While he tolerated this blond brood, he never would permit the slightest intimacy. Desnoyers and his wife often had to come to their rescue, accusing the grandfather of injustice. And in order to pour the vials of his wrath out on someone, the old plainsman would hunt up Celedonio, the best of his listeners, who invariably replied, "Yes, Patron. That's so, Patron."

"They're not to blame," agreed the old man, "but I can't abide them! Besides, they are so like their father, so fair, with hair like a shredded carrot, and the two oldest wearing specs as if they were court clerks! . . . They don't seem like folks with those glasses; they look like sharks."

Madariaga had never seen any sharks, but he imagined them, without knowing why, with round, glassy eyes, like the bottoms of bottles.

By the time he was eight years old, Julio was a famous little equestrian. "To horse, peoncito," his grandfather would cry, and away they would race, streaking like lightning across the fields, midst thousands and thousands of horned herds. The "peoncito," proud of his title, obeyed the master in everything, and so learned to whirl the lasso over the steers, leaving them bound and conquered. Upon making his pony take a deep ditch or creep along the edge of the cliffs, he sometimes fell under his mount, but clambered up gamely.

"Ah, fine cowboy!" exclaimed the grandfather bursting with pride in his exploits. "Here are five dollars for you to give a handkerchief to some china."

The old man, in his increasing mental confusion, did not gauge his gifts exactly with the lad's years; and the infantile horseman, while keeping the money, was wondering what china was referred to, and why he should make her a present.

Desnoyers finally had to drag his son away from the baleful teachings of his grandfather. It was simply useless to have masters come to the house, or to send Julio to the country school. Madariaga would always steal his grandson away, and then they would scour the plains together. So when the boy was eleven years old, his father placed him in a big school in the Capital.

The grandfather then turned his attention to Julio's three-year-old sister, exhibiting her before him as he had her brother, as he took her from ranch to ranch. Everybody called Chicha's little girl Chichi, but the grandfather bestowed on her the same nickname that he had given her brother, the "peoncito." And Chichi, who was growing up wild, vigorous and wilful, breakfasting on meat and talking in her sleep of roast beef, readily fell in with the old man's tastes. She was dressed like a boy, rode astride like a man, and in order to win her grandfather's praises as "fine cowboy," carried a knife in the back of her belt. The two raced the fields from sun to sun, Madariaga following the flying pigtail of the little Amazon as though it were a flag. When nine years old she, too, could lasso the cattle with much dexterity.

What most irritated the ranchman was that his family would remember his age. He received as insults his son-in-law's counsels to remain quietly at home, becoming more aggressive and reckless as he advanced in years, exaggerating his activity, as if he wished to drive Death away. He accepted no help except from his harum-scarum "Peoncito." When Karl's children, great hulking youngsters, hastened to his assistance and offered to hold his stirrup, he would repel them with snorts of indignation.

"So you think I am no longer able to help myself, eh! . . . There's still enough life in me to make those who are waiting for me to die, so as to grab my dollars, chew their disappointment a long while yet!"

Since the German and his wife were kept pointedly apart from the family life, they had to put up with these allusions in silence. Karl, needing protection, constantly shadowed the Frenchman, improving every opportunity to overwhelm him with his eulogies. He never could thank him enough for all that he had done for him. He was his only champion. He longed for a chance to prove his gratitude, to die for him if necessary. His wife admired him with enthusiasm as "the most gifted knight in the world." And Desnoyers received their devotion in gratified silence, accepting the German as an excellent comrade. As he controlled absolutely the family fortune, he aided Karl very generously without arousing the resentment of the old man. He also took the initiative in bringing about the realization of Karl's pet ambition—a visit to the Fatherland. So many years in America! . . . For the very reason that Desnoyers himself had no desire to return to Europe, he wished to facilitate Karl's trip, and gave him the means to make the journey with his entire family. The father-in-law had no curiosity as to who paid the expenses. "Let them go!" he said gleefully, "and may they never return!"

Their absence was not a very long one, for they spent their year's allowance in three months. Karl, who had apprised his parents of the great fortune which his marriage had brought him, wished to make an impression as a millionaire, in full enjoyment of his riches. Elena returned radiant, speaking with pride of her relatives—of the baron, Colonel of Hussars, of the Captain of the Guard, of the Councillor at Court—asserting that all countries were most insignificant when compared with her husband's. She even affected a certain condescension toward Desnoyers, praising him as "a very worthy man, but without ancient lineage or distinguished family—and French, besides."

Karl, on the other hand, showed the same devotion as before, keeping himself submissively in the background when with his brother-in-law who had the keys of the cash box and was his only defense against the browbeating old Patron. . . . He had left his two older sons in a school in Germany. Years afterwards they reached an equal footing with the other grandchildren of the Spaniard who always begrudged them their existence, "perfect frights, with carroty hair, and eyes like a shark."

Suddenly the old man became very lonely, for they had also carried off his second "Peoncito." The good Chicha could not tolerate her daughter's growing up like a boy, parading 'round on horseback all the time, and glibly repeating her grandfather's vulgarities. So she was now in a convent in the Capital, where the Sisters had to battle valiantly in order to tame the mischievous rebellion of their wild little pupil.

When Julio and Chichi returned to the ranch for their vacations, the grandfather again concentrated his fondness on the first, as though the girl had merely been a substitute. Desnoyers was becoming indignant at his son's dissipated life. He was no longer at college, and his existence was that of a student in a rich family who makes up for parental parsimony with all sorts of imprudent borrowings.

But Madariaga came to the defense of his grandson. "Ah, the fine cowboy!" . . . Seeing him again on the ranch, he admired the dash of the good looking youth, testing his muscles in order to convince himself of their strength, and making him to recount his nightly escapades as ringleader of a band of toughs in the Capital. He longed to go to Buenos Aires himself, just to see the youngster in the midst of this gay, wild life. But alas! he was not seventeen like his grandson; he had already passed eighty.

"Come here, you false prophet! Tell me how many children you have. . . . You must have a great many children, you know!"

"Father!" protested Chicha who was always hanging around, fearing her parent's bad teachings.

"Stop nagging at me!" yelled the irate old fellow in a towering temper. "I know what I'm saying."

Paternity figured largely in all his amorous fancies. He was almost blind, and the loss of his sight was accompanied by an increasing mental upset. His crazy senility took on a lewd character, expressing itself in language which scandalized or amused the community.

"Oh, you rascal, what a pretty fellow you are!" he said, leering at Julio with eyes which could no longer distinguish things except in a shadowy way. "You are the living image of my poor dead wife. . . . Have a good time, for Grandpa is always here with his money! If you could only count on what your father gives you, you would live like a hermit. These Frenchies are a close-fisted lot! But I am looking out for you. Peoncito! Spend and enjoy yourself—that's what your Granddaddy has piled up the silver for!"

When the Desnoyers children returned to the Capital, he spent his lonesome hours in going from ranch to ranch. A young half-breed would set the water for his shrub-tea to boiling on the hearth, and the old man would wonder confusedly if she were his daughter. Another, fifteen years old, would offer him a gourd filled with the bitter liquid and a silver pipe with which to sip it. . . . A grandchild, perhaps—he wasn't sure. And so he passed the afternoons, silent and sluggish, drinking gourd after gourd of shrub tea, surrounded by families who stared at him with admiration and fear.

Every time he mounted his horse for these excursions, his older daughter would protest. "At eighty-four years! Would it not be better for him to remain quietly at home. . . ." Some day something terrible would happen. . . . And the terrible thing did happen. One evening the Patron's horse came slowly home without its rider. The old man had fallen on the sloping highway, and when they found him, he was dead. Thus died the centaur as he had lived, with the lash hanging from his wrist, with his legs bowed by the saddle.

A Spanish notary, almost as old as he, produced the will. The family was somewhat alarmed at seeing what a voluminous document it was. What terrible bequests had Madariaga dictated? The reading of the first part tranquilized Karl and Elena. The old father had left considerable more to the wife of Desnoyers, but there still remained an enormous share for the Romantica and her children.

"I do this," he said, "in memory of my poor dead wife, and so that people won't talk."

After this, came eighty-six legacies. Eighty-five dark-hued individuals (women and men), who had lived on the ranch for many years as tenants and retainers, were to receive the last paternal munificence of the old patriarch. At the head of these was Celedonio whom Madariaga had greatly enriched in his lifetime for no heavier work than listening to him and repeating, "That's so, Patron, that's true!" More than a million dollars were represented by these bequests in lands and herds. The one who completed the list of beneficiaries was Julio Desnoyers. The grandfather had made special mention of this namesake, leaving him a plantation "to meet his private expenses, making up for that which his father would not give him."

"But that represents hundreds of thousands of dollars!" protested Karl, who had been making himself almost obnoxious in his efforts to assure himself that his wife had not been overlooked in the will.

The days following the reading of this will were very trying ones for the family. Elena and her children kept looking at the other group as though they had just waked up, contemplating them in an entirely new light. They seemed to forget what they were going to receive in their envy of the much larger share of their relatives.

Desnoyers, benevolent and conciliatory, had a plan. An expert in administrative affairs, he realized that the distribution among the heirs was going to double the expenses without increasing the income. He was calculating, besides, the complications and disbursements necessary for a judicial division of nine immense ranches, hundreds of thousands of cattle, deposits in the banks, houses in the city, and debts to collect. Would it not be better for them all to continue living as before? . . . Had they not lived most peaceably as a united family? . . .

The German received this suggestion by drawing himself up haughtily. No; to each one should be given what was his. Let each live in his own sphere. He wished to establish himself in Europe, spending his wealth freely there. It was necessary for him to return to "his world."

As they looked squarely at each other, Desnoyers saw an unknown Karl, a Karl whose existence he had never suspected when he was under his protection, timid and servile. The Frenchman, too, was beginning to see things in a new light.

"Very well," he assented. "Let each take his own. That seems fair to me."

CHAPTER III

THE DESNOYERS FAMILY

The "Madariagan succession," as it was called in the language of the legal men interested in prolonging it in order to augment their fees—was divided into two groups, separated by the ocean. The Desnoyers moved to Buenos Aires. The Hartrotts moved to Berlin as soon as Karl could sell all the legacy, to re-invest it in lands and industrial enterprises in his own country.

Desnoyers no longer cared to live in the country. For twenty years, now, he had been the head of an enormous agricultural and stock raising business, overseeing hundreds of men in the various ranches. The parcelling out of the old man's fortune among Elena and the other legatees had considerably constricted the radius of his authority, and it angered him to see established on the neighboring lands so many foreigners, almost all Germans, who had bought of Karl. Furthermore, he was getting old, his wife's inheritance amounted to about twenty millions of dollars, and perhaps his brother-in-law was showing the better judgment in returning to Europe.

So he leased some of the plantations, handed over the superintendence of others to those mentioned in the will who considered themselves left-handed members of the family—of which Desnoyers as the Patron received their submissive allegiance—and moved to Buenos Aires.

By this move, he was able to keep an eye on his son who continued living a dissipated life without making any headway in his engineering studies. Then, too, Chichi was now almost a woman—her robust development making her look older than she was—and it was not expedient to keep her on the estate to become a rustic senorita like her mother.

Dona Luisa had also tired of ranch life, the social triumphs of her sister making her a little restless. She was incapable of feeling jealous, but material ambitions made her anxious that her children should not bring up the rear of the procession in which the other grandchildren were cutting such a dashing figure.

During the year, most wonderful reports from Germany were finding their way to the Desnoyers home in the Capital. "The aunt from Berlin," as the children called her, kept sending long letters filled with accounts of dances, dinners, hunting parties and titles—many high-sounding and military titles;— "our brother, the Colonel," "our cousin, the Baron," "our uncle, the Intimate Councillor," "our great-uncle, the Truly Intimate." All the extravagances of the German social ladder, which incessantly manufactures new titles in order to satisfy the thirst for honors of a people divided into castes, were enumerated with delight by the old Romantica. She even mentioned her husband's secretary (a nobody) who, through working in the public offices, had acquired the title of Rechnungarath, Councillor of Calculations. She also referred with much pride to the retired Oberpedell which she had in her house, explaining that that meant "Superior Porter."

The news about her children was no less glorious. The oldest was the wise one of the family. He was devoted to philology and the historical sciences, but his sight was growing weaker all the time because of his omnivorous reading. Soon he would be a Doctor, and before he was thirty, a Herr Professor. The mother lamented that he had not military aspirations, considering that his tastes had somewhat distorted the lofty destinies of the family. Professorships, sciences and literature were more properly the perquisites of the Jews, unable, because of their race, to obtain preferment in the army; but she was trying to console herself by keeping in mind that a celebrated professor could, in time, acquire a social rank almost equal to that of a colonel.

Her other four sons would become officers. Their father was preparing the ground so that they might enter the Guard or some aristocratic regiment without any of the members being able to vote against their admission. The two daughters would surely marry, when they had reached a suitable age with officers of the Hussars whose names bore the magic "von" of petty nobility, haughty and charming gentlemen about whom the daughter of Misia Petrona waxed most enthusiastic.

The establishment of the Hartrotts was in keeping with these new relationships. In the home in Berlin, the servants wore knee-breeches and white wigs on the nights of great banquets. Karl had bought an old castle with pointed towers, ghosts in the cellars, and various legends of assassinations, assaults and abductions which enlivened its history in an interesting way. An architect, decorated with many foreign orders, and bearing the title of "Councillor of Construction," was engaged to modernize the mediaeval edifice without sacrificing its terrifying aspect. The Romantica described in anticipation the receptions in the gloomy salon, the light diffused by electricity, simulating torches, the crackling of the emblazoned hearth with its imitation logs bristling with flames of gas, all the splendor of modern luxury combined with the souvenirs of an epoch of omnipotent nobility—the best, according to her, in history. And the hunting parties, the future hunting parties! . . . in an annex of sandy and loose soil with pine woods—in no way comparable to the rich ground of their native ranch, but which had the honor of being trodden centuries ago by the Princes of Brandenburg, founders of the reigning house of Prussia. And all this advancement in a single year! . . .

They had, of course, to compete with other oversea families who had amassed enormous fortunes in the United States, Brazil or the Pacific coast; but these were Germans "without lineage," coarse plebeians who were struggling in vain to force themselves into the great world by making donations to the imperial works. With all their millions, the very most that they could ever hope to attain would be to marry their daughters with ordinary soldiers. Whilst Karl! . . . The relatives of Karl! . . . and the Romantica let her pen run on, glorifying a family in whose bosom she fancied she had been born.

From time to time were enclosed with Elena's effusions brief, crisp notes directed to Desnoyers. The brother-in-law continued giving an account of his operations the same as when living on the ranch under his protection. But with this deference was now mixed a badly concealed pride, an evident desire to retaliate for his times of voluntary humiliation. Everything that he was doing was grand and glorious. He had invested his millions in the industrial enterprises of modern Germany. He was stockholder of munition factories as big as towns, and of navigation companies launching a ship every half year. The Emperor was interesting himself in these works, looking benevolently on all those who wished to aid him. Besides this, Karl was buying land. At first sight, it seemed foolish to have sold the fertile fields of their inheritance in order to acquire sandy Prussian wastes that yielded only to much artificial fertilizing; but by becoming a land owner, he now belonged to the "Agrarian Party," the aristocratic and conservative group par excellence, and thus he was living in two different but equally distinguished worlds—that of the great industrial friends of the Emperor, and that of the Junkers, knights of the countryside, guardians of the old traditions and the supply-source of the officials of the King of Prussia.

On hearing of these social strides, Desnoyers could not but think of the pecuniary sacrifices which they must represent. He knew Karl's past, for on the ranch, under an impulse of gratitude, the German had one day revealed to the Frenchman the cause of his coming to America. He was a former officer in the German army, but the desire of living ostentatiously without other resources than his salary, had dragged him into committing such reprehensible acts as abstracting funds belonging to the regiment, incurring debts of honor and paying for them with forged signatures. These crimes had not been officially prosecuted through consideration of his father's memory, but the members of his division had submitted him to a tribunal of honor. His brothers and friends had advised him to shoot himself as the only remedy; but he loved life and had fled to South America where, in spite of humiliations, he had finally triumphed.

Wealth effaces the spots of the past even more rapidly than Time. The news of his fortune on the other side of the ocean made his family give him a warm reception on his first voyage home; introducing him again into their world. Nobody could remember shameful stories about a few hundred marks concerning a man who was talking about his father-in-law's lands, more extensive than many German principalities. Now, upon installing himself definitely in his country, all was forgotten. But, oh, the contributions levied upon his vanity . . . Desnoyers shrewdly guessed at the thousands of marks poured with both hands into the charitable works of the Empress, into the imperialistic propagandas, into the societies of veterans, into the clubs of aggression and expansion organized by German ambition.

The frugal Frenchman, thrifty in his expenditures and free from social ambitions, smiled at the grandeurs of his brother-in-law. He considered Karl an excellent companion although of a childish pride. He recalled with satisfaction the years that they had passed together in the country. He could not forget the German who was always hovering around him, affectionate and submissive as a younger brother. When his family commented with a somewhat envious vivacity upon the glories of their Berlin relatives, Desnoyers would say smilingly, "Leave them in peace; they are paying very dear for their whistle."

But the enthusiasm which the letters from Germany breathed finally created an atmosphere of disquietude and rebellion. Chichi led the attack. Why were they not going to Europe like other folks? all their friends had been there. Even the Italian and Spanish shopkeepers were making the voyage, while she, the daughter of a Frenchman, had never seen Paris! . . . Oh, Paris. The doctors in attendance on melancholy ladies were announcing the existence of a new and terrible disease, "the mania for Paris." Dona Luisa supported her daughter. Why had she not gone to live in Europe like her sister, since she was the richer of the two? Even Julio gravely declared that in the old world he could study to better advantage. America is not the land of the learned.

Infected by the general unrest, the father finally began to wonder why the idea of going to Europe had not occurred to him long before. Thirty-four years without going to that country which was not his! . . . It was high time to start! He was living too near to his business. In vain the retired ranchman had tried to keep himself indifferent to the money market. Everybody was coining money around him. In the club, in the theatre, wherever he went, the people were talking about purchases of lands, of sales of stock, of quick negotiations with a triple profit, of portentous balances. The amount of money that he was keeping idle in the banks was beginning to weigh upon him. He finally ended by involving himself in some speculation; like a gambler who cannot see the roulette wheel without putting his hand in his pocket.

His family was right. "To Paris!" For in the Desnoyers' mind, to go to Europe meant, of course, to go to Paris. Let the "aunt from Berlin" keep on chanting the glories of her husband's country! "It's sheer nonsense!" exclaimed Julio who had made grave geographical and ethnic comparisons in his nightly forays. "There is no place but Paris!" Chichi saluted with an ironical smile the slightest doubt of it—"Perhaps they make as elegant fashions in Germany as in Paris? . . . Bah!" Dona Luisa took up her children's cry. "Paris!" . . . Never had it even occurred to her to go to a Lutheran land to be protected by her sister.

"Let it be Paris, then!" said the Frenchman, as though he were speaking of an unknown city.

He had accustomed himself to believe that he would never return to it. During the first years of his life in America, the trip would have been an impossibility because of the military service which he had evaded. Then he had vague news of different amnesties. After the time for conscription had long since passed, an inertness of will had made him consider a return to his country as somewhat absurd and useless. On the other side, nothing remained to attract him. He had even lost track of those country relatives with whom his mother had lived. In his heaviest hours he had tried to occupy his activity by planning an enormous mausoleum, all of marble, in La Recoleta, the cemetery of the rich, in order to move thither the remains of Madariaga as founder of the dynasty, following him with all his own when their hour should come. He was beginning to feel the weight of age. He was nearly seventy years old, and the rude life of the country, the horseback rides in the rain, the rivers forded upon his swimming horse, the nights passed in the open air, had brought on a rheumatism that was torturing his best days.

His family, however, reawakened his enthusiasm. "To Paris!" . . . He began to fancy that he was twenty again, and forgetting his habitual parsimony, wished his household to travel like royalty, in the most luxurious staterooms, and with personal servants. Two copper-hued country girls, born on the ranch and elevated to the rank of maids to the senora and her daughter, accompanied them on the voyage, their oblique eyes betraying not the slightest astonishment before the greatest novelties.

Once in Paris, Desnoyers found himself quite bewildered. He confused the names of streets, proposed visits to buildings which had long since disappeared, and all his attempts to prove himself an expert authority on Paris were attended with disappointment. His children, guided by recent reading up, knew Paris better than he. He was considered a foreigner in his own country. At first, he even felt a certain strangeness in using his native tongue, for he had remained on the ranch without speaking a word of his language for years at a time. He was used to thinking in Spanish, and translating his ideas into the speech of his ancestors spattered his French with all kinds of Creole dialect.

"Where a man makes his fortune and raises his family, there is his true country," he said sententiously, remembering Madariaga.

The image of that distant country dominated him with insistent obsession as soon as the impressions of the voyage had worn off. He had no French friends, and upon going into the street, his feet instinctively took him to the places where the Argentinians gathered together. It was the same with them. They had left their country only to feel, with increasing intensity, the desire to talk about it all the time. There he read the papers, commenting on the rising prices in the fields, on the prospects for the next harvests and on the sales of cattle. Returning home, his thoughts were still in America, and he chuckled with delight as he recalled the way in which the two chinas had defied the professional dignity of the French cook, preparing their native stews and other dishes in Creole style.

He had settled the family in an ostentatious house in the avenida Victor Hugo, for which he paid a rental of twenty-eight thousand francs. Dona Luisa had to go and come many times before she could accustom herself to the imposing aspect of the concierges—he, decorated with gold trimmings on his black uniform and wearing white whiskers like a notary in a comedy, she with a chain of gold upon her exuberant bosom, and receiving the tenants in a red and gold salon. In the rooms above was ultra-modern luxury, gilded and glacial, with white walls and glass doors with tiny panes which exasperated Desnoyers, who longed for the complicated carvings and rich furniture in vogue during his youth. He himself directed the arrangement and furnishings of the various rooms which always seemed empty.

Chichi protested against her father's avarice when she saw him buying slowly and with much calculation and hesitation. "Avarice, no!" he retorted, "it is because I know the worth of things."

Nothing pleased him that he had not acquired at one-third of its value. Beating down those who overcharged but proved the superiority of the buyer. Paris offered him one delightful spot which he could not find anywhere else in the world—the Hotel Drouot. He would go there every afternoon that he did not find other important auctions advertised in the papers. For many years, there was no famous failure in Parisian life, with its consequent liquidation, from which he did not carry something away. The use and need of these prizes were matters of secondary interest, the great thing was to get them for ridiculous prices. So the trophies from the auction-rooms now began to inundate the apartment which, at the beginning, he had been furnishing with such desperate slowness.

His daughter now complained that the home was getting overcrowded. The furnishings and ornaments were handsome, but too many . . . far too many! The white walls seemed to scowl at the magnificent sets of chairs and the overflowing glass cabinets. Rich and velvety carpets over which had passed many generations, covered all the compartments. Showy curtains, not finding a vacant frame in the salons, adorned the doors leading into the kitchen. The wall mouldings gradually disappeared under an overlay of pictures, placed close together like the scales of a cuirass. Who now could accuse Desnoyers of avarice? . . . He was investing far more than a fashionable contractor would have dreamed of spending.

The underlying idea still was to acquire all this for a fourth of its price—an exciting bait which lured the economical man into continuous dissipation. He could sleep well only when he had driven a good bargain during the day. He bought at auction thousands of bottles of wine consigned by bankrupt firms, and he who scarcely ever drank, packed his wine cellars to overflowing, advising his family to use the champagne as freely as ordinary wine. The failure of a furrier induced him to buy for fourteen thousand francs pelts worth ninety thousand. In consequence, the entire Desnoyers family seemed suddenly to be suffering as frightfully from cold as though a polar iceberg had invaded the avenida Victor Hugo. The father kept only one fur coat for himself but ordered three for his son. Chichi and Dona Luisa appeared arrayed in all kinds of silky and luxurious skins—one day chinchilla, other days blue fox, marten or seal.

The enraptured buyer would permit no one but himself to adorn the walls with his new acquisitions, using the hammer from the top of a step-ladder in order to save the expense of a professional picture hanger. He wished to set his children the example of economy. In his idle hours, he would change the position of the heaviest pieces of furniture, trying every kind of combination. This employment reminded him of those happy days when he handled great sacks of wheat and bundles of hides on the ranch. Whenever his son noticed that he was looking thoughtfully at a monumental sideboard or heavy piece, he prudently betook himself to other haunts.

Desnoyers stood a little in awe of the two house-men, very solemn, correct creatures always in dress suit, who could not hide their astonishment at seeing a man with an income of more than a million francs engaged in such work. Finally it was the two coppery maids who aided their Patron, the three working contentedly together like companions in exile.

Four automobiles completed the luxuriousness of the family. The children would have been more content with one—small and dashing, in the very latest style. But Desnoyers was not the man to let a bargain slip past him, so one after the other, he had picked up the four, tempted by the price. They were as enormous and majestic as coaches of state. Their entrance into a street made the passers-by turn and stare. The chauffeur needed two assistants to help him keep this flock of mastodons in order, but the proud owner thought only of the skill with which he had gotten the best of the salesmen, anxious to get such monuments out of their sight.

To his children he was always recommending simplicity and economy. "We are not as rich as you suppose. We own a good deal of property, but it produces a scanty income."

And then, after refusing a domestic expenditure of two hundred francs, he would put five thousand into an unnecessary purchase just because it would mean a great loss to the seller. Julio and his sister kept protesting to their mother, Dona Luisa—Chichi even going so far as to announce that she would never marry a man like her father.

"Hush, hush!" exclaimed the scandalized Creole. "He has his little peculiarities, but he is very good. Never has he given me any cause for complaint. I only hope that you may be lucky enough to find his equal."

Her husband's quarrelsomeness, his irritable character and his masterful will all sank into insignificance when she thought of his unvarying fidelity. In so many years of married life . . . nothing! His faithfulness had been unexceptional even in the country where many, surrounded by beasts, and intent on increasing their flocks, had seemed to become contaminated by the general animalism. She remembered her father only too well! . . . Even her sister was obliged to live in apparent calmness with the vainglorious Karl, quite capable of disloyalty not because of any special lust, but just to imitate the doings of his superiors.

Desnoyers and his wife were plodding through life in a routine affection, reminding Dona Luisa, in her limited imagination, of the yokes of oxen on the ranch who refused to budge whenever another animal was substituted for the regular companion. Her husband certainly was quick tempered, holding her responsible for all the whims with which he exasperated his children, yet he could never bear to have her out of his sight. The afternoons at the hotel Drouot would be most insipid for him unless she was at his side, the confidante of his plans and wrathful outbursts.

"To-day there is to be a sale of jewels; shall we go?"

He would make this proposition in such a gentle and coaxing voice—the voice that Dona Luisa remembered in their first talks around the old home. And so they would go together, but by different routes;—she in one of the monumental vehicles because, accustomed to the leisurely carriage rides of the ranch, she no longer cared to walk; and Desnoyers—although owner of the four automobiles, heartily abominating them because he was conservative and uneasy with the complications of new machinery—on foot under the pretext that, through lack of work, his body needed the exercise. When they met in the crowded salesrooms, they proceeded to examine the jewels together, fixing beforehand, the price they would offer. But he, quick to become exasperated by opposition, always went further, hurling numbers at his competitors as though they were blows. After such excursions, the senora would appear as majestic and dazzling as a basilica of Byzantium—ears and neck decorated with great pearls, her bosom a constellation of brilliants, her hands radiating points of light of all colors of the rainbow.

"Too much, mama," Chichi would protest. "They will take you for a pawnbroker's lady!" But the Creole, satisfied with her splendor, the crowning glory of a humble life, attributed her daughter's faultfinding to envy. Chichi was only a girl now, but later on she would thank her for having collected all these gems for her.

Already the home was unable to accommodate so many purchases. In the cellars were piled up enough paintings, furniture, statues, and draperies to equip several other dwellings. Don Marcelo began to complain of the cramped space in an apartment costing twenty-eight thousand francs a year—in reality large enough for a family four times the size of his. He was beginning to deplore being obliged to renounce some very tempting furniture bargains when a real estate agent smelled out the foreigner and relieved him of his embarrassment. Why not buy a castle? . . .

The entire family was delighted with the idea. An historic castle, the most historic that could be found, would supplement their luxurious establishment. Chichi paled with pride. Some of her friends had castles. Others, of old colonial family, who were accustomed to look down upon her for her country bringing up, would now cry with envy upon learning of this acquisition which was almost a patent of nobility. The mother smiled in the hope of months in the country which would recall the simple and happy life of her youth. Julio was less enthusiastic. The "old man" would expect him to spend much time away from Paris, but he consoled himself by reflecting that the suburban place would provide excuse for frequent automobile trips.

Desnoyers thought of the relatives in Berlin. Why should he not have his castle like the others? . . . The bargains were alluring. Historic mansions by the dozen were offered him. Their owners, exhausted by the expense of maintaining them, were more than anxious to sell. So he bought the castle of Villeblanche-sur-Marne, built in the time of the religious wars—a mixture of palace and fortress with an Italian Renaissance facade, gloomy towers with pointed hoods, and moats in which swans were swimming.

He could now live with some tracts of land over which to exercise his authority, struggling again with the resistance of men and things. Besides, the vast proportions of the rooms of the castle were very tempting and bare of furniture. This opportunity for placing the overflow from his cellars plunged him again into buying. With this atmosphere of lordly gloom, the antiques would harmonize beautifully, without that cry of protest which they always seemed to make when placed in contact with the glaring white walls of modern habitations. The historic residence required an endless outlay; on that account it had changed owners so many times.

But he and the land understood each other beautifully. . . . So at the same time that he was filling the salons, he was going to begin farming and stock-raising in the extensive parks—a reproduction in miniature of his enterprises in South America. The property ought to be made self-supporting. Not that he had any fear of the expenses, but he did not intend to lose money on the proposition.

The acquisition of the castle brought Desnoyers a true friendship—the chief advantage in the transaction. He became acquainted with a neighbor, Senator Lacour, who twice had been Minister of State, and was now vegetating in the senate, silent during its sessions, but restless and voluble in the corridors in order to maintain his influence. He was a prominent figure of the republican nobility, an aristocrat of the new regime that had sprung from the agitations of the Revolution, just as the titled nobility had won their spurs in the Crusades. His great-grandfather had belonged to the Convention. His father had figured in the Republic of 1848. He, as the son of an exile who had died in banishment, had when very young marched behind the grandiloquent figure of Gambetta, and always spoke in glowing terms of the Master, in the hope that some of his rays might be reflected on his disciple. His son Rene, a pupil of the Ecole Centrale regarded his father as "a rare old sport," laughing a little at his romantic and humanitarian republicanism. He, nevertheless, was counting much on that same official protection treasured by four generations of Lacours dedicated to the service of the Republic, to assist him when he became an engineer.

Don Marcelo who used to look uneasily upon any new friendship, fearing a demand for a loan, gave himself up with enthusiasm to intimacy with this "grand man." The personage admired riches and recognized, besides, a certain genius in this millionaire from the other side of the sea accustomed to speaking of limitless pastures and immense herds. Their intercourse was more than the mere friendliness of a country neighborhood, and continued on after their return to Paris. Finally Rene visited the home on the avenida Victor Hugo as though it were his own.

The only disappointments in Desnoyers' new life came from his children. Chichi irritated him because of the independence of her tastes. She did not like antiques, no matter how substantial and magnificent they might be, much preferring the frivolities of the latest fashion. She accepted all her father's gifts with great indifference. Before an exquisite blonde piece of lace, centuries old, picked up at auction, she made a wry face, saying, "I would much rather have had a new dress costing three hundred francs." She and her brother were solidly opposed to everything old.

Now that his daughter was already a woman, he had confided her absolutely to the care of Dona Luisa. But the former "Peoncito" was not showing much respect for the advice and commands of the good natured Creole. She had taken up roller-skating with enthusiasm, regarding it as the most elegant of diversions.

She would go every afternoon to the Ice Palace, Dona Luisa chaperoning her, although to do this she was obliged to give up accompanying her husband to his sales. Oh, the hours of deadly weariness before that frozen oval ring, watching the white circle of balancing human monkeys gliding by on runners to the sound of an organ! . . . Her daughter would pass and repass before her tired eyes, rosy from the exercise, spirals of hair escaped from her hat, streaming out behind, the folds of her skirt swinging above her skates—handsome, athletic and Amazonian, with the rude health of a child who, according to her father, "had been weaned on beefsteaks."

Finally Dona Luisa rebelled against this troublesome vigilance, preferring to accompany her husband on his hunt for underpriced riches. Chichi went to the skating rink with one of the dark-skinned maids, passing the afternoons with her sporty friends of the new world. Together they ventilated their ideas under the glare of the easy life of Paris, freed from the scruples and conventions of their native land. They all thought themselves older than they were, delighting to discover in each other unsuspected charms. The change from the other hemisphere had altered their sense of values. Some were even writing verses in French. And Desnoyers became alarmed, giving free rein to his bad humor, when Chichi of evenings, would bring forth as aphorisms that which she and her friends had been discussing, as a summary of their readings and observations.— "Life is life, and one must live! . . . I will marry the man I love, no matter who he may be. . . ."

But the daughter's independence was as nothing compared to the worry which the other child gave the Desnoyers. Ay, that other one! . . . Julio, upon arriving in Paris, had changed the bent of his aspirations. He no longer thought of becoming an engineer; he wished to become an artist. Don Marcelo objected in great consternation, but finally yielded. Let it be painting! The important thing was to have some regular profession. The father, while he considered property and wealth as sacred rights, felt that no one should enjoy them who had not worked to acquire them.

Recalling his apprenticeship as a wood carver, he began to hope that the artistic instincts which poverty had extinguished in him were, perhaps, reappearing in his son. What if this lazy boy, this lively genius, hesitating before taking up his walk in life, should turn out to be a famous painter, after all! . . . So he agreed to all of Julio's caprices, the budding artist insisting that for his first efforts in drawing and coloring, he needed a separate apartment where he could work with more freedom. His father, therefore, established him near his home, in the rue de la Pompe in the former studio of a well-known foreign painter. The workroom and its annexes were far too large for an amateur, but the owner had died, and Desnoyers improved the opportunity offered by the heirs, and bought at a remarkable bargain, the entire plant, pictures and furnishings.

Dona Luisa at first visited the studio daily like a good mother, caring for the well-being of her son that he may work to better advantage. Taking off her gloves, she emptied the brass trays filled with cigar stubs and dusted the furniture powdered with the ashes fallen from the pipes. Julio's visitors, long-haired young men who spoke of things that she could not understand, seemed to her rather careless in their manners. . . . Later on she also met there women, very lightly clad, and was received with scowls by her son. Wasn't his mother ever going to let him work in peace? . . . So the poor lady, starting out in the morning toward the rue de la Pompe, stopped midway and went instead to the church of Saint Honore d'Eylau.

The father displayed more prudence. A man of his years could not expect to mingle with the chums of a young artist. In a few months' time, Julio passed entire weeks without going to sleep under the paternal roof. Finally he installed himself permanently in his studio, occasionally making a flying trip home that his family might know that he was still in existence. . . . Some mornings, Desnoyers would arrive at the rue de la Pompe in order to ask a few questions of the concierge. It was ten o'clock; the artist was sleeping. Upon returning at midday, he learned that the heavy sleep still continued. Soon after lunch, another visit to get better news. It was two o'clock, the young gentleman was just arising. So the father would retire, muttering stormily—"But when does this painter ever paint?" . . .

At first Julio had tried to win renown with his brush, believing that it would prove an easy task. In true artist fashion, he collected his friends around him, South American boys with nothing to do but enjoy life, scattering money ostentatiously so that everybody might know of their generosity. With serene audacity, the young canvas-dauber undertook to paint portraits. He loved good painting, "distinctive" painting, with the cloying sweetness of a romance, that copied only the forms of women. He had money, a good studio, his father was standing behind him ready to help—why shouldn't he accomplish as much as many others who lacked his opportunities? . . .

So he began his work by coloring a canvas entitled, "The Dance of the Hours," a mere pretext for copying pretty girls and selecting buxom models. These he would sketch at a mad speed, filling in the outlines with blobs of multi-colored paint, and up to this point all went well. Then he would begin to vacillate, remaining idle before the picture only to put it in the corner in hope of later inspiration. It was the same way with his various studies of feminine heads. Finding that he was never able to finish anything, he soon became resigned, like one who pants with fatigue before an obstacle waiting for a providential interposition to save him. The important thing was to be a painter . . . even though he might not paint anything. This afforded him the opportunity, on the plea of lofty aestheticism, of sending out cards of invitation and asking light women to his studio. He lived during the night. Don Marcelo, upon investigating the artist's work, could not contain his indignation. Every morning the two Desnoyers were accustomed to greet the first hours of dawn—the father leaping from his bed, the son, on his way home to his studio to throw himself upon his couch not to wake till midday.

The credulous Dona Luisa would invent the most absurd explanations to defend her son. Who could tell? Perhaps he had the habit of painting during the night, utilizing it for original work. Men resort to so many devilish things! . . .

Desnoyers knew very well what these nocturnal gusts of genius were amounting to—scandals in the restaurants of Montmartre, and scrimmages, many scrimmages. He and his gang, who believed that at seven a full dress or Tuxedo was indispensable, were like a band of Indians, bringing to Paris the wild customs of the plains. Champagne always made them quarrelsome. So they broke and paid, but their generosities were almost invariably followed by a scuffle. No one could surpass Julio in the quick slap and the ready card. His father heard with a heavy heart the news brought him by some friends thinking to flatter his vanity—his son was always victorious in these gentlemanly encounters; he it was who always scratched the enemy's skin. The painter knew more about fencing than art. He was a champion with various weapons; he could box, and was even skilled in the favorite blows of the prize fighters of the slums. "Useless as a drone, and as dangerous, too," fretted his father. And yet in the back of his troubled mind fluttered an irresistible satisfaction—an animal pride in the thought that this hare-brained terror was his own.

For a while, he thought that he had hit upon a way of withdrawing his son from such an existence. The relatives in Berlin had visited the Desnoyers in their castle of Villeblanche. With good-natured superiority, Karl von Hartrott had appreciated the rich and rather absurd accumulations of his brother-in-law. They were not bad; he admitted that they gave a certain cachet to the home in Paris and to the castle. They smacked of the possessions of titled nobility. But Germany! . . . The comforts and luxuries in his country! . . . He just wished his brother-in-law to admire the way he lived and the noble friendships that embellished his opulence. And so he insisted in his letters that the Desnoyers family should return their visit. This change of environment might tone Julio down a little. Perhaps his ambition might waken on seeing the diligence of his cousins, each with a career. The Frenchman had, besides, an underlying belief in the more corrupt influence of Paris as compared with the purity of the customs in Patriarchal Germany.

They were there four months. In a little while Desnoyers felt ready to retreat. Each to his own kind; he would never be able to understand such people. Exceedingly amiable, with an abject amiability and evident desire to please, but constantly blundering through a tactless desire to make their grandeur felt. The high-toned friends of Hartrott emphasized their love for France, but it was the pious love that a weak and mischievous child inspires, needing protection. And they would accompany their affability with all manner of inopportune memories of the wars in which France had been conquered. Everything in Germany—a monument, a railroad station, a simple dining-room device, instantly gave rise to glorious comparisons. "In France, you do not have this," "Of course, you never saw anything like this in America."

Don Marcelo came away fatigued by so much condescension, and his wife and daughter refused to be convinced that the elegance of Berlin could be superior to Paris. Chichi, with audacious sacrilege, scandalized her cousins by declaring that she could not abide the corseted officers with immovable monocle, who bowed to the women with such automatic rigidity, blending their gallantries with an air of superiority.

Julio, guided by his cousins, was saturated in the virtuous atmosphere of Berlin. With the oldest, "The Sage," he had nothing to do. He was a poor creature devoted to his books who patronized all the family with a protecting air. It was the others, the sub-lieutenants or military students, who proudly showed him the rounds of German joy.

Julio was accordingly introduced to all the night restaurants—imitations of those in Paris, but on a much larger scale. The women who in Paris might be counted by the dozens appeared here in hundreds. The scandalous drunkenness here never came by chance, but always by design as an indispensable part of the gaiety. All was grandiose, glittering, colossal. The libertines diverted themselves in platoons, the public got drunk in companies, the harlots presented themselves in regiments. He felt a sensation of disgust before these timid and servile females, accustomed to blows, who were so eagerly trying to reimburse themselves for the losses and exposures of their business. For him, it was impossible to celebrate with hoarse ha-has, like his cousins, the discomfiture of these women when they realized that they had wasted so many hours without accomplishing more than abundant drinking. The gross obscenity, so public and noisy, like a parade of riches, was loathsome to Julio. "There is nothing like this in Paris," his cousins repeatedly exulted as they admired the stupendous salons, the hundreds of men and women in pairs, the thousands of tipplers. "No, there certainly was nothing like that in Paris." He was sick of such boundless pretension. He seemed to be attending a fiesta of hungry mariners anxious at one swoop to make amends for all former privations. Like his father, he longed to get away. It offended his aesthetic sense.

Don Marcelo returned from this visit with melancholy resignation. Those people had undoubtedly made great strides. He was not such a blind patriot that he could not admit what was so evident. Within a few years they had transformed their country, and their industry was astonishing . . . but, well . . . it was simply impossible to have anything to do with them. Each to his own, but may they never take a notion to envy their neighbor! . . . Then he immediately repelled this last suspicion with the optimism of a business man.

"They are going to be very rich," he thought. "Their affairs are prospering, and he that is rich does not hunt quarrels. That war of which some crazy fools are always dreaming would be an impossible thing."

Young Desnoyers renewed his Parisian existence, living entirely in the studio and going less and less to his father's home. Dona Luisa began to speak of a certain Argensola, a very learned young Spaniard, believing that his counsels might prove most helpful to Julio. She did not know exactly whether this new companion was friend, master or servant. The studio habitues also had their doubts. The literary ones always spoke of Argensola as a painter. The painters recognized only his ability as a man of letters. He was among those who used to come up to the studio of winter afternoons, attracted by the ruddy glow of the stove and the wines secretly provided by the mother, holding forth authoritatively before the often-renewed bottle and the box of cigars lying open on the table. One night, he slept on the divan, as he had no regular quarters. After that first night, he lived entirely in the studio.

Julio soon discovered in him an admirable reflex of his own personality. He knew that Argensola had come third-class from Madrid with twenty francs in his pocket, in order to "capture glory," to use his own words. Upon observing that the Spaniard was painting with as much difficulty as himself, with the same wooden and childish strokes, which are so characteristic of the make-believe artists and pot-boilers, the routine workers concerned themselves with color and other rank fads. Argensola was a psychological artist, a painter of souls. And his disciple, felt astonished and almost displeased on learning what a comparatively simple thing it was to paint a soul. Upon a bloodless countenance, with a chin as sharp as a dagger, the gifted Spaniard would trace a pair of nearly round eyes, and at the centre of each pupil he would aim a white brush stroke, a point of light . . . the soul. Then, planting himself before the canvas, he would proceed to classify this soul with his inexhaustible imagination, attributing to it almost every kind of stress and extremity. So great was the sway of his rapture that Julio, too, was able to see all that the artist flattered himself into believing that he had put into the owlish eyes. He, also, would paint souls . . . souls of women.

In spite of the ease with which he developed his psychological creations, Argensola preferred to talk, stretched on a divan, or to read, hugging the fire while his friend and protector was outside. Another advantage this fondness for reading gave young Desnoyers was that he was no longer obliged to open a volume, scanning the index and last pages "just to get the idea." Formerly when frequenting society functions, he had been guilty of coolly asking an author which was his best book—his smile of a clever man—giving the writer to understand that he merely enquired so as not to waste time on the other volumes. Now it was no longer necessary to do this; Argensola would read for him. As soon as Julio would see him absorbed in a book, he would demand an immediate share: "Tell me the story." So the "secretary," not only gave him the plots of comedies and novels, but also detailed the argument of Schopenhauer or of Nietzsche . . . Dona Luisa almost wept on hearing her visitors—with that benevolence which wealth always inspires—speak of her son as "a rather gay young man, but wonderfully well read!"

In exchange for his lessons, Argensola received, much the same treatment as did the Greek slaves who taught rhetoric to the young patricians of decadent Rome. In the midst of a dissertation, his lord and friend would interrupt him with—"Get my dress suit ready. I am invited out this evening."

At other times, when the instructor was luxuriating in bodily comfort, with a book in one hand near the roaring stove, seeing through the windows the gray and rainy afternoon, his disciple would suddenly appear saying, "Quick, get out! . . . There's a woman coming!"

And Argensola, like a dog who gets up and shakes himself, would disappear to continue his reading in some miserable little coffee house in the neighborhood.

In his official capacity, this widely gifted man often descended from the peaks of intellectuality to the vulgarities of everyday life. He was the steward of the lord of the manor, the intermediary between the pocketbook and those who appeared bill in hand. "Money!" he would say laconically at the end of the month, and Desnoyers would break out into complaints and curses. Where on earth was he to get it, he would like to know. His father was as regular as a machine, and would never allow the slightest advance upon the following month. He had to submit to a rule of misery. Three thousand francs a month!— what could any decent person do with that? . . . He was even trying to cut THAT down, to tighten the band, interfering in the running of his house, so that Dona Luisa could not make presents to her son. In vain he had appealed to the various usurers of Paris, telling them of his property beyond the ocean. These gentlemen had the youth of their own country in the hollow of their hand and were not obliged to risk their capital in other lands. The same hard luck pursued him when, with sudden demonstrations of affection, he had tried to convince Don Marcelo that three thousand francs a month was but a niggardly trifle.

The millionaire fairly snorted with indignation. "Three thousand francs a trifle!" And the debts besides, that he often had to pay for his son! . . .

"Why, when I was your age," . . . he would begin saying—but Julio would suddenly bring the dialogue to a close. He had heard his father's story too many times. Ah, the stingy old miser! What he had been giving him all these months was no more than the interest on his grandfather's legacy. . . . And by the advice of Argensola he ventured to get control of the field. He was planning to hand over the management of his land to Celedonio, the old overseer, who was now such a grandee in his country that Julio ironically called him "my uncle."

Desnoyers accepted this rebellion coldly. "It appears just to me. You are now of age!" Then he promptly reduced to extremes his oversight of his home, forbidding Dona Luisa to handle any money. Henceforth he regarded his son as an adversary, treating him during his lightning apparitions at the avenue Victor Hugo with glacial courtesy as though he were a stranger.

For a while a transitory opulence enlivened the studio. Julio had increased his expenses, considering himself rich. But the letters from his uncle in America soon dissipated these illusions. At first the remittances exceeded very slightly the monthly allowance that his father had made him. Then it began to diminish in an alarming manner. According to Celedonio, all the calamities on earth seemed to be falling upon his plantation. The pasture land was yielding scantily, sometimes for lack of rain, sometimes because of floods, and the herds were perishing by hundreds. Julio required more income, and the crafty half-breed sent him what he asked for, but simply as a loan, reserving the return until they should adjust their accounts.

In spite of such aid, young Desnoyers was suffering great want. He was gambling now in an elegant circle, thinking thus to compensate for his periodical scrimpings; but this resort was only making the remittances from America disappear with greater rapidity. . . . That such a man as he was should be tormented so for the lack of a few thousand francs! What else was a millionaire father for?

If the creditors began threatening, the poor youth had to bring the secretary into play, ordering him to see the mother immediately; he himself wished to avoid her tears and reproaches. So Argensola would slip like a pickpocket up the service stairway of the great house on the avenue Victor Hugo. The place in which he transacted his ambassadorial business was the kitchen, with great danger that the terrible Desnoyers might happen in there, on one of his perambulations as a laboring man, and surprise the intruder.

Dona Luisa would weep, touched by the heartrending tales of the messenger. What could she do! She was as poor as her maids; she had jewels, many jewels, but not a franc. Then Argensola came to the rescue with a solution worthy of his experience. He would smooth the way for the good mother, leaving some of her jewels at the Mont-de-Piete. He knew the way to raise money on them. So the lady accepted his advice, giving him, however, only jewels of medium value as she suspected that she might never see them again. Later scruples made her at times refuse flatly. Suppose Don Marcelo should ever find it out, what a scene! . . . But the Spaniard deemed it unseemly to return empty-handed, and always bore away a basket of bottles from the well-stocked wine-cellar of the Desnoyers.

Every morning Dona Luisa went to Saint-Honore-d'Eylau to pray for her son. She felt that this was her own church. It was a hospitable and familiar island in the unexplored ocean of Paris. Here she could exchange discreet salutations with her neighbors from the different republics of the new world. She felt nearer to God and the saints when she could hear in the vestibule conversations in her language.

It was, moreover, a sort of salon in which took place the great events of the South American colony. One day was a wedding with flowers, orchestra and chanting chorals. With Chichi beside her, she greeted those she knew, congratulating the bride and groom. Another day it was the funeral of an ex-president of some republic, or some other foreign dignitary ending in Paris his turbulent existence. Poor President! Poor General! . . .

Dona Luisa remembered the dead man. She had seen him many times in that church devoutly attending mass and she was indignant at the evil tongues which, under the cover of a funeral oration, recalled the shootings and bank failures in his country. Such a good and religious gentleman! May God receive his soul in glory! . . . And upon going out into the square, she would look with tender eyes upon the young men and women on horseback going to the Bois de Boulogne, the luxurious automobiles, the morning radiant in the sunshine, all the primeval freshness of the early hours—realizing what a beautiful thing it is to live.

Her devout expression of gratitude for mere existence usually included the monument in the centre of the square, all bristling with wings as if about to fly away from the ground. Victor Hugo! . . . It was enough for her to have heard this name on the lips of her son to make her contemplate the statue with a family interest. The only thing that she knew about the poet was that he had died. Of this she was almost sure, and she imagined that in life, he was a great friend of Julio's because she had so often heard her son repeat his name.

Ay, her son! . . . All her thoughts, her conjectures, her desires, converged on him and her strong-willed husband. She longed for the men to come to an understanding and put an end to a struggle in which she was the principal victim. Would not God work this miracle? . . . Like an invalid who goes from one sanitarium to another in pursuit of health, she gave up the church on her street to attend the Spanish chapel on the avenue Friedland. Here she considered herself even more among her own.

In the midst of the fine and elegant South American ladies who looked as if they had just escaped from a fashion sheet, her eyes sought other women, not so well dressed, fat, with theatrical ermine and antique jewelry. When these high-born dames met each other in the vestibule, they spoke with heavy voices and expressive gestures, emphasizing their words energetically. The daughter of the ranch ventured to salute them because she had subscribed to all their pet charities, and upon seeing her greeting returned, she felt a satisfaction which made her momentarily forget her woes. They belonged to those families which her father had so greatly admired without knowing why. They came from the "mother country," and to the good Chicha were all Excelentisimas or Altisimas, related to kings. She did not know whether to give them her hand or bend the knee, as she had vaguely heard was the custom at court. But soon she recalled her preoccupation and went forward to wrestle in prayer with God. Ay, that he would mercifully remember her! That he would not long forget her son! . . .

It was Glory that remembered Julio, stretching out to him her arms of light, so that he suddenly awoke to find himself surrounded by all the honors and advantages of celebrity. Fame cunningly surprises mankind on the most crooked and unexpected of roads. Neither the painting of souls nor a fitful existence full of extravagant love affairs and complicated duels had brought Desnoyers this renown. It was Glory that put him on his feet.

A new pleasure for the delight of humanity had come from the other side of the seas. People were asking one another in the mysterious tones of the initiated who wish to recognize a familiar spirit, "Do you know how to tango? . . ." The tango had taken possession of the world. It was the heroic hymn of a humanity that was suddenly concentrating its aspirations on the harmonious rhythm of the thigh joints, measuring its intelligence by the agility of its feet. An incoherent and monotonous music of African inspiration was satisfying the artistic ideals of a society that required nothing better. The world was dancing . . . dancing . . . dancing.

A negro dance from Cuba introduced into South America by mariners who shipped jerked beef to the Antilles, conquered the entire earth in a few months, completely encircling it, bounding victoriously from nation to nation . . . like the Marseillaise. It was even penetrating into the most ceremonious courts, overturning all traditions of conservation and etiquette like a song of the Revolution—the revolution of frivolity. The Pope even had to become a master of the dance, recommending the "Furlana" instead of the "Tango," since all the Christian world, regardless of sects, was united in the common desire to agitate its feet with the tireless frenzy of the "possessed" of the Middle Ages.

Julio Desnoyers, upon meeting this dance of his childhood in full swing in Paris, devoted himself to it with the confidence that an old love inspires. Who could have foretold that when as a student, he was frequenting the lowest dance halls in Buenos Aires, watched by the police, that he was really serving an apprenticeship to Glory? . . .

From five to seven, in the salons of the Champs d'Elysees where it cost five francs for a cup of tea and the privilege of joining in the sacred dance, hundreds of eyes followed him with admiration. "He has the key," said the women, appraising his slender elegance, medium stature, and muscular springs. And he, in abbreviated jacket and expansive shirt bosom, with his small, girlish feet encased in high-heeled patent leathers with white tops, danced gravely, thoughtfully, silently, like a mathematician working out a problem, under the lights that shed bluish tones upon his plastered, glossy locks. Ladies asked to be presented to him in the sweet hope that their friends might envy them when they beheld them in the arms of the master. Invitations simply rained upon Julio. The most exclusive salons were thrown open to him so that every afternoon he made a dozen new acquaintances. The fashion had brought over professors from the other side of the sea, compatriots from the slums of Buenos Aires, haughty and confused at being applauded like famous lecturers or tenors; but Julio triumphed over these vulgarians who danced for money, and the incidents of his former life were considered by the women as deeds of romantic gallantry.

"You are killing yourself," Argensola would say. "You are dancing too much."

The glory of his friend and master was only making more trouble for him. His placid readings before the fire were now subject to daily interruptions. It was impossible to read more than a chapter. The celebrated man was continually ordering him to betake himself to the street. "A new lesson," sighed the parasite. And when he was alone in the studio numerous callers—all women, some inquisitive and aggressive, others sad, with a deserted air—were constantly interrupting his thoughtful pursuits.

One of them terrified the occupants of the studio with her insistence. She was a North American of uncertain age, somewhere between thirty-two and fifty-nine, with short skirts that whenever she sat down, seemed to fly up as if moved by a spring. Various dances with Desnoyers and a visit to the rue de la Pompe she seemed to consider as her sacred rights, and she pursued the master with the desperation of an abandoned zealot. Julio had made good his escape upon learning that this beauty of youthful elegance—when seen from the back—had two grandchildren. "MASTER Desnoyers has gone out," Argensola would invariably say upon receiving her. And, thereupon she would burst into tears and threats, longing to kill herself then and there that her corpse might frighten away those other women who would come to rob her of what she considered her special privilege. Now it was Argensola who sped his companion to the street when he wished to be alone. He had only to remark casually, "I believe that Yankee is coming," and the great man would beat a hasty retreat, oftentimes in his desperate flight availing himself of the back stairs.

At this time began to develop the most important event in Julio's existence. The Desnoyers family was to be united with that of Senator Lacour. Rene, his only son, had succeeded in awakening in Chichi a certain interest that was almost love. The dignitary enjoyed thinking of his son allied to the boundless plains and immense herds whose description always affected him like a marvellous tale. He was a widower, but he enjoyed giving at his home famous banquets and parties. Every new celebrity immediately suggested to him the idea of giving a dinner. No illustrious person passing through Paris, polar explorer or famous singer, could escape being exhibited in the dining room of Lacour. The son of Desnoyers—at whom he had scarcely glanced before—now inspired him with sudden interest. The senator was a thoroughly up-to-date man who did not classify glory nor distinguish reputations. It was enough for him that a name should be on everybody's lips for him to accept it with enthusiasm. When Julio responded to his invitation, he presented him with pride to his friends, and came very near to calling him "dear master." The tango was monopolizing all conversation nowadays. Even in the Academy they were taking it up in order to demonstrate that the youth of ancient Athens had diverted itself in a somewhat similar way. . . . And Lacour had dreamed all his life of an Athenian republic.

At these reunions, Desnoyers became acquainted with the Lauriers. He was an engineer who owned a motor-factory for automobiles in the outskirts of Paris—a man about thirty-five, tall, rather heavy and silent, with a deliberate air as though he wished to see deeply into men and things. She was of a light, frivolous character, loving life for the satisfactions and pleasures which it brought her, appearing to accept with smiling conformity the silent and grave adoration of her husband. She could not well do less with a man of his merits. Besides, she had brought to the marriage a dowry of three hundred thousand francs, a capital which had enabled the engineer to enlarge his business. The senator had been instrumental in arranging this marriage. He was interested in Laurier because he was the son of an old friend.

Upon Marguerite Laurier the presence of Julio flashed like a ray of sunlight in the tiresome salon of Lacour. She was dancing the fad of the hour and frequenting the tango teas where reigned the adored Desnoyers. And to think that she was being entertained with this celebrated and interesting man that the other women were raving about! . . . In order that he might not take her for a mere middle-class woman like the other guests at the senator's party, she spoke of her modistes, all from the rue de la Paix, declaring gravely that no woman who had any self-respect could possibly walk through the streets wearing a gown costing less than eight hundred francs, and that the hat of a thousand francs— but a few years ago, an astonishing novelty—was nowadays a very ordinary affair.

This acquaintanceship made the "little Laurier," as her friends called her notwithstanding her tallness, much sought by the master of the dance, in spite of the looks of wrath and envy hurled at her by the others. What a triumph for the wife of a simple engineer who was used to going everywhere in her mother's automobile! . . . Julio at first had supposed her like all the others who were languishing in his arms, following the rhythmic complications of the dance, but he soon found that she was very different. Her coquetry after the first confidential words, but increased his admiration. He really had never before been thrown with a woman of her class. Those of his first social period were the habituees of the night restaurants paid for their witchery. Now Glory was tossing into his arms ladies of high position but with an unconfessable past, anxious for novelties although exceedingly mature. This middle class woman who would advance so confidently toward him and then retreat with such capricious outbursts of modesty, was a new type for him.

The tango salons soon began to suffer a great loss. Desnoyers was permitting himself to be seen there with less frequency, handing Glory over to the professionals. Sometimes entire weeks slipped by without the five-to-seven devotees being able to admire his black locks and his tiny patent leathers twinkling under the lights in time with his graceful movements.

Marguerite was also avoiding these places. The meetings of the two were taking place in accordance with what she had read in the love stories of Paris. She was going in search of Julio, fearing to be recognized, tremulous with emotion, selecting her most inconspicuous suit, and covering her face with a close veil—"the veil of adultery," as her friends called it. They had their trysts in the least-frequented squares of the district, frequently changing the places, like timid birds that at the slightest disturbance fly to perch a little further away. Sometimes they would meet in the Buttes Chaumont, at others they preferred the gardens on the left bank of the Seine, the Luxembourg, and even the distant Parc de Montsouris. She was always in tremors of terror lest her husband might surprise them, although she well knew that the industrious engineer was in his factory a great distance away. Her agitated aspect, her excessive precautions in order to slip by unseen, only served to attract the attention of the passers-by. Although Julio was waxing impatient with the annoyance of this wandering love affair which only amounted to a few fugitive kisses, he finally held his peace, dominated by Marguerite's pleadings.

She did not wish merely to be one in the procession of his sweethearts; it was necessary to convince herself first that this love was going to last forever. It was her first slip and she wanted it to be the last. Ay, her former spotless reputation! . . . What would people say! . . . The two returned to their adolescent period, loving each other as they had never loved before, with the confident and childish passion of fifteen-year-olds.

Julio had leaped from childhood to libertinism, taking his initiation into life at a single bound. She had desired marriage in order to acquire the respect and liberty of a married woman, but feeling towards her husband only a vague gratitude. "We end where others begin," she had said to Desnoyers.

Their passion took the form of an intense, reciprocal and vulgar love. They felt a romantic sentimentality in clasping hands or exchanging kisses on a garden bench in the twilight. He was treasuring a ringlet of Marguerite's—although he doubted its genuineness, with a vague suspicion that it might be one of the latest wisps of fashion. She would cuddle down with her head on his shoulder, as though imploring his protection, although always in the open air. If Julio ever attempted greater intimacy in a carriage, madame would repel him most vigorously. A contradictory duality appeared to inspire her actions. Every morning, on awaking, she would decide to yield, but then when near him, her middle-class respectability, jealous of its reputation, kept her faithful to her mother's teachings.

One day she agreed to visit his studio with the interest that the haunts of the loved one always inspires. "Promise that you will not take advantage of me." He readily promised, swearing that everything should be as Marguerite wished. . . . But from that day they were no longer seen in the gardens, nor wandering around persecuted by the winter winds. They preferred the studio, and Argensola had to rearrange his existence, seeking the stove of another artist friend, in order to continue his reading.

This state of things lasted two months. They never knew what secret force suddenly disturbed their tranquility. Perhaps one of her friends, guessing at the truth, had told the husband anonymously. Perhaps it was she herself unconsciously, with her inexpressible happiness, her tardy returns home when dinner was already served, and the sudden aversion which she showed toward the engineer in their hours alone, trying to keep her heart faithful to her lover. To divide her interest between her legal companion and the man she loved was a torment that her simple and vehement enthusiasm could not tolerate.

While she was hurrying one night through the rue de la Pompe, looking at her watch and trembling with impatience at not finding an automobile or even a cab, a man stood in front of her. . . . Etienne Laurier! She always shuddered with fear on recalling that hour. For a moment she believed that he was going to kill her. Serious men, quiet and diffident, are most terrible in their explosions of wrath. Her husband knew everything. With the same patience that he employed in solving his industrial problems, he had been studying her day by day, without her ever suspecting the watchfulness behind that impassive countenance. Then he had followed her in order to complete the evidence of his misfortune.

Marguerite had never supposed that he could be so common and noisy in his anger. She had expected that he would accept the facts coldly with that slight tinge of philosophical irony usually shown by distinguished men, as the husbands of her friends had done. But the poor engineer who, outside of his work, saw only his wife, loving her as a woman, and adoring her as a dainty and superior being, a model of grace and elegance, could not endure the thought of her downfall, and cried and threatened without reserve, so that the scandal became known throughout their entire circle of friends. The senator felt greatly annoyed in remembering that it was in his exclusive home that the guilty ones had become acquainted; but his displeasure was visited upon the husband. What lack of good taste! . . . Women will be women, and everything is capable of adjustment. But before the imprudent outbursts of this frantic devil no elegant solution was possible, and there was now nothing to do but to begin divorce proceedings.

Desnoyers, senior, was very indignant upon learning of this last escapade of his son. He had always had a great liking for Laurier. That instinctive bond which exists between men of industry, patient and silent, had made them very congenial. At the senator's receptions he had always talked with the engineer about the progress of his business, interesting himself in the development of that factory of which he always spoke with the affection of a father. The millionaire, in spite of his reputation for miserliness, had even volunteered his disinterested support if at any time it should become necessary to enlarge the plant. And it was this good man's happiness that his son, a frivolous and useless dancer, was going to steal! . . .

At first Laurier spoke of a duel. His wrath was that of a work horse who breaks the tight reins of his laboring outfit, tosses his mane, neighs wildly and bites. The father was greatly distressed at the possibility of such an outcome. . . . One scandal more! Julio had dedicated the greater part of his existence to the handling of arms.

"He will kill the poor man!" he said to the senator. "I am sure that he will kill him. It is the logic of life; the good-for-nothing always kill those who amount to anything."

But there was no killing. The Father of the Republic knew how to handle the clashing parties, with the same skill that he always employed in the corridors of the Senate during a ministerial crisis. The scandal was hushed up. Marguerite went to live with her mother and took the first steps for a divorce.

Some evenings, when the studio clock was striking seven, she would yawn and say sadly: "I must go. . . . I have to go, although this is my true home. . . . Ah, what a pity that we are not married!"

And he, feeling a whole garden of bourgeois virtues, hitherto ignored, bursting into bloom, repeated in a tone of conviction:

"That's so; why are we not married!"

Their wishes could be realized. The husband was facilitating the step by his unexpected intervention. So young Desnoyers set forth for South America in order to raise the money and marry Marguerite.

CHAPTER IV

THE COUSIN FROM BERLIN

The studio of Julio Desnoyers was on the top floor, both the stairway and the elevator stopping before his door. The two tiny apartments at the back were lighted by an interior court, their only means of communication being the service stairway which went on up to the garrets.

While his comrade was away, Argensola had made the acquaintance of those in the neighboring lodgings. The largest of the apartments was empty during the day, its occupants not returning till after they had taken their evening meal in a restaurant. As both husband and wife were employed outside, they could not remain at home except on holidays. The man, vigorous and of a martial aspect, was superintendent in a big department store. . . . He had been a soldier in Africa, wore a military decoration, and had the rank of sub-lieutenant in the Reserves. She was a blonde, heavy and rather anaemic, with bright eyes and a sentimental expression. On holidays she spent long hours at the piano, playing musical reveries, always the same. At other times Argensola saw her through the interior window working in the kitchen aided by her companion, the two laughing over their clumsiness and inexperience in preparing the Sunday dinner.

The concierge thought that this woman was a German, but she herself said that she was Swiss. She was a cashier in a shop—not the one in which her husband was employed. In the mornings they left home together, separating in the Place d'Etoile. At seven in the evening they met here, greeting each other with a kiss, like lovers who meet for the first time; and then after supper, they returned to their nest in the rue de la Pompe. All Argensola's attempts at friendliness with these neighbors were repulsed because of their self-centredness. They responded with freezing courtesy; they lived only for themselves.

The other apartment of two rooms was occupied by a single man. He was a Russian or Pole who almost always returned with a package of books, and passed many hours writing near the patio window. From the very first the Spaniard took him to be a mysterious man, probably a very distinguished one—a true hero of a novel. The foreign appearance of this Tchernoff made a great impression upon him—his dishevelled beard, and oily locks, his spectacles upon a large nose that seemed deformed by a dagger-thrust. There emanated from him, like an invisible nimbus, an odor of cheap wine and soiled clothing.

When Argensola caught a glimpse of him through the service door he would say to himself, "Ah, Friend Tchernoff is returning," and thereupon he would saunter out to the stairway in order to have a chat with his neighbor. For a long time the stranger discouraged all approach to his quarters, which fact led the Spaniard to infer that he devoted himself to alchemy and kindred mysteries. When he finally was allowed to enter he saw only books, many books, books everywhere—scattered on the floor, heaped upon benches, piled in corners, overflowing on to broken-down chairs, old tables, and a bed that was only made up now and then when the owner, alarmed by the increasing invasion of dust and cobwebs, was obliged to call in the aid of his friend, the concierge.

Argensola finally realized, not without a certain disenchantment, that there was nothing mysterious in the life of the man. What he was writing near the window were merely translations, some of them ordered, others volunteer work for the socialist periodicals. The only marvellous thing about him was the quantity of languages that he knew.

"He knows them all," said the Spaniard, when describing their neighbor to Desnoyers. "He has only to hear of a new one to master it. He holds the key, the secret of all languages, living or dead. He speaks Castilian as well as we do, and yet he has never been in a Spanish-speaking country."

Argensola again felt a thrill of mystery upon reading the titles of many of the volumes. The majority were old books, many of them in languages that he was not able to decipher, picked up for a song at second-hand shops or on the book stands installed upon the parapets of the Seine. Only a man holding the key of tongues could get together such volumes. An atmosphere of mysticism, of superhuman insight, of secrets intact for many centuries appeared to emanate from these heaps of dusty volumes with worm-eaten leaves. And mixed with these ancient tomes were others red and conspicuous, pamphlets of socialistic propaganda, leaflets in all the languages of Europe and periodicals—many periodicals, with revolutionary titles.

Tchernoff did not appear to enjoy visits and conversation. He would smile enigmatically into his black beard, and was very sparing with his words so as to shorten the interview. But Argensola possessed the means of winning over this sullen personage. It was only necessary for him to wink one eye with the expressive invitation, "Do we go?" and the two would soon be settled on a bench in the kitchen of Desnoyers' studio, opposite a bottle which had come from the avenue Victor Hugo. The costly wines of Don Marcelo made the Russian more communicative, although, in spite of this aid, the Spaniard learned little of his neighbor's real existence. Sometimes he would mention Jaures and other socialistic orators. His surest means of existence was the translation of periodicals or party papers. On various occasions the name of Siberia escaped from his lips, and he admitted that he had been there a long time; but he did not care to talk about a country visited against his will. He would merely smile modestly, showing plainly that he did not wish to make any further revelations.

The morning after the return of Julio Desnoyers, while Argensola was talking on the stairway with Tchernoff, the bell rang. How annoying! The Russian, who was well up in advanced politics, was just explaining the plans advanced by Jaures. There were still many who hoped that war might be averted. He had his motives for doubting it. . . . He, Tchernoff, was commenting on these illusions with the smile of a flat-nosed sphinx when the bell rang for a second time, so that Argensola was obliged to break away from his interesting friend, and run to open the main door.

A gentleman wished to see Julio. He spoke very correct French, though his accent was a revelation for Argensola. Upon going into the bedroom in search of his master, who was just arising, he said confidently, "It's the cousin from Berlin who has come to say good-bye. It could not be anyone else."

When the three came together in the studio, Desnoyers presented his comrade, in order that the visitor might not make any mistake in regard to his social status.

"I have heard him spoken of. The gentleman is Argensola, a very deserving youth."

Doctor Julius von Hartrott said this with the self-sufficiency of a man who knows everything and wishes to be agreeable to an inferior, conceding him the alms of his attention.

The two cousins confronted each other with a curiosity not altogether free from distrust. Although closely related, they knew each other very slightly, tacitly admitting complete divergence in opinions and tastes.

After slowly examining the Sage, Argensola came to the conclusion that he looked like an officer dressed as a civilian. He noticed in his person an effort to imitate the soldierly when occasionally discarding uniform—the ambition of every German burgher wishing to be taken for the superior class. His trousers were narrow, as though intended to be tucked into cavalry boots. His coat with two rows of buttons had the contracted waist with very full skirt and upstanding lapels, suggesting vaguely a military great coat. The reddish moustachios, strong jaw and shaved head completed his would-be martial appearance; but his eyes, large, dark-circled and near-sighted, were the eyes of a student taking refuge behind great thick glasses which gave him the aspect of a man of peace.

Desnoyers knew that he was an assistant professor of the University, that he had published a few volumes, fat and heavy as bricks, and that he was a member of an academic society collaborating in documentary research directed by a famous historian. In his lapel he was wearing the badge of a foreign order.

Julio's respect for the learned member of the family was not unmixed with contempt. He and his sister Chichi had from childhood felt an instinctive hostility toward the cousins from Berlin. It annoyed him, too, to have his family everlastingly holding up as a model this pedant who only knew life as it is in books, and passed his existence investigating what men had done in other epochs, in order to draw conclusions in harmony with Germany's views. While young Desnoyers had great facility for admiration, and reverenced all those whose "arguments" Argensola had doled out to him, he drew the line at accepting the intellectual grandeur of this illustrious relative.

During his stay in Berlin, a German word of vulgar invention had enabled him to classify this prig. Heavy books of minute investigation were every month being published by the dozens in the Fatherland. There was not a professor who could resist the temptation of constructing from the simplest detail an enormous volume written in a dull, involved style. The people, therefore, appreciating that these near-sighted authors were incapable of any genial vision of comradeship, called them Sitzfleisch haben, because of the very long sittings which their works represented. That was what this cousin was for him, a mere Sitzfleisch haben.

Doctor von Hartrott, on explaining his visit, spoke in Spanish. He availed himself of this language used by the family during his childhood, as a precaution, looking around repeatedly as if he feared to be heard. He had come to bid his cousin farewell. His mother had told him of his return, and he had not wished to leave Paris without seeing him. He was leaving in a few hours, since matters were growing more strained.

"But do you really believe that there will be war?" asked Desnoyers.

"War will be declared to-morrow or the day after. Nothing can prevent it now. It is necessary for the welfare of humanity."

Silence followed this speech, Julio and Argensola looking with astonishment at this peaceable-looking man who had just spoken with such martial arrogance. The two suspected that the professor was making this visit in order to give vent to his opinions and enthusiasms. At the same time, perhaps, he was trying to find out what they might think and know, as one of the many viewpoints of the people in Paris.

"You are not French," he added looking at his cousin. "You were born in Argentina, so before you I may speak the truth."

"And were you not born there?" asked Julio smiling.

The Doctor made a gesture of protest, as though he had just heard something insulting. "No, I am a German. No matter where a German may be born, he always belongs to his mother country." Then turning to Argensola— "This gentleman, too, is a foreigner. He comes from noble Spain, which owes to us the best that it has—the worship of honor, the knightly spirit."

The Spaniard wished to remonstrate, but the Sage would not permit, adding in an oracular tone:

"You were miserable Celts, sunk in the vileness of an inferior and mongrel race whose domination by Rome but made your situation worse. Fortunately you were conquered by the Goths and others of our race who implanted in you a sense of personal dignity. Do not forget, young man, that the Vandals were the ancestors of the Prussians of to-day."

Again Argensola tried to speak, but his friend signed to him not to interrupt the professor who appeared to have forgotten his former reserve and was working up to an enthusiastic pitch with his own words.

"We are going to witness great events," he continued. "Fortunate are those born in this epoch, the most interesting in history! At this very moment, humanity is changing its course. Now the true civilization begins."

The war, according to him, was going to be of a brevity hitherto unseen. Germany had been preparing herself to bring about this event without any long, economic world-disturbance. A single month would be enough to crush France, the most to be feared of their adversaries. Then they would march against Russia, who with her slow, clumsy movements could not oppose an immediate defense. Finally they would attack haughty England, so isolated in its archipelago that it could not obstruct the sweep of German progress. This would make a series of rapid blows and overwhelming victories, requiring only a summer in which to play this magnificent role. The fall of the leaves in the following autumn would greet the definite triumph of Germany.

With the assurance of a professor who does not expect his dictum to be refuted by his hearers, he explained the superiority of the German race. All mankind was divided into two groups—dolicephalous and the brachicephalous, according to the shape of the skull. Another scientific classification divided men into the light-haired and dark-haired. The dolicephalous (arched heads) represented purity of race and superior mentality. The brachicephalous (flat heads) were mongrels with all the stigma of degeneration. The German, dolicephalous par excellence, was the only descendant of the primitive Aryans. All the other nations, especially those of the south of Europe called "latins," belonged to a degenerate humanity.

The Spaniard could not contain himself any longer. "But no person with any intelligence believes any more in those antique theories of race! What if there no longer existed a people of absolutely pure blood, owing to thousands of admixtures due to historical conquests!" . . . Many Germans bore the identical ethnic marks which the professor was attributing to the inferior races.

"There is something in that," admitted Hartrott, "but although the German race may not be perfectly pure, it is the least impure of all races and, therefore, should have dominion over the world."

His voice took on an ironic and cutting edge when speaking of the Celts, inhabitants of the lands of the South. They had retarded the progress of Humanity, deflecting it in the wrong direction. The Celt is individualistic and consequently an ungovernable revolutionary who tends to socialism. Furthermore, he is a humanitarian and makes a virtue of mercy, defending the existence of the weak who do not amount to anything.

The illustrious German places above everything else, Method and Power. Elected by Nature to command the impotent races, he possesses all the qualifications that distinguish the superior leader. The French Revolution was merely a clash between Teutons and Celts. The nobility of France were descended from Germanic warriors established in the country after the so-called invasion of the barbarians. The middle and lower classes were the Gallic-Celtic element. The inferior race had conquered the superior, disorganizing the country and perturbing the world. Celtism was the inventor of Democracy, of the doctrines of Socialism and Anarchy. Now the hour of Germanic retaliation was about to strike, and the Northern race would re-establish order, since God had favored it by demonstrating its indisputable superiority.

"A nation," he added, "can aspire to great destinies only when it is fundamentally Teutonic. The less German it is, the less its civilization amounts to. We represent 'the aristocracy of humanity,' 'the salt of the earth,' as our William said."

Argensola was listening with astonishment to this outpouring of conceit. All the great nations had passed through the fever of Imperialism. The Greeks aspired to world-rule because they were the most civilized and believed themselves the most fit to give civilization to the rest of mankind. The Romans, upon conquering countries, implanted law and the rule of justice. The French of the Revolution and the Empire justified their invasions on the plea that they wished to liberate mankind and spread abroad new ideas. Even the Spaniards of the sixteenth century, when battling with half of Europe for religious unity and the extermination of heresy, were working toward their ideals obscure and perhaps erroneous, but disinterested.

All the nations of history had been struggling for something which they had considered generous and above their own interests. Germany alone, according to this professor, was trying to impose itself upon the world in the name of racial superiority—a superiority that nobody had recognized, that she was arrogating to herself, coating her affirmations with a varnish of false science.

"Until now wars have been carried on by the soldiery," continued Hartrott. "That which is now going to begin will be waged by a combination of soldiers and professors. In its preparation the University has taken as much part as the military staff. German science, leader of all sciences, is united forever with what the Latin revolutionists disdainfully term militarism. Force, mistress of the world, is what creates right, that which our truly unique civilization imposes. Our armies are the representatives of our culture, and in a few weeks we shall free the world from its decadence, completely rejuvenating it."

The vision of the immense future of his race was leading him on to expose himself with lyrical enthusiasm. William I, Bismarck, all the heroes of past victories, inspired his veneration, but he spoke of them as dying gods whose hour had passed. They were glorious ancestors of modest pretensions who had confined their activities to enlarging the frontiers, and to establishing the unity of the Empire, afterwards opposing themselves with the prudence of valetudinarians to the daring of the new generation. Their ambitions went no further than a continental hegemony . . . but now William II had leaped into the arena, the complex hero that the country required.

"Lamprecht, my master, has pictured his greatness. It is tradition and the future, method and audacity. Like his grandfather, the Emperor holds the conviction of what monarchy by the grace of God represents, but his vivid and modern intelligence recognizes and accepts modern conditions. At the same time that he is romantic, feudal and a supporter of the agrarian conservatives, he is also an up-to-date man who seeks practical solutions and shows a utilitarian spirit. In him are correctly balanced instinct and reason."

Germany, guided by this hero, had, according to Hartrott, been concentrating its strength, and recognizing its true path. The Universities supported him even more unanimously than the army. Why store up so much power and maintain it without employment? . . . The empire of the world belongs to the German people. The historians and philosophers, disciples of Treitschke, were taking it upon themselves to frame the rights that would justify this universal domination. And Lamprecht, the psychological historian, like the other professors, was launching the belief in the absolute superiority of the Germanic race. It was just that it should rule the world, since it only had the power to do so. This "telurian germanization" was to be of immense benefit to mankind. The earth was going to be happy under the dictatorship of a people born for mastery. The German state, "tentacular potency," would eclipse with its glory the most imposing empire of the past and present. Gott mit uns!

"Who will be able to deny, as my master says, that there exists a Christian, German God, the 'Great Ally,' who is showing himself to our enemies, the foreigners, as a strong and jealous divinity?" . . .

Desnoyers was listening to his cousin with astonishment and at the same time looking at Argensola who, with a flutter of his eyes, seemed to be saying to him, "He is mad! These Germans are simply mad with pride."

Meanwhile, the professor, unable to curb his enthusiasm, continued expounding the grandeur of his race. From his viewpoint, the providential Kaiser had shown inexplicable weakenings. He was too good and too kind. "Deliciae generis humani," as had said Professor Lasson, another of Hartrott's masters. Able to overthrow everything with his annihilating power, the Emperor was limiting himself merely to maintaining peace. But the nation did not wish to stop there, and was pushing its leader until it had him started. It was useless now to put on the brakes. "He who does not advance recedes";—that was the cry of PanGermanism to the Emperor. He must press on in order to conquer the entire world.

"And now war comes," continued the pedant. "We need the colonies of the others, even though Bismarck, through an error of his stubborn old age, exacted nothing at the time of universal distribution, letting England and France get possession of the best lands. We must control all countries that have Germanic blood and have been civilized by our forbears."

Hartrott enumerated these countries. Holland and Belgium were German. France, through the Franks, was one-third Teutonic blood. Italy. . . . Here the professor hesitated, recalling the fact that this nation was still an ally, certainly a little insecure, but still united by diplomatic bonds. He mentioned, nevertheless, the Longobards and other races coming from the North. Spain and Portugal had been populated by the ruddy Goth and also belonged to the dominant race. And since the majority of the nations of America were of Spanish and Portuguese origin, they should also be included in this recovery.

"It is a little premature to think of these last nations just yet," added the Doctor modestly, "but some day the hour of justice will sound. After our continental triumph, we shall have time to think of their fate. . . . North America also should receive our civilizing influence, for there are living millions of Germans who have created its greatness."

He was talking of the future conquests as though they were marks of distinction with which his country was going to favor other countries. These were to continue living politically the same as before with their individual governments, but subject to the Teutons, like minors requiring the strong hand of a master. They would form the Universal United States, with an hereditary and all-powerful president—the Emperor of Germany—receiving all the benefits of Germanic culture, working disciplined under his industrial direction. .

. . But the world is ungrateful, and human badness always opposes itself to progress.

"We have no illusions," sighed the professor, with lofty sadness. "We have no friends. All look upon us with jealousy, as dangerous beings, because we are the most intelligent, the most active, and have proved ourselves superior to all others. . . . But since they no longer love us, let them fear us! As my friend Mann says, although Kultur is the spiritual organization of the world, it does not exclude bloody savagery when that becomes necessary. Kultur sanctifies the demon within us, and is above morality, reason and science. We are going to impose Kultur by force of the cannon."

Argensola continued, saying with his eyes, "They are crazy, crazy with pride! . . . What can the world expect of such people!"

Desnoyers here intervened in order to brighten this gloomy monologue with a little optimism. War had not yet been positively declared. The diplomats were still trying to arrange matters. Perhaps it might all turn out peaceably at the last minute, as had so often happened before. His cousin was seeing things entirely distorted by an aggressive enthusiasm.

Oh, the ironical, ferocious and cutting smile of the Doctor! Argensola had never known old Madariaga, but it, nevertheless, occurred to him that in this fashion sharks must smile, although he, too, had never seen a shark.

"It is war," boomed Hartrott. "When I left Germany, fifteen days ago, I knew that war was inevitable."

The certainty with which he said this dissipated all Julio's hope. Moreover, this man's trip, on the pretext of seeing his mother, disquieted him. . . . On what mission had Doctor Julius von Hartrott come to Paris? . . .

"Well, then," asked Desnoyers, "why so many diplomatic interviews? Why does the German government intervene at all—although in such a lukewarm way—in the struggle between Austria and Servia. . . . Would it not be better to declare war right out?"

The professor replied with simplicity: "Our government undoubtedly wishes that the others should declare the war. The role of outraged dignity is always the most pleasing one and justifies all ulterior resolutions, however extreme they may seem. There are some of our people who are living comfortably and do not desire war. It is expedient to make them believe that those who impose it upon us are our enemies so that they may feel the necessity of defending themselves. Only superior minds reach the conviction of the great advancement that can be accomplished by the sword alone, and that war, as our grand Treitschke says, is the highest form of progress."

Again he smiled with a ferocious expression. Morality, from his point of view, should exist among individuals only to make them more obedient and disciplined, for morality per se impedes governments and should be suppressed as a useless obstacle. For the State there exists neither truth nor falsehood; it only recognizes the utility of things. The glorious Bismarck, in order to consummate the war with France, the base of German grandeur, had not hesitated to falsify a telegraphic despatch.

"And remember, that he is the most glorious hero of our time! History looks leniently upon his heroic feat. Who would accuse the one who triumphs? . . . Professor Hans Delbruck has written with reason, 'Blessed be the hand that falsified the telegram of Ems!'"

It was convenient to have the war break out immediately, in order that events might result favorably for Germany, whose enemies are totally unprepared. Preventive war was recommended by General Bernhardi and other illustrious patriots. It would be dangerous indeed to defer the declaration of war until the enemies had fortified themselves so that they should be the ones to make war. Besides, to the Germans what kind of deterrents could law and other fictions invented by weak nations possibly be? . . . No; they had the Power, and Power creates new laws. If they proved to be the victors, History would not investigate too closely the means by which they had conquered. It was Germany that was going to win, and the priests of all cults would finally sanctify with their chants the blessed war—if it led to triumph.

"We are not making war in order to punish the Servian regicides, nor to free the Poles, nor the others oppressed by Russia, stopping there in admiration of our disinterested magnanimity. We wish to wage it because we are the first people of the earth and should extend our activity over the entire planet. Germany's hour has sounded. We are going to take our place as the powerful Mistress of the World, the place which Spain occupied in former centuries, afterwards France, and England to-day. What those people accomplished in a struggle of many years we are going to bring about in four months. The storm-flag of the Empire is now going to wave over nations and oceans; the sun is going to shine on a great slaughter. . . .

"Old Rome, sick unto death, called 'barbarians' the Germans who opened the grave. The world to-day also smells death and will surely call us barbarians. . . . So be it! When Tangiers and Toulouse, Amberes and Calais have become submissive to German barbarism . . . then we will speak further of this matter. We have the power, and who has that needs neither to hesitate nor to argue. . . . Power! . . . That is the beautiful word—the only word that rings true and clear. . . . Power! One sure stab and all argument is answered forever!"

"But are you so sure of victory?" asked Desnoyers. "Sometimes Destiny gives us great surprises. There are hidden forces that we must take into consideration or they may overturn the best-laid plans."

The smile of the Doctor became increasingly scornful and arrogant. Everything had been foreseen and studied out long ago with the most minute Germanic method. What had they to fear? . . . The enemy most to be reckoned with was France, incapable of resisting the enervating moral influences, the sufferings, the strain and the privations of war;—a nation physically debilitated and so poisoned by revolutionary spirit that it had laid aside the use of arms through an exaggerated love of comfort.

"Our generals," he announced, "are going to leave her in such a state that she will never again cross our path."

There was Russia, too, to consider, but her amorphous masses were slow to assemble and unwieldy to move. The Executive Staff of Berlin had timed everything by measure for crushing France in four weeks, and would then lead its enormous forces against the Russian empire before it could begin action.

"We shall finish with the bear after killing the cock," affirmed the professor triumphantly.

But guessing at some objection from his cousin, he hastened on—"I know what you are going to tell me. There remains another enemy, one that has not yet leaped into the lists but which all the Germans are waiting for. That one inspires more hatred than all the others put together, because it is of our blood, because it is a traitor to the race. . . . Ah, how we loathe it!"

And in the tone in which these words were uttered throbbed an expression of hatred and a thirst for vengeance which astonished both listeners.

"Even though England attack us," continued Hartrott, "we shall conquer, notwithstanding. This adversary is not more terrible than the others. For the past century she has ruled the world. Upon the fall of Napoleon she seized the continental hegemony, and will fight to keep it. But what does her energy amount to? . . . As our Bernhardi says, the English people are merely a nation of renters and sportsmen. Their army is formed from the dregs of the nation. The country lacks military spirit. We are a people of warriors, and it will be an easy thing for us to conquer the English, debilitated by a false conception of life."

The Doctor paused and then added: "We are counting on the internal corruption of our enemies, on their lack of unity. God will aid us by sowing confusion among these detested people. In a few days you will see His hand. Revolution is going to break out in France at the same time as war. The people of Paris will build barricades in the streets and the scenes of the Commune will repeat themselves. Tunis, Algiers and all their other possessions are about to rise against the metropolis."

Argensola seized the opportunity to smile with an aggressive incredulity.

"I repeat it," insisted Hartrott, "that this country is going to have internal revolution and colonial insurrection. I know perfectly well what I am talking about. . . . Russia also will break out into revolution with a red flag that will force the Czar to beg for mercy on his knees. You have only to read in the papers of the recent strikes in Saint Petersburg, and the manifestations of the strikers with the pretext of President Poincare's visit. . . . England will see her appeals to her colonies completely ignored. India is going to rise against her, and Egypt, too, will seize this opportunity for her emancipation."

Julio was beginning to be impressed by these affirmations enunciated with such oracular certainty, and he felt almost irritated at the incredulous Argensola, who continued looking insolently at the seer, repeating with his winking eyes, "He is insane—insane with pride." The man certainly must have strong reasons for making such awful prophecies. His presence in Paris just at this time was difficult for Desnoyers to understand, and gave to his words a mysterious authority.

"But the nations will defend themselves," he protested to his cousin. "Victory will not be such a very simple thing as you imagine."

"Yes, they will defend themselves, and the struggle will be fiercely contested. It appears that, of late years, France has been paying some attention to her army. We shall undoubtedly encounter some resistance; triumph may be somewhat difficult, but we are going to prevail. . . . You have no idea to what extent the offensive power of Germany has attained. Nobody knows with certainty beyond the frontiers. If our foes should comprehend it in all its immensity, they would fall on their knees beforehand to beg for mercy, thus obviating the necessity for useless sacrifices."

There was a long silence. Julius von Hartrott appeared lost in reverie. The very thought of the accumulated strength of his race submerged him in a species of mystic adoration.

"The preliminary victory," he suddenly exclaimed, "we gained some time ago. Our enemies, therefore, hate us, and yet they imitate us. All that bears the stamp of Germany is in demand throughout the world. The very countries that are trying to resist our arms copy our methods in their universities and admire our theories, even those which do not attain success in Germany. Oftentimes we laugh among ourselves, like the Roman augurs, upon seeing the servility with which they follow us! . . . And yet they will not admit our superiority!"

For the first time, Argensola's eyes and general expression approved the words of Hartrott. What he had just said was only too true—the world was a victim of "the German superstition." An intellectual cowardice, the fear of Force had made it admire en masse and indiscriminately, everything of Teutonic origin, just because of the intensity of its glitter—gold mixed with talcum. The so-called Latins, dazed with admiration, were, with unreasonable pessimism, becoming doubtful of their ability, and thus were the first to decree their own death. And the conceited Germans merely had to repeat the words of these pessimists in order to strengthen their belief in their own superiority.

With that Southern temperament, which leaps rapidly from one extreme to another, many Latins had proclaimed that in the world of the future, there would be no place for the Latin peoples, now in their death-agony—adding that Germany alone preserved the latent forces of civilization. The French who declaimed among themselves, with the greatest exaggeration, unconscious that folks were listening the other side of the door, had proclaimed repeatedly for many years past, that France was degenerating rapidly and would soon vanish from the earth. . . . Then why should they resent the scorn of their enemies. . . . Why shouldn't the Germans share in their beliefs?

The professor, misinterpreting the silent agreement of the Spaniard who until then had been listening with such a hostile smile, added:

"Now is the time to try out in France the German culture, implanting it there as conquerors."

Here Argensola interrupted, "And what if there is no such thing as German culture, as a celebrated Teuton says?" It had become necessary to contradict this pedant who had become insufferable with his egotism. Hartrott almost jumped from his chair on hearing such a doubt.

"What German is that?"

"Nietzsche."

The professor looked at him pityingly. Nietzsche had said to mankind, "Be harsh!" affirming that "a righteous war sanctifies every cause." He had exalted Bismarck; he had taken part in the war of '70; he was glorifying Germany when he spoke of "the smiling lion," and "the blond beast." But Argensola listened with the tranquillity of one sure of his ground. Oh, hours of placid reading near the studio chimney, listening to the rain beating against the pane! . . .

"The philosopher did say that," he admitted, "and he said many other very different things, like all great thinkers. His doctrine is one of pride, but of individual pride, not that of a nation or race. He always spoke against 'the insidious fallacy of race.'"

Argensola recalled his philosophy word for word. Culture, according to Nietzsche, was "unity of style in all the manifestations of life." Science did not necessarily include culture. Great knowledge might be accompanied with great barbarity, by the absence of style or by the chaotic confusion of all styles. Germany, according to the philosopher, had no genuine culture owing to its lack of style. "The French," he had said, "were at the head of an authentic and fruitful culture, whatever their valor might be, and until now everybody had drawn upon it." Their hatreds were concentrated within their own country. "I cannot endure Germany. The spirit of servility and pettiness penetrates everywhere. . . . I believe only in French culture, and what the rest of Europe calls culture appears to me to be a mistake. The few individual cases of lofty culture that I met in Germany were of French origin."

"You know," continued Argensola, "that in quarrelling with Wagner about the excess of Germanism in his art, Nietzsche proclaimed the necessity of mediterraneanizing music. His ideal was a culture for all Europe, but with a Latin base."

Julius von Hartrott replied most disdainfully to this, repeating the Spaniard's very words. Men who thought much said many things. Besides, Nietzsche was a poet, completely demented at his death, and was no authority among the University sages. His fame had only been recognized in foreign lands. . . . And he paid no further attention to the youth, ignoring him as though he had evaporated into thin air after his presumption. All the professor's attention was now concentrated on Desnoyers.

"This country," he resumed, "is dying from within. How can you doubt that revolution will break out the minute war is declared? . . . Have you not noticed the agitation of the boulevard on account of the Caillaux trial? Reactionaries and revolutionists have been assaulting each other for the past three days. I have seen them challenging one another with shouts and songs as if they were going to come to blows right in the middle of the street. This division of opinion will become accentuated when our troops cross the frontier. It will then be civil war. The anti-militarists are clamoring mournfully, believing that it is in the power of the government to prevent the clash. . . . A country degenerated by democracy and by the inferiority of the triumphant Celt, greedy for full liberty! . . . We are the only free people on earth because we know how to obey."

This paradox made Julio smile. Germany the only free people! . . .

"It is so," persisted Hartrott energetically. "We have the liberty best suited to a great people—economical and intellectual liberty."

"And political liberty?"

The professor received this question with a scornful shrug.

"Political liberty! . . . Only decadent and ungovernable people, inferior races anxious for equality and democratic confusion, talk about political liberty. We Germans do not need it. We are a nation of masters who recognize the sacredness of government, and we wish to be commanded by those of superior birth. We possess the genius of organization."

That, according to the Doctor, was the grand German secret, and the Teutonic race upon taking possession of the world, would share its discovery with all. The nations would then be so organized that each individual would give the maximum of service to society. Humanity, banded in regiments for every class of production, obeying a superior officer, like machines contributing the greatest possible output of labor—there you have the perfect state! Liberty was a purely negative idea if not accompanied with a positive concept which would make it useful.

The two friends listened with astonishment to this description of the future which Teutonic superiority was offering to the world. Every individual submitted to intensive production, the same as a bit of land from which its owner wishes to get the greatest number of vegetables. . . . Mankind reduced to mechanics. . . . No useless operations that would not produce immediate results. . . . And the people who heralded this awful idea were the very philosophers and idealists who had once given contemplation and reflection the first place in their existence! . . .

Hartrott again harked back to the inferiority of their racial enemies. In order to combat successfully, it required self-assurance, an unquenchable confidence in the superiority of their own powers.

"At this very hour in Berlin, everyone is accepting war, everyone is believing that victory is sure, while HERE! . . . I do not say that the French are afraid; they have a brave past that galvanizes them at certain times—but they are so depressed that it is easy to guess that they will make almost any sacrifices in order to evade what is coming upon them. The people first will shout with enthusiasm, as it always cheers that which carries it to perdition. The upper classes have no faith in the future; they are keeping quiet, but the presentiment of disaster may easily be conjectured. Yesterday I was talking with your father. He is French, and he is rich. He was indignant against the government of his country for involving the nation in the European conflict in order to defend a distant and uninteresting people. He complains of the exalted patriots who have opened the abyss between Germany and France, preventing a reconciliation. He says that Alsace and Lorraine are not worth what a war would cost in men and money. . . . He recognizes our greatness and is convinced that we have progressed so rapidly that the other countries cannot come up to us. . . . And as your father thinks, so do many others—all those who are wrapped in creature comfort, and fear to lose it. Believe me, a country that hesitates and fears war is conquered before the first battle."

Julio evinced a certain disquietude, as though he would like to cut short the conversation.

"Just leave my father out of it! He speaks that way to-day because war is not yet an accomplished fact, and he has to contradict and vent his indignation on whoever comes near him. To-morrow he will say just the opposite. . . . My father is a Latin."

The professor looked at his watch. He must go; there were still many things which he had to do before going to the station. The Germans living in Paris had fled in great bands as though a secret order had been circulating among them. That afternoon the last of those who had been living ostensibly in the Capital would depart.

"I have come to see you because of our family interest, because it was my duty to give you fair warning. You are a foreigner, and nothing holds you here. If you are desirous of witnessing a great historic event, remain—but it will be better for you to go. The war is going to be ruthless, very ruthless, and if Paris attempts resistance, as formerly, we shall see terrible things. Modes of offense have greatly changed."

Desnoyers made a gesture of indifference.

"The same as your father," observed the professor. "Last night he and all your family responded in the same way. Even my mother prefers to remain with her sister, saying that the Germans are very good, very civilized and there is nothing to apprehend in their triumph."

This good opinion seemed to be troubling the Doctor.

"They don't understand what modern warfare means. They ignore the fact that our generals have studied the art of overcoming the enemy and they will apply it mercilessly. Ruthlessness is the only means, since it perturbs the intelligence of the enemy, paralyzes his action and pulverizes his resistance. The more ferocious the war, the more quickly it is concluded. To punish with cruelty is to proceed humanely. Therefore, Germany is going to be cruel with a cruelty hitherto unseen, in order that the conflict may not be prolonged."

He had risen and was standing, cane and straw hat in hand. Argensola was looking at him with frank hostility. The professor, obliged to pass near him, did so with a stiff and disdainful nod.

Then he started toward the door, accompanied by his cousin. The farewell was brief.

"I repeat my counsel. If you do not like danger, go! It may be that I am mistaken, and that this nation, convinced of the uselessness of defense, may give itself up voluntarily. . . . At any rate, we shall soon see. I shall take great pleasure in returning to Paris when the flag of the Empire is floating over the Eiffel

Tower, a mere matter of three or four weeks, certainly by the beginning of September."

France was going to disappear from the map. To the Doctor, her death was a foregone conclusion.

"Paris will remain," he admitted benevolently, "the French will remain, because a nation is not easily suppressed; but they will not retain their former place. We shall govern the world; they will continue to occupy themselves in inventing fashions, in making life agreeable for visiting foreigners; and in the intellectual world, we shall encourage them to educate good actresses, to produce entertaining novels and to write witty comedies. . . . Nothing more."

Desnoyers laughed as he shook his cousin's hand, pretending to take his words as a paradox.

"I mean it," insisted Hartrott. "The last hour of the French Republic as an important nation has sounded. I have studied it at close range, and it deserves no better fate. License and lack of confidence above—sterile enthusiasm below."

Upon turning his head, he again caught Argensola's malicious smile.

"We know all about that kind of study," he added aggressively. "We are accustomed to examine the nations of the past, to dissect them fibre by fibre, so that we recognize at a glance the psychology of the living."

The Bohemian fancied that he saw a surgeon talking self-sufficiently about the mysteries of the will before a corpse. What did this pedantic interpreter of dead documents know about life? . . .

When the door closed, he approached his friend who was returning somewhat dismayed. Argensola no longer considered Doctor Julius von Hartrott crazy.

"What a brute!" he exclaimed, throwing up his hands. "And to think that they are at large, these originators of gloomy errors! . . . Who would ever believe that they belong to the same land that produced Kant, the pacifist, the serene Goethe and Beethoven! . . . To think that for so many years, we have believed that they were forming a nation of dreamers and philosophers occupied in working disinterestedly for all mankind! . . ."

The sentence of a German geographer recurred to him: "The German is bicephalous; with one head he dreams and poetizes while with the other he thinks and executes."

Desnoyers was now beginning to feel depressed at the certainty of war. This professor seemed to him even worse than the Herr Counsellor and the other Germans that he had met on the steamer. His distress was not only because of his selfish thought as to how the catastrophe was going to affect his plans with Marguerite. He was suddenly discovering that in this hour of uncertainty he loved France. He recognized it as his father's native land and the scene of the great Revolution. . . . Although he had never mixed in political campaigns, he was a republican at heart, and had often ridiculed certain of his friends who adored kings and emperors, thinking it a great sign of distinction.

Argensola tried to cheer him up.

"Who knows? . . . This is a country of surprises. One must see the Frenchman when he tries to remedy his want of foresight. Let that barbarian of a cousin of yours say what he will—there is order, there is enthusiasm. . . . Worse off than we were those who lived in the days before Valmy. Entirely disorganized, their only defense battalions of laborers and countrymen handling a gun for the first time. . . . But, nevertheless, the Europe of the old monarchies could not for twenty years free themselves from these improvised warriors!"

CHAPTER V

IN WHICH APPEAR THE FOUR HORSEMEN

The two friends now lived a feverish life, considerably accelerated by the rapidity with which events succeeded each other. Every hour brought forth an astonishing bit of news—generally false—which changed opinions very suddenly. As soon as the danger of war seemed arrested, the report would spread that mobilization was going to be ordered within a few minutes.

Within each twenty-four hours were compressed the disquietude, anxiety and nervous waste of a normal year. And that which was aggravating the situation still more was the uncertainty, the expectation of the event, feared but still invisible, the distress on account of a danger continually threatening but never arriving.

History in the making was like a stream overflowing its banks, events overlapping each other like the waves of an inundation. Austria was declaring war with Servia while the diplomats of the great powers were continuing their efforts to stem the tide. The electric web girdling the planet was vibrating incessantly in the depths of the ocean and on the peaks of the continents, transmitting alternate hopes and fears.

Russia was mobilizing a part of its army. Germany, with its troops in readiness under the pretext of manoeuvres, was decreeing the state of "threatened war." The Austrians, regardless of the efforts of diplomacy, were beginning the bombardment of Belgrade. William II, fearing that the intervention of the Powers might settle the differences between the Czar and the Emperor of Austria, was forcing the course of events by declaring war upon Russia. Then Germany began isolating herself, cutting off railroad and telegraphic communications in order to shroud in mystery her invading forces.

France was watching this avalanche of events, temperate in its words and enthusiasm. A cool and grave resolution was noticeable everywhere. Two generations had come into the world, informed as soon as they reached a reasonable age, that some day there would undoubtedly be war. Nobody wanted it; the adversary imposed it. . . . But all were accepting it with the firm intention of fulfilling their duty.

During the daytime Paris was very quiet, concentrating the mind on the work in hand. Only a few groups of exalted patriots, following the tricolored flag, were passing through the place de la Concorde, in order to salute the statue of Strasbourg. The people were accosting each other in a friendly way in the streets. Everybody seemed to know everybody else, although they might not have met before. Eye attracted eye, and smiles appeared to broaden mutually with the sympathy of a common interest. The women were sad but speaking cheerily in order to hide their emotions. In the long summer twilight, the boulevards were filling with crowds. Those from the outlying districts were converging toward the centre of the city, as in the remote revolutionary days, banding together in groups, forming an endless multitude from which came shouts and songs. These manifestations were passing through the centre under the electric lights that were just being turned on, the processions generally lasting until midnight, with the national banner floating above the walking crowds, escorted by the flags of other nations.

It was on one of these nights of sincere enthusiasm that the two friends heard an unexpected, astonishing piece of news. "They have killed Jaures!" The groups were repeating it from one to another with an amazement which seemed to overpower their grief. "Jaures assassinated! And what for?" The best popular element, which instinctively seeks an explanation of every proceeding, remained in suspense, not knowing which way to turn. The tribune dead, at the very moment that his word as welder of the people was most needed! . . .

Argensola thought immediately of Tchernoff. "What will our neighbors say?" . . . The quiet, orderly people of Paris were fearing a revolution, and for a few moments Desnoyers believed that his cousin's auguries were about to be fulfilled. This assassination, with its retaliations, might be the signal for civil war. But the masses of the people, worn out with grief at the death of their hero, were waiting in tragic silence. All were seeing, beyond his dead body, the image of the country.

By the following morning, the danger had vanished. The laboring classes were talking of generals and war, showing each other their little military memorandums, announcing the date of their departure as soon as the order of mobilization should be published. "I go the second day." "I the first." Those of the standing army who were on leave were recalled individually to the barracks. All these events were tending in the same direction—war.

The Germans were invading Luxembourg; the Germans were ordering their armies to invade the French frontier when their ambassador was still in Paris making promises of peace. On the day after the death of Jaures, the first of August, the people were crowding around some pieces of paper, written by hand and in evident haste. These papers were copies of other larger printed sheets, headed by two crossed flags. "It has come; it is now a fact!". . . It was the order for general mobilization. All France was about to take up arms, and chests seemed to expand with a sigh of relief. Eyes were sparkling with excitement. The nightmare was at last over! . . . Cruel reality was preferable to the uncertainty of days and days, each as long as a week.

In vain President Poincare, animated by a last hope, was explaining to the French that "mobilization is not necessarily war, that a call to arms may be simply a preventive measure." "It is war, inevitable war," said the populace with a fatalistic expression. And those who were going to start that very night or the following day were the most eager and enthusiastic.—"Now those who seek us are going to find us! Vive la France!" The Chant du Depart, the martial hymn of the volunteers of the first Republic, had been exhumed by the instinct of a people which seek the voice of Art in its most critical moments. The stanzas of the conservative Chenier, adapted to a music of warlike solemnity, were resounding through the streets, at the same time as the Marseillaise:

La Republique nous appelle.
Sachons vaincre ou sachons perir;
Un francais doit vivre pour elle.
Pour elle un francais doit mourir.

The mobilization began at midnight to the minute. At dusk, groups of men began moving through the streets towards the stations. Their families were walking beside them, carrying the valise or bundle of clothes. They were escorted by the friends of their district, the tricolored flag borne aloft at the head of these platoons. The Reserves were donning their old uniforms which presented all the difficulties of suits long ago forgotten. With new leather belts and their revolvers at their sides, they were betaking themselves to the railway which was to carry them to the point of concentration. One of their children was carrying the old sword in its cloth sheath. The wife was hanging on his arm, sad and proud at the same time, giving her last counsels in a loving whisper.

Street cars, automobiles and cabs rolled by with crazy velocity. Nobody had ever seen so many vehicles in the Paris streets, yet if anybody needed one, he called in vain to the conductors, for none wished to serve mere civilians. All means of transportation were for military men, all roads ended at the railroad stations. The heavy trucks of the administration, filled with sacks, were saluted with general enthusiasm. "Hurrah for the army!" The soldiers in mechanic's garb, on top of the swaying pyramid, replied to the cheers, waving their arms and uttering shouts that nobody pretended to understand.

Fraternity had created a tolerance hitherto unknown. The crowds were pressing forward, but in their encounters, invariably preserved good order. Vehicles were running into each other, and when the conductors resorted to the customary threats, the crowds would intervene and make them shake hands. "Three cheers for France!" The pedestrians, escaping between the wheels of the automobiles were laughing and good-naturedly reproaching the chauffeur with, "Would you kill a Frenchman on his way to his regiment?" and the conductor would reply, "I, too, am going in a few hours. This is my last trip." As night approached, cars and cabs were running with increasing irregularity, many of the employees having abandoned their posts to take leave of their families and make the train. All the life of Paris was concentrating itself in a half-dozen human rivers emptying in the stations.

Desnoyers and Argensola met in a boulevard cafe toward midnight. Both were exhausted by the day's emotions and under that nervous depression which follows noisy and violent spectacles. They needed to rest. War was a fact, and now that it was a certainty, they felt no anxiety to get further news. Remaining in the cafe proved impossible. In the hot and smoky atmosphere, the occupants were singing and shouting and waving tiny flags. All the battle hymns of the past and present were here intoned in chorus, to an accompaniment of glasses and plates. The rather cosmopolitan clientele was reviewing the European nations. All, absolutely all, were going to enroll themselves on the side of France. "Hurrah! . . . Hurrah!" . . . An old man and his wife were seated at a table near the two friends. They were tenants, of an orderly, humdrum walk in life, who perhaps in all their existence had never been awake at such an hour. In the general enthusiasm they had come to the boulevards "in order to see war a little closer." The foreign tongue used by his neighbors gave the husband a lofty idea of their importance.

"Do you believe that England is going to join us?" . . .

Argensola knew as much about it as he, but he replied authoritatively, "Of course she will. That's a sure thing!" The old man rose to his feet: "Hurrah for England!" and he began chanting a forgotten patriotic song, marking time with his arms in a spirited way, to the great admiration of his old wife, and urging all to join in the chorus that very few were able to follow.

The two friends had to take themselves home on foot. They could not find a vehicle that would stop for them; all were hurrying in the opposite direction toward the stations. They were both in a bad humor, but Argensola couldn't keep his to himself.

"Ah, these women!" Desnoyers knew all about his relations (so far honorable) with a midinette from the rue Taitbout. Sunday strolls in the suburbs of Paris, various trips to the moving picture shows, comments upon the fine points of the latest novel published in the sheets of a popular paper, kisses of farewell when she took the night train from Bois Colombes in order to sleep at home—that was all. But Argensola was wickedly counting on Father Time to mellow the sharpest virtues. That evening they had taken some refreshment with a French friend who was going the next morning to join his regiment. The girl had sometimes seen him with Argensola without noticing him particularly, but now she suddenly began admiring him as though he were another person. She had given up the idea of returning home that night; she wanted to see how a war begins. The three had dined together, and all her interest had centred upon the one who was going away. She even took offense, with sudden modesty, when Argensola tried as he had often done before, to squeeze her hand under the table. Meanwhile she was almost leaning her head on the shoulder of the future hero, enveloping him with admiring gaze.

"And they have gone. . . . They have gone away together!" said the Spaniard bitterly. "I had to leave them in order not to make my hard luck any worse. To have worked so long . . . for another!"

He was silent for a few minutes, then changing the trend of his ideas, he added: "I recognize, nevertheless, that her behavior is beautiful. The generosity of these women when they believe that the moment for sacrifice has come! She is terribly afraid of her father, and yet she stays away from home all night with a person whom she hardly knows, and whom she was not even thinking of in the middle of the afternoon! . . . The entire nation feels gratitude toward those who are going to imperil their lives, and she, poor child, wishing to do something, too, for those destined for death, to give them a little pleasure in their last hour . . . is giving the best she has, that which she can never recover. I have sketched her role poorly, perhaps. . . . Laugh at me if you want to, but admit that it is beautiful."

Desnoyers laughed heartily at his friend's discomfiture, in spite of the fact that he, too, was suffering a good deal of secret annoyance. He had seen Marguerite but once since the day of his return. The only news of her that he had received was by letter. . . . This cursed war! What an upset for happy people! Marguerite's mother was ill. She was brooding over the departure of her son, an officer, on the first day of the mobilization. Marguerite, too, was uneasy about her brother and did not think it expedient to come to the studio while her mother was grieving at home. When was this situation ever to end? . . .

That check for four hundred thousand francs which he had brought from America was also worrying him. The day before, the bank had declined to pay it for lack of the customary official advice. Afterward they said that they had received the advice, but did not give him the money. That very afternoon, when the trust companies had closed their doors, the government had already declared a moratorium, in order to prevent a general bankruptcy due to the general panic. When would they pay him? . . . Perhaps when the war which had not yet begun was ended—perhaps never. He had no other money available except the two thousand francs left over from his travelling expenses. All of his friends were in the same distressing situation, unable to draw on the sums which they had in the banks. Those who had any money were obliged to go from shop to shop, or form in line at the bank doors, in order to get a bill changed. Oh, this war! This stupid war!

In the Champs Elysees, they saw a man with a broad-brimmed hat who was walking slowly ahead of them and talking to himself. Argensola recognized him as he passed near the street lamp, "Friend Tchernoff." Upon returning their greeting, the Russian betrayed a slight odor of wine. Uninvited, he had adjusted his steps to theirs, accompanying them toward the Arc de Triomphe.

Julio had merely exchanged silent nods with Argensola's new acquaintance when encountering him in the vestibule; but sadness softens the heart and makes us seek the friendship of the humble as a refreshing shelter. Tchernoff, on the contrary, looked at Desnoyers as though he had known him all his life.

The man had interrupted his monologue, heard only by the black masses of vegetation, the blue shadows perforated by the reddish tremors of the street lights, the summer night with its cupola of warm breezes and twinkling stars. He took a few steps without saying anything, as a mark of consideration to his companions, and then renewed his arguments, taking them up where he had broken off, without offering any explanation, as though he were still talking to himself. . . .

"And at this very minute, they are shouting with enthusiasm the same as they are doing here, honestly believing that they are going to defend their outraged country, wishing to die for their families and firesides that nobody has threatened."

"Who are 'they,' Tchernoff?" asked Argensola.

The Russian stared at him as though surprised at such a question.

"They," he said laconically.

The two understood. . . . THEY! It could not be anyone else.

"I have lived ten years in Germany," he continued, connecting up his words, now that he found himself listened to. "I was daily correspondent for a paper in Berlin and I know these people. Passing along these thronged boulevards, I have been seeing in my imagination what must be happening there at this hour. They, too, are singing and shouting with enthusiasm as they wave their flags. On the outside, they seem just alike—but oh, what a difference within! . . . Last night the people beset a few babblers in the boulevard who were yelling, 'To Berlin!'— a slogan of bad memories and worse taste. France does not wish conquests; her only desire is to be respected, to live in peace without humiliations or disturbances. To-night two of the mobilized men said on leaving, 'When we enter Germany we are going to make it a republic!' . . . A republic is not a perfect thing, but it is better tha living under an irresponsible monarchy by the grace of God. It at least presupposes tranquillity and absence of the personal ambitions that disturb life. I was impressed by the generous thought of these laboring men who, instead of wishing to exterminate their enemies, were planning to give them something better."

Tchernoff remained silent a few minutes, smiling ironically at the picture which his imagination was calling forth.

"In Berlin, the masses are expressing their enthusiasm in the lofty phraseology befitting a superior people. Those in the lowest classes, accustomed to console themselves for humiliations with a gross materialism, are now crying 'Nach Paris! We are going to drink champagne gratis!' The pietistic burgher, ready to do anything to attain a new honor, and the aristocracy which has given the world the greatest scandals of recent years, are also shouting, 'Nach Paris!' To them Paris is the Babylon of the deadly sin, the city of the Moulin Rouge and the restaurants of Montmartre, the only places that they know. . . . And my comrades of the Social-Democracy, they are also cheering, but to another tune.—'To-morrow! To St. Petersburg! Russian ascendency, the menace of civilization, must be obliterated!' The Kaiser waving the tyranny of another country as a scarecrow to his people! . . . What a joke!"

And the loud laugh of the Russian sounded through the night like the noise of wooden clappers.

"We are more civilized than the Germans," he said, regaining his self-control.

Desnoyers, who had been listening with great interest, now gave a start of surprise, saying to himself, "This Tchernoff has been drinking."

"Civilization," continued the Socialist, "does not consist merely in great industry, in many ships, armies and numerous universities that only teach science. That is material civilization. There is another, a superior one, that elevates the soul and does not permit human dignity to suffer without protesting against continual humiliations. A Swiss living in his wooden chalet and considering himself the equal of the other men of his country, is more civilized than the Herr Professor who gives precedence to a lieutenant, or to a Hamburg millionaire who, in turn, bends his neck like a lackey before those whose names are prefixed by a von."

Here the Spaniard assented as though he could guess what Tchernoff was going to say.

"We Russians endure great tyranny. I know something about that. I know the hunger and cold of Siberia. . . . But opposed to our tyranny has always existed a revolutionary protest. Part of the nation is half-barbarian, but the rest has a superior mentality, a lofty moral spirit which faces danger and sacrifice because of liberty and truth. . . . And Germany? Who there has ever raised a protest in order to defend human rights? What revolutions have ever broken out in Prussia, the land of the great despots?

"Frederick William, the founder of militarism, when he was tired of beating his wife and spitting in his children's plates, used to sally forth, thong in hand, in order to cowhide those subjects who did not get out of his way in time. His son, Frederick the Great, declared that he died, bored to death with governing a nation of slaves. In two centuries of Prussian history, one single revolution—the barricades of 1848—a bad Berlinish copy of the Paris revolution, and without any result. Bismarck corrected with a heavy hand so as to crush completely the last attempts at protest—if such ever really existed. And when his friends were threatening him with revolution, the ferocious Junker, merely put his hands on his hips and roared with the most insolent of horse laughs. A revolution in Prussia! . . . Nothing at all, as he knew his people!"

Tchernoff was not a patriot. Many a time Argensola had heard him railing against his country, but now he was indignant in view of the contempt with which Teutonic haughtiness was treating the Russian nation. Where, in the last forty years of imperial grandeur, was that universal supremacy of which the Germans were everlastingly boasting? . . .

Excellent workers in science; tenacious and short-sighted academicians, each wrapped in his specialty!—Benedictines of the laboratory who experimented painstakingly and occasionally hit upon something, in spite of enormous blunders given out as truths, because they were their own . . . that was all! And side by side with such patient laboriosity, really worthy of respect—what charlatanism! What great names exploited as a shop sample! How many sages turned into proprietors of sanatoriums! . . . A Herr Professor discovers the cure of tuberculosis, and the tubercular keep on dying as before. Another labels with a number the invincible remedy for the most unconfessable of diseases, and the genital scourge continues afflicting the world. And all these errors were representing great fortunes, each saving panacea bringing into existence an industrial corporation selling its products at high prices—as though suffering were a privilege of the rich. How different from the bluff Pasteur and other clever men of the inferior races who have given their discoveries to the world without stooping to form monopolies!

"German science," continued Tchernoff, "has given much to humanity, I admit that; but the science of other nations has done as much. Only a nation puffed up with conceit could imagine that it has done everything for civilization, and the others nothing. . . . Apart from their learned specialists, what genius has been produced in our day by this Germany which believes itself so transcendent? Wagner, the last of the romanticists, closes an epoch and belongs to the past. Nietzsche took pains to proclaim his Polish origin and abominated Germany, a country, according to him, of middle-class pedants. His Slavism was so pronounced that he even prophesied the overthrow of the Prussians by the Slavs. . . . And there are others. We, although a savage people, have given the world of modern times an admirable moral grandeur. Tolstoi and Dostoievsky are world-geniuses. What names can the Germany of William II put ahead of these? . . . His country was the country of music, but the Russian musicians of to-day are more original than the mere followers of Wagner, the copyists who take refuge in orchestral exasperations in order to hide their mediocrity. . . . In its time of stress the German nation had men of genius, before Pan-Germanism had been born, when the Empire did not exist. Goethe, Schiller, Beethoven were subjects of little principalities. They received influence from other countries and contributed their share to the universal civilization like citizens of the world, without insisting that the world should, therefore, become Germanized."

Czarism had committed atrocities. Tchernoff knew that by experience, and did not need the Germans to assure him of it. But all the illustrious classes of Russia were enemies of that tyranny and were protesting against it. Where in Germany were the intellectual enemies of Prussian Czarism? They were either holding their peace, or breaking forth into adulation of the anointed of the Lord—a musician and comedian like Nero, of a sharp and superficial intelligence, who believed that by merely skimming through anything he knew it all. Eager to strike a spectacular pose in history, he had finally afflicted the world with the greatest of calamities.

"Why must the tyranny that weighs upon my country necessarily be Russian? The worst Czars were imitators of Prussia. Every time that the Russian people of our day have attempted to revindicate their rights, the reactionaries have used the Kaiser as a threat, proclaiming that he would come to their aid. One-half of the Russian aristocracy is German; the functionaries who advise and support despotism are Germans; German, too, are the generals who have distinguished themselves by massacring the people; German are the officials who undertake to punish the laborers' strikes and the rebellion of their allies. The reactionary Slav is brutal, but he has the fine sensibility of a race in which many princes have become Nihilists. He raises the lash with facility, but then he repents and oftentimes weeps. I have seen Russian officials kill themselves rather than march against the people, or through remorse for slaughter committed. The German in the service of the Czar feels no scruples, nor laments his conduct. He kills coldly, with the minuteness and exactitude with which he does everything. The Russian is a barbarian who strikes and regrets; German civilization shoots without hesitation. Our Slav Czar, in a humanitarian dream, favored the Utopian idea of universal peace, organizing the Conference of The Hague. The Kaiser of culture, meanwhile, has been working years and years in the erection and establishment of a destructive organ of an immensity heretofore unknown, in order to crush all Europe. The Russian is a humble Christian, socialistic, democratic, thirsting for justice; the German prides himself upon his Christianity, but is an idolator like the German of other centuries. His religion loves blood and maintains castes; his true worship is that of Odin;—only that nowadays, the god of slaughter has changed his name and calls himself, 'The State'!"

Tchernoff paused an instant—perhaps in order to increase the wonder of his companions—and then said with simplicity:

"I am a Christian."

Argensola, who already knew the ideas and history of the Russian, started with astonishment, and Julio persisted in his suspicion, "Surely Tchernoff is drunk."

"It is true," declared the Russian earnestly, "that I do not worry about God, nor do I believe in dogmas, but my soul is Christian as is that of all revolutionists. The philosophy of modern democracy is lay Christianity. We Socialists love the humble, the needy, the weak. We defend their right to life and well-being, as did the greatest lights of the religious world who saw a brother in every unfortunate. We exact respect for the poor in the name of justice; the others ask for it in the name of charity. That only separates us. But we strive that mankind may, by common consent, lead a better life, that the strong may sacrifice for the weak, the lofty for the lowly, and the world be ruled by brotherliness, seeking the greatest equality possible."

The Slav reviewed the history of human aspirations. Greek thought had brought comfort, a sense of well-being on the earth—but only for the few, for the citizens of the little democracies, for the free men, leaving the slaves and barbarians who constituted the majority, in their misery. Christianity, the religion of the lowly, had recognized the right of happiness for all mankind, but this happiness was placed in heaven, far from this world, this "vale of tears." The Revolution and its heirs, the Socialists, were trying to place happiness in the immediate realities of earth, like the ancients, but making all humanity participants in it like the Christians.

"Where is the 'Christianity of modern Germany? . . . There is far more genuine Christian spirit in the fraternal laity of the French Republic, defender of the weak, than in the religiosity of the conservative Junkers. Germany has made a god in her own image, believing that she adores it, but in reality adoring her own image. The German God is a reflex of the German State which considers war as the first activity of a nation and the noblest of occupations. Other Christian peoples, when they have to go to war, feel the contradiction that exists between their conduct and the teachings of the Gospel, and excuse themselves by showing the cruel necessity which impels them. Germany declares that war is acceptable to God. I have heard German sermons proving that Jesus was in favor of Militarism.

"Teutonic pride, the conviction that its race is providentially destined to dominate the world, brings into working unity their Protestants, Catholics and Jews.

"Far above their differences of dogma is that God of the State which is German—the Warrior God to whom William is probably referring as 'my worthy Ally.' Religions always tend toward universality. Their aim is to place humanity in relationship with God, and to sustain these relations among mankind. Prussia has retrograded to barbarism, creating for its personal use a second Jehovah, a divinity hostile to the greater part of the human race who makes his own the grudges and ambitions of the German people."

Tchernoff then explained in his own way the creation of this Teutonic God, ambitious, cruel and vengeful. The Germans were comparatively recent Christians. Their Christianity was not more than six centuries old. When the Crusades were drawing to a close, the Prussians were still living in paganism. Pride of race, impelling them to war, had revived these dead divinities. The God of the Gospel was now adorned by the Germans with lance and shield like the old Teutonic god who was a military chief.

"Christianity in Berlin wears helmet and riding boots. God at this moment is seeing Himself mobilized the same as Otto, Fritz and Franz, in order to punish the enemies of His chosen people. That the Lord has commanded, 'Thou shalt not kill,' and His Son has said to the world, 'Blessed are the peacemakers,' no longer matters. Christianity, according to its German priests of all creeds, can only influence the individual betterment of mankind, and should not mix itself in affairs of state. The Prussian God of the State is 'the old German God,' the lineal descendant of the ferocious Germanic mythology, a mixture of divinities hungry for war."

In the silence of the avenue, the Russian evoked the ruddy figures of the implacable gods, that were going to awake that night upon hearing the hum of arms and smelling the acrid odor of blood. Thor, the brutal god with the little head, was stretching his biceps and clutching the hammer that crushed cities. Wotan was sharpening his lance which had the lightning for its handle, the thunder for its blade. Odin, the one-eyed, was gaping with gluttony on the mountain-tops, awaiting the dead warriors that would crowd around his throne. The dishevelled Valkyries, fat and perspiring, were beginning to gallop from cloud to cloud, hallooing to humanity that they might carry off the corpses doubled like saddle bags, over the haunches of their flying nags.

"German religiosity," continued the Russian, "is the disavowal of Christianity. In its eyes, men are no longer equal before God. Their God is interested only in the strong, and favors them with his support so that they may dare anything. Those born weak must either submit or disappear. Neither are nations equal, but are divided into leaders and inferior races whose destiny is to be sifted out and absorbed by their superiors. Since God has thus ordained, it is unnecessary to state that the grand world-leader is Germany."

Argensola here interrupted to observe that German pride believed itself championed not only by God but by science, too.

"I know that," interposed the Russian without letting him finish— "generalization, inequality, selection, the struggle for life, and all that. . . . The Germans, so conceited about their special worth, erect upon distant ground their intellectual monuments, borrowing of the foreigner their foundation material whenever they undertake a new line of work. A Frenchman and an Englishman, Gobineau and Chamberlain, have given them the arguments with which to defend the superiority of their race. With the rubbish left over from Darwin and Spencer, their old Haeckel has built up his doctrine of 'Monism' which, applied to politics, scientifically consecrates Prussian pride and recognizes its right to rule the world by force."

"No, a thousand times no!" he exclaimed after a brief silence. "The struggle for existence with its procession of cruelties may be true among the lower species, but it should not be true among human creatures. We are rational beings and ought to free ourselves from the fatality of environment, moulding it to our convenience. The animal does not know law, justice or compassion; he lives enslaved in the obscurity of his instincts. We think, and thought signifies liberty. Force does not necessarily have to be cruel; it is strongest when it does not take advantage of its power, and is kindly. All have a right to the life into which they are born, and since among individuals there exist the haughty and the humble, the mighty and the weak, so should exist nations, large and small, old and young. The end of our existence is not combat nor killing in order that others may afterwards kill us, and, perhaps, be killed themselves. Civilized peoples ought unanimously to adopt the idea of southern Europe, striving for the most peaceful and sweetest form of life possible."

A cruel smile played over the Russian's beard.

"But there exists that Kultur, diametrically opposed to civilization, which the Germans wish to palm off upon us. Civilization is refinement of spirit, respect of one's neighbor, tolerance of foreign opinion, courtesy of manner. Kultur is the action of a State that organizes and assimilates individuals and communities in order to utilize them for its own ends; and these ends consist mainly in placing 'The State' above other states, overwhelming them with their grandeur— or what is the same thing—with their haughty and violent pride."

By this time, the three had reached the place de l'Etoile. The dark outline of the Arc de Triomphe stood forth clearly in the starry expanse. The avenues extended in all directions, a double file of lights. Those around the monument illuminated its gigantic bases and the feet of the sculptured groups. Further up, the vaulted spaces were so locked in shadow that they had the black density of ebony.

Upon passing under the Arch, which greatly intensified the echo of their footsteps, they came to a standstill. The night breeze had a wintry chill as it whistled past, and the curved masses seemed melting into the diffused blue of space. Instinctively the three turned to glance back at the Champs Elysees. They saw only a river of shadow on which were floating rosaries of red stars among the two long, black scarfs formed by the buildings. But they were so well acquainted with this panorama that in imagination they mentally saw the majestic sweep of the avenue, the double row of palaces, the place de la Concorde in the background with the Egyptian obelisk, and the trees of the Tuileries.

"How beautiful it is!" exclaimed Tchernoff who was seeing something beyond the shadows. "An entire civilization, loving peace and pleasure, has passed through here."

A memory greatly affected the Russian. Many an afternoon, after lunch, he had met in this very spot a robust man, stocky, with reddish beard and kindly eyes—a man who looked like a giant who had just stopped growing. He was always accompanied by a dog. It was Jaures, his friend Jaures, who before going to the senate was accustomed to taking a walk toward the Arch from his home in Passy.

"He liked to come just where we are now! He loved to look at the avenues, the distant gardens, all of Paris which can be seen from this height; and filled with admiration, he would often say to me, 'This is magnificent—one of the most beautiful perspectives that can be found in the entire world.' . . . Poor Jaures!"

Through association of ideas, the Russian evoked the image of his compatriot, Michael Bakounine, another revolutionist, the father of anarchy, weeping with emotion at a concert after hearing the symphony with Beethoven chorals directed by a young friend of his, named Richard Wagner. "When our revolution comes," he cried, clasping the hand of the master, "whatever else may perish, this must be saved at any cost!"

Tchernoff roused himself from his reveries to look around him and say with sadness:

"THEY have passed through here!"

Every time that he walked through the Arch, the same vision would spring up in his mind. THEY were thousands of helmets glistening in the sun, thousands of heavy boots lifted with mechanical rigidity at the same time; horns, fifes, drums large and small, clashing against the majestic silence of these stones—the warlike march from Lohengrin sounding in the deserted avenues before the closed houses.

He, who was a foreigner, always felt attracted by the spell exerted by venerable buildings guarding the glory of a bygone day. He did not wish to know who had erected it. As soon as its pride is flattered, mankind tries immediately to solidify it. Then Humanity intervenes with a broader vision that changes the original significance of the work, enlarges it and strips it of its first egotistical import. The Greek statues, models of the highest beauty, had been originally mere images of the temple, donated by the piety of the devotees of those times. Upon evoking Roman grandeur, everybody sees in imagination the enormous Coliseum, circle of butcheries, or the arches erected to the glory of the inept Caesars. The representative works of nations have two significations—the interior or immediate one which their creators gave them, and the exterior or universal interest, the symbolic value which the centuries have given them.

"This Arch," continued Tchernoff, "is French within, with its names of battles and generals open to criticism. On the outside, it is the monument of the people who carried through the greatest revolution for liberty ever known. The glorification of man is there below in the column of the place Vendome. Here there is nothing individual. Its builders erected it to the memory of la Grande Armee and that Grand Army was the people in arms who spread revolution throughout Europe. The artists, great inventors, foresaw the true significance of this work. The warriors of Rude who are chanting the Marseillaise in the group at the left are not professional soldiers, they are armed citizens, marching to work out their sublime and violent mission. Their nudity makes them appear to me like sans-culottes in Grecian helmets. . . . Here there is more than the glory and egoism of a great nation. All Europe is awake to new life, thanks to these Crusaders of Liberty. . . . The nations call to mind certain images. If I think of Greece, I see the columns of the Parthenon; Rome, Mistress of the World, is the Coliseum and the Arch of Trajan; and revolutionary France is the Arc de Triomphe."

The Arch was even more, according to the Russian. It represented a great historical retaliation; the nations of the South, called the Latin races, replying, after many centuries, to the invasion which had destroyed the Roman jurisdiction—the Mediterranean peoples spreading themselves as conquerors through the lands of the ancient barbarians. Retreating immediately, they had swept away the past like a tidal wave—the great surf depositing all that it contained. Like the waters of certain rivers which fructify by overflowing, this recession of the human tide had left the soil enriched with new and generous ideas.

"If THEY should return!" added Tchernoff with a look of uneasiness. "If they again should tread these stones! . . . Before, they were simple-minded folk, stunned by their rapid good-fortune, who passed through here like a farmer through a salon. They were content with money for the pocket and two provinces which should perpetuate the memory of their victory. . . . But now they will not be the soldiers only who march against Paris. At the tail of the armies come the maddened canteen-keepers, the Herr Professors, carrying at the side the little keg of wine with the powder which crazes the barbarian, the wine of Kultur. And in the vans come also an enormous load of scientific savagery, a new philosophy which glorifies Force as a principle and sanctifier of everything, denies liberty, suppresses the weak and places the entire world under the charge of a minority chosen by God, just because it possesses the surest and most rapid methods of slaughter. Humanity may well tremble for the future if again resounds under this archway the tramp of boots following a march of Wagner or any other Kapellmeister."

They left the Arch, following the avenue Victor Hugo. Tchernoff walking along in dogged silence as though the vision of this imaginary procession had overwhelmed him. Suddenly he continued aloud the course of his reflections.

"And if they should enter, what does it matter? . . . On that account, the cause of Right will not die. It suffers eclipses, but is born again; it may be ignored and trampled under foot, but it does not, therefore, cease to exist, and all good souls recognize it as the only rule of life. A nation of madmen wishes to place might upon the pedestal that others have raised to Right. Useless endeavor! The eternal hope of mankind will ever be the increasing power of more liberty, more brotherliness, more justice."

The Russian appeared to calm himself with this statement. He and his friends spoke of the spectacle which Paris was presenting in its preparation for war. Tchernoff bemoaned the great suffering produced by the catastrophe, the thousands and thousands of domestic tragedies that were unrolling at that moment. Apparently nothing had changed. In the centre of the city and around the stations, there was unusual agitation, but the rest of the immense city did not appear affected by the great overthrow of its existence. The solitary street was presenting its usual aspect, the breeze was gently moving the leaves. A solemn peace seemed to be spreading itself through space. The houses appeared wrapped in slumber, but behind the closed windows might be surmised the insomnia of the reddened eyes, the sighs from hearts anguished by the threatened danger, the tremulous agility of the hands preparing the war outfit, perhaps the last loving greetings exchanged without pleasure, with kisses ending in sobs.

Tchernoff thought of his neighbors, the husband and wife who occupied the other interior apartment behind the studio. She was no longer playing the piano. The Russian had overheard disputes, the banging of doors locked with violence, and the footsteps of a man in the middle of the night, fleeing from a woman's cries. There had begun to develop on the other side of the wall a regulation drama—a repetition of hundreds of others, all taking place at the same time.

"She is a German," volunteered the Russian. "Our concierge has ferreted out her nationality. He must have gone by this time to join his regiment. Last night I could hardly sleep. I heard the lamentations through the thin wall partition, the steady, desperate weeping of an abandoned child, and the voice of a man who was vainly trying to quiet her! . . . Ah, what a rain of sorrows is now falling upon the world!"

That same evening, on leaving the house, he had met her by her door. She appeared like another woman, with an old look as though in these agonizing hours she had been suffering for fifteen years. In vain the kindly Tchernoff had tried to cheer her up, urging her to accept quietly her husband's absence so as not to harm the little one who was coming.

"For the unhappy creature is going to be a mother," he said sadly. "She hides her condition with a certain modesty, but from my window, I have often seen her making the dainty layette."

The woman had listened to him as though she did not understand. Words were useless before her desperation. She could only sob as though talking to herself, "I am a German. . . . He has gone; he has to go away. . . . Alone! . . . Alone forever!" . . .

"She is thinking all the time of her nationality which is separating her from her husband; she is thinking of the concentration camp to which they will take her with her compatriots. She is fearful of being abandoned in the enemy's country obliged to defend itself against the attack of her own country. . . . And all this when she is about to become a mother. What miseries! What agonies!"

The three reached the rue de la Pompe and on entering the house, Tchernoff began to take leave of his companions in order to climb the service stairs; but Desnoyers wished to prolong the conversation. He dreaded being alone with his friend, still chagrined over the evening's events. The conversation with the Russian interested him, so they all went up in the elevator together. Argensola suggested that this would be a good opportunity to uncork one of the many bottles which he was keeping in the kitchen. Tchernoff could go home through the studio door that opened on the stairway.

The great window had its glass doors wide open; the transoms on the patio side were also open; a breeze kept the curtains swaying, moving, too, the old lanterns, moth-eaten flags and other adornments of the romantic studio. They seated themselves around the table, near a window some distance from the light which was illuminating the other end of the big room. They were in the shadow, with their backs to the interior court. Opposite them were tiled roofs and an enormous rectangle of blue shadow, perforated by the sharp-pointed stars. The city lights were coloring the shadowy space with a bloody reflection.

Tchernoff drank two glasses, testifying to the excellence of the liquid by smacking his lips. The three were silent with the wondering and thoughtful silence which the grandeur of the night imposes. Their eyes were glancing from star to star, grouping them in fanciful lines, forming them into triangles or squares of varying irregularity. At times, the twinkling radiance of a heavenly body appeared to broaden the rays of light, almost hypnotizing them.

The Russian, without coming out of his revery, availed himself of another glass. Then he smiled with cruel irony, his bearded face taking on the semblance of a tragic mask peeping between the curtains of the night.

"I wonder what those men up there are thinking!" he muttered. "I wonder if any star knows that Bismarck ever existed! . . . I wonder if the planets are aware of the divine mission of the German nation!"

And he continued laughing.

Some far-away and uncertain noise disturbed the stillness of the night, slipping through some of the chinks that cut the immense plain of roofs. The three turned their heads so as to hear better. . . . The sound of voices cut through the thick silence of night—a masculine chorus chanting a hymn, simple, monotonous and solemn. They guessed at what it must be, although they could not hear very well. Various single notes floating with greater intensity on the night wind, enabled Argensola to piece together the short song, ending in a melodious, triumphant yell—a true war song:

C'est l'Alsace et la Lorraine,
C'est l'Alsace qu'il nous faut,
Oh, oh, oh, oh.

A new band of men was going away through the streets below, toward the railway station, the gateway of the war. They must be from the outlying districts, perhaps from the country, and passing through silence-wrapped Paris, they felt like singing of the great national hope, that those who were watching behind the dark facades might feel comforted, knowing that they were not alone.

"Just as it is in the opera," said Julio listening to the last notes of the invisible chorus dying away into the night.

Tchernoff continued drinking, but with a distracted air, his eyes fixed on the red cloud that floated over the roofs.

The two friends conjectured his mental labor from his concentrated look, and the low exclamations which were escaping him like the echoes of an interior monologue. Suddenly he leaped from thought to word without any forewarning, continuing aloud the course of his reasoning.

"And when the sun arises in a few hours, the world will see coursing through its fields the four horsemen, enemies of mankind. . . . Already their wild steeds are pawing the ground with impatience; already the ill-omened riders have come together and are exchanging the last words before leaping into the saddle."

"What horsemen are these?" asked Argensola.

"Those which go before the Beast."

The two friends thought this reply as unintelligible as the preceding words. Desnoyers again said mentally, "He is drunk," but his curiosity forced him to ask, "What beast is that?"

"That of the Apocalypse."

There was a brief silence, but the Russian's terseness of speech did not last long. He felt the necessity of expressing his enthusiasm for the dreamer on the island rock of Patmos. The poet of great and mystic vision was exerting, across two thousand years, his influence over this mysterious revolutionary, tucked away on the top floor of a house in Paris. John had foreseen it all. His visions, unintelligible to the masses, nevertheless held within them the mystery of great human events.

Tchernoff described the Apocalyptic beast rising from the depths of the sea. He was like a leopard, his feet like those of a bear, his mouth like the snout of a lion. He had seven heads and ten horns. And upon the horns were ten crowns, and upon each of his heads the name of a blasphemy. The evangelist did not say just what these blasphemies were, perhaps they differed according to the epochs, modified every thousand years when the beast made a new apparition. The Russian seemed to be reading those that were flaming on the heads of the monster—blasphemies against humanity, against justice, against all that makes life sweet and bearable. "Might is superior to Right!" . . . "The weak should not exist." . . . "Be harsh in order to be great." . . . And the Beast in all its hideousness was attempting to govern the world and make mankind render him homage!

"But the four horsemen?" persisted Desnoyers.

The four horsemen were preceding the appearance of the monster in John's vision.

The seven seals of the book of mystery were broken by the Lamb in the presence of the great throne where was seated one who shone like jasper. The rainbow round about the throne was in sight like unto an emerald. Twenty-four thrones were in a semicircle around the great throne, and upon them twenty-four elders with white robes and crowns of gold. Four enormous animals, covered with eyes and each having six wings, seemed to be guarding the throne. The sounding of trumpets was greeting the breaking of the first seal.

"Come and see," cried one of the beasts in a stentorian tone to the vision-seeing poet. . . . And the first horseman appeared on a white horse. In his hand he carried a bow, and a crown was given unto him. He was Conquest, according to some, the Plague according to others. He might be both things at the same time. He wore a crown, and that was enough for Tchernoff.

"Come forth," shouted the second animal, removing his thousand eyes. And from the broken seal leaped a flame-colored steed. His rider brandished over his head an enormous sword. He was War. Peace fled from the world before his furious gallop; humanity was going to be exterminated.

And when the third seal was broken, another of the winged animals bellowed like a thunder clap, "Come and see!" And John saw a black horse. He who mounted it held in his hand a scale in order to weigh the maintenance of mankind. He was Famine.

The fourth animal saluted the breaking of the fourth seal with a great roaring—"Come and see!" And there appeared a pale-colored horse. His rider was called Death, and power was given him to destroy with the sword and with hunger and with death, and with the beasts of the earth.

The four horsemen were beginning their mad, desolating course over the heads of terrified humanity.

Tchernoff was describing the four scourges of the earth exactly as though he were seeing them. The horseman on the white horse was clad in a showy and barbarous attire. His Oriental countenance was contracted with hatred as if smelling out his victims. While his horse continued galloping, he was bending his bow in order to spread pestilence abroad. At his back swung the brass quiver filled with poisoned arrows, containing the germs of all diseases—those of private life as well as those which envenom the wounded soldier on the battlefield.

The second horseman on the red steed was waving the enormous, two-edged sword over his hair bristling with the swiftness of his course. He was young, but the fierce scowl and the scornful mouth gave him a look of implacable ferocity. His garments, blown open by the motion of his wild race, disclosed the form of a muscular athlete.

Bald, old and horribly skinny was the third horseman bouncing up and down on the rawboned back of his black steed. His shrunken legs clanked against the thin flanks of the lean beast. In one withered hand he was holding the scales, symbol of the scarcity of food that was going to become as valuable as gold.

The knees of the fourth horseman, sharp as spurs, were pricking the ribs of the pale horse. His parchment-like skin betrayed the lines and hollows of his skeleton. The front of his skull-like face was twisted with the sardonic laugh of destruction. His cane-like arms were whirling aloft a gigantic sickle. From his angular shoulders was hanging a ragged, filthy shroud.

And the furious cavalcade was passing like a hurricane over the immense assemblage of human beings. The heavens showed above their heads, a livid, dark-edged cloud from the west. Horrible monsters and deformities were swarming in spirals above the furious horde, like a repulsive escort. Poor Humanity, crazed with fear, was fleeing in all directions on hearing the thundering pace of the Plague, War, Hunger and Death. Men and women, young and old, were knocking each other down and falling to the ground overwhelmed by terror, astonishment and desperation. And the white horse, the red, the black and the pale, were crushing all with their relentless, iron tread—the athletic man was hearing the crashing of his broken ribs, the nursing babe was writhing at its mother's breast, and the aged and feeble were closing their eyes forever with a childlike sob.

"God is asleep, forgetting the world," continued the Russian. "It will be a long time before he awakes, and while he sleeps the four feudal horsemen of the Beast will course through the land as its only lords."

Tchernoff was overpowered by the intensity of his dramatic vision. Springing from his seat, he paced up and down with great strides; but his picture of the fourfold catastrophe revealed by the gloomy poet's trance, seemed to him very weak indeed. A great painter had given corporeal form to these terrible dreams.

"I have a book," he murmured, "a rare book." . . .

And suddenly he left the studio and went to his own quarters. He wanted to bring the book to show to his friends. Argensola accompanied him, and they returned in a few minutes with the volume, leaving the doors open behind them, so as to make a stronger current of air among the hollows of the facades and the interior patio.

Tchernoff placed his precious book under the light. It was a volume printed in 1511, with Latin text and engravings. Desnoyers read the title, "The Apocalypse Illustrated." The engravings were by Albert Durer, a youthful effort, when the master was only twenty-seven years old. The three were fascinated by the picture portraying the wild career of the Apocalyptic horsemen. The quadruple scourge, on fantastic mounts, seemed to be precipitating itself with a realistic sweep, crushing panic-stricken humanity.

Suddenly something happened which startled the three men from their contemplative admiration—something unusual, indefinable, a dreadful sound which seemed to enter directly into their brains without passing through their ears—a clutch at the heart. Instinctively they knew that something very grave had just happened.

They stared at each other silently for a few interminable seconds.

Through the open door, a cry of alarm came up from the patio.

With a common impulse, the three ran to the interior window, but before reaching them, the Russian had a presentiment.

"My neighbor! . . . It must be my neighbor. Perhaps she has killed herself!"

Looking down, they could see lights below, people moving around a form stretched out on the tiled floor. The alarm had instantly filled all the court windows, for it was a sleepless night—a night of nervous apprehension when everyone was keeping a sad vigil.

"She has killed herself," said a voice which seemed to come up from a well. "The German woman has committed suicide."

The explanation of the concierge leaped from window to window up to the top floor.

The Russian was shaking his head with a fatalistic expression. The unhappy woman had not taken the death-leap of her own accord. Someone had intensified her desperation, someone had pushed her. . . . The horsemen! The four horsemen of the Apocalypse! . . . Already they were in the saddle! Already they were beginning their merciless gallop of destruction!

The blind forces of evil were about to be let loose throughout the world.

The agony of humanity, under the brutal sweep of the four horsemen, was already begun!

PART II

CHAPTER I

WHAT DON MARCELO ENVIED

Upon being convinced that war really was inevitable, the elder Desnoyers was filled with amazement. Humanity had gone crazy. Was it possible that war could happen in these days of so many railroads, so many merchant marines, so many inventions, so much activity developed above and below the earth? . . . The nations would ruin themselves forever. They were now accustomed to luxuries and necessities unknown a century ago. Capital was master of the world, and war was going to wipe it out. In its turn, war would be wiped out in a few months' time through lack of funds to sustain it. His soul of a business man revolted before the hundreds of thousands of millions that this foolhardy event was going to convert into smoke and slaughter.

As his indignation had to fix upon something close at hand, he made his own countrymen responsible for this insanity. Too much talk about la revanche! The very idea of worrying for forty-four years over the two lost provinces when the nation was mistress of enormous and undeveloped lands in other countries! . . . Now they were going to pay the penalty for such exasperating and clamorous foolishness.

For him war meant disaster writ large. He had no faith in his country. France's day had passed. Now the victors were of the Northern peoples, and especially that Germany which he had seen so close, admiring with a certain terror its discipline and its rigorous organization. The former working-man felt the conservative and selfish instinct of all those who have amassed millions. He scorned political ideals, but through class interest he had of late years accepted the declarations against the scandals of the government. What could a corrupt and disorganized Republic do against the solidest and strongest empire in the world? . . .

"We are going to our deaths," he said to himself. "Worse than '70! . . . We are going to see horrible things!"

The good order and enthusiasm with which the French responded to their country's call and transformed themselves into soldiers were most astonishing to him. This moral shock made his national faith begin to revive. The great majority of Frenchmen were good after all; the nation was as valiant as in former times. Forty-four years of suffering and alarm had developed their old bravery. But the leaders? Where were they going to get leaders to march to victory? . . .

Many others were asking themselves the same question. The silence of the democratic government was keeping the country in complete ignorance of their future commanders. Everybody saw the army increasing from hour to hour: very few knew the generals. One name was beginning to be repeated from mouth to mouth, "Joffre . . . Joffre." His first pictures made the curious crowds struggle to get a glimpse of them. Desnoyers studied them very carefully. "He looks like a very capable person." His methodical instincts were gratified by the grave and confident look of the general of the Republic. Suddenly he felt the great confidence that efficient-looking bank directors always inspired in him. He could entrust his interests to this gentleman, sure that he would not act impulsively.

Finally, against his will, Desnoyers was drawn into the whirlpool of enthusiasm and emotion. Like everyone around him, he lived minutes that were hours, and hours that were years. Events kept on overlapping each other; within a week the world seemed to have made up for its long period of peace.

The old man fairly lived in the street, attracted by the spectacle of the multitude of civilians saluting the multitude of uniformed men departing for the seat of war.

At night he saw the processions passing through the boulevards. The tricolored flag was fluttering its colors under the electric lights. The cafes were overflowing with people, sending forth from doors and windows the excited, musical notes of patriotic songs. Suddenly, amidst applause and cheers, the crowd would make an opening in the street. All Europe was passing here; all Europe—less the arrogant enemy—and was saluting France in her hour of danger with hearty spontaneity. Flags of different nations were filing by, of all tints of the rainbow, and behind them were the Russians with bright and mystical eyes; the English, with heads uncovered, intoning songs of religious gravity; the Greeks and Roumanians of aquiline profile; the Scandinavians, white and red; the North Americans, with the noisiness of a somewhat puerile enthusiasm; the Hebrews without a country, friends of the nation of socialistic revolutions; the Italians, as spirited as a choir of heroic tenors; the Spanish and South Americans, tireless in their huzzas. They were students and apprentices who were completing their courses in the schools and workshops, and refugees who, like shipwrecked mariners, had sought shelter on the hospitable strand of Paris. Their cheers had no special significance, but they were all moved by their desire to show their love for the Republic. And Desnoyers, touched by the sight, felt that France was still of some account in the world, that she yet exercised a moral force among the nations, and that her joys and sorrows were still of interest to humanity.

"In Berlin and Vienna, too," he said to himself, "they must also be cheering enthusiastically at this moment . . . but Germans only, no others. Assuredly no foreigner is joining in their demonstrations."

The nation of the Revolution, legislator of the rights of mankind, was harvesting the gratitude of the throngs, but was beginning to feel a certain remorse before the enthusiasm of the foreigners who were offering their blood for France. Many were lamenting that the government should delay twenty days, until after they had finished the operations of mobilization, in admitting the volunteers. And he, a Frenchman born, a few hours before, had been mistrusting his country! . . .

In the daytime the popular current was running toward the Gare de l'Est. Crowded against the gratings was a surging mass of humanity stretching its tentacles through the nearby streets. The station that was acquiring the importance of a historic spot appeared like a narrow tunnel through which a great human river was trying to flow with many rippling encounters and much heavy pressure against its banks. A large part of France in arms was coursing through this exit from Paris toward the battlefields at the frontier.

Desnoyers had been in the station only twice, when going and coming from Germany. Others were now taking the same road. The crowds were swarming in from the environs of the city in order to see the masses of human beings in geometric bodies, uniformly clad, disappearing within the entrance with flash of steel and the rhythm of clanking metal. The crystal archways that were glistening in the sun like fiery mouths were swallowing and swallowing people. When night fell the processions were still coming on, by light of the electric lamps. Through the iron grills were passing thousands and thousands of draught horses; men with their breasts crossed with metal and bunches of horsehair hanging from their helmets, like paladins of bygone centuries; enormous cases that were serving as cages for the aeronautic condors; strings of cannon, long and narrow, painted grey and protected, by metal screens, more like astronomical instruments than mouths of death; masses and masses of red kepis (military caps) moving in marching rhythm, rows and rows of muskets, some black and stark like reed plantations, others ending in bayonets like shining spikes. And over all these restless fields of seething throngs, the flags of the regiments were fluttering in the air like colored birds; a white body, a blue wing, or a red one, a cravat of gold on the neck, and above, the metal tip pointing toward the clouds.

Don Marcelo would return home from these send-offs vibrating with nervous fatigue, as one who had just participated in a scene of racking emotion. In spite of his tenacious character which always stood out against admitting a mistake, the old man began to feel ashamed of his former doubts. The nation was quivering with life; France was a grand nation; appearances had deceived him as well as many others. Perhaps the most of his countrymen were of a light and flippant character, given to excessive interest in the sensuous side of life; but when danger came they were fulfilling their duty simply, without the necessity of the harsh force to which the iron-clad organizations were submitting their people.

On leaving home on the morning of the fourth day of the mobilization Desnoyers, instead of betaking himself to the centre of the city, went in the opposite direction toward the rue de la Pompe. Some imprudent words dropped by Chichi, and the uneasy looks of his wife and sister-in-law made him suspect that Julio had returned from his trip. He felt the necessity of seeing at least the outside of the studio windows, as if they might give him news. And in order to justify a trip so at variance with his policy of ignoring his son, he remembered that the carpenter lived in the same street.

"I must hunt up Robert. He promised a week ago that he would come here."

This Robert was a husky young fellow who, to use his own words, was "emancipated from boss tyranny," and was working independently in his own home. A tiny, almost subterranean room was serving him for dwelling and workshop. A woman he called "my affinity" was looking carefully after his hearth and home, with a baby boy clinging to her skirts. Desnoyers was accustomed to humor Robert's tirades against his fellow citizens because the man had always humored his whimseys about the incessant rearrangement of his furniture. In the luxurious apartment in the avenue Victor Hugo the carpenter would sing La Internacional while using hammer and saw, and his employer would overlook his audacity of speech because of the cheapness of his work.

Upon arriving at the shop he found the man with cap over one ear, broad trousers like a mameluke's, hobnailed boots and various pennants and rosettes fastened to the lapels of his jacket.

"You've come too late, Boss," he said cheerily. "I am just going to close the factory. The Proprietor has been mobilized, and in a few hours will join his regiment."

And he pointed to a written paper posted on the door of his dwelling like the printed cards on all establishments, signifying that employer and employees had obeyed the order of mobilization.

It had never occurred to Desnoyers that his carpenter might become a soldier, since he was so opposed to all kinds of authority. He hated the flics, the Paris police, with whom he had, more than once, exchanged fisticuffs and clubbings. Militarism was his special aversion. In the meetings against the despotism of the barracks he had always been one of the noisiest participants. And was this revolutionary fellow going to war naturally and voluntarily? . . .

Robert spoke enthusiastically of his regiment, of life among comrades with Death but four steps away.

"I believe in my ideas, Boss, the same as before," he explained as though guessing the other's thought. "But war is war and teaches many things—among others that Liberty must be accompanied with order and authority. It is necessary that someone direct that the rest may follow—willingly, by common consent . . . but they must follow. When war actually comes one sees things very differently from when living at home doing as one pleases."

The night that they assassinated Jaures he howled with rage, announcing that the following morning the murder would be avenged. He had hunted up his associates in the district in order to inform them what retaliation was being planned against the malefactors. But war was about to break out. There was something in the air that was opposing civil strife, that was placing private grievances in momentary abeyance, concentrating all minds on the common weal.

"A week ago," he exclaimed, "I was an anti-militarist! How far away that seems now—as if a year had gone by! I keep thinking as before! I love peace and hate war like all my comrades. But the French have not offended anybody, and yet they threaten us, wishing to enslave us. . . . But we French can be fierce, since they oblige us to be, and in order to defend ourselves it is just that nobody should shirk, that all should obey. Discipline does not quarrel with Revolution. Remember the armies of the first Republic—all citizens, Generals as well as soldiers, but Hoche, Kleber and the others were rough-hewn, unpolished benefactors who knew how to command and exact obedience."

The carpenter was well read. Besides the papers and pamphlets of "the Idea," he had also read on stray sheets the views of Michelet and other liberal actors on the stage of history.

"We are going to make war on War," he added. "We are going to fight so that this war will be the last."

This statement did not seem to be expressed with sufficient clearness, so he recast his thought.

"We are going to fight for the future; we are going to die in order that our grandchildren may not have to endure a similar calamity. If the enemy triumphs, the war-habit will triumph, and conquest will be the only means of growth. First they will overcome Europe, then the rest of the world. Later on, those who have been pillaged will rise up in their wrath. More wars! . . . We do not want conquests. We desire to regain Alsace and Lorraine, for their inhabitants wish to return to us . . . and nothing more. We shall not imitate the enemy, appropriating territory and jeopardizing the peace of the world. We had enough of that with Napoleon; we must not repeat that experience. We are going to fight for our immediate security, and at the same time for the security of the world—for the life of the weaker nations. If this were a war of aggression, of mere vanity, of conquest, then we Socialists would bethink ourselves of our anti-militarism. But this is self-defense, and the government has not been at fault. Since we are attacked, we must be united in our defensive."

The carpenter, who was also anti-clerical, was now showing a more generous tolerance, an amplitude of ideas that embraced all mankind. The day before he had met at the administration office a Reservist who was just leaving to join his regiment. At a glance he saw that this man was a priest.

"I am a carpenter," he had said to him, by way of introduction, "and you, comrade, are working in the churches?"

He employed this figure of speech in order that the priest might not suspect him of anything offensive. The two had clasped hands.

"I do not take much stock in the clerical cowl," Robert explained to Desnoyers. "For some time I have not been on friendly terms with religion. But in every walk of life there must be good people, and the good people ought to understand each other in a crisis like this. Don't you think so, Boss?"

The war coincided with his socialistic tendencies. Before this, when speaking of future revolution, he had felt a malign pleasure in imagining all the rich deprived of their fortunes and having to work in order to exist. Now he was equally enthusiastic at the thought that all Frenchmen would share the same fate without class distinction.

"All with knapsacks on their backs and eating at mess."

And he was even extending this military sobriety to those who remained behind the army. War was going to cause great scarcity of provisions, and all would have to come down to very plain fare.

"You, too, Boss, who are too old to go to war—you, with all your millions, will have to eat the same as I. . . . Admit that it is a beautiful thing."

Desnoyers was not offended by the malicious satisfaction that his future privations seemed to inspire in the carpenter. He was very thoughtful. A man of his stamp, an enemy of existing conditions, who had no property to defend, was going to war—to death, perhaps—because of a generous and distant ideal, in order that future generations might never know the actual horrors of war! To do this, he was not hesitating at the sacrifice of his former cherished beliefs, all that he had held sacred till now. . . . And he who belonged to the privileged class, who possessed so many tempting things, requiring defense, had given himself up to doubt and criticism! . . .

Hours after, he again saw the carpenter, near the Arc de Triomphe. He was one of a group of workmen looking much as he did, and this group was joining others and still others that represented every social class—well-dressed citizens, stylish and anaemic young men, graduate students with worn jackets, pale faces and thick glasses, and youthful priests who were smiling rather shamefacedly as though they had been caught at some ridiculous escapade. At the head of this human herd was a sergeant, and as a rear guard, various soldiers with guns on their shoulders. Forward march, Reservists! . . .

And a musical cry, a solemn harmony like a Greek chant, menacing and monotonous, surged up from this mass with open mouths, swinging arms, and legs that were opening and shutting like compasses.

Robert was singing the martial chorus with such great energy that his eyes and Gallic moustachios were fairly trembling. In spite of his corduroy suit and his bulging linen hand bag, he had the same grand and heroic aspect as the figures by Rude in the Arc de Triomphe. The "affinity" and the boy were trudging along the sidewalk so as to accompany him to the station. For a moment he took his eyes from them to speak with a companion in the line, shaven and serious-looking, undoubtedly the priest whom he had met the day before. Now they were talking confidentially, intimately, with that brotherliness which contact with death inspires in mankind.

The millionaire followed the carpenter with a look of respect, immeasurably increased since he had taken his part in this human avalanche. And this respect had in it something of envy, the envy that springs from an uneasy conscience.

Whenever Don Marcelo passed a bad night, suffering from nightmare, a certain terrible thing—always the same—would torment his imagination. Rarely did he dream of mortal peril to his family or self. The frightful vision was always that certain notes bearing his signature were presented for collection which he, Marcelo Desnoyers, the man always faithful to his bond, with a past of immaculate probity, was not able to pay. Such a possibility made him tremble, and long after waking his heart would be oppressed with terror. To his imagination this was the greatest disgrace that a man could suffer.

Now that war was overturning his existence with its agitations, the same agonies were reappearing. Completely awake, with full powers of reasoning, he was suffering exactly the same distress as when in his horrible dreams he saw his dishonored signature on a protested document.

All his past was looming up before his eyes with such extraordinary clearness that it seemed as though until then his mind must have been in hopeless confusion. The threatened land of France was his native country. Fifteen centuries of history had been working for him, in order that his opening eyes might survey progress and comforts that his ancestors did not even know. Many generations of Desnoyers had prepared for his advent into life by struggling with the land and defending it that he might be born into a free family and fireside. . . . And when his turn had come for continuing this effort, when his time had arrived in the rosary of generations—he had fled like a debtor evading payment! . . . On coming into his fatherland he had contracted obligations with the human group to whom he owed his existence. This obligation should be paid with his arms, with any sacrifice that would repel danger . . . and he had eluded the acknowledgment of his signature, fleeing his country and betraying his trust to his forefathers! Ah, miserable coward! The material success of his life, the riches acquired in a remote country, were comparatively of no importance. There are failures that millions cannot blot out. The uneasiness of his conscience was proving it now. Proof, too, was in the envy and respect inspired by this poor mechanic marching to meet his death with others equally humble, all kindled with the satisfaction of duty fulfilled, of sacrifice accepted.

The memory of Madariaga came to his memory.

"Where we make our riches, and found a family—there is our country."

No, the statement of the centaur was not correct. In normal times, perhaps. Far from one's native land when it is not exposed to danger, one may forget it for a few years. But he was living now in France, and France was being obliged to defend herself against enemies wishing to overpower her. The sight of all her people rising en masse was becoming an increasingly shameful torture for Desnoyers, making him think all the time of what he should have done in his youth, of what he had dodged.

The veterans of '70 were passing through the streets, with the green and black ribbon in their lapel, souvenirs of the privations of the Siege of Paris, and of heroic and disastrous campaigns. The sight of these men, satisfied with their past, made him turn pale. Nobody was recalling his, but he knew it, and that was enough. In vain his reason would try to lull this interior tempest. . . . Those times were different; then there was none of the present unanimity; the Empire was unpopular . . . everything was lost. . . . But the recollection of a celebrated sentence was fixing itself in his mind as an obsession—"France still remained!" Many had thought as he did in his youth, but they had not, therefore, evaded military service. They had stood by their country in a last and desperate resistance.

Useless was his excuse-making reasoning. Nobler thoughts showed him the fallacy of this beating around the bush. Explanations and demonstrations are unnecessary to the understanding of patriotic and religious ideals; true patriotism does not need them. One's country . . . is one's country. And the laboring man, skeptical and jesting, the self-centred farmer, the solitary pastor, all had sprung to action at the sound of this conjuring word, comprehending it instantly, without previous instruction.

"It is necessary to pay," Don Marcelo kept repeating mentally. "I ought to pay my debt."

As in his dreams, he was constantly feeling the anguish of an upright and desperate man who wishes to meet his obligations.

Pay! . . . and how? It was now very late. For a moment the heroic resolution came into his head of offering himself as a volunteer, of marching with his bag at his side in some one of the groups of future combatants, the same as the carpenter. But the uselessness of the sacrifice came immediately into his mind. Of what use would it be? . . . He looked robust and was well-preserved for his age, but he was over seventy, and only the young make good soldiers. Combat is but one incident in the struggle. Equally necessary are the hardship and self-denial in the form of interminable marches, extremes of temperature, nights in the open air, shoveling earth, digging trenches, loading carts, suffering hunger. . . . No; it was too late. He could not even leave an illustrious name that might serve as an example.

Instinctively he glanced behind. He was not alone in the world; he had a son who could assume his father's debt . . . but that hope only lasted a minute. His son was not French; he belonged to another people; half of his blood was from another source. Besides, how could the boy be expected to feel as he did? Would he even understand if his father should explain it to him? . . . It was useless to expect anything from this lady-killing, dancing clown, from this fellow of senseless bravado, who was constantly exposing his life in duels in order to satisfy a silly sense of honor.

Oh, the meekness of the bluff Senor Desnoyers after these reflections! . . . His family felt alarmed at seeing the humility and gentleness with which he moved around the house. The two men-servants had gone to join their regiments, and to them the most surprising result of the declaration of war was the sudden kindness of their master, the lavishness of his farewell gifts, the paternal care with which he supervised their preparations for departure. The terrible Don Marcelo embraced them with moist eyes, and the two had to exert themselves to prevent his accompanying them to the station.

Outside of his home he was slipping about humbly as though mutely asking pardon of the many people around him. To him they all appeared his superiors. It was a period of economic crisis; for the time being, the rich also were experiencing what it was to be poor and worried; the banks had suspended operations and were paying only a small part of their deposits. For some weeks the millionaire was deprived of his wealth, and felt restless before the uncertain future. How long would it be before they could send him money from South America? Was war going to take away fortunes as well as lives? . . . And yet Desnoyers had never appreciated money less, nor disposed of it with greater generosity.

Numberless mobilized men of the lower classes who were going alone toward the station met a gentleman who would timidly stop them, put his hand in his pocket and leave in their right hand a bill of twenty francs, fleeing immediately before their astonished eyes. The working-women who were returning weeping from saying good-bye to their husbands saw this same gentleman smiling at the children who were with them, patting their cheeks and hastening away, leaving a five-franc piece in their hands.

Don Marcelo, who had never smoked, was now frequenting the tobacco shops, coming out with hands and pockets filled in order that he might, with lavish generosity, press the packages upon the first soldier he met. At times the recipient, smiling courteously, would thank him with a few words, revealing his superior breeding—afterwards passing the gift on to others clad in cloaks as coarse and badly cut as his own. The mobilization, universally obligatory, often caused him to make these mistakes.

The rough hands pressing his with a grateful clasp, left him satisfied for a few moments. Ah, if he could only do more! . . . The Government in mobilizing its vehicles had appropriated three of his monumental automobiles, and Desnoyers felt very sorry that they were not also taking the fourth mastodon. Of what use were they to him? The shepherds of this monstrous herd, the chauffeur and his assistants, were now in the army. Everybody was marching away. Finally he and his son would be the only ones left—two useless creatures.

He roared with wrath on learning of the enemy's entrance into Belgium, considering this the most unheard-of treason in history. He suffered agonies of shame at remembering that at first he had held the exalted patriots of his country responsible for the war. . . . What perfidy, methodically carried out after long years of preparation! The accounts of the sackings, fires and butcheries made him turn pale and gnash his teeth. To him, to Marcelo Desnoyers, might happen the very same thing that Belgium was enduring, if the barbarians should invade France. He had a home in the city, a castle in the country, and a family. Through association of ideas, the women assaulted by the soldiery, made him think of Chichi and the dear Dona Luisa. The mansions in flames called to his mind the rare and costly furnishings accumulated in his expensive dwellings— the armorial bearings of his social elevation. The old folk that were shot, the women foully mutilated, the children with their hands cut off, all the horrors of a war of terror, aroused the violence of his character.

And such things could happen with impunity in this day and generation! . . .

In order to convince himself that punishment was near, that vengeance was overtaking the guilty ones, he felt the necessity of mingling daily with the people crowding around the Gare de l'Est.

Although the greater part of the troops were operating on the frontiers, that was not diminishing the activity in Paris. Entire battalions were no longer going off, but day and night soldiers were coming to the station singly or in groups. These were Reserves without uniform on their way to enroll themselves with their companies, officials who until then had been busy with the work of the mobilization, platoons in arms destined to fill the great gaps opened by death.

The multitude, pressed against the railing, was greeting those who were going off, following them with their eyes while they were crossing the large square. The latest editions of the daily papers were announced with hoarse yells, and instantly the dark throng would be spotted with white, all reading with avidity the printed sheets. Good news: "Vive la France!" A doubtful despatch, foreshadowing calamity: "No matter! We must press on at all costs! The Russians will close in behind them!" And while these dialogues, inspired by the latest news were taking place, many young girls were going among the groups offering little flags and tricolored cockades—and passing through the patio, men and still more men were disappearing behind the glass doors, on their way to the war.

A sub-lieutenant of the Reserves, with his bag on his shoulder, was accompanied by his father toward the file of policemen keeping the crowds back. Desnoyers saw in the young officer a certain resemblance to his son. The father was wearing in his lapel the black and green ribbon of 1870—a decoration which always filled Desnoyers with remorse. He was tall and gaunt, but was still trying to hold himself erect, with a heavy frown. He wanted to show himself fierce, inhuman, in order to hide his emotion.

"Good-bye, my boy! Do your best."

"Good-bye, father."

They did not clasp hands, and each was avoiding looking at the other. The official was smiling like an automaton. The father turned his back brusquely, and threading his way through the throng, entered a cafe, where for some time he needed the most retired seat in the darkest earner to hide his emotion.

AND DON MARCELO ENVIED HIS GRIEF.

Some of the Reservists came along singing, preceded by a flag. They were joking and jostling each other, betraying in excited actions, long halts at all the taverns along the way. One of them, without interrupting his song, was pressing the hand of an old woman marching beside him, cheerful and dry-eyed. The mother was concentrating all her strength in order, with feigned happiness, to accompany this strapping lad to the last minute.

Others were coming along singly, separated from their companies, but not on that account alone. The gun was hanging from the shoulder, the back overlaid by the hump of the knapsack, the red legs shooting in and out of the turned-back folds of the blue cloak, and the smoke of a pipe under the visor of the kepis. In front of one of these men, four children were walking along, lined up according to size. They kept turning their heads to admire their father, suddenly glorified by his military trappings. At his side was marching his wife, affable and resigned, feeling in her simple soul a revival of love, an ephemeral Spring, born of the contact with danger. The man, a laborer of Paris, who a few months before was singing La Internacional, demanding the abolishment of armies and the brotherhood of all mankind, was now going in quest of death. His wife, choking back her sobs, was admiring him greatly. Affection and commiseration made her insist upon giving him a few last counsels. In his knapsack she had put his best handkerchiefs, the few provisions in the house and all the money. Her man was not to be uneasy about her and the children; they would get along all right. The government and kind neighbors would look after them.

The soldier in reply was jesting over the somewhat misshapen figure of his wife, saluting the coming citizen, and prophesying that he would be born in a time of great victory. A kiss to the wife, an affectionate hair-pull for his offspring, and then he had joined his comrades. . . . No tears. Courage! . . . Vive la France!

The final injunctions of the departing were now heard. Nobody was crying. But as the last red pantaloons disappeared, many hands grasped the iron railing convulsively, many handkerchiefs were bitten with gnashing teeth, many faces were hidden in the arms with sobs of anguish.

AND DON MARCELO ENVIED THESE TEARS.

The old woman, on losing the warm contact of her son's hand from her withered one, turned in the direction which she believed to be that of the hostile country, waving her arms with threatening fury.

"Ah, the assassin! . . . the bandit!"

In her wrathful imagination she was again seeing the countenance so often displayed in the illustrated pages of the periodicals—moustaches insolently aggressive, a mouth with the jaw and teeth of a wolf, that laughed . . . and laughed as men must have laughed in the time of the cave-men.

AND DON MARCELO ENVIED THIS WRATH!

CHAPTER II

NEW LIFE

When Marguerite was able to return to the studio in the rue de la Pompe, Julio, who had been living in a perpetual bad humor, seeing everything in the blackest colors, suddenly felt a return of his old optimism.

The war was not going to be so cruel as they all had at first imagined. The days had passed by, and the movements of the troops were beginning to be less noticeable. As the number of men diminished in the streets, the feminine population seemed to have increased. Although there was great scarcity of money, the banks still remaining closed, the necessity for it was increasingly great, in order to secure provisions. Memories of the famine of the siege of '70 tormented the imagination. Since war had broken out with the same enemy, it seemed but logical to everybody to expect a repetition of the same happenings. The storehouses were besieged by women who were securing stale food at exorbitant prices in order to store it in their homes. Future hunger was producing more terror than immediate dangers.

For young Desnoyers these were about all the transformations that war was creating around him. People would finally become accustomed to the new existence. Humanity has a certain reserve force of adaptation which enables it to mould itself to circumstances and continue existing. He was hoping to continue his life as though nothing had happened. It was enough for him that Marguerite should continue faithful to their past. Together they would see events slipping by them with the cruel luxuriousness of those who, from an inaccessible height, contemplate a flood without the slightest risk to themselves.

This selfish attitude had also become habitual to Argensola.

"Let us be neutral," the Bohemian would say. "Neutrality does not necessarily mean indifference. Let us enjoy the great spectacle, since nothing like it will ever happen again in our lifetime."

It was unfortunate that war should happen to come when they had so little money. Argensola was hating the banks even more than the Central Powers, distinguishing with special antipathy the trust company which was delaying payment of Julio's check. How lovely it would have been with this sum available, to have forestalled events by laying in every class of commodity! In order to supplement the domestic scrimping, he again had to solicit the aid of Dona Luisa. War had lessened Don Marcelo's precautions, and the family was now living in generous unconcern. The mother, like other house mistresses, had stored up provisions for months and months to come, buying whatever eatables she was able to lay hands on. Argensola took advantage of this abundance, repeating his visits to the home in the avenue Victor Hugo, descending its service stairway with great packages which were swelling the supplies in the studio.

He felt all the joys of a good housekeeper in surveying the treasures piled up in the kitchen—great tins of canned meat, pyramids of butter crocks, and bags of dried vegetables. He had accumulated enough there to maintain a large family. The war had now offered a new pretext for him to visit Don Marcelo's wine-vaults.

"Let them come!" he would say with a heroic gesture as he took stock of his treasure trove. "Let them come when they will! We are ready for them!"

The care and increase of his provisions, and the investigation of news were the two functions of his existence. It seemed necessary to procure ten, twelve, fifteen papers a day; some because they were reactionary, and the novelty of seeing all the French united filled him with enthusiasm; others because they were radical and must be better informed of the news received from the government. They generally appeared at midday, at three, at four and at five in the afternoon. An half hour's delay in the publication of the sheet raised great hopes in the public, on the qui vive for stupendous news. All the last supplements were snatched up; everybody had his pockets stuffed with papers, waiting anxiously the issue of extras in order to buy them, too. Yet all the sheets were saying approximately the same thing.

Argensola was developing a credulous, enthusiastic soul, capable of admitting many improbable things. He presumed that this same spirit was probably animating everybody around him. At times, his old critical attitude would threaten to rebel, but doubt was repulsed as something dishonorable. He was living in a new world, and it was but natural that extraordinary things should occur that could be neither measured nor explained by the old processes of reasoning. So he commented with infantile joy on the marvellous accounts in the daily papers—of combats between a single Belgian platoon and entire regiments of enemies, putting them to disorderly flight; of the German fear of the bayonet that made them run like hares the instant that the charge sounded; of the inefficiency of the German artillery whose projectiles always missed fire.

It was logical and natural that little Belgium should conquer gigantic Germany—a repetition of David and Goliath—with all the metaphors and images that this unequal contest had inspired across so many centuries. Like the greater part of the nation, he had the mentality of a reader of tales of chivalry who feels himself defrauded if the hero, single-handed, fails to cleave a thousand enemies with one fell stroke. He purposely chose the most sensational papers, those which published many stories of single encounters, of individual deeds about which nobody could know with any degree of certainty.

The intervention of England on the seas made him imagine a frightful famine, coming providentially like a thunder-clap to torture the enemy. He honestly believed that ten days of this maritime blockade would convert Germany into a group of shipwrecked sailors floating on a raft. This vision made him repeat his visits to the kitchen to gloat over his packages of provisions.

"Ah, what they would give in Berlin for my treasures!" . . .

Never had Argensola eaten with greater avidity. Consideration of the great privations suffered by the adversary was sharpening his appetite to a monstrous capacity. White bread, golden brown and crusty, was stimulating him to an almost religious ecstasy.

"If friend William could only get his claws on this!" he would chuckle to his companion.

So he chewed and swallowed with increasing relish; solids and liquids on passing through his mouth seemed to be acquiring a new flavor, rare and divine. Distant hunger for him was a stimulant, a sauce of endless delight.

While France was inspiring his enthusiasm, he was conceding greater credit to Russia. "Ah, those Cossacks!" . . . He was accustomed to speak of them as intimate friends. He loved to describe the unbridled gallop of the wild horsemen, impalpable as phantoms, and so terrible in their wrath that the enemy could not look them in the face. The concierge and the stay-at-homes used to listen to him with all the respect due to a foreign gentleman, knowing much of the great outside world with which they were not familiar.

"The Cossacks will adjust the accounts of these bandits!" he would conclude with absolute assurance. "Within a month they will have entered Berlin."

And his public composed of women—wives and mothers of those who had gone to war—would modestly agree with him, with that irresistible desire which we all feel of placing our hopes on something distant and mysterious. The French would defend the country, reconquering, besides the lost territories, but the Cossacks—of whom so many were speaking but so few had seen—were going to give the death blow. The only person who knew them at first hand was Tchernoff, and to Argensola's astonishment, he listened to his words without showing any enthusiasm. The Cossacks were for him simply one body of the Russian army—good enough soldiers, but incapable of working the miracles that everybody was expecting from them.

"That Tchernoff!" exclaimed Argensola. "Since he hates the Czar, he thinks the entire country mad. He is a revolutionary fanatic. . . . And I am opposed to all fanaticisms."

Julio was listening absent-mindedly to the news brought by his companion, the vibrating statements recited in declamatory tones, the plans of the campaign traced out on an enormous map fastened to the wall of the studio and bristling with tiny flags that marked the camps of the belligerent armies. Every issue of the papers obliged the Spaniard to arrange a new dance of the pins on the map, followed by his comments of bomb-proof optimism.

"We have entered into Alsace; very good! . . . It appears now that we abandon Alsace. Splendid! I suspect the cause. It is in order to enter again in a better place, getting at the enemy from behind. . . . They say that Liege has fallen. What a lie! . . . And if it does fall, it doesn't matter. Just an incident, nothing more! The others remain . . . the others! . . . that are advancing on the Eastern side, and are going to enter Berlin."

The news from the Russian front was his favorite, but obliged him to remain in suspense every time that he tried to find on the map the obscure names of the places where the admired Cossacks were exhibiting their wonderful exploits.

Meanwhile Julio was continuing the course of his own reflections. Marguerite! . . . She had come back at last, and yet each time seemed to be drifting further away from him. . . .

In the first days of the mobilization, he had haunted her neighborhood, trying to appease his longing by this illusory proximity. Marguerite had written to him, urging patience. How fortunate it was that he was a foreigner and would not have to endure the hardship of war! Her brother, an officer in the artillery Reserves, was going at almost any minute. Her mother, who made her home with this bachelor son, had kept an astonishing serenity up to the last minute, although she had wept much while the war was still but a possibility. She herself had prepared the soldier's outfit so that the small valise might contain all that was indispensable for campaign life. But Marguerite had divined her poor mother's secret struggles not to reveal her despair, in moist eyes and trembling hands. It was impossible to leave her alone at such a time. . . . Then had come the farewell. "God be with you, my son! Do your duty, but be prudent." Not a tear nor a sign of weakness. All her family had advised her not to accompany her son to the railway station, so his sister had gone with him. And upon returning home, Marguerite had found her mother rigid in her arm chair, with a set face, avoiding all mention of her son, speaking of the friends who also had sent their boys to the war, as if they only could comprehend her torture. "Poor Mama! I ought to be with her now more than ever. . . . To-morrow, if I can, I shall come to see you."

When at last she returned to the rue de la Pompe, her first care was to explain to Julio the conservatism of her tailored suit, the absence of jewels in the adornment of her person. "The war, my dear! Now it is the chic thing to adapt oneself to the depressing conditions, to be frugal and inconspicuous like soldiers. Who knows what we may expect!" Her infatuation with dress still accompanied her in every moment of her life.

Julio noticed a persistent absent-mindedness about her. It seemed as though her spirit, abandoning her body, was wandering to far-away places. Her eyes were looking at him, but she seldom saw him. She would speak very slowly, as though wishing to weigh every word, fearful of betraying some secret. This spiritual alienation did not, however, prevent her slipping bodily along the smooth path of custom, although afterwards she would seem to feel a vague remorse. "I wonder if it is right to do this! . . . Is it not wrong to live like this when so many sorrows are falling on the world?" Julio hushed her scruples with:

"But if we are going to marry as soon as possible! . . . If we are already the same as husband and wife!"

She replied with a gesture of strangeness and dismay. To marry! . . . Ten days ago she had had no other wish. Now the possibility of marriage was recurring less and less in her thoughts. Why think about such remote and uncertain events? More immediate things were occupying her mind.

The farewell to her brother in the station was a scene which had fixed itself ineradicably in her memory. Upon going to the studio she had planned not to speak about it, foreseeing that she might annoy her lover with this account; but alas, she had only to vow not to mention a thing, to feel an irresistible impulse to talk about it.

She had never suspected that she could love her brother so dearly. Her former affection for him had been mingled with a silent sentiment of jealousy because her mother had preferred the older child. Besides, he was the one who had introduced Laurier to his home; the two held diplomas as industrial engineers and had been close friends from their school days. . . . But upon seeing the boy ready to depart, Marguerite suddenly discovered that this brother, who had always been of secondary interest to her, was now occupying a preeminent place in her affections.

"He was so handsome, so interesting in his lieutenant's uniform! . . . He looked like another person. I will admit to you that I was very proud to walk beside him, leaning on his arm. People thought that we were married. Seeing me weep, some poor women tried to console me saying, 'Courage, Madame. . . . Your man will come back.' He just laughed at hearing these mistakes. The only thing that was really saddening him was thinking about our mother."

They had separated at the door of the station. The sentries would not let her go any further, so she had handed over his sword that she had wished to carry till the last moment.

"It is lovely to be a man!" she exclaimed enthusiastically. "I would love to wear a uniform, to go to war, to be of some real use!"

She tried not to say more about it, as though she suddenly realized the inopportuneness of her last words. Perhaps she noticed the scowl on Julio's face.

She was, however, so wrought up by the memory of that farewell that, after a long pause, she was unable to resist the temptation of again putting her thought into words.

At the station entrance, while she was kissing her brother for the last time, she had an encounter, a great surprise. "He" had approached, also clad as an artillery officer, but alone, having to entrust his valise to a good-natured man from the crowd.

Julio shot her a questioning look. Who was "he"? He suspected, but feigned ignorance, as though fearing to learn the truth.

"Laurier," she replied laconically, "my former husband."

The lover displayed a cruel irony. It was a cowardly thing to ridicule this man who had responded to the call of duty. He recognized his vileness, but a malign and irresistible instinct made him keep on with his sneers in order to discredit the man before Marguerite. Laurier a soldier!—He must cut a pretty figure dressed in uniform!

"Laurier, the warrior!" he continued in a voice so sarcastic and strange that it seemed to be coming from somebody else. . . . "Poor creature!"

She hesitated in her response, not wishing to exasperate Desnoyers any further. But the truth was uppermost in her mind, and she said simply:

"No . . . no, he didn't look so bad. Quite the contrary. Perhaps it was the uniform, perhaps it was his sadness at going away alone, completely alone, without a single hand to clasp his. I didn't recognize him at first. Seeing my brother, he started toward us; but then when he saw me, he went his own way . . . . Poor man! I feel sorry for him!"

Her feminine instinct must have told her that she was talking too much, and she cut her chatter suddenly short. The same instinct warned her that Julio's countenance was growing more and more saturnine, and his mouth taking a very bitter curve. She wanted to console him and added:

"What luck that you are a foreigner and will not have to go to the war! How horrible it would be for me to lose you!" . . .

She said it sincerely. . . . A few moments before she had been envying men, admiring the gallantry with which they were exposing their lives, and now she was trembling before the idea that her lover might have been one of these.

This did not please his amorous egoism—to be placed apart from the rest as a delicate and fragile being only fit for feminine adoration. He preferred to inspire the envy that she had felt on beholding her brother decked out in his warlike accoutrement. It seemed to him that something was coming between him and Marguerite that would never disappear, that would go on expanding, repelling them in contrary directions . . . far . . . very far, even to the point of not recognizing each other when their glances met.

He continued to be conscious of this impalpable obstacle in their following interviews. Marguerite was extremely affectionate in her speech, and would look at him with moist and loving eyes. But her caressing hands appeared more like those of a mother than a lover, and her tenderness was accompanied with a certain disinterestedness and extraordinary modesty. She seemed to prefer remaining obstinately in the studio, declining to go into the other rooms.

"We are so comfortable here. . . . I would rather not. . . . It is not worth while. I should feel remorse afterwards. . . . Why think of such things in these anxious times!"

The world around her seemed saturated with love, but it was a new love—a love for the man who is suffering, desire for abnegation, for sacrifice. This love called forth visions of white caps, of tremulous hands healing shell-riddled and bleeding flesh.

Every advance on Julio's part but aroused in Marguerite a vehement and modest protest as though they were meeting for the first time.

"It is impossible," she protested. "I keep thinking of my brother, and of so many that I know that may be dying at this very minute."

News of battles were beginning to arrive, and blood was beginning to flow in great quantities.

"No, no, I cannot," she kept repeating.

And when Julio finally triumphed, he found that her thoughts were still following independently the same line of mental stress.

One afternoon, Marguerite announced that henceforth she would see him less frequently. She was attending classes now, and had only two free days.

Desnoyers listened, dumbfounded. Classes? . . . What were her studies? . . .

She seemed a little irritated at his mocking expression. . . . Yes, she was studying; for the past week she had been attending classes. Now the lessons were going to be more regular; the course of instruction had been fully organized, and there were many more instructors.

"I wish to be a trained nurse. I am distressed over my uselessness. . . . Of what good have I ever been till now?" . . .

She was silent for a few moments as though reviewing her past.

"At times I almost think," she mused, "that war, with all its horrors, still has some good in it. It helps to make us useful to our fellowmen. We look at life more seriously; trouble makes us realize that we have come into the world for some purpose. . . . I believe that we must not love life only for the pleasures that it brings us. We ought to find satisfaction in sacrifice, in dedicating ourselves to others, and this satisfaction—I don't know just why, perhaps because it is new— appears to me superior to all other things."

Julio looked at her in surprise, trying to imagine what was going on in that idolized and frivolous head. What ideas were forming back of that thoughtful forehead which until then had merely reflected the slightest shadow of thoughts as swift and flitting as birds? . . .

But the former Marguerite was still alive. He saw her constantly reappearing in a funny way among the sombre preoccupations with which war was overshadowing all lives.

"We have to study very hard in order to earn our diplomas as nurses. Have you noticed our uniform? . . . It is most distinctive, and the white is so becoming both to blondes and brunettes. Then the cap which allows little curls over the ears—the fashionable coiffure—and the blue cape over the white suit, make a splendid contrast. With this outfit, a woman well shod, and with few jewels, may present a truly chic appearance. It is a mixture of nun and great lady which is vastly becoming."

She was going to study with a regular fury in order to become really useful . . . and sooner to wear the admired uniform.

Poor Desnoyers! . . . The longing to see her, and the lack of occupation in these interminable afternoons which hitherto had been employed so delightfully, compelled him to haunt the neighborhood of the unoccupied palace where the government had just established the training school for nurses. Stationing himself at the corner, watching the fluttering skirts and quick steps of the feminine feet on the sidewalk, he imagined that the course of time must have turned backward, and that he was still but eighteen—the same as when he used to hang around the establishments of some celebrated modiste. The groups of women that at certain hours came out of the palace suggested these former days. They were dressed extremely quietly, the aspect of many of them as humble as that of the seamstresses. But they were ladies of the well-to-do class, some even coming in automobiles driven by chauffeurs in military uniform, because they were ministerial vehicles.

These long waits often brought him unexpected encounters with the elegant students who were going and coming.

"Desnoyers!" some feminine voices would exclaim behind him. "Isn't it Desnoyers?"

And he would find himself obliged to relieve their doubts, saluting the ladies who were looking at him as though he were a ghost. They were friends of a remote epoch, of six months ago—ladies who had admired and pursued him, trusting sweetly to his masterly wisdom to guide them through the seven circles of the science of the tango. They were now scrutinizing him as if between their last encounter and the present moment had occurred a great cataclysm, transforming all the laws of existence—as if he were the sole survivor of a vanished race.

Eventually they all asked the same questions—"Are you not going to the war? . . . How is it that you are not wearing a uniform?"

He would attempt to explain, but at his first words, they would interrupt him:

"That's so. . . . You are a foreigner."

They would say it with a certain envy, doubtless thinking of their loved ones now suffering the privations and dangers of war. . . . But the fact that he was a foreigner would instantly create a vague atmosphere of spiritual aloofness, an alienation that Julio had not known in the good old days when people sought each other without considering nationality, without feeling that disavowal of danger which isolates and concentrates human groups.

The ladies generally bade him adieu with malicious suspicion. What was he doing hanging around there? In search of his usual lucky adventure? . . . And their smiles were rather grave, the smiles of older folk who know the true significance of life and commiserate the deluded ones still seeking diversion in frivolities.

This attitude was as annoying to Julio as though it were a manifestation of pity. They were supposing him still exercising the only function of which he was capable; he wasn't good for anything else. On the other hand, these empty heads, still keeping something of their old appearance, now appeared animated by the grand sentiment of maternity—an abstract maternity which seemed to be extending to all the men of the nation—a desire for self-sacrifice, of knowing first-hand the privations of the lowly, and aiding all the ills that flesh is heir to.

This same yearning was inspiring Marguerite when she came away from her lessons. She was advancing from one overpowering dread to another, accepting the first rudiments of surgery as the greatest of scientific marvels. At the same time, she was astonished at the avidity with which she was assimilating these hitherto unsuspected mysteries. Sometimes with a funny assumption of assurance, she would even believe she had mistaken her vocation.

"Who knows but what I was born to be a famous doctor?" she would exclaim.

Her great fear was that she might lose her self-control when the time came to put her newly acquired knowledge into practice. To see herself before the foul odors of decomposing flesh, to contemplate the flow of blood—a horrible thing for her who had always felt an invincible repugnance toward all the unpleasant conditions of ordinary life! But these hesitations were short, and she was suddenly animated by a dashing energy. These were times of sacrifice. Were not the men snatched every day from the comforts of sensuous existence to endure the rude life of a soldier? . . . She would be, a soldier in petticoats, facing pain, battling with it, plunging her hands into putrefaction, flashing like a ray of sunlight into the places where soldiers were expecting the approach of death.

She proudly narrated to Desnoyers all the progress that she was making in the training school, the complicated bandages that she was learning to adjust, sometimes over a mannikin, at others over the flesh of an employee, trying to play the part of a sorely wounded patient. She, so dainty, so incapable in her own home of the slightest physical effort, was learning the most skilful ways of lifting a human body from the ground and carrying it on her back. Who knew but that she might render this very service some day on the battlefield! She was ready for the greatest risks, with the ignorant audacity of women impelled by flashes of heroism. All her admiration was for the English army nurses, slender women of nervous vigor whose photographs were appearing in the papers, wearing pantaloons, riding boots and white helmets.

Julio listened to her with astonishment. Was this woman really Marguerite? . . . War was obliterating all her winning vanities. She was no longer fluttering about in bird-like fashion. Her feet were treading the earth with resolute firmness, calm and secure in the new strength which was developing within. When one of his caresses would remind her that she was a woman, she would always say the same thing,

"What luck that you are a foreigner! . . . What happiness to know that you do not have to go to war!"

In her anxiety for sacrifice, she wanted to go to the battlefields, and yet at the same time, she was rejoicing to see her lover exempt from military duty. This preposterous lack of logic was not gratefully received by Julio but irritated him as an unconscious offense.

"One might suppose that she was protecting me!" he thought. "She is the man and rejoices that I, the weak comrade, should be protected from danger. . . . What a grotesque situation!" . . .

Fortunately, at times when Marguerite presented herself at the studio, she was again her old self, making him temporarily forget his annoyance. She would arrive with the same joy in a vacation that the college student or the employee feels on a holiday. Responsibility was teaching her to know the value of time.

"No classes to-day!" she would call out on entering; and tossing her hat on a divan, she would begin a dance-step, retreating with infantile coquetry from the arms of her lover.

But in a few minutes she would recover her customary gravity, the serious look that had become habitual with her since the outbreak of hostilities. She spoke often of her mother, always sad, but striving to hide her grief and keeping herself up in the hope of a letter from her son; she spoke, too, of the war, commenting on the latest events with the rhetorical optimism of the official dispatches. She could describe the first flag taken from the enemy as minutely as though it were a garment of unparalleled elegance. From a window, she had seen the Minister of War. She was very much affected when repeating the story of some fugitive Belgians recently arrived at the hospital. They were the only patients that she had been able to assist until now. Paris was not receiving the soldiers wounded in battle; by order of the Government, they were being sent from the front to the hospitals in the South.

She no longer evinced toward Julio the resistance of the first few days. Her training as a nurse was giving her a certain passivity. She seemed to be ignoring material attractions, stripping them of the spiritual importance which she had hitherto attributed to them. She wanted to make Julio happy, although her mind was concentrated on other matters.

One afternoon, she felt the necessity of communicating certain news which had been filling her mind since the day before. Springing up from the couch, she hunted for her handbag which contained a letter. She wanted to read it again to tell its contents to somebody with that irresistible impulse which forestalls confession.

It was a letter which her brother had sent her from the Vosges. In it he spoke of Laurier more than of himself. They belonged to different batteries, but were in the same division and had taken part in the same combats. The officer was filled with admiration for his former brother-in-law. Who could have guessed that a future hero was hidden within that silent and tranquil engineer! . . . But he was a genuine hero, just the same! All the officials had agreed with Marguerite's brother on seeing how calmly he fulfilled his duty, facing death with the same coolness as though he were in his factory near Paris.

He had asked for the dangerous post of lookout, slipping as near as possible to the enemy's lines in order to verify the exactitude of the artillery discharge, rectifying it by telephone. A German shell had demolished the house on the roof of which he was concealed, and Laurier, on crawling out unhurt from the ruins, had readjusted his telephone and gone tranquilly on, continuing the same work in the shelter of a nearby grove. His battery, picked out by the enemy's aeroplanes, had received the concentrated fire of the artillery opposite. In a few minutes all the force were rolling on the ground—the captain and many soldiers dead, officers wounded and almost all the gunners. There only remained as chief, Laurier, the Impassive (as his comrades nicknamed him), and aided by the few artillerymen still on their feet, he continued firing under a rain of iron and fire, so as to cover the retreat of a battalion.

"He has been mentioned twice in dispatches," Marguerite continued reading. "I do not believe that it will be long before they give him the cross. He is valiant in every way. Who would have supposed all this a few weeks ago?" . . .

She did not share the general astonishment. Living with Laurier had many times shown her the intrepidity of his character, the fearlessness concealed under that placid exterior. On that account, her instincts had warned her against rousing her husband's wrath in the first days of her infidelity. She still remembered the way he looked the night he surprised her leaving Julio's home. His was the passion that kills, and, nevertheless, he had not attempted the least violence with her. . . . The memory of his consideration was awakening in Marguerite a sentiment of gratitude. Perhaps he had loved her as no other man had.

Her eyes, with an irresistible desire for comparison, sought Julio's, admiring his youthful grace and distinction. The image of Laurier, heavy and ordinary, came into her mind as a consolation. Certainly the officer whom she had seen at the station when saying good-bye to her brother, did not seem to her like her old husband. But Marguerite wished to forget the pallid lieutenant with the sad countenance who had passed before her eyes, preferring to remember him only as the manufacturer preoccupied with profits and incapable of comprehending what she was accustomed to call "the delicate refinements of a chic woman." Decidedly Julio was the more fascinating. She did not repent of her past. She did not wish to repent of it.

And her loving selfishness made her repeat once more the same old exclamation—"How fortunate that you are a foreigner! . . . What a relief to know that you are safe from the dangers of war!"

Julio felt the usual exasperation at hearing this. He came very near to closing his beloved's mouth with his hand. Was she trying to make fun of him? . . . It was fairly insulting to place him apart from other men.

Meanwhile, with blind irrelevance, she persisted in talking about Laurier, commenting upon his achievements.

"I do not love him, I never have loved him. Do not look so cross! How could the poor man ever be compared with you? You must admit, though, that his new existence is rather interesting. I rejoice in his brave deeds as though an old friend had done them, a family visitor whom I had not seen for a long time. . . . The poor man deserved a better fate. He ought to have married some other woman, some companion more on a level with his ideals. . . . I tell you that I really pity him!"

And this pity was so intense that her eyes filled with tears, awakening the tortures of jealousy in her lover. After these interviews, Desnoyers was more ill-tempered and despondent than ever.

"I am beginning to realize that we are in a false position," he said one morning to Argensola. "Life is going to become increasingly painful. It is difficult to remain tranquil, continuing the same old existence in the midst of a people at war."

His companion had about come to the same conclusion. He, too, was beginning to feel that the life of a young foreigner in Paris was insufferable, now that it was so upset by war.

"One has to keep showing passports all the time in order that the police may be sure that they have not discovered a deserter. In the street car, the other afternoon, I had to explain that I was a Spaniard to some girls who were wondering why I was not at the front. . . . One of them, as soon as she learned my nationality, asked me with great simplicity why I did not offer myself as a volunteer. . . . Now they have invented a word for the stay-at-homes, calling them Les Embusques, the hidden ones. . . . I am sick and tired of the ironical looks shot at me wherever I go; it makes me wild to be taken for an Embusque."

A flash of heroism was galvanizing the impressionable Bohemian. Now that everybody was going to the war, he was wishing to do the same thing. He was not afraid of death; the only thing that was disturbing him was the military service, the uniform, the mechanical obedience to bugle-call, the blind subservience to the chiefs. Fighting was not offering any difficulties for him but his nature capriciously resented everything in the form of discipline. The foreign groups in Paris were trying to organize each its own legion of volunteers and he, too, was planning his—a battalion of Spaniards and South Americans, reserving naturally the presidency of the organizing committee for himself, and later the command of the body.

He had inserted notices in the papers, making the studio in the rue de la Pompe the recruiting office. In ten days, two volunteers had presented themselves; a clerk, shivering in midsummer, who stipulated that he should be an officer because he was wearing a suitable jacket, and a Spanish tavern-keeper who at the very outset had wished to rob Argensola of his command on the futile pretext that he was a soldier in his youth while the Bohemian was only an artist. Twenty Spanish battalions were attempted with the same result in different parts of Paris. Each enthusiast wished to be commander of the others, with the individual haughtiness and aversion to discipline so characteristic of the race. Finally the future generalissimos, decided to enlist as simple volunteers . . . but in a French regiment.

"I am waiting to see what the Garibaldis do," said Argensola modestly. "Perhaps I may go with them."

This glorious name made military service conceivable to him. But then he vacillated; he would certainly have to obey somebody in this body of volunteers, and he did not believe in an obedience that was not preceded by long discussions. . . . What next!

"Life has changed in a fortnight," he continued. "It seems as if we were living in another planet; our former achievements are not appreciated. Others, most obscure and poor, those who formerly had the least consideration, are now promoted to the first ranks. The refined man of complex spirituality has disappeared for who knows how many years! . . . Now the simple-minded man climbs triumphantly to the top, because, though his ideas are limited, they are sure and he knows how to obey. We are no longer the style."

Desnoyers assented. It was so; they were no longer fashionable. None knew that better than he, for he who was once the sensation of the day, was now passing as a stranger among the very people who a few months before had raved over him.

"Your reign is over," laughed Argensola. "The fact that you are a handsome fellow doesn't help you one bit nowadays. In a uniform and with a cross on my breast, I could soon get the best of you in a rival love affair. In times of peace, the officers only set the girls of the provinces to dreaming; but now that we are at war, there has awakened in every woman the ancestral enthusiasm that her remote grandmothers used to feel for the strong and aggressive beast. . . . The high-born dames who a few months ago were complicating their desires with psychological subtleties, are now admiring the military man with the same simplicity that the maid has for the common soldier. Before a uniform, they feel the humble and servile enthusiasm of the female of the lower animals before the crests, foretops and gay plumes of the fighting males. Look out, master! . . . We shall have to follow the new course of events or resign ourselves to everlasting obscurity. The tango is dead."

And Desnoyers agreed that truly they were two beings on the other side of the river of life which at one bound had changed its course. There was no longer any place in the new existence for that poor painter of souls, nor for that hero of a frivolous life who, from five to seven every afternoon, had attained the triumphs most envied by mankind.

CHAPTER III

THE RETREAT

War had extended one of its antennae even to the avenue Victor Hugo. It was a silent war in which the enemy, bland, shapeless and gelatinous, seemed constantly to be escaping from the hands only to renew hostilities a little later on.

"I have Germany in my own house," growled Marcelo Desnoyers.

"Germany" was Dona Elena, the wife of von Hartrott. Why had not her son—that professor of inexhaustible sufficiency whom he now believed to have been a spy—taken her home with him? For what sentimental caprice had she wished to stay with her sister, losing the opportunity of returning to Berlin before the frontiers were closed?

The presence of this woman in his home was the cause of many compunctions and alarms. Fortunately, the chauffeur and all the men-servants were in the army. The two chinas received an order in a threatening tone. They must be very careful when talking to the French maids—not the slightest allusion to the nationality of Dona Elena's husband nor to the residence of her family. Dona Elena was an Argentinian. But in spite of the silence of the maids, Don Marcelo was always in fear of some outburst of exalted patriotism, and that his wife's sister might suddenly find herself confined in a concentration camp under suspicion of having dealings with the enemy.

Frau von Hartrott made his uneasiness worse. Instead of keeping a discreet silence, she was constantly introducing discord into the home with her opinions.

During the first days of the war, she kept herself locked in her room, joining the family only when summoned to the dining room. With tightly puckered mouth and an absent-minded air, she would then seat herself at the table, pretending not to hear Don Marcelo's verbal outpourings of enthusiasm. He enjoyed describing the departure of the troops, the moving scenes in the streets and at the stations, commenting on events with an optimism sure of the first news of the war. Two things were beyond all discussion. The bayonet was the secret of the French, and the Germans were shuddering with terror before its fatal, glistening point. . . . The '75 cannon had proved itself a unique jewel, its shots being absolutely sure. He was really feeling sorry for the enemy's artillery since its projectiles so seldom exploded even when well aimed. . . . Furthermore, the French troops had entered victoriously into Alsace; many little towns were already theirs.

"Now it is as it was in the '70's," he would exult, brandishing his fork and waving his napkin. "We are going to kick them back to the other side of the Rhine—kick them! . . . That's the word."

Chichi always agreed gleefully while Dona Elena was raising her eyes to heaven, as though silently calling upon somebody hidden in the ceiling to bear witness to such errors and blasphemies.

The kind Dona Luisa always sought her out afterwards in the retirement of her room, believing it necessary to give sisterly counsel to one living so far from home. The Romantica did not maintain her austere silence before the sister who had always venerated her superior instruction; so now the poor lady was overwhelmed with accounts of the stupendous forces of Germany, enunciated with all the authority of a wife of a great Teutonic patriot, and a mother of an almost celebrated professor. According to her graphic picture, millions of men were now surging forth in enormous streams, thousands of cannons were filing by, and tremendous mortars like monstrous turrets. And towering above all this vast machinery of destruction was a man who alone was worth an army, a being who knew everything and could do everything, handsome, intelligent, and infallible as a god—the Emperor.

"The French just don't know what's ahead of them," declared Dona Elena. "We are going to annihilate them. It is merely a matter of two weeks. Before August is ended, the Emperor will have entered Paris."

Senora Desnoyers was so greatly impressed by these dire prophecies that she could not hide them from her family. Chichi waxed indignant at her mother's credulity and her aunt's Germanism. Martial fervor was flaming up in the former Peoncito. Ay, if the women could only go to war! . . . She enjoyed picturing herself on horseback in command of a regiment of dragoons, charging the enemy with other Amazons as dashing and buxom as she. Then her fondness for skating would predominate over her tastes for the cavalry, and she would long to be an Alpine hunter, a diable bleu among those who slid on long runners, with musket slung across the back and alpenstock in hand, over the snowy slopes of the Vosges.

But the government did not appreciate the valorous women, and she could obtain no other part in the war but to admire the uniform of her true-love, Rene Lacour, converted into a soldier. The senator's son certainly looked beautiful. He was tall and fair, of a rather feminine type recalling his dead mother. In his fiancee's opinion, Rene was just "a little sugar soldier." At first she had been very proud to walk the streets by the side of this warrior, believing that his uniform had greatly augmented his personal charm, but little by little a revulsion of feeling was clouding her joy. The senatorial prince was nothing but a common soldier. His illustrious father, fearful that the war might cut off forever the dynasty of the Lacours, indispensable to the welfare of the State, had had his son mustered into the auxiliary service of the army. By this arrangement, his heir need not leave Paris, ranking about as high as those who were kneading the bread or mending the soldiers' cloaks. Only by going to the front could he claim—as a student of the Ecole Centrale—his title of sub-lieutenant in the Artillery Reserves.

"What happiness for me that you have to stay in Paris! How delighted I am that you are just a private! . . ."

And yet, at the same time, Chichi was thinking enviously of her friends whose lovers and brothers were officers. They could parade the streets, escorted by a gold-trimmed kepis that attracted the notice of the passers-by and the respectful salute of the lower ranks.

Each time that Dona Luisa, terrified by the forecasts of her sister, undertook to communicate her dismay to her daughter, the girl would rage up and down, exclaiming:—

"What lies my aunt tells you! . . . Since her husband is a German, she sees everything as he wishes it to be. Papa knows more; Rene's father is better informed about these things. We are going to give them a thorough hiding! What fun it will be when they hit my uncle and all my snippy cousins in Berlin! . . ."

"Hush," groaned her mother. "Do not talk such nonsense. The war has turned you as crazy as your father."

The good lady was scandalized at hearing the outburst of savage desires that the mere mention of the Kaiser always aroused in her daughter. In times of peace, Chichi had rather admired this personage. "He's not so bad-looking," she had commented, "but with a very ordinary smile." Now all her wrath was concentrated upon him. The thousands of women that were weeping through his fault! The mothers without sons, the wives without husbands, the poor children left in the burning towns! . . . Ah, the vile wretch! . . . And she would brandish her knife of the old Peoncito days—a dagger with silver handle and sheath richly chased, a gift that her grandfather had exhumed from some forgotten souvenirs of his childhood in an old valise. The very first German that she came across was doomed to death. Dona Luisa was terrified to find her flourishing this weapon before her dressing mirror. She was no longer yearning to be a cavalryman nor a diable bleu. She would be entirely content if they would leave her, alone in some closed space with the detested monster. In just five minutes she would settle the universal conflict.

"Defend yourself, Boche," she would shriek, standing at guard as in her childhood she had seen the peons doing on the ranch.

And with a knife-thrust above and below, she would pierce his imperial vitals. Immediately there resounded in her imagination, shouts of joy, the gigantic sigh of millions of women freed at last from the bloody nightmare— thanks to her playing the role of Judith or Charlotte Corday, or a blend of all the heroic women who had killed for the common weal. Her savage fury made her continue her imaginary slaughter, dagger in hand. Second stroke!—the Crown Prince rolling to one side and his head to the other. A rain of dagger thrusts!— all the invincible generals of whom her aunt had been boasting fleeing with their insides in their hands—and bringing up the rear, that fawning lackey who wished to receive the same things as those of highest rank—the uncle from Berlin. . . . Ay, if she could only get the chance to make these longings a reality!

"You are mad," protested her mother. "Completely mad! How can a ladylike girl talk in such a way?" . . .

Surprising her niece in the ecstasy of these delirious ravings, Dona Elena would raise her eyes to heaven, abstaining thenceforth from communicating her opinions, reserving them wholly for the mother.

Don Marcelo's indignation took another bound when his wife repeated to him the news from her sister. All a lie! . . . The war was progressing finely. On the Eastern frontier the French troops had advanced through the interior of Alsace and Lorraine.

"But—Belgium is invaded, isn't it?" asked Dona Luisa. "And those poor Belgians?"

Desnoyers retorted indignantly.

"That invasion of Belgium is treason. . . . And a treason never amounts to anything among decent people."

He said it in all good faith as though war were a duel in which the traitor was henceforth ruled out and unable to continue his outrages. Besides, the heroic resistance of Belgium was nourishing the most absurd illusions in his heart. The Belgians were certainly supernatural men destined to the most stupendous achievements. . . . And to think that heretofore he had never taken this plucky little nation into account! . . . For several days, he considered Liege a holy city before whose walls the Teutonic power would be completely confounded. Upon the fall of Liege, his unquenchable faith sought another handle. There were still remaining many other Lieges in the interior. The Germans might force their way further in; then we would see how many of them ever succeeded in getting out. The entry into Brussels did not disquiet him. An unprotected city! . . . Its surrender was a foregone conclusion. Now the Belgians would be better able to defend Antwerp. Neither did the advance of the Germans toward the French frontier alarm him at all. In vain his sister-in-law, with malicious brevity, mentioned in the dining-room the progress of the invasion, so confusedly outlined in the daily papers. The Germans were already at the frontier.

"And what of that?" yelled Don Marcelo. "Soon they will meet someone to talk to! Joffre is going to meet them. Our armies are in the East, in the very place where they ought to be, on the true frontier, at the door of their home. But they have to deal with a treacherous and cowardly opponent that instead of marching face to face, leaps the walls of the corral like sheep-stealers. . . . Their underhand tricks won't do them any good, though! The French are already in Belgium and adjusting the accounts of the Germans. We shall smash them so effectually that never again will they be able to disturb the peace of the world. And that accursed individual with the rampant moustache we are going to put in a cage, and exhibit in the place de la Concorde!"

Inspired by the paternal braggadocio, Chichi also launched forth exultingly an imaginary series of avenging torments and insults as a complement to this Imperial Exhibition.

These allusions to the Emperor aggravated Frau von Hartrott more than anything else. In the first days of the war, her sister had surprised her weeping before the newspaper caricatures and leaflets sold in the streets.

"Such an excellent man . . . so knightly . . . such a good father to his family! He wasn't to blame for anything. It was his enemies who forced him to assume the offensive."

Her veneration for exalted personages was making her take the attacks upon this admired grandee as though they were directed against her own family.

One night in the dining room, she abandoned her tragic silence. Certain sarcasms, shot by Desnoyers at her hero, brought the tears to her eyes, and this sentimental indulgence turned her thoughts upon her sons who were undoubtedly taking part in the invasion.

Her brother-in-law was longing for the extermination of all the enemy. "May every barbarian be exterminated! . . . every one of the bandits in pointed helmets who have just burned Louvain and other towns, shooting defenceless peasants, old men, women and children!"

"You forget that I am a mother," sobbed Frau von Hartrott. "You forget that among those whose extermination you are imploring, are my sons."

Her violent weeping made Desnoyers realize more than ever the abyss yawning between him and this woman lodged in his own house. His resentment, however, overleapt family considerations. . . . She might weep for her sons all she wanted to; that was her right. But these sons were aggressors and wantonly doing evil. It was the other mothers who were inspiring his pity—those who were living tranquilly in their smiling little Belgian towns when their sons were suddenly shot down, their daughters violated and their houses burned to the ground.

As though this description of the horrors of war were a fresh insult to her, Dona Elena wept harder than ever. What falsehoods! The Kaiser was an excellent man. His soldiers were gentlemen, the German army was a model of civilization and goodness. Her husband had belonged to this army, her sons were marching in its ranks. And she knew her sons—well-bred and incapable of wrong-doing. These Belgian calumnies she could no longer listen to . . . and, with dramatic abandon, she flung herself into the arms of her sister.

Senor Desnoyers raged against the fate that condemned him to live under the same roof with this woman. What an unfortunate complication for the family! . . . and the frontiers were closed, making it impossible to get rid of her!

"Very well, then," he thundered. "Let us talk no more about it. We shall never reach an understanding, for we belong to two different worlds. It's a great pity that you can't go back to your own people."

After that, he refrained from mentioning the war in his sister-in-law's presence. Chichi was the only one keeping up her aggressive and noisy enthusiasm. Upon reading in the papers the news of the shootings, sackings, burning of cities, and the dolorous flight of those who had seen their all reduced to ashes, she again felt the necessity of assuming the role of lady-assassin. Ay, if she could only once get her hands on one of those bandits! . . . What did the men amount to anyway if they couldn't exterminate the whole lot? . . .

Then she would look at Rene in his exquisitely fresh uniform, sweet-mannered and smiling as though all war meant to him was a mere change of attire, and she would exclaim enigmatically:

"What luck that you will never have to go to the front! . . . How fine that you don't run any risks!"

And her lover would accept these words as but another proof of her affectionate interest.

One day Don Marcelo was able to appreciate the horrors of the war without leaving Paris. Three thousand Belgian refugees were quartered provisionally in the circus before being distributed among the provinces. When Desnoyers entered this place, he saw in the vestibule the same posters which had been flaunting their spectacular gayeties when he had visited it a few months before with his family.

Now he noticed the odor from a sick and miserable multitude crowded together—like the exhalation from a prison or poorhouse infirmary. He saw a throng that seemed crazy or stupefied with grief. They did not know exactly where they were; they had come thither, they didn't know how. The terrible spectacle of the invasion was still so persistent in their minds that it left room for no other impression. They were still seeing the helmeted men in their peaceful hamlets, their homes in flames, the soldiery firing upon those who were fleeing, the mutilated women done to death by incessant adulterous assault, the old men burned alive, the children stabbed in their cradles by human beasts inflamed by alcohol and license. . . . Some of the octogenarians were weeping as they told how the soldiers of a civilized nation were cutting off the breasts from the women in order to nail them to the doors, how they had passed around as a trophy a new-born babe spiked on a bayonet, how they had shot aged men in the very armchair in which they were huddled in their sorrowful weakness, torturing them first with their jests and taunts.

They had fled blindly, pursued by fire and shot, as crazed with terror as the people of the middle ages trying not to be ridden down by the hordes of galloping Huns and Mongols. And this flight had been across the country in its loveliest festal array, in the most productive of months, when the earth was bristling with ears of grain, when the August sky was most brilliant, and when the birds were greeting the opulent harvest with their glad songs!

In that circus, filled with the wandering crowds, the immense crime was living again. The children were crying with a sound like the bleating of lambs; the men were looking wildly around with terrified eyes; the frenzied women were howling like the insane. Families had become separated in the terror of flight. A mother of five little ones now had but one. The parents, as they realized the number missing, were thinking with anguish of those who had disappeared. Would they ever find them again? . . . Or were they already dead? . . .

Don Marcelo returned home, grinding his teeth and waving his cane in an alarming manner. Ah, the bandits! . . . If only his sister-in-law could change her sex! Why wasn't she a man? . . . It would be better still if she could suddenly assume the form of her husband, von Hartrott. What an interesting interview the two brothers-in-law would have! . . .

The war was awakening religious sentiment in the men and increasing the devotion of the women. The churches were filled. Dona Luisa was no longer confining herself to those of her neighborhood. With the courage induced by extraordinary events, she was traversing Paris afoot and going from the

Madeleine to Notre Dame, or to the Sacre Coeur on the heights of Montmartre. Religious festivals were now thronged like popular assemblies. The preachers were tribunes. Patriotic enthusiasm interrupted many sermon with applause.

Each morning on opening the papers, before reading the war news, Senora Desnoyers would hunt other notices. "Where was Father Amette going to be to-day?" Then, under the arched vaultings of that temple, would she unite her voice with the devout chorus imploring supernatural intervention. "Lord, save France!" Patriotic religiosity was putting Sainte Genevieve at the head of the favored ones, so from all these fiestas, Dona Luisa, tremulous with faith, would return in expectation of a miracle similar to that which the patron saint of Paris had worked before the invading hordes of Attila.

Dona Elena was also visiting the churches, but those nearest the house. Her brother-in-law saw her one afternoon entering Saint-Honoree d'Eylau. The building was filled with the faithful, and on the altar was a sheaf of flags—France and the allied nations. The imploring crowd was not composed entirely of women. Desnoyers saw men of his age, pompous and grave, moving their lips and fixing steadfast eyes on the altar on which were reflected like lost stars, the flames of the candles. And again he felt envy. They were fathers who were recalling their childhood prayers, thinking of their sons in battle. Don Marcelo, who had always considered religion with indifference, suddenly recognized the necessity of faith. He wanted to pray like the others, with a vague, indefinite supplication, including all beings who were struggling and dying for a land that he had not tried to defend.

He was scandalized to see von Hartrott's wife kneeling among these people raising her eyes to the cross in a look of anguished entreaty. She was begging heaven to protect her husband, the German who perhaps at this moment was concentrating all his devilish faculties on the best organization for crushing the weak; she was praying for her sons, officers of the King of Prussia, who revolver in hand were entering villages and farmlands, driving before them a horror-stricken crowd, leaving behind them fire and death. And these orisons were going to mingle with those of the mothers who were praying for the youth trying to check the onslaught of the barbarians—with the petitions of these earnest men, rigid in their tragic grief! . . .

He had to make a great effort not to protest aloud, and he left the church. His sister-in-law had no right to kneel there among those people.

"They ought to put her out!" he growled indignantly. "She is compromising God with her absurd entreaties."

But in spite of his annoyance, he had to endure her living in his household, and at the same time had taken great pains to prevent her nationality being known outside.

It was a severe trial for Don Marcelo to be obliged to keep silent when at table with his family. He had to avoid the hysterics of his sister-in-law who promptly burst into sighs and sobs at the slightest allusion to her hero; and he feared equally the complaints of his wife, always ready to defend her sister, as though she were the victim. . . . That a man in his own home should have to curb his tongue and speak tactfully! . . .

The only satisfaction permitted him was to announce the military moves. The French had entered Belgium. "It appears that the Boches have had a good set-back." The slightest clash of cavalry, a simple encounter with the advance troops, he would glorify as a decisive victory. "In Lorraine, too, we are making great headway!" . . . But suddenly the fountain of his bubbling optimism seemed to become choked up. To judge from the periodicals, nothing extraordinary was occurring. They continued publishing war-stories so as to keep enthusiasm at fever-heat, but nothing definite. The Government, too, was issuing communications of vague and rhetorical verbosity. Desnoyers became alarmed, his instinct warning him of danger. "There is something wrong," he thought. "There's a spring broken somewhere!"

This lack of encouraging news coincided exactly with the sudden rise in Dona Elena's spirits. With whom had that woman been talking? Whom did she meet when she was on the street? . . . Without dropping her pose as a martyr, with the same woebegone look and drooping mouth, she was talking, and talking treacherously. The torment of Don Marcelo in being obliged to listen to the enemy harbored within his gates! . . . The French had been vanquished in Lorraine and in Belgium at the same time. A body of the army had deserted the colors; many prisoners, many cannon were captured. "Lies! German exaggerations!" howled Desnoyers. And Chichi with the derisive ha-ha's of an insolent girl, drowned out the triumphant communications of the aunt from Berlin. "I don't know, of course," said the unwelcome lodger with mock humility. "Perhaps it is not authentic. I have heard it said." Her host was furious. Where had she heard it said? Who was giving her such news? . . .

And in order to ventilate his wrath, he broke forth into tirades against the enemy's espionage, against the carelessness of the police force in permitting so many Germans to remain hidden in Paris. Then he suddenly became quiet, thinking of his own behavior in this line. He, too, was involuntarily contributing toward the maintenance and support of the foe.

The fall of the ministry and the constitution of a government of national defense made it apparent that something very important must have taken place. The alarms and tears of Dona Luisa increased his nervousness. The good lady was no longer returning from the churches, cheered and strengthened. Her confidential talks with her sister were filling her with a terror that she tried in vain to communicate to her husband. "All is lost. . . . Elena is the only one that knows the truth."

Desnoyers went in search of Senator Lacour. He would know all the ministers; no one could be better informed. "Yes, my friend," said the important man sadly. "Two great losses at Morhange and Charleroi, at the East and the North. The enemy is going to invade French soil! . . . But our army is intact, and will retreat in good order. Good fortune may still be ours. A great calamity, but all is not lost."

Preparations for the defense of Paris were being pushed forward . . . rather late. The forts were supplying themselves with new cannon. Houses, built in the danger zone in the piping times of peace, were now disappearing under the blows of the official demolition. The trees on the outer avenues were being felled in order to enlarge the horizon. Barricades of sacks of earth and tree trunks were heaped at the doors of the old walls. The curious were skirting the suburbs in order to gaze at the recently dug trenches and the barbed wire fences. The Bois de Boulogne was filled with herds of cattle. Near heaps of dry alfalfa steers and sheep were grouped in the green meadows. Protection against famine was uppermost in the minds of a people still remembering the suffering of 1870. Every night, the street lighting was less and less. The sky, on the other hand, was streaked incessantly by the shafts from the searchlights. Fear of aerial invasion was increasing the public uneasiness. Timid people were speaking of Zeppelins, attributing to them irresistible powers, with all the exaggeration that accompanies mysterious dangers.

In her panic, Dona Luisa greatly distressed her husband, who was passing the days in continual alarm, yet trying to put heart into his trembling and anxious wife. "They are going to come, Marcelo; my heart tells me so. The girl! . . . the girl!" She was accepting blindly all the statements made by her sister, the only thing that comforted her being the chivalry and discipline of those troops to which her nephews belonged. The news of the atrocities committed against the women of Belgium were received with the same credulity as the enemy's advances announced by Elena. "Our girl, Marcelo. . . . Our girl!" And the girl, object of so much solicitude, would laugh with the assurance of vigorous youth on hearing of her mother's anxiety. "Just let the shameless fellows come! I shall take great pleasure in seeing them face to face!" And she clenched her right hand as though it already clutched the avenging knife.

The father became tired of this situation. He still had one of his monumental automobiles that an outside chauffeur could manage. Senator Lacour obtained the necessary passports and Desnoyers gave his wife her orders in a tone that admitted of no remonstrance. They must go to Biarritz or to some of the summer resorts in the north of Spain. Almost all the South American families had already gone in the same direction. Dona Luisa tried to object. It was impossible for her to separate herself from her husband. Never before, in their many years of married life, had they once been separated. But a harsh negative from Don Marcelo cut her pleadings short. He would remain. Then the poor senora ran to the rue de la Pompe. Her son! . . . Julio scarcely listened to his mother. Ay! he, too, would stay. So finally the imposing automobile lumbered toward the South carrying Dona Luisa, her sister who hailed with delight this withdrawal before the admired troops of the Emperor, and Chichi, pleased that the war was necessitating an excursion to the fashionable beaches frequented by her friends.

Don Marcelo was at last alone. The two coppery maids had followed by rail the flight of their mistresses. At first the old man felt a little bewildered by this solitude, which obliged him to eat uncomfortable meals in a restaurant and pass the nights in enormous and deserted rooms still bearing traces of their former occupants. The other apartments in the building had also been vacated. All the tenants were foreigners, who had discreetly decamped, or French families surprised by the war when summering at their country seats.

Instinctively he turned his steps toward the rue de la Pompe gazing from afar at the studio windows. What was his son doing? . . . Undoubtedly continuing his gay and useless life. Such men only existed for their own selfish folly.

Desnoyers felt satisfied with the stand he had taken. To follow the family would be sheer cowardice. The memory of his youthful flight to South America was sufficient martyrdom; he would finish his life with all the compensating bravery that he could muster. "No, they will not come," he said repeatedly, with the optimism of enthusiasm. "I have a presentiment that they will never reach Paris. And even if they DO come!" . . . The absence of his family brought him a joyous valor and a sense of bold youthfulness. Although his age might prevent his going to war in the open air, he could still fire a gun, immovable in a trench, without fear of death. Let them come! . . . He was longing for the struggle with the anxiety of a punctilious business man wishing to cancel a former debt as soon as possible.

In the streets of Paris he met many groups of fugitives. They were from the North and East of France, and had escaped before the German advance. Of all the tales told by this despondent crowd—not knowing where to go and dependent upon the charity of the people—he was most impressed with those dealing with the disregard of property. Shootings and assassinations made him clench his fists, with threats of vengeance; but the robberies authorized by the heads, the wholesale sackings by superior order, followed by fire, appeared to him so unheard-of that he was silent with stupefaction, his speech seeming to be temporarily paralyzed. And a people with laws could wage war in this fashion, like a tribe of Indians going to combat in order to rob! . . . His adoration of property rights made him beside himself with wrath at these sacrileges.

He began to worry about his castle at Villeblanche. All that he owned in Paris suddenly seemed to him of slight importance to what he had in his historic mansion. His best paintings were there, adorning the gloomy salons; there, too, the furnishings captured from the antiquarians after an auctioneering battle, and the crystal cabinets, the tapestries, the silver services.

He mentally reviewed all of these objects, not letting a single one escape his inventory. Things that he had forgotten came surging up in his memory, and the fear of losing them seemed to give them greater lustre, increasing their size, and intensifying their value. All the riches of Villeblanche were concentrated in one certain acquisition which Desnoyers admired most of all; for, to his mind, it stood for all the glory of his immense fortune—in fact, the most luxurious appointment that even a millionaire could possess.

"My golden bath," he thought. "I have there my tub of gold."

This bath of priceless metal he had procured, after much financial wrestling, from an auction, and he considered the purchase the culminating achievement of his wealth. No one knew exactly its origin; perhaps it had been the property of luxurious princes; perhaps it owed its existence to the caprice of a demi-mondaine fond of display. He and his had woven a legend around this golden cavity adorned with lions' claws, dolphins and busts of naiads. Undoubtedly it was once a king's! Chichi gravely affirmed that it had been Marie Antoinette's, and the entire family thought that the home on the avenue Victor Hugo was altogether too modest and plebeian to enshrine such a jewel. They therefore agreed to put it in the castle, where it was greatly venerated, although it was useless and solemn as a museum piece. . . . And was he to permit the enemy in their advance toward the Marne to carry off this priceless treasure, as well as the other gorgeous things which he had accumulated with such patience Ah, no! His soul of a collector would be capable of the greatest heroism before he would let that go.

Each day was bringing a fresh sheaf of bad news. The papers were saying little, and the Government was so veiling its communications that the mind was left in great perplexity. Nevertheless, the truth was mysteriously forcing its way, impelled by the pessimism of the alarmists, and the manipulation of the enemy's spies who were remaining hidden in Paris. The fatal news was being passed along in whispers. "They have already crossed the frontier. . . ." "They are already in Lille." . . . They were advancing at the rate of thirty-five miles a day. The name of von Kluck was beginning to have a familiar ring. English and French were retreating before the enveloping progression of the invaders. Some were expecting another Sedan. Desnoyers was following the advance of the Germans, going daily to the Gare du Nord. Every twenty-four hours was lessening the radius of travel. Bulletins announcing that tickets would not be sold for the Northern districts served to indicate how these places were falling, one after the other, into the power of the invader. The shrinkage of national territory was going on with such methodical regularity that, with watch in hand, and allowing an advance of thirty-five miles daily, one might gauge the hour when the lances of the first Uhlans would salute the Eiffel tower. The trains were running full, great bunches of people overflowing from their coaches.

In this time of greatest anxiety, Desnoyers again visited his friend, Senator Lacour, in order to astound him with the most unheard-of petitions. He wished to go immediately to his castle. While everybody else was fleeing toward Paris he earnestly desired to go in the opposite direction. The senator couldn't believe his ears.

"You are beside yourself!" he exclaimed. "It is necessary to leave Paris, but toward the South. I will tell you confidentially, and you must not tell because it is a secret—we are leaving at any minute; we are all going, the President, the Government, the Chambers. We are going to establish ourselves at Bordeaux as in 1870. The enemy is surely approaching; it is only a matter of days . . . of hours. We know little of just what is happening, but all the news is bad. The army still holds firm, is yet intact, but retreating . . . retreating, all the time yielding ground. . . . Believe me, it will be better for you to leave Paris. Gallieni will defend it, but the defense is going to be hard and horrible. . . . Although

Paris may surrender, France will not necessarily surrender. The war will go on if necessary even to the frontiers of Spain . . . but it is sad . . . very sad!"

And he offered to take his friend with him in that flight to Bordeaux of which so few yet knew. Desnoyers shook his head. No; he wanted to go the castle of Villeblanche. His furniture . . . his riches . . . his parks.

"But you will be taken prisoner!" protested the senator. "Perhaps they will kill you!"

A shrug of indifference was the only response. He considered himself energetic enough to struggle against the entire German army in the defense of his property. The important thing was to get there, and then—just let anybody dare to touch his things! . . . The senator looked with astonishment at this civilian infuriated by the lust of possession. It reminded him of some Arab merchants that he had once known, ordinarily mild and pacific, who quarrelled and killed like wild beasts when Bedouin thieves seized their wares. This was not the moment for discussion, and each must map out his own course. So the influential senator finally yielded to the desire of his friend. If such was his pleasure, let him carry it through! So he arranged that his mad petitioner should depart that very night on a military train that was going to meet the army.

That journey put Don Marcelo in touch with the extraordinary movement which the war had developed on the railroads. His train took fourteen hours to cover the distance normally made in two. It was made up of freight cars filled with provisions and cartridges, with the doors stamped and sealed. A third-class car was occupied by the train escort, a detachment of provincial guards. He was installed in a second-class compartment with the lieutenant in command of this guard and certain officials on their way to join their regiments after having completed the business of mobilization in the small towns in which they were stationed before the war. The crowd, habituated to long detentions, was accustomed to getting out and settling down before the motionless locomotive, or scattering through the nearby fields.

In the stations of any importance all the tracks were occupied by rows of cars. High-pressure engines were whistling, impatient to be off. Groups of soldiers were hesitating before the different trains, making mistakes, getting out of one coach to enter others. The employees, calm but weary-looking, were going from side to side, giving explanations about mountains of all sorts of freight and arranging them for transport. In the convoy in which Desnoyers was placed the Territorials were sleeping, accustomed to the monotony of acting as guard. Those in charge of the horses had opened the sliding doors, seating themselves on the floor with their legs hanging over the edge. The train went very slowly during the night, across shadowy fields, stopping here and there before red lanterns and announcing its presence by prolonged whistling.

In some stations appeared young girls clad in white with cockades and pennants on their breasts. Day and night they were there, in relays, so that no train should pass through without a visit. They offered, in baskets and trays, their gifts to the soldiers—bread, chocolate, fruit. Many, already surfeited, tried to resist, but had to yield eventually before the pleading countenance of the maidens. Even Desnoyers was laden down with these gifts of patriotic enthusiasm.

He passed a great part of the night talking with his travelling companions. Only the officers had vague directions as to where they were to meet their regiments, for the operations of war were daily changing the situation. Faithful to duty, they were passing on, hoping to arrive in time for the decisive combat. The Chief of the Guard had been over the ground, and was the only one able to give any account of the retreat. After each stop the train made less progress. Everybody appeared confused. Why the retreat? . . . The army had undoubtedly suffered reverses, but it was still united and, in his opinion, ought to seek an engagement where it was. The retreat was leaving the advance of the enemy unopposed. To what point were they going to retreat? . . . They who two weeks before were discussing in their garrisons the place in Belgium where their adversaries were going to receive their death blow and through what places their victorious troops would invade Germany! . . .

Their admission of the change of tactics did not reveal the slightest discouragement. An indefinite but firm hope was hovering triumphantly above their vacillations. The Generalissimo was the only one who possessed the secret of events. And Desnoyers approved with the blind enthusiasm inspired by those in whom we have confidence. Joffre! . . . That serious and calm leader would finally bring things out all right. Nobody ought to doubt his ability; he was the kind of man who always says the decisive word.

At daybreak Don Marcelo left the train. "Good luck to you!" And he clasped the hands of the brave young fellows who were going to die, perhaps in a very short time. Finding the road unexpectedly open, the train started immediately and Desnoyers found himself alone in the station. In normal times a branch road would have taken him on to Villeblanche, but the service was now suspended for lack of a train crew. The employees had been transferred to the lines crowded with the war transportation.

In vain he sought, with most generous offers, a horse, a simple cart drawn by any kind of old beast, in order to continue his trip. The mobilization had appropriated the best, and all other means of transportation had disappeared with the flight of the terrified. He would have to walk the eight miles. The old man did not hesitate. Forward March! And he began his course along the dusty, straight, white highway running between an endless succession of plains. Some groups of trees, some green hedges and the roofs of various farms broke the monotony of the countryside. The fields were covered with stubble from the recent harvest. The haycocks dotted the ground with their yellowish cones, now beginning to darken and take on a tone of oxidized gold. In the valleys the birds were flitting about, shaking off the dew of dawn.

The first rays of the sun announced a very hot day. Around the hay stacks Desnoyers saw knots of people who were getting up, shaking out their clothes, and awaking those who were still sleeping. They were fugitives camping near the station in the hope that some train would carry them further on, they knew not where. Some had come from far-away districts; they had heard the cannon, had seen war approaching, and for several days had been going forward, directed by chance. Others, infected with the contagion of panic, had fled, fearing to know the same horrors. . . . Among them he saw mothers with their little ones in their arms, and old men who could only walk with a cane in one hand and the other arm in that of some member of the family, and a few old women, withered and motionless as mummies, who were sleeping as they were trundled along in wheelbarrows. When the sun awoke this miserable band they gathered themselves together with heavy step, still stiffened by the night. Many were going toward the station in the hope of a train which never came, thinking that, perhaps, they might have better luck during the day that was just dawning. Some were continuing their way down the track, hoping that fate might be more propitious in some other place.

Don Marcelo walked all the morning long. The white, rectilinear ribbon of roadway was spotted with approaching groups that on the horizon line looked like a file of ants. He did not see a single person going in his direction. All were fleeing toward the South, and on meeting this city gentleman, well-shod, with walking stick and straw hat, going on alone toward the country which they were abandoning in terror, they showed the greatest astonishment. They concluded that he must be some functionary, some celebrity from the Government.

At midday he was able to get a bit of bread, a little cheese and a bottle of white wine from a tavern near the road. The proprietor was at the front, his wife sick and moaning in her bed. The mother, a rather deaf old woman surrounded by her grandchildren, was watching from the doorway the procession of fugitives which had been filing by for the last three days. "Monsieur, why do they flee?" she said to Desnoyers. "War only concerns the soldiers. We countryfolk have done no wrong to anybody, and we ought not to be afraid."

Four hours later, on descending one of the hills that bounded the valley of the Marne, he saw afar the roofs of Villeblanche clustered around the church, and further on, beyond a little grove, the slatey points of the round towers of his castle.

The streets of the village were deserted. Only on the outer edges of the square did he see some old women sitting as in the placid evenings of bygone summers. Half of the neighborhood had fled; the others were staying by their firesides through sedentary routine, or deceiving themselves with a blind optimism. If the Prussians should approach, what could they do to them? . . . They would obey their orders without attempting any resistance, and it is impossible to punish people who obey. . . . Anything would be preferable to losing the homes built by their forefathers which they had never left.

In the square he saw the mayor and the principal inhabitants grouped together. Like the women, they all stared in astonishment at the owner of the castle. He was the most unexpected of apparitions. While so many were fleeing toward Paris, this Parisian had come to join them and share in their fate. A smile of affection, a look of sympathy began to appear on the rough, bark-like countenances of the suspicious rustics. For a long time Desnoyers had been on bad terms with the entire village. He had harshly insisted on his rights, showing no tolerance in matters touching his property. He had spoken many times of bringing suit against the mayor and sending half of the neighborhood to prison, so his enemies had retaliated by treacherously invading his lands, poaching in his hunting preserves, and causing him great trouble with counter-suits and involved claims. His hatred of the community had even united him with the priest because he was on terms of permanent hostility with the mayor. But his relations with the Church turned out as fruitless as his struggles with the State. The priest was a kindly old soul who bore a certain resemblance to Renan, and seemed interested only in getting alms for his poor out of Don Marcelo, even carrying his good-natured boldness so far as to try to excuse the marauders on his property.

How remote these struggles of a few months ago now seemed to him! . . . The millionaire was greatly surprised to see the priest, on leaving his house to enter the church, greet the mayor as he passed, with a friendly smile.

After long years of hostile silence they had met on the evening of August first at the foot of the church tower. The bell was ringing the alarm, announcing the mobilization to the men who were in the field—and the two enemies had instinctively clasped hands. All French! This affectionate unanimity also came to meet the detested owner of the castle. He had to exchange greetings first on one side, then on the other, grasping many a horny hand. Behind his back the people broke out into kindly excuses—"A good man, with no fault except a little bad temper. . . ." And in a few minutes Monsieur Desnoyers was basking in the delightful atmosphere of popularity.

As the iron-willed old gentleman approached his castle he concluded that, although the fatigue of the long walk was making his knees tremble, the trip had been well worth while. Never had his park appeared to him so extensive and so majestic as in that summer twilight, never so glistening white the swans that were gliding double over the quiet waters, never so imposing the great group of towers whose inverted images were repeated in the glassy green of the moats. He felt eager to see at once the stables with their herds of animals; then a brief glance showed him that the stalls were comparatively empty. Mobilization had carried off his best work horses; the driving and riding horses also had disappeared. Those in charge of the grounds and the various stable boys were also in the army. The Warden, a man upwards of fifty and consumptive, was the only one of the personnel left at the castle. With his wife and daughter he was keeping the mangers filled, and from time to time was milking the neglected cows.

Within the noble edifice he again congratulated himself on the adamantine will which had brought him thither. How could he ever give up such riches! . . . He gloated over the paintings, the crystals, the draperies, all bathed in gold by the splendor of the dying day, and he felt more than proud to be their possessor. This pride awakened in him an absurd, impossible courage, as though he were a gigantic being from another planet, and all humanity merely an ant hill that he could grind under foot. Just let the enemy come! He could hold his own against the whole lot! . . . Then, when his common sense brought him out of his heroic delirium, he tried to calm himself with an equally illogical optimism. They would not come. He did not know why it was, but his heart told him that they would not get that far.

He passed the following morning reconnoitering the artificial meadows that he had made behind the park, lamenting their neglected condition due to the departure of the men, trying himself to open the sluice gates so as to give some water to the pasture lands which were beginning to dry up. The grape vines were extending their branches the length of their supports, and the full bunches, nearly ripe, were beginning to show their triangular lusciousness among the leaves. Ay, who would gather this abundant fruit! . . .

By afternoon he noted an extraordinary amount of movement in the village. Georgette, the Warden's daughter, brought the news that many enormous automobiles and soldiers, French soldiers, were beginning to pass through the main street. In a little while a procession began filing past on the high road near the castle, leading to the bridge over the Marne. This was composed of motor trucks, open and closed, that still had their old commercial signs under their covering of dust and spots of mud. Many of them displayed the names of business firms in Paris, others the names of provincial establishments. With these industrial vehicles requisitioned by mobilization were others from the public service which produced in Desnoyers the same effect as a familiar face in a throng of strangers. On their upper parts were the names of their old routes:— "Madeleine-Bastille, Passy-Bourne," etc. Probably he had travelled many times in these very vehicles, now shabby and aged by twenty days of intense activity, with dented planks and twisted metal, perforated like sieves, but rattling crazily on.

Some of the conveyances displayed white discs with a red cross in the center; others had certain letters and figures comprehensible only to those initiates in the secrets of military administration. Within these vehicles—the only new and strong motors—he saw soldiers, many soldiers, but all wounded, with head and legs bandaged, ashy faces made still more tragic by their growing beards, feverish eyes looking fixedly ahead, mouths so sadly immobile that they seemed carven by agonizing groans. Doctors and nurses were occupying various carriages in this convoy escorted by several platoons of horsemen. And mingled with the slowly moving horses and automobiles were marching groups of foot-soldiers, with cloaks unbuttoned or hanging from their shoulders like capes— wounded men who were able to walk and joke and sing, some with arms in splints across their breasts, others with bandaged heads with clotted blood showing through the thin white strips.

The millionaire longed to do something for these brave fellows, but he had hardly begun to distribute some bottles of wine and loaves of bread before a doctor interposed, upbraiding him as though he had committed a crime. His gifts might result fatally. So he had to stand beside the road, sad and helpless, looking after the sorrowful convoy. . . . By nightfall the vehicles filled with the sick were no longer filing by.

He now saw hundreds of drays, some hermetically sealed with the prudence that explosive material requires, others with bundles and boxes that were sending out a stale odor of provisions. Then came great herds of cattle raising thick, whirling clouds of dust in the narrow parts of the road, prodded on by the sticks and yells of the shepherds in kepis.

His thoughts kept him wakeful all night. This, then, was the retreat of which the people of Paris were talking, but in which many wished not to believe—the retreat reaching even there and continuing its indefinite retirement, since nobody knew what its end might be. . . . His optimism aroused a ridiculous hope. Perhaps this was only the retreat of the hospitals and stores which always follows an army. The troops, wishing to be rid of impedimenta, were sending them forward by railway and highway. That must be it. So all through the night, he interpreted the incessant bustle as the passing of vehicles filled with the wounded, with munitions and eatables, like those which had filed by in the afternoon.

Toward morning he fell asleep through sheer weariness, and when he awoke late in the day his first glance was toward the road. He saw it filled with men and horses dragging some rolling objects. But these men were carrying guns and were formed in battalions and regiments. The animals were pulling the pieces of artillery. It was an army. . . . It was the retreat!

Desnoyers ran to the edge of the road to be more convinced of the truth.

Alas, they were regiments such as he had seen leaving the stations of Paris. . . . But with what a very different aspect! The blue cloaks were now ragged and yellowing garments, the trousers faded to the color of a half-baked brick, the shoes great cakes of mud. The faces had a desperate expression, with layers of dust and sweat in all their grooves and openings, with beards of recent growth, sharp as spikes, with an air of great weariness showing the longing to drop down somewhere forever, killing or dying, but without going a step further. They were tramping . . . tramping . . . tramping! Some marches had lasted thirty hours at a stretch. The enemy was on their tracks, and the order was to go on and not to fight, freeing themselves by their fleet-footedness from the involved movements of the invader.

The chiefs suspected the discouraged exhaustion of their men. They might exact of them complete sacrifice of life—but to order them to march day and night, forever fleeing before the enemy when they did not consider themselves vanquished, when they were animated by that ferocious wrath which is the mother of heroism! . . . Their despairing expressions mutely sought the nearest officers, the leaders, even the colonel. They simply could go no further! Such a long, devastating march in such a few days, and what for? . . . The superior officers, who knew no more than their men, seemed to be replying with their eyes, as though they possessed a secret—"Courage! One more effort! . . . This is going to come to an end very soon."

The vigorous beasts, having no imagination, were resisting less than the men, but their aspect was deplorable. How could these be the same strong horses with glossy coats that he had seen in the Paris processions at the beginning of the previous month? A campaign of twenty days had aged and exhausted them; their dull gaze seemed to be imploring pity. They were weak and emaciated, the outline of their skeletons so plainly apparent that it made their eyes look larger. Their harness, as they moved, showed the skin raw and bleeding. Yet they were pushing on with a mighty effort, concentrating their last powers, as though human demands were beyond their obscure instincts. Some could go no further and suddenly collapsed from sheer fatigue. Desnoyers noticed that the artillerymen rapidly unharnessed them, pushing them out of the road so as to leave the way open for the rest. There lay the skeleton-like frames with stiffened legs and glassy eyes staring fixedly at the first flies already attracted by their miserable carrion.

The cannons painted gray, the gun-carriages, the artillery equipment, all that Don Marcelo had seen clean and shining with the enthusiastic friction that man has given to arms from remote epochs—even more persistent than that which woman gives to household utensils—were now dirty, overlaid with the marks of endless use, with the wreckage of unavoidable neglect. The wheels were deformed with mud, the metal darkened by the smoke of explosion, the gray paint spotted with mossy dampness.

In the free spaces in this file, in the parentheses opened between battery and regiment, were sandwiched crowds of civilians—miserable groups driven on by the invasion, populations of entire towns that had disintegrated, following the army in its retreat. The approach of a new division would make them leave the road temporarily, continuing their march in the adjoining fields. Then at the slightest opening in the troops they would again slip along the white and even surface of the highway. They were mothers who were pushing hand-carts heaped high with pyramids of furniture and tiny babies, the sick who could hardly drag themselves along, old men carried on the shoulders of their grandsons, old women with little children clinging to their skirts—a pitiful, silent brood.

Nobody now opposed the liberality of the owner of the castle. His entire vintage seemed to be overflowing on the highway. Casks from the last grape-gathering were rolled out to the roadside, and the soldiers filled the metal ladles hanging from their belts with the red stream. Then the bottled wine began making its appearance by order of date, and was instantly lost in the river of men continually flowing by. Desnoyers observed with much satisfaction the effects of his munificence. The smiles were reappearing on the despairing faces, the French jest was leaping from row to row, and on resuming their march the groups began to sing.

Then he went to see the officers who in the village square were giving their horses a brief rest before rejoining their columns. With perplexed countenances and heavy eyes they were talking among themselves about this retreat, so incomprehensible to them all. Days before in Guise they had routed their pursuers, and yet now they were continually withdrawing in obedience to a severe and endless order. "We do not understand it," they were saying. "We do not understand." An ordered and methodical tide was dragging back these men who wanted to fight, yet had to retreat. All were suffering the same cruel doubt. "We do not understand."

And doubt was making still more distressing this day-and-night march with only the briefest rests—because the heads of the divisions were in hourly fear of being cut off from the rest of the army. "One effort more, boys! Courage! Soon we shall rest!" The columns in their retirement were extending hundreds of miles. Desnoyers was seeing only one division. Others and still others were doing exactly this same thing at that very hour, their recessional extending across half of France. All, with the same disheartened obedience, were falling back, the men exclaiming the same as the officials, "We don't understand. We don't understand!"

Don Marcelo soon felt the same sadness and bewilderment as these soldiers. He didn't understand, either. He saw the obvious thing, what all were able to see—the territory invaded without the Germans encountering any stubborn resistance;—entire counties, cities, villages, hamlets remaining in the power of the enemy, at the back of an army that was constantly withdrawing. His enthusiasm suddenly collapsed like a pricked balloon, and all his former pessimism returned. The troops were displaying energy and discipline; but what did that amount to if they had to keep retreating all the time, unable on account of strict orders to fight or defend the land? "Just as it was in the '70's," he sighed. "Outwardly there is more order, but the result is going to be the same."

As though a negative reply to his faint-heartedness, he overheard the voice of a soldier reassuring a farmer: "We are retreating, yes—only that we may pounce upon the Boches with more strength. Grandpa Joffre is going to put them in his pocket when and where he will."

The mere sound of the Marshal's name revived Don Marcelo's hope. Perhaps this soldier, who was keeping his faith intact in spite of the interminable and demoralizing marches, was nearer the truth than the reasoning and studious officers.

He passed the rest of the day making presents to the last detachments of the column. His wine cellars were gradually emptying. By order of dates, he continued distributing thousands of bottles stored in the subterranean parts of the castle. By evening he was giving to those who appeared weakest bottles covered with the dust of many years. As the lines filed by the men seemed weaker and more exhausted. Stragglers were now passing, painfully drawing their raw and bleeding feet from their shoes. Some had already freed themselves from these torture cases and were marching barefoot, with their heavy boots hanging from their shoulders, and staining the highway with drops of blood. Although staggering with deadly fatigue, they kept their arms and outfits, believing that the enemy was near.

Desnoyers' liberality stupefied many of them. They were accustomed to crossing their native soil, having to struggle with the selfishness of the producer. Nobody had been offering anything. Fear of danger had made the country folk hide their eatables and refuse to lend the slightest aid to their compatriots who were fighting for them.

The millionaire slept badly this second night in his pompous bed with columns and plushes that had belonged to Henry IV—according to the declarations of the salesmen. The troops no longer were marching past. From time to time there straggled by a single battalion, a battery, a group of horsemen—the last forces of the rear guard that had taken their position on the outskirts of the village in order to cover the retreat. The profound silence that followed the turmoil of transportation awoke in his mind a sense of doubt and disquietude. What was he doing there when the soldiers had gone? Was he not crazy to remain there? . . . But immediately there came galloping into his mind the great riches which the castle contained. If he could only take it all away! . . . That was impossible now through want of means and time. Besides, his stubborn will looked upon such flight as a shameful concession. "We must finish what we have begun!" he said to himself. He had made the trip on purpose to guard his own, and he must not flee at the approach of danger. . . .

The following morning, when he went down into the village, he saw hardly any soldiers. Only a single detachment of dragoons was still in the neighborhood; the horsemen were scouring the woods and pushing forward the stragglers at the same time that they were opposing the advance of the enemy. The troopers had obstructed the street with a barricade of carts and furniture. Standing behind this crude barrier, they were watching the white strip of roadway which ran between the two hills covered with trees. Occasionally there sounded stray shots like the snapping of cords. "Ours," said the troopers. These were the last detachments of sharpshooters firing at the advancing Uhlans. The cavalry of the rear guard had the task of opposing a continual resistance to the enemy, repelling the squads of Germans who were trying to work their way along to the retreating columns.

Desnoyers saw approaching along the highroad the last stragglers from the infantry. They were not walking, they rather appeared to be dragging themselves forward, with the firm intention of advancing, but were betrayed by emaciated legs and bleeding feet. Some had sunk down for a moment by the roadside, agonized with weariness, in order to breathe without the weight of their knapsacks, and draw their swollen feet from their leather prisons, and wipe off the sweat; but upon trying to renew their march, they found it impossible to rise. Their bodies seemed made of stone. Fatigue had brought them to a condition bordering on catalepsy so, unable to move, they were seeing dimly the rest of the army passing on as a fantastic file—battalions, more battalions, batteries, troops of horses. Then the silence, the night, the sleep on the stones and dust, shaken by most terrible nightmare. At daybreak they were awakened by bodies of horsemen exploring the ground, rounding up the remnants of the retreat. Ay, it was impossible to move! The dragoons, revolver in hand, had to resort to threats in order to rouse them! Only the certainty that the pursuer was near and might make them prisoners gave them a momentary vigor. So they were forcing themselves up by superhuman effort, staggering, dragging their legs, and supporting themselves on their guns as though they were canes.

Many of these were young men who had aged in an hour and changed into confirmed invalids. Poor fellows! They would not go very far! Their intention was to follow on, to join the column, but on entering the village they looked at the houses with supplicating eyes, desiring to enter them, feeling such a craving for immediate relief that they forgot even the nearness of the enemy.

Villeblanche was now more military than before the arrival of the troops. The night before a great part of the inhabitants had fled, having become infected with the same fear that was driving on the crowds following the army. The mayor and the priest remained. Reconciled with the owner of the castle through his unexpected presence in their midst, and admiring his liberality, the municipal official approached to give him some news. The engineers were mining the bridge over the Marne. They were only waiting for the dragoons to cross before blowing it up. If he wished to go, there was still time.

Again Desnoyers hesitated. Certainly it was foolhardy to remain there. But a glance at the woods over whose branches rose the towers of his castle, settled his doubts. No, no. . . . "We must finish what we have begun!"

The very last band of troopers now made their appearance, coming out of the woods by different paths. They were riding their horses slowly, as though they deplored this retreat. They kept looking behind, carbine in hand, ready to halt and shoot. The others who had been occupying the barricade were already on their mounts. The division reformed, the commands of the officers were heard and a quick trot, accompanied by the clanking of metal, told Don Marcelo that the last of the army had left.

He remained near the barricade in a solitude of intense silence, as though the world were suddenly depopulated. Two dogs, abandoned by the flight of their masters, leaped and sniffed around him, coaxing him for protection. They were unable to get the desired scent in that land trodden down and disfigured by the transit of thousands of men. A family cat was watching the birds that were beginning to return to their haunts. With timid flutterings they were picking at what the horses had left, and an ownerless hen was disputing the banquet with the winged band, until then hidden in the trees and roofs. The silence intensified the rustling of the leaves, the hum of the insects, the summer respiration of the sunburnt soil which appeared to have contracted timorously under the weight of the men in arms.

Desnoyers was losing exact track of the passing of time. He was beginning to believe that all which had gone before must have been a bad dream. The calm surrounding him made what had been happening here seem most improbable.

Suddenly he saw something moving at the far end of the road, at the very highest point where the white ribbon of the highway touched the blue of the horizon. There were two men on horseback, two little tin soldiers who appeared to have escaped from a box of toys. He had brought with him a pair of field glasses that had often surprised marauders on his property, and by their aid he saw more clearly the two riders clad in greenish gray! They were carrying lances and wearing helmets ending in a horizontal plate . . . They! He could not doubt it: before his eyes were the first Uhlans!

For some time they remained motionless, as though exploring the horizon. Then, from the obscure masses of vegetation that bordered the roadside, others and still others came sallying forth in groups. The little tin soldiers no longer were showing their silhouettes against the horizon's blue; the whiteness of the highway was now making their background, ascending behind their heads. They came slowly down, like a band that fears ambush, examining carefully everything around.

The advisability of prompt retirement made Don Marcelo bring his investigations to a close. It would be most disastrous for him if they surprised him here. But on lowering his glasses something extraordinary passed across his field of vision. A short distance away, so that he could almost touch them with his hand, he saw many men skulking along in the shadow of the trees on both sides of the road. His surprise increased as he became convinced that they were Frenchmen, wearing kepis. Where were they coming from? . . . He examined more closely with his spy glass. They were stragglers in a lamentable state of body and a picturesque variety of uniforms—infantry, Zouaves, dragoons without their horses. And with them were forest guards and officers from the villages that had received too late the news of the retreat—altogether about fifty. A few were fresh and vigorous, others were keeping themselves up by supernatural effort. All were carrying arms.

They finally made the barricade, looking continually behind them, in order to watch, in the shelter of the trees, the slow advance of the Uhlans. At the head of this heterogeneous troop was an official of the police, old and fat, with a revolver in his right hand, his moustache bristling with excitement, and a murderous glitter in his heavy-lidded blue eyes. The band was continuing its advance through the village, slipping over to the other side of the barricade of carts without paying much attention to their curious countryman, when suddenly sounded a loud detonation, making the horizon vibrate and the houses tremble.

"What is that?" asked the officer, looking at Desnoyers for the first time. He explained that it was the bridge which had just been blown up. The leader received the news with an oath, but his confused followers, brought together by chance, remained as indifferent as though they had lost all contact with reality.

"Might as well die here as anywhere," continued the official. Many of the fugitives acknowledged this decision with prompt obedience, since it saved them the torture of continuing their march. They were almost rejoicing at the explosion which had cut off their progress. Instinctively they were gathering in the places most sheltered by the barricade. Some entered the abandoned houses whose doors the dragoons had forced in order to utilize the upper floors. All seemed satisfied to be able to rest, even though they might soon have to fight. The officer went from group to group giving his orders. They must not fire till he gave the word.

Don Marcelo watched these preparations with the immovability of surprise. So rapid and noiseless had been the apparition of the stragglers that he imagined he must still be dreaming. There could be no danger in this unreal situation; it was all a lie. And he remained in his place without understanding the deputy who was ordering his departure with roughest words. Obstinate civilian! . . .

The reverberation of the explosion had filled the highway with horsemen. They were coming from all directions, forming themselves into the advance group. The Uhlans were galloping around under the impression that the village was abandoned.

"Fire!"

Desnoyers was enveloped in a rain of crackling noises, as though the trunks of all the trees had split before his eyes.

The impetuous band halted suddenly. Some of their men were rolling on the ground. Some were bending themselves double, trying to get across the road without being seen. Others remained stretched out on their backs or face downward with their arms in front. The riderless horses were racing wildly across the fields with reins dragging, urged on by the loose stirrups.

And after this rude shock which had brought them surprise and death, the band disappeared, instantly swallowed up by the trees.

CHAPTER IV

NEAR THE SACRED GROTTO

Argensola had found a new occupation even more exciting than marking out on the map the manoeuvres of the armies.

"I am now devoting myself to the taube," he announced. "It appears from four to five with the precision a punctilious guest coming to take tea."

Every afternoon at the appointed hour, a German aeroplane was flying over Paris dropping bombs. This would-be intimidation was producing no terror, the people accepting the visit as an interesting and extraordinary spectacle. In vain the aviators were flinging in the city streets German flags bearing ironic messages, giving accounts of the defeat of the retreating army and the failures of the Russian offensive. Lies, all lies! In vain they were dropping bombs, destroying garrets, killing or wounding old men, women and babes. "Ah, the bandits!" The crowds would threaten with their fists the malign mosquito, scarcely visible 6,000 feet above them, and after this outburst, they would follow it with straining eyes from street to street, or stand motionless in the square in order to study its evolutions.

The most punctual of all the spectators was Argensola. At four o'clock he was in the place de la Concorde with upturned face and wide-open eyes, in most cordial good-fellowship with all the bystanders. It was as though they were holding season tickets at the same theatre, becoming acquainted through seeing each other so often. "Will it come? . . . Will it not come to-day?" The women appeared to be the most vehement, some of them rushing up, flushed and breathless, fearing that they might have arrived too late for the show. . . . A great cry—"There it comes! . . . There it is!" And thousands of hands were pointing to a vague spot on the horizon. With field glasses and telescopes they were aiding their vision, the popular venders offering every kind of optical instruments and for an hour the thrilling spectacle of an aerial hunt was played out, noisy and useless.

The great insect was trying to reach the Eiffel Tower, and from its base would come sharp reports, at the same time that the different platforms spit out a fierce stream of shrapnel. As it zigzagged over the city, the discharge of rifles would crackle from roof and street. Everyone that had arms in his house was firing—the soldiers of the guard, and the English and Belgians on their way through Paris. They knew that their shots were perfectly useless, but they were firing for the fun of retorting, hoping at the same time that one of their chance shots might achieve a miracle; but the only miracle was that the shooters did not kill each other with their precipitate and ineffectual fire. As it was, a few passers-by did fall, wounded by balls from unknown sources.

Argensola would tear from street to street following the evolutions of the inimical bird, trying to guess where its projectiles would fall, anxious to be the first to reach the bombarded house, excited by the shots that were answering from below. And to think that he had no gun like those khaki-clad Englishmen or those Belgians in barrick cap, with tassel over the front! . . . Finally the taube tired of manoeuvering, would disappear. "Until to-morrow!" ejaculated the Spaniard. "Perhaps to-morrow's show may be even more interesting!"

He employed his free hours between his geographical observations and his aerial contemplations in making the rounds of the stations, watching the crowds of travellers making their escape from Paris. The sudden vision of the truth—after the illusion which the Government had been creating with its optimistic dispatches, the certainty that the Germans were actually near when a week before they had imagined them completely routed, the taubes flying over Paris, the mysterious threat of the Zeppelins—all these dangerous signs were filling a part of the community with frenzied desperation. The railroad stations, guarded by the soldiery, were only admitting those who had secured tickets in advance. Some had been waiting entire days for their turn to depart. The most impatient were starting to walk, eager to get outside of the city as soon as possible. The roads were black with the crowds all going in the same directions. Toward the South they were fleeing by automobile, in carriages, in gardeners' carts, on foot.

Argensola surveyed this hegira with serenity. He would remain because he had always admired those men who witnessed the Siege of Paris in 1870. Now it was going to be his good fortune to observe an historical drama, perhaps even more interesting. The wonders that he would be able to relate in the future! . . . But the distraction and indifference of his present audience were annoying him greatly. He would hasten back to the studio, in feverish excitement, to communicate the latest gratifying news to Desnoyers who would listen as though he did not hear him. The night that he informed him that the Government, the Chambers, the Diplomatic Corps, and even the actors of the Comedie Francaise were going that very hour on special trains for Bordeaux, his companion merely replied with a shrug of indifference.

Desnoyers was worrying about other things. That morning he had received a note from Marguerite—only two lines scrawled in great haste. She was leaving, starting immediately, accompanied by her mother. Adieu! . . . and nothing more. The panic had caused many love-affairs to be forgotten, had broken off long intimacies, but Marguerite's temperament was above such incoherencies from mere flight. Julio felt that her terseness was very ominous. Why not mention the place to which she was going? . . .

In the afternoon, he took a bold step which she had always forbidden. He went to her home and talked a long time with the concierge in order to get some news. The good woman was delighted to work off on him the loquacity so brusquely cut short by the flight of tenants and servants. The lady on the first floor (Marguerite's mother) had been the last to abandon the house in spite of the fact that she was really sick over her son's departure. They had left the day before without saying where they were going. The only thing that she knew was that they took the train in the Gare d'Orsay. They were going toward the South like all the rest of the rich.

And she supplemented her revelations with the vague news that the daughter had seemed very much upset by the information that she had received from the front. Someone in the family was wounded. Perhaps it was the brother, but she really didn't know. With so many surprises and strange things happening, it was difficult to keep track of everything. Her husband, too, was in the army and she had her own affairs to worry about.

"Where can she have gone?" Julio asked himself all day long. "Why does she wish to keep me in ignorance of her whereabouts?"

When his comrade told him that night about the transfer of the seat of government, with all the mystery of news not yet made public, Desnoyers merely replied:

"They are doing the best thing. . . . I, too, will go tomorrow if I can."

Why remain longer in Paris? His family was away. His father, according to Argensola's investigations, also had gone off without saying whither. Now Marguerite's mysterious flight was leaving him entirely alone, in a solitude that was filling him with remorse.

That afternoon, when strolling through the boulevards, he had stumbled across a friend considerably older than himself, an acquaintance in the fencing club which he used to frequent. This was the first time they had met since the beginning of the war, and they ran over the list of their companions in the army. Desnoyers' inquiries were answered by the older man. So-and-so? . . . He had been wounded in Lorraine and was now in a hospital in the South. Another friend? . . . Dead in the Vosges. Another? . . . Disappeared at Charleroi. And thus had continued the heroic and mournful roll-call. The others were still living, doing brave things. The members of foreign birth, young Poles, English residents in Paris and South Americans, had finally enlisted as volunteers. The club might well be proud of its young men who had practised arms in times of peace, for now they were all jeopardizing their existence at the front. Desnoyers turned his face away as though he feared to meet in the eyes of his friend, an ironical and questioning expression. Why had he not gone with the others to defend the land in which he was living? . . .

"To-morrow I will go," repeated Julio, depressed by this recollection.

But he went toward the South like all those who were fleeing from the war. The following morning Argensola was charged to get him a railroad ticket for Bordeaux. The value of money had greatly increased, but fifty francs, opportunely bestowed, wrought the miracle and procured a bit of numbered cardboard whose conquest represented many days of waiting.

"It is good only for to-day," said the Spaniard, "you will have to take the night train."

Packing was not a very serious matter, as the trains were refusing to admit anything more than hand-luggage. Argensola did not wish to accept the liberality of Julio who tried to leave all his money with him. Heroes need very little and the painter of souls was inspired with heroic resolution, The brief harangue of Gallieni in taking charge of the defense of Paris, he had adopted as his own. He intended to keep up his courage to the last, just like the hardy general.

"Let them come," he exclaimed with a tragic expression. "They will find me at my post!" . . .

His post was the studio from which he could witness the happenings which he proposed relating to coming generations. He would entrench himself there with the eatables and wines. Besides he had the plan—just as soon as his partner should disappear—of bringing to live there with him certain lady-friends who were wandering around in search of a problematical dinner, and feeling timid in the solitude of their own quarters. Danger often gathers congenial folk together and adds a new attractiveness to the pleasures of a community. The tender affections of the prisoners of the Terror, when they were expecting momentarily to be conducted to the guillotine, flashed through his mind. Let us drain Life's goblet at one draught since we have to die! . . . The studio of the rue de la Pompe was about to witness the mad and desperate revels of a castaway bark well-stocked with provisions.

Desnoyers left the Gare d'Orsay in a first-class compartment, mentally praising the good order with which the authorities had arranged everything, so that every traveller could have his own seat. At the Austerlitz station, however, a human avalanche assaulted the train. The doors were broken open, packages and children came in through the windows like projectiles. The people pushed with the unreason of a crowd fleeing before a fire. In the space reserved for eight persons, fourteen installed themselves; the passageways were heaped with mountains of bags and valises that served later travellers for seats. All class distinctions had disappeared. The villagers invaded by preference the best coaches, believing that they would there find more room. Those holding first-class tickets hunted up the plainer coaches in the vain hope of travelling without being crowded. On the cross roads were waiting from the day before long trains made up of cattle cars. All the stables on wheels were filled with people seated on the wooden floor or in chairs brought from their homes. Every train load was an encampment eager to take up its march; whenever it halted, layers of greasy papers, hulls and fruit skins collected along its entire length.

The invaders, pushing their way in, put up with many annoyances and pardoned one another in a brotherly way. "In war times, war measures," they would always say as a last excuse. And each one was pressing closer to his neighbor in order to make a few more inches of room, and helping to wedge his scanty baggage among the other bundles swaying most precariously above. Little by little, Desnoyers was losing all his advantage as a first comer. These poor people who had been waiting for the train from four in the morning till eight at night, awakened his pity. The women, groaning with weariness, were standing in the corridors, looking with ferocious envy at those who had seats. The children were bleating like hungry kids. Julio finally gave up his place, sharing with the needy and improvident the bountiful supply of eatables with which Argensola had provided him. The station restaurants had all been emptied of food.

During the train's long wait, soldiers only were seen on the platform, soldiers who were hastening at the call of the trumpet, to take their places again in the strings of cars which were constantly steaming toward Paris. At the signal stations, long war trains were waiting for the road to be clear that they might continue their journey. The cuirassiers, wearing a yellow vest over their steel breastplate, were seated with hanging legs in the doorways of the stable cars, from whose interior came repeated neighing. Upon the flat cars were rows of gun carriages. The slender throats of the cannon of '75 were pointed upwards like telescopes.

Young Desnoyers passed the night in the aisle, seated on a valise, noting the sodden sleep of those around him, worn out by weariness and exhaustion. It was a cruel and endless night of jerks, shrieks and stops punctuated by snores. At every station, the trumpets were sounding precipitously as though the enemy were right upon them. The soldiers from the South were hurrying to their posts, and at brief intervals another detachment of men was dragged along the rails toward Paris. They all appeared gay, and anxious to reach the scene of slaughter as soon as possible. Many were regretting the delays, fearing that they might arrive too late. Leaning out of the window, Julio heard the dialogues and shouts on the platforms impregnated with the acrid odor of men and mules. All were evincing an unquenchable confidence. "The Boches! very numerous, with huge cannons, with many mitrailleuse . . . but we only have to charge with our bayonets to make them run like rabbits!"

The attitude of those going to meet death was in sharp contrast to the panic and doubt of those who were deserting Paris. An old and much-decorated gentleman, type of a jubilee functionary, kept questioning Desnoyers whenever the train started on again—"Do you believe that they will get as far as Tours?" Before receiving his reply, he would fall asleep. Brutish sleep was marching down the aisles with leaden feet. At every junction, the old man would start up and suddenly ask, "Do you believe that we will get as far as Bordeaux?" . . . And his great desire not to halt until, with his family, he had reached an absolutely secure refuge, made him accept as oracles all the vague responses.

At daybreak, they saw the Territorialists guarding the roads. They were armed with old muskets, and were wearing the red kepis as their only military distinction. They were following the opposite course of the military trains.

In the station at Bordeaux, the civilian crowds struggling to get out or to enter other cars, were mingling with the troops. The trumpets were incessantly sounding their brazen notes, calling the soldiers together. Many were men of darkest coloring, natives with wide gray breeches and red caps above their black or bronzed faces.

Julio saw a train bearing wounded from the battles of Flanders and Lorraine. Their worn and dirty uniforms were enlivened by the whiteness of the bandages sustaining the wounded limbs or protecting the broken heads. All were trying to smile, although with livid mouths and feverish eyes, at their first glimpse of the land of the South as it emerged from the mist bathed in the sunlight, and covered with the regal vestures of its vineyards. The men from the North stretched out their hands for the fruit that the women were offering them, tasting with delight the sweet grapes of the country.

For four days the distracted lover lived in Bordeaux, stunned and bewildered by the agitation of a provincial city suddenly converted into a capital. The hotels were overcrowded, many notables contenting themselves with servants' quarters.

There was not a vacant seat in the cafes; the sidewalks could not accommodate the extraordinary assemblage. The President was installed in the Prefecture; the State Departments were established in the schools and museums; two theatres were fitted up for the future reunions of the Senate and the Chamber of Deputies. Julio was lodged in a filthy, disreputable hotel at the end of a foul-smelling alley. A little Cupid adorned the crystals of the door, and the looking-glass in his room was scratched with names and unspeakable phrases—souvenirs of the occupants of an hour . . . and yet many grand ladies, hunting in vain for temporary residence, would have envied him his good fortune.

All his investigations proved fruitless. The friends whom he encountered in the fugitive crowd were thinking only of their own affairs. They could talk of nothing but incidents of the installation, repeating the news gathered from the ministers with whom they were living on familiar terms, or mentioning with a mysterious air, the great battle which was going on stretching from the vicinity of Paris to Verdun. A pupil of his days of glory, whose former elegance was now attired in the uniform of a nurse, gave him some vague information. "The little Madame Laurier? . . . I remember hearing that she was living somewhere near here. . . . Perhaps in Biarritz." Julio needed no more than this to continue his journey. To Biarritz!

The first person that he encountered on his arrival was Chichi. She declared that the town was impossible because of the families of rich Spaniards who were summering there. "The Boches are in the majority, and I pass a miserable existence quarrelling with them. . . . I shall finally have to live alone." Then he met his mother—embraces and tears. Afterwards he saw his Aunt Elena in the hotel parlors, most enthusiastic over the country and the summer colony.

She could talk at great length with many of them about the decadence of France. They were all expecting to receive the news from one moment to another, that the Kaiser had entered the Capital. Ponderous men who had never done anything in all their lives, were criticizing the defects and indolence of the Republic. Young men whose aristocracy aroused Dona Elena's enthusiasm, broke forth into apostrophes against the corruption of Paris, corruption that they had studied thoroughly, from sunset to sunrise, in the virtuous schools of Montmartre. They all adored Germany where they had never been, or which they knew only through the reels of the moving picture films. They criticized events as though they were witnessing a bull fight. "The Germans have the snap! You can't fool with them! They are fine brutes!" And they appeared to admire this inhumanity as the most admirable characteristic. "Why will they not say that in their own home on the other side of the frontier?" Chichi would protest. "Why do they come into their neighbor's country to ridicule his troubles? . . . Possibly they consider it a sign of their wonderful good-breeding!"

But Julio had not gone to Biarritz to live with his family. . . . The very day of his arrival, he saw Marguerite's mother in the distance. She was alone. His inquiries developed the information that her daughter was living in Pau. She was a trained nurse taking care of a wounded member of the family. "Her brother . .

. undoubtedly it is her brother," thought Julio. And he again continued his trip, this time going to Pau.

His visits to the hospitals there were also unavailing. Nobody seemed to know Marguerite. Every day a train was arriving with a new load of bleeding flesh, but her brother was not among the wounded. A Sister of Charity, believing that he was in search of someone of his family, took pity on him and gave him some helpful directions. He ought to go to Lourdes; there were many of the wounded there and many of the military nurses. So Desnoyers immediately took the short cut between Pau and Lourdes.

He had never visited the sacred city whose name was so frequently on his mother's lips. For Dona Luisa, the French nation was Lourdes. In her discussions with her sister and other foreign ladies who were praying that France might be exterminated for its impiety, the good senora always summed up her opinions in the same words:—"When the Virgin wished to make her appearance in our day, she chose France. This country, therefore, cannot be as bad as you say. . . . When I see that she appears in Berlin, we will then re-discuss the matter."

But Desnoyers was not there to confirm his mother's artless opinions. Just as soon as he had found a room in a hotel near the river, he had hastened to the big hostelry, now converted into a hospital. The guard told him that he could not speak to the Director until the afternoon. In order to curb his impatience he walked through the street leading to the basilica, past all the booths and shops with pictures and pious souvenirs which have converted the place into a big bazaar. Here and in the gardens adjoining the church, he saw wounded convalescents with uniforms stained with traces of the combat. Their cloaks were greatly soiled in spite of repeated brushings. The mud, the blood and the rain had left indelible spots and made them as stiff as cardboard. Some of the wounded had cut their sleeves in order to avoid the cruel friction on their shattered arms, others still showed on their trousers the rents made by the devastating shells.

They were fighters of all ranks and of many races—infantry, cavalry, artillerymen; soldiers from the metropolis and from the colonies; French farmers and African sharpshooters; red heads, faces of Mohammedan olive and the black countenances of the Sengalese, with eyes of fire, and thick, bluish blubber lips; some showing the good-nature and sedentary obesity of the middle-class man suddenly converted into a warrior; others sinewy, alert, with the aggressive profile of men born to fight, and experienced in foreign fields.

The city, formerly visited by the hopeful, Catholic sick, was now invaded by a crowd no less dolorous but clad in carnival colors. All, in spite of their physical distress, had a certain air of good cheer and satisfaction. They had seen Death very near, slipping out from his bony claws into a new joy and zest in life. With their cloaks adorned with medals, their theatrical Moorish garments, their kepis and their African headdresses, this heroic band presented, nevertheless, a lamentable aspect.

Very few still preserved the noble vertical carriage, the pride of the superior human being. They were walking along bent almost double, limping, dragging themselves forward by the help of a staff or friendly arm. Others had to let themselves be pushed along, stretched out on the hand-carts which had so often conducted the devout sick from the station to the Grotto of the Virgin. Some were feeling their way along, blindly, leaning on a child or nurse. The first encounters in Belgium and in the East, a mere half-dozen battles, had been enough to produce these physical wrecks still showing a manly nobility in spite of the most horrible outrages. These organisms, struggling so tenaciously to regain their hold on life, bringing their reviving energies out into the sunlight, represented but the most minute part of the number mowed down by the scythe of Death. Back of them were thousands and thousands of comrades groaning on hospital beds from which they would probably never rise. Thousands and thousands were hidden forever in the bosom of the Earth moistened by their death agony—fatal land which, upon receiving a hail of projectiles, brought forth a harvest of bristling crosses!

War now showed itself to Desnoyers with all its cruel hideousness. He had been accustomed to speak of it heretofore as those in robust health speak of death, knowing that it exists and is horrible, but seeing it afar off . . . so far off that it arouses no real emotion. The explosion of the shells were accompanying their destructive brutality with a ferocious mockery, grotesquely disfiguring the human body. He saw wounded objects just beginning to recover their vital force who were but rough skeletons of men, frightful caricatures, human rags, saved from the tomb by the audacities of science—trunks with heads which were dragged along on wheeled platforms; fragments of skulls whose brains were throbbing under an artificial cap; beings without arms and without legs, resting in the bottom of little wagons, like bits of plaster models or scraps from the dissecting room; faces without noses that looked like skulls with great, black nasal openings. And these half-men were talking, smoking, laughing, satisfied to see the sky, to feel the caress of the sun, to have come back to life, dominated by that sovereign desire to live which trustingly forgets present misery in the confident hope of something better.

So strongly was Julio impressed that for a little while he forgot the purpose which had brought him thither. . . . If those who provoke war from diplomatic chambers or from the tables of the Military Staff could but see it—not in the field of battle fired with the enthusiasm which prejudices judgments—but in cold blood, as it is seen in the hospitals and cemeteries, in the wrecks left in its trail! . . .

To Julio's imagination this terrestrial globe appeared like an enormous ship sailing through infinity. Its crews—poor humanity—had spent century after century in exterminating each other on the deck. They did not even know what existed under their feet, in the hold of the vessel. To occupy the same portion of the surface in the sunlight seemed to be the ruling desire of each group. Men, considered superior human beings, were pushing these masses to extermination in order to scale the last bridge and hold the helm, controlling the course of the boat. And all those who felt the overmastering ambition for absolute command knew the same thing . . . nothing. Not one of them could say with certainty what lay beyond the visible horizon, nor whither the ship was drifting. The sullen hostility of mystery surrounded them all; their life was precarious, necessitating incessant care in order to maintain it, yet in spite of that, the crew for ages and ages, had never known an instant of agreement, of team work, of clear reason. Periodically half of them would clash with the other half. They killed each other that they might enslave the vanquished on the rolling deck floating over the abyss; they fought that they might cast their victims from the vessel, filling its wake with cadavers. And from the demented throng there were still springing up gloomy sophistries to prove that a state of war was the perfect state, that it ought to go on forever, that it was a bad dream on the part of the crew to wish to regard each other as brothers with a common destiny, enveloped in the same unsteady environment of mystery. . . . Ah, human misery!

Julio was drawn out of these pessimistic reflections by the childish glee which many of the convalescents were evincing. Some were Mussulmans, sharpshooters from Algeria and Morocco. In Lourdes, as they might be anywhere, they were interested only in the gifts which the people were showering upon them with patriotic affection. They all surveyed with indifference the basilica inhabited by "the white lady," their only preoccupation being to beg for cigars and sweets.

Finding themselves regaled by the dominant race, they became greatly puffed up, daring everything like mischievous children. What pleased them most was the fact that the ladies would take them by the hand. Blessed war that permitted them to approach and touch these white women, perfumed and smiling as they appeared in their dreams of the paradise of the blest! "Lady . . . Lady," they would sigh, looking at them with dark, sparkling eyes. And not content with the hand, their dark paws would venture the length of the entire arm while the ladies laughed at this tremulous adoration. Others would go through the crowds, offering their right hand to all the women. "We touch hands." . . . And then they would go away satisfied after receiving the hand clasp.

Desnoyers wandered a long time around the basilica where, in the shadow of the trees, were long rows of wheeled chairs occupied by the wounded. Officers and soldiers rested many hours in the blue shade, watching their comrades who were able to use their legs. The sacred grotto was resplendent with the lights from hundreds of candles. Devout crowds were kneeling in the open air, fixing their eyes in supplication on the sacred stones whilst their thoughts were flying far away to the fields of battle, making their petitions with that confidence in divinity which accompanies every distress. Among the kneeling mass were many soldiers with bandaged heads, kepis in hand and tearful eyes.

Up and down the double staircase of the basilica were flitting women, clad in white, with spotless headdresses that fluttered in such a way that they appeared like flying doves. These were the nurses and Sisters of Charity guiding the steps of the injured. Desnoyers thought he recognized Marguerite in every one of them, but the prompt disillusion following each of these discoveries soon made him doubtful about the outcome of his journey. She was not in Lourdes, either. He would never find her in that France so immeasurably expanded by the war that it had converted every town into a hospital.

His afternoon explorations were no more successful. The employees listened to his interrogations with a distraught air. He could come back again; just now they were taken up with the announcement that another hospital train was on the way. The great battle was still going on near Paris. They had to improvise lodgings for the new consignment of mutilated humanity. In order to pass away the time until his return, Desnoyers went back to the garden near the grotto. He was planning to return to Pau that night; there was evidently nothing more to do at Lourdes. In what direction should he now continue his search?

Suddenly he felt a thrill down his back—the same indefinable sensation which used to warn him of her presence when they were meeting in the gardens of Paris. Marguerite was going to present herself unexpectedly as in the old days without his knowing from exactly what spot—as though she came up out of the earth or descended from the clouds.

After a second's thought he smiled bitterly. Mere tricks of his desire! Illusions! . . . Upon turning his head he recognized the falsity of his hope. Nobody was following his footsteps; he was the only being going down the center of the avenue. Near him, in the diaphanous white of a guardian angel, was a nurse. Poor blind man! . . . Desnoyers was passing on when a quick movement on the part of the white-clad woman, an evident desire to escape notice, to hide her face by looking at the plants, attracted his attention. He was slow in recognizing her. Two little ringlets escaping from the band of her cap made him guess the hidden head of hair; the feet shod in white were the signs which enabled him to reconstruct the person somewhat disfigured by the severe uniform. Her face was pale and sad. There wasn't a trace left in it of the old vanities that used to give it its childish, doll-like beauty. In the depths of those great, dark-circled eyes life seemed to be reflected in new forms. . . . Marguerite!

They stared at one another for a long while, as though hypnotized with surprise. She looked alarmed when Desnoyers advanced a step toward her. No . . . No! Her eyes, her hands, her entire body seemed to protest, to repel his approach, to hold him motionless. Fear that he might come near her, made her go toward him. She said a few words to the soldier who remained on the bench, receiving across the bandage on his face a ray of sunlight which he did not appear to feel. Then she rose, going to meet Julio, and continued forward, indicating by a gesture that they must find some place further on where the wounded man could not hear them.

She led the way to a side path from which she could see the blind man confided to her care. They stood motionless, face to face. Desnoyers wished to say many things; many . . . but he hesitated, not knowing how to frame his complaints, his pleadings, his endearments. Far above all these thoughts towered one, fatal, dominant and wrathful.

"Who is that man?"

The spiteful accent, the harsh voice with which he said these words surprised him as though they came from someone else's mouth.

The nurse looked at him with her great limpid eyes, eyes that seemed forever freed from contractions of surprise or fear. Her response slipped from her with equal directness.

"It is Laurier. . . . It is my husband."

Laurier! . . . Julio looked doubtfully and for a long time at the soldier before he could be convinced. That blind officer motionless on the bench, that figure of heroic grief, was Laurier! . . . At first glance, he appeared prematurely old with roughened and bronzed skin so furrowed with lines that they converged like rays around all the openings of his face. His hair was beginning to whiten on the temples and in the beard which covered his cheeks. He had lived twenty years in that one month. . . . At the same time he appeared younger, with a youthfulness that was radiating an inward vigor, with the strength of a soul which has suffered the most violent emotions and, firm and serene in the satisfaction of duty fulfilled, can no longer know fear.

As Desnoyers contemplated him, he felt both admiration and jealousy. He was ashamed to admit the aversion inspired by the wounded man, so sorely wounded that he was unable to see what was going on around him. His hatred was a form of cowardice, terrifying in its persistence. How pensive were Marguerite's eyes if she took them off her patient for a few seconds! . . . She had never looked at him in that way. He knew all the amorous gradations of her glance, but her fixed gaze at this injured man was something entirely different, something that he had never seen before.

He spoke with the fury of a lover who discovers an infidelity.

"And for this thing you have run away without warning, without a word! . . . You have abandoned me in order to go in search of him. . . . Tell me, why did you come? . . . Why did you come?". . .

"I came because it was my duty."

Then she spoke like a mother who takes advantage of a parenthesis of surprise in an irascible child's temper, in order to counsel self-control, and explained how it had all happened. She had received the news of Laurier's wounding just as she and her mother were preparing to leave Paris. She had not hesitated an instant; her duty was to hasten to the aid of this man. She had been doing a great deal of thinking in the last few weeks; the war had made her ponder much on the values in life. Her eyes had been getting glimpses of new horizons; our destiny is not mere pleasure and selfish satisfaction; we ought to take our part in pain and sacrifice.

She had wanted to work for her country, to share the general stress, to serve as other women did; and since she was disposed to devote herself to strangers, was it not natural that she should prefer to help this man whom she had so greatly wronged? . . . There still lived in her memory the moment in which she had seen him approach the station, completely alone among so many who had the consolation of loving arms when departing in search of death. Her pity had become still more acute on hearing of his misfortune. A shell had exploded near him, killing all those around him. Of his many wounds, the only serious one was that on his face. He had completely lost the sight of one eye; and the doctors were keeping the other bound up hoping to save it. But she was very doubtful about it; she was almost sure that Laurier would be blind.

Marguerite's voice trembled when saying this as if she were going to cry, although her eyes were tearless. They did not now feel the irresistible necessity for tears. Weeping had become something superfluous, like many other luxuries of peaceful days. Her eyes had seen so much in so few days! . . .

"How you love him!" exclaimed Julio.

Fearing that they might be overheard and in order to keep him at a distance, she had been speaking as though to a friend. But her lover's sadness broke down her reserve.

"No, I love you. . . . I shall always love you."

The simplicity with which she said this and her sudden tenderness of tone revived Desnoyers' hopes.

"And the other one?" he asked anxiously.

Upon receiving her reply, it seemed to him as though something had just passed across the sun, veiling its light temporarily. It was as though a cloud had drifted over the land and over his thoughts, enveloping them in an unbearable chill.

"I love him, too."

She said it with a look that seemed to implore pardon, with the sad sincerity of one who has given up lying and weeps in foreseeing the injury that the truth must inflict.

He felt his hard wrath suddenly dwindling like a crumbling mountain. Ah, Marguerite! His voice was tremulous and despairing. Could it be possible that everything between these two was going to end thus simply? Were her former vows mere lies? . . . They had been attracted to each other by an irresistible affinity in order to be together forever, to be one. . . . And now, suddenly hardened by indifference, were they to drift apart like two unfriendly bodies? . . . What did this absurdity about loving him at the same time that she loved her former husband mean, anyway?

Marguerite hung her head, murmuring desperately:

"You are a man, I am a woman. You would never understand me, no matter what I might say. Men are not able to comprehend certain of our mysteries. . . . A woman would be better able to appreciate the complexity."

Desnoyers felt that he must know his fate in all its cruelty. She might speak without fear. He felt strong enough to bear the blow. . . . What had Laurier said when he found that he was being so tenderly cared for by Marguerite? . . .

"He does not know who I am. . . . He believes me to be a war-nurse, like the rest, who pities him seeing him alone and blind with no relatives to write to him or visit him. . . . At certain times, I have almost suspected that he guesses the truth. My voice, the touch of my hands made him shiver at first, as though with an unpleasant sensation. I have told him that I am a Belgian lady who has lost her loved ones and is alone in the world. He has told me his life story very sketchily, as if he desired to forget a hated past. . . . Never one disagreeable word about his former wife. There are nights when I think that he knows me, that he takes advantage of his blindness in order to prolong his feigned ignorance, and that distresses me. I long for him to recover his sight, for the doctors to save that doubtful eye—and yet at the same time, I feel afraid. What will he say when he recognizes me? . . . But no; it is better that he should see, no matter what may result. You cannot understand my anxiety, you cannot know what I am suffering."

She was silent for an instant, trying to regain her self-control, again tortured with the agony of her soul.

"Oh, the war!" she resumed. "What changes in our life! Two months ago, my present situation would have appeared impossible, unimaginable. . . . I caring for my husband, fearing that he would discover my identity and leave me, yet at the same time, wishing that he would recognize me and pardon me. . . . It is only one week that I have been with him. I disguise my voice when I can, and avoid words that may reveal the truth . . . but this cannot keep up much longer. It is only in novels that such painful situations turn out happily."

Doubt suddenly overwhelmed her.

"I believe," she continued, "that he has recognized me from the first. . . . He is silent and feigns ignorance because he despises me . . . because he can never bring himself to pardon me. I have been so bad! . . . I have wronged him so!". . .

She was recalling the long and reflective silences of the wounded man after she had dropped some imprudent words. After two days of submission to her care, he had been somewhat rebellious, avoiding going out with her for a walk. Because of his blind helplessness, and comprehending the uselessness of his resistance, he had finally yielded in passive silence.

"Let him think what he will!" concluded Marguerite courageously. "Let him despise me! I am here where I ought to be. I need his forgiveness, but if he does not pardon me, I shall stay with him just the same. . . . There are moments when I wish that he may never recover his sight, so that he may always need me, so that I may pass my life at his side, sacrificing everything for him."

"And I?" said Desnoyers.

Marguerite looked at him with clouded eyes as though she were just awaking. It was true—and the other one? . . . Kindled by the proposed sacrifice which was to be her expiation, she had forgotten the man before her.

"You!" she said after a long pause. "You must leave me. . . . Life is not what we have thought it. Had it not been for the war, we might, perhaps, have realized our dream, but now! . . . Listen carefully and try to understand. For the remainder of my life, I shall carry the heaviest burden, and yet at the same time it will be sweet, since the more it weighs me down the greater will my atonement be. Never will I leave this man whom I have so grievously wronged, now that he is more alone in the world and will need protection like a child. Why do you come to share my fate? How could it be possible for you to live with a nurse constantly at the side of a blind and worthy man whom we would constantly offend with our passion? . . . No, it is better for us to part. Go your way, alone and untrammelled. Leave me; you will meet other women who will make you more happy than I. Yours is the temperament that finds new pleasures at every step."

She stood firmly to her decision. Her voice was calm, but back of it trembled the emotion of a last farewell to a joy which was going from her forever. The man would be loved by others . . . and she was giving him up! . . . But the noble sadness of the sacrifice restored her courage. Only by this renunciation could she expiate her sins.

Julio dropped his eyes, vanquished and perplexed. The picture of the future outlined by Marguerite terrified him. To live with her as a nurse taking advantage of her patient's blindness would be to offer him fresh insult every day. . . . Ah, no! That would be villainy, indeed! He was now ashamed to recall the malignity with which, a little while before, he had regarded this innocent unfortunate. He realized that he was powerless to contend with him. Weak and helpless as he was sitting there on the garden bench, he was stronger and more deserving of respect than Julio Desnoyers with all his youth and elegance. The victim had amounted to something in his life; he had done what Julio had not dared to do.

This sudden conviction of his inferiority made him cry out like an abandoned child, "What will become of me?" . . .

Marguerite, too—contemplating the love which was going from her forever, her vanished hopes, the future illumined by the satisfaction of duty fulfilled but monotonous and painful—cried out:

"And I. . . . What will become of me?" . . .

As though he had suddenly found a solution which was reviving his courage, Desnoyers said:

"Listen, Marguerite: I can read your soul. You love this man, and you do well. He is superior to me, and women are always attracted by superiority. . . . I am a coward. Yes, do not protest, I am a coward with all my youth, with all my strength. Why should you not have been impressed by the conduct of this man! . . . But I will atone for past wrongs. This country is yours, Marguerite; I will fight for it. Do not say no. . . ."

And moved by his hasty heroism, he outlined the plan more definitely. He was going to be a soldier. Soon she would hear him well spoken of. His idea was either to be stretched on the battlefield in his first encounter, or to astound the world by his bravery. In this way the impossible situation would settle itself— either the oblivion of death or glory.

"No, no!" interrupted Marguerite in an anguished tone. "You, no! One is enough. . . . How horrible! You, too, wounded, mutilated forever, perhaps dead! . . . No, you must live. I want you to live, even though you might belong to another. . . . Let me know that you exist, let me see you sometimes, even though you may have forgotten me, even though you may pass me with indifference, as if you did not know me."

In this outburst her deep love for him rang true—her heroic and inflexible love which would accept all penalties for herself, if only the beloved one might continue to live.

But then, in order that Julio might not feel any false hopes, she added:—"Live; you must not die; that would be for me another torment. . . . But live without me. No matter how much we may talk about it, my destiny beside the other one is marked out forever."

"Ah, how you love him! . . . How you have deceived me!"

In a last desperate attempt at explanation she again repeated what she had said at the beginning of their interview. She loved Julio . . . and she loved her husband. They were different kinds of love. She could not say which was the stronger, but misfortune was forcing her to choose between the two, and she was accepting the most difficult, the one demanding the greatest sacrifices.

"You are a man, and you will never be able to understand me. . . . A woman would comprehend me."

It seemed to Julio, as he looked around him, as though the afternoon were undergoing some celestial phenomenon. The garden was still illuminated by the sun, but the green of the trees, the yellow of the ground, the blue of the sky, all appeared to him as dark and shadowy as though a rain of ashes were falling.

"Then . . . all is over between us?"

His pleading, trembling voice charged with tears made her turn her head to hide her emotion. Then in the painful silence the two despairs formed one and the same question, as if interrogating the shades of the future: "What will become of me?" murmured the man. And like an echo her lips repeated, "What will become of me?"

All had been said. Hopeless words came between the two like an obstacle momentarily increasing in size, impelling them in opposite directions. Why prolong the painful interview? . . . Marguerite showed the ready and energetic decision of a woman who wishes to bring a scene to a close. "Good-bye!" Her face had assumed a yellowish cast, her pupils had become dull and clouded like the glass of a lantern when the light dies out. "Good-bye!" She must go to her patient.

She went away without looking at him, and Desnoyers instinctively went in the opposite direction. As he became more self-controlled and turned to look at her again, he saw her moving on and giving her arm to the blind man, without once turning her head.

He now felt convinced that he should never see her again, and became oppressed by an almost suffocating agony. And could two beings, who had formerly considered the universe concentrated in their persons, thus easily be separated forever? . . .

His desperation at finding himself alone made him accuse himself of stupidity. Now his thoughts came tumbling over each other in a tumultuous throng, and each one of them seemed to him sufficient to have convinced Marguerite. He certainly had not known how to express himself. He would have to talk with her again . . . and he decided to remain in Lourdes.

He passed a night of torture in the hotel, listening to the ripple of the river among its stones. Insomnia had him in his fierce jaws, gnawing him with interminable agony. He turned on the light several times, but was not able to read. His eyes looked with stupid fixity at the patterns of the wall paper and the pious pictures around the room which had evidently served as the lodging place of some rich traveller. He remained motionless and as abstracted as an Oriental who thinks himself into an absolute lack of thought. One idea only was dancing in the vacuum in his skull—"I shall never see her again. . . . Can such a thing be possible?"

He drowsed for a few seconds, only to be awakened with the sensation that some horrible explosion was sending him through the air. And so, with sweats of anguish, he wakefully passed the hours until in the gloom of his room the dawn showed a milky rectangle of light, and began to be reflected on the window curtains.

The velvet-like caress of day finally closed his eyes. Upon awaking he found that the morning was well advanced, and he hurried to the garden of the grotto. . . . Oh, the hours of tremulous and unavailing waiting, believing that he recognized Marguerite in every white-clad lady that came along, guiding a wounded patient!

By afternoon, after a lunch whose dishes filed past him untouched, he returned to the garden in search of her. Beholding her in the distance with the blind man leaning on her arm, a feeling of faintness came over him. She looked to him taller, thinner, her face sharper, with two dark hollows in her cheeks and her eyes bright with fever, the lids drawn with weariness. He suspected that she, too, had passed an anguished night of tenacious, self-centred thought, of grievous stupefaction like his own, in the room of her hotel. Suddenly he felt all the weight of insomnia and listlessness, all the depressing emotion of the cruel sensations experienced in the last few hours. Oh, how miserable they both were! . . .

She was walking warily, looking from one side to the other, as though foreseeing danger. Upon discovering him she clung to her charge, casting upon her former lover a look of entreaty, of desperation, imploring pity. . . Ay, that look!

He felt ashamed of himself; his personality appeared to be unrolling itself before him, and he surveyed himself with the eyes of a judge. What was this seduced and useless man, called Julio Desnoyers, doing there, tormenting with his presence a poor woman, trying to turn her from her righteous repentance, insisting on his selfish and petty desires when all humanity was thinking of other things? . . . His cowardice angered him. Like a thief taking advantage of the sleep of his victim, he was stalking around this brave and true man who could not see him, who could not defend himself, in order to rob him of the only affection that he had in the world which had so miraculously returned to him! Very well, Gentleman Desnoyers! . . . Ah, what a scoundrel he was!

Such subconscious insults made him draw himself erect, in haughty, cruel and inexorable defiance against that other I who so richly deserved the judge's scorn.

He turned his head away; he could not meet Marguerite's piteous eyes; he feared their mute reproach. Neither did he dare to look at the blind man in his shabby and heroic uniform, with his countenance aged by duty and glory. He feared him like remorse.

So the vanquished lover turned his back on the two and went away with a firm step. Good-bye, Love! Goodbye, Happiness! . . . He marched quickly and bravely on; a miracle had just taken place within him! he had found the right road at last!

To Paris! . . . A new impetus was going to fill the vacuum of his objectless existence.

CHAPTER V

THE INVASION

Don Marcelo was fleeing to take refuge in his castle when he met the mayor of Villeblanche. The noise of the firing had made him hurry to the barricade. When he learned of the apparition of the group of stragglers he threw up his hands in despair. They were crazy. Their resistance was going to be fatal for the village, and he ran on to beg them to cease.

For some time nothing happened to disturb the morning calm. Desnoyers had climbed to the top of his towers and was surveying the country with his field glasses. He couldn't make out the highway through the nearest group of trees, but he suspected that underneath their branches great activity was going on—masses of men on guard, troops preparing for the attack. The unexpected defense of the fugitives had upset the advance of the invasion. Desnoyers thought despairingly of that handful of mad fellows and their stubborn chief. What was their fate going to be? . . .

Focussing his glasses on the village, he saw the red spots of kepis waving like poppies over the green of the meadows. They were the retreating men, now convinced of the uselessness of their resistance. Perhaps they had found a ford or forgotten boat by which they might cross the Maine, and so were continuing their retreat toward the river. At any minute now the Germans were going to enter Villeblanche.

Half an hour of profound silence passed by. The village lay silhouetted against a background of hills—a mass of roofs beneath the church tower finished with its cross and iron weather cock. Everything seemed as tranquil as in the best days of peace. Suddenly he noticed that the grove was vomiting forth something noisy and penetrating—a bubble of vapor accompanied by a deafening report. Something was hurtling through the air with a strident curve. Then a roof in the village opened like a crater, vomiting forth flying wood, fragments of plaster and broken furniture. All the interior of the house seemed to be escaping in a stream of smoke, dirt and splinters.

The invaders were bombarding Villeblanche before attempting attack, as though fearing to encounter persistent resistance in its streets. More projectiles fell. Some passed over the houses, exploding between the hamlet and the castle. The towers of the Desnoyers property were beginning to attract the aim of the artillerymen. The owner was therefore about to abandon his dangerous observatory when he saw something white like a tablecloth or sheet floating from the church tower. His neighbors had hoisted this signal of peace in order to avoid bombardment. A few more missiles fell and then there was silence.

When Don Marcelo reached his park he found the Warden burying at the foot of a tree the sporting rifles still remaining in his castle. Then he went toward the great iron gates. The enemies were going to come, and he had to receive them. While uneasily awaiting their arrival his compunctions again tormented him. What was he doing there? Why had he remained? . . . But his obstinate temperament immediately put aside the promptings of fear. He was there because he had to guard his own. Besides, it was too late now to think about such things.

Suddenly the morning stillness was broken by a sound like the deafening tearing of strong cloth. "Shots, Master," said the Warden. "Firing! It must be in the square."

A few minutes after they saw running toward them a woman from the village, an old soul, dried up and darkened by age, who was panting from her great exertion, and looking wildly around her. She was fleeing blindly, trying to escape from danger and shut out horrible visions. Desnoyers and the Keeper's family listened to her explanations interrupted with hiccoughs of terror.

The Germans were in Villeblanche. They had entered first in an automobile driven at full speed from one end of the village to the other. Its mitrailleuse was firing at random against closed houses and open doors, knocking down all the people in sight. The old woman flung up her arms with a gesture of terror. . . . Dead . . . many dead . . . wounded . . . blood! Then other iron-plated vehicles had stopped in the square, and behind them cavalrymen, battalions of infantry, many battalions coming from everywhere. The helmeted men seemed furious; they accused the villagers of having fired at them. In the square they had struck the mayor and villagers who had come forward to meet them. The priest, bending over some of the dying, had also been trodden under foot. . . . All prisoners! The Germans were talking of shooting them.

The old dame's words were cut short by the rumble of approaching automobiles.

"Open the gates," commanded the owner to the Warden. The massive iron grill work swung open, and was never again closed. All property rights were at an end.

An enormous automobile, covered with dust and filled with men, stopped at the entrance. Behind them sounded the horns of other vehicles that were putting on the brakes. Desnoyers saw soldiers leaping out, all wearing the greenish-gray uniform with a sheath of the same tone covering the pointed casque. The one who marched at their head put his revolver to the millionaire's forehead.

"Where are the sharpshooters?" he asked.

He was pale with the pallor of wrath, vengeance and fear. His face was trembling under the influence of his triple emotion. Don Marcelo explained slowly, contemplating at a short distance from his eyes the black circle of the threatening tube. He had not seen any sharpshooters. The only inhabitants of the castle were the Warden with his family and himself, the owner of the castle.

The officer surveyed the edifice and then examined Desnoyers with evident astonishment as though he thought his appearance too unpretentious for a proprietor. He had taken him for a simple employee, and his respect for social rank made him lower his revolver.

He did not, however, alter his haughty attitude. He pressed Don Marcelo into the service as a guide, making him search ahead of him while forty soldiers grouped themselves at his back. They advanced in two files to the shelter of the trees which bordered the central avenue, with their guns ready to shoot, and looking uneasily at the castle windows as though expecting to receive from them hidden shots. Desnoyers marched tranquilly through the centre, and the official, who had been imitating the precautions of his men, finally joined him when he was crossing the drawbridge.

The armed men scattered through the rooms in search of the enemy. They ran their bayonets through beds and divans. Some, with automatic destructiveness, slit the draperies and the rich bed coverings. The owner protested; what was the sense in such useless destruction? . . . He was suffering unbearable torture at seeing the enormous boots spotting the rugs with mud, on hearing the clash of guns and knapsacks against the most fragile, choicest pieces of furniture. Poor historic mansion! . . .

The officer looked amazed that he should protest for such trifling cause, but he gave orders in German and his men ceased their rude explorations. Then, in justification of this extraordinary respect, he added in French:

"I believe that you are going to have the honor of entertaining here the general of our division."

The certainty that the castle did not hold any hidden enemies made him more amiable. He, nevertheless, persisted in his wrath against the sharpshooters. A group of the villagers had opened fire upon the Uhlans when they were entering unsuspiciously after the retreat of the French.

Desnoyers felt it necessary to protest. They were neither inhabitants nor sharpshooters; they were French soldiers. He took good care to be silent about their presence at the barricade, but he insisted that he had distinguished their uniforms from a tower of the castle.

The official made a threatening face.

"You, too? . . . You, who appear a reasonable man, can repeat such yarns as these?" And in order to close the conversation, he said, arrogantly: "They were wearing uniforms, then, if you persist in saying so, but they were sharpshooters just the same. The French Government has distributed arms and uniforms among the farmers that they may assassinate us. . . . Belgium did the same thing. . . . But we know their tricks, and we know how to punish them, too!"

The village was going to be burned. It was necessary to avenge the four German dead lying on the outskirts of Villeblanche, near the barricade. The mayor, the priest, the principal inhabitants would all be shot.

By the time they reached the top floor Desnoyers could see floating above the boughs of his park dark clouds whose outlines were reddened by the sun. The top of the bell tower was the only thing that he could distinguish at that distance. Around the iron weathercock were flying long thin fringes like black cobwebs lifted by the breeze. An odor of burning wood came toward the castle.

The German greeted this spectacle with a cruel smile. Then on descending to the park, he ordered Desnoyers to follow him. His liberty and his dignity had come to an end. Henceforth he was going to be an underling at the beck and call of these men who would dispose of him as their whims directed. Ay, why had he remained? . . . He obeyed, climbing into an automobile beside the officer, who was still carrying his revolver in his right hand. His men distributed themselves through the castle and outbuildings, in order to prevent the flight of an imaginary enemy. The Warden and his family seemed to be saying good-bye to him with their eyes. Perhaps they were taking him to his death. . . .

Beyond the castle woods a new world was coming into existence. The short cut to Villeblanche seemed to Desnoyers a leap of millions of leagues, a fall into a red planet where men and things were covered with the film of smoke and the glare of fire. He saw the village under a dark canopy spotted with sparks and glowing embers. The bell tower was burning like an enormous torch; the roof of the church was breaking into flames with a crashing fury. The glare of the holocaust seemed to shrivel and grow pale in the impassive light of the sun.

Running across the fields with the haste of desperation were shrieking women and children. The animals had escaped from the stables, and driven forth by the flames were racing wildly across the country. The cow and the work horse were dragging their halters broken by their flight. Their flanks were smoking and smelt of burnt hair. The pigs, the sheep and the chickens were all tearing along mingled with the cats and the dogs. All the domestic animals were returning to a brute existence, fleeing from civilized man. Shots were heard and hellish ha-ha's. The soldiers outside of the village were making themselves merry in this hunt for fugitives. Their guns were aimed at beasts and were hitting people.

Desnoyers saw men, many men, men everywhere. They were like gray ants, marching in endless files towards the South, coming out from the woods, filling the roads, crossing the fields. The green of vegetation was disappearing under their tread; the dust was rising in spirals behind the dull roll of the cannons and the measured trot of thousands of horses. On the roadside several battalions had halted, with their accompaniment of vehicles and draw horses. They were resting before renewing their march. He knew this army. He had seen it in Berlin on parade, and yet it seemed to have changed its former appearance. There now remained very little of the heavy and imposing glitter, of the mute and vainglorious haughtiness which had made his relatives-in-law weep with admiration. War, with its realism, had wiped out all that was theatrical about this formidable organization of death. The soldiers appeared dirty and tired, out. The respiration of fat and sweaty bodies, mixed with the strong smell of leather, floated over the regiments. All the men had hungry faces.

For days and nights they had been following the heels of an enemy which was always just eluding their grasp. In this forced advance the provisions of the administration would often arrive so late at the cantonments that they could depend only on what they happened to have in their knapsacks. Desnoyers saw them lined up near the road devouring hunks of black bread and mouldy sausages. Some had scattered through the fields to dig up beet roots and other tubers, chewing with loud crunchings the hard pulp to which the grit still adhered. An ensign was shaking the fruit trees using as a catch-all the flag of his regiment. That glorious standard, adorned with souvenirs of 1870, was serving as a receptacle for green plums. Those who were seated on the ground were improving this rest by drawing their perspiring, swollen feet from high boots which were sending out an insufferable smell.

The regiments of infantry which Desnoyers had seen in Berlin reflecting the light on metal and leather straps, the magnificent and terrifying Hussars, the Cuirassiers in pure white uniform like the paladins of the Holy Grail, the artillerymen with breasts crossed with white bands, all the military variations that on parade had drawn forth the Hartrotts' sighs of admiration—these were now all unified and mixed together, of uniform color, all in greenish mustard like the dusty lizards that, slipping along, try to be confounded with the earth.

The persistency of the iron discipline was easily discernible. A word from the chiefs, the sound of a whistle, and they all grouped themselves together, the human being disappearing in the throngs of automatons; but danger, weariness, and the uncertainty of triumph had for the time being brought officers and men nearer together, obliterating caste distinction. The officers were coming part way out of their overbearing, haughty seclusion, and were condescending to talk with the lower orders so as to revive their courage. One effort more and they would overwhelm both French and English, repeating the triumph of Sedan, whose anniversary they were going to celebrate in a few days! They were going to enter Paris; it was only a matter of a week. Paris! Great shops filled with luxurious things, famous restaurants, women, champagne, money. . . . And the men, flattered that their commanders were stooping to chat with them, forgot fatigue and hunger, reviving like the throngs of the Crusade before the image of Jerusalem. "Nach Paris!" The joyous shout circulated from the head to the tail of the marching columns. "To Paris! To Paris!"

The scarcity of their food supply was here supplemented by the products of a country rich in wines. When sacking houses they rarely found eatables, but invariably a wine cellar. The humble German, the perpetual beer drinker, who had always looked upon wine as a privilege of the rich, could now open up casks with blows from his weapons, even bathing his feet in the stream of precious liquid. Every battalion left as a souvenir of its passing a wake of empty bottles; a halt in camp sowed the land with glass cylinders. The regimental trucks, unable to renew their stores of provisions, were accustomed to seize the wine in all the towns. The soldier, lacking bread, would receive alcohol. . . .

This donation was always accompanied by the good counsels of the officers—War is war; no pity toward our adversaries who do not deserve it. The French were shooting their prisoners, and their women were putting out the eyes of the wounded. Every dwelling was a den of traps. The simple-hearted and innocent German entering therein was going to certain death. The beds were made over subterranean caves, the wardrobes were make-believe doors, in every corner was lurking an assassin. This traitorous nation, which was arranging its ground like the scenario of a melodrama, would have to be chastised. The municipal officers, the priests, the schoolmasters were directing and protecting the sharpshooters.

Desnoyers was shocked at the indifference with which these men were stalking around the burning village. They did not appear to see the fire and destruction; it was just an ordinary spectacle, not worth looking at. Ever since they had crossed the frontier, smoldering and blasted villages, fired by the advance guard, had marked their halting places on Belgian and French soil.

When entering Villeblanche the automobile had to lower its speed. Burned walls were bulging out over the street and half-charred beams were obstructing the way, obliging the vehicle to zigzag through the smoking rubbish. The vacant lots were burning like fire pans between the houses still standing, with doors broken, but not yet in flames. Desnoyers saw within these rectangular spaces partly burned wood, chairs, beds, sewing machines, iron stoves, all the household goods of the well-to-do countryman, being consumed or twisted into shapeless masses. Sometimes he would spy an arm sticking out of the ruins, beginning to burn like a long wax candle. No, it could not be possible . . . and then the smell of cooking flesh began to mingle with that of the soot, wood and plaster.

He closed his eyes, not able to look any longer. He thought for a moment he must be dreaming. It was unbelievable that such horrors could take place in less than an hour. Human wickedness at its worst he had supposed incapable of changing the aspect of a village in such a short time.

An abrupt stoppage of the motor made him look around involuntarily. This time the obstruction was the dead bodies in the street—two men and a woman. They had probably fallen under the rain of bullets from the machine gun which had passed through the town preceding the invasion. Some soldiers were seated a little beyond them, with their backs to the victims, as though ignoring their presence. The chauffeur yelled to them to clear the track; with their guns and feet they pushed aside the bodies still warm, at every turn leaving a trail of blood. The space was hardly opened before the vehicle shot through . . . a thud, a leap—the back wheels had evidently crushed some very fragile obstacle.

Desnoyers was still huddled in his seat, benumbed and with closed eyes. The horror around him made him think of his own fate. Whither was this lieutenant taking him? . . .

He soon saw the town hall flaming in the square; the church was now nothing but a stone shell, bristling with flames. The houses of the prosperous villagers had had their doors and windows chopped out by axe-blows. Within them soldiers were moving about methodically. They entered empty-handed and came out loaded with furniture and clothing. Others, in the upper stories, were flinging out various objects; accompanying their trophies with jests and guffaws. Suddenly they had to come out flying, for fire was breaking out with the violence and rapidity of an explosion. Following their footsteps was a group of men with big boxes and metal cylinders. Someone at their head was pointing out the buildings into whose broken windows were to be thrown the lozenges and liquid streams which would produce catastrophe with lightning rapidity.

Out of one of these flaming buildings two men, who seemed but bundles of rags, were being dragged by some Germans. Above the blue sleeves of their military cloaks Don Marcelo could distinguish blanched faces and eyes immeasurably distended with suffering. Their legs were dragging on the ground, sticking out between the tatters of their red pantaloons. One of them still had on his kepis. Blood was gushing from different parts of their bodies and behind them, like white serpents, were trailing their loosened bandages. They were wounded Frenchmen, stragglers who had remained in the village because too weak to keep up with the retreat. Perhaps they had joined the group which, finding its escape cut off, had attempted that insane resistance.

Wishing to make that matter more clearly understood, Desnoyers looked at the official beside him, attempting to speak; but the officer silenced him instantly: "French sharpshooters in disguise who are going to get the punishment they deserve." The German bayonets were sunk deep into their bodies. Then blows with the guns fell on the head of one of them . . . and these blows were repeated with dull thumps upon their skulls, crackling as they burst open.

Again the old man wondered what his fate would be. Where was this lieutenant taking him across such visions of horror? . . .

They had reached the outskirts of the village, where the dragoons had built their barricade. The carts were still there, but at one side of the road. They climbed out of the automobile, and he saw a group of officers in gray, with sheathed helmets like the others. The one who had brought him to this place was standing rigidly erect with one hand to his visor, speaking to a military man standing a few paces in front of the others. He looked at this man, who was scrutinizing him with his little hard blue eyes that had carved his spare, furrowed countenance with lines. He must be the general. His arrogant and piercing gaze was sweeping him from head to foot. Don Marcelo felt a presentiment that his life was hanging on this examination; should an evil suggestion, a cruel caprice flash across this brain, he was surely lost. The general shrugged his shoulders and said a few words in a contemptuous tone, then entered his automobile with two of his aids, and the group disbanded.

The cruel uncertainty, the interminable moments before the official returned to his side, filled Desnoyers with dread.

"His Excellency is very gracious," announced the lieutenant. "He might have shot you, but he pardons you and yet you people say that we are savages!" . . .

With involuntary contempt, he further explained that he had conducted him thither fully expecting that he would be shot. The General was planning to punish all the prominent residents of Villeblanche, and he had inferred, on his own initiative, that the owner of the castle must be one of them.

"Military duty, sir. . . . War exacts it."

After this excuse the petty official renewed his eulogies of His Excellency. He was going to make his headquarters in Don Marcelo's property, and on that account granted him his life. He ought to thank him. . . . Then again his face trembled with wrath. He pointed to some bodies lying near the road. They were the corpses of Uhlans, covered with some cloaks from which were protruding the enormous soles of their boots.

"Plain murder!" he exclaimed. "A crime for which the guilty are going to pay dearly!"

His indignation made him consider the death of four soldiers as an unheard-of and monstrous outrage—as though in was only the enemy ought to fall, keeping safe and sound the lives of his compatriots.

A band of infantry commanded by an officer approached. As their ranks opened, Desnoyers saw the gray uniforms roughly pushing forward some of the inhabitants. Their clothes were torn and some had blood on face and hands. He recognized them one by one as they were lined up against the mud wall, at twenty paces from the firing squad of soldiers—the mayor, the priest, the forest guard, and some rich villagers whose houses he had seen falling in flames.

"They are going to shoot them . . . in order to prevent any doubt about it," the lieutenant explained. "I wanted you to see this. It will serve as an object lesson. In this way, you will feel more appreciative of the leniency of His Excellency."

The prisoners were mute. Their voices had been exhausted in vain protest. All their life was concentrated in their eyes, looking around them in stupefaction. . . . And was it possible that they would kill them in cold blood without hearing their testimony, without admitting the proofs of their innocence!

The certainty of approaching death soon gave almost all of them a noble serenity. It was useless to complain. Only one rich countryman, famous for his avarice, was whimpering desperately, saying over and over, "I do not wish to die. . . . I do not want to die!"

Trembling and with eyes overflowing with tears, Desnoyers hid himself behind his implacable guide. He knew them all, he had battled with them all, and repented now of his former wrangling. The mayor had a red stain on his forehead from a long skin wound. Upon his breast fluttered a tattered tricolor; the municipality had placed it there that he might receive the invaders who had torn most of it away. The priest was holding his little round body as erect as possible, wishing to embrace in a look of resignation the victims, the executioners, earth and heaven. He appeared larger than usual and more imposing. His black girdle, broken by the roughness of the soldiers, left his cassock loose and floating. His waving, silvery hair was dripping blood, spotting with its red drops the white clerical collar.

Upon seeing him cross the fatal field with unsteady step, because of his obesity, a savage roar cut the tragic silence. The unarmed soldiers, who had hastened to witness the execution, greeted the venerable old man with shouts of laughter. "Death to the priest!" . . . The fanaticism of the religious wars vibrated through their mockery. Almost all of them were devout Catholics or fervent Protestants, but they believed only in the priests of their own country. Outside of Germany, everything was despicable—even their own religion.

The mayor and the priest changed their places in the file, seeking one another. Each, with solemn courtesy, was offering the other the central place in the group.

"Here, your Honor, is your place as mayor—at the head of all."

"No, after you, Monsieur le cure."

They were disputing for the last time, but in this supreme moment each one was wishing to yield precedence to the other.

Instinctively they had clasped hands, looking straight ahead at the firing squad, that had lowered its guns in a rigid, horizontal line. Behind them sounded laments—"Good-bye, my children. . . . Adieu, life! . . . I do not wish to die! . . . I do not want to die! . . ."

The two principal men felt the necessity of saying something, of closing the page of their existence with an affirmation.

"Vive la Republique!" cried the mayor.

"Vive la France!" said the priest.

Desnoyers thought that both had said the same thing. Two uprights flashed up above their heads—the arm of the priest making the sign of the cross, and the sabre of the commander of the shooters, glistening at the same instant. . . . A dry, dull thunderclap, followed by some scattering, tardy shots.

Don Marcelo's compassion for that forlorn cluster of massacred humanity was intensified on beholding the grotesque forms which many assumed in the moment of death. Some collapsed like half-emptied sacks; others rebounded from the ground like balls; some leaped like gymnasts, with upraised arms, falling on their backs, or face downward, like a swimmer. In that human heap, he saw limbs writhing in the agony of death. Some soldiers advanced like hunters bagging their prey. From the palpitating mass fluttered locks of white hair, and a feeble hand, trying to repeat the sacred sign. A few more shots and blows on the livid, mangled mass . . . and the last tremors of life were extinguished forever.

The officer had lit a cigar.

"Whenever you wish," he said to Desnoyers with ironical courtesy.

They re-entered the automobile in order to return to the castle by the way of Villeblanche. The increasing number of fires and the dead bodies in the streets no longer impressed the old man. He had seen so much! What could now affect his sensibilities? . . . He was longing to get out of the village as soon as possible to try to find the peace of the country. But the country had disappeared under the invasion—soldier's, horses, cannons everywhere. Wherever they stopped to rest, they were destroying all that they came in contact with. The marching battalions, noisy and automatic as a machine were preceded by the fifes and drums, and every now and then, in order to cheer their drooping spirits, were breaking into their joyous cry, "Nach Paris!"

The castle, too, had been disfigured by the invasion. The number of guards had greatly increased during the owner's absence. He saw an entire regiment of infantry encamped in the park. Thousands of men were moving about under the trees, preparing the dinner in the movable kitchens. The flower borders of the gardens, the exotic plants, the carefully swept and gravelled avenues were all broken and spoiled by this avalanche of men, beasts and vehicles.

A chief wearing on his sleeve the band of the military administration was giving orders as though he were the proprietor. He did not even condescend to look at this civilian walking beside the lieutenant with the downcast look of a prisoner. The stables were vacant. Desnoyers saw his last animals being driven off with sticks by the helmeted shepherds. The costly progenitors of his herds were all beheaded in the park like mere slaughter-house animals. In the chicken houses and dovecotes, there was not a single bird left. The stables were filled with thin horses who were gorging themselves before overflowing mangers. The feed from the barns was being lavishly distributed through the avenue, much of it lost before it could be used. The cavalry horses of various divisions were turned loose in the meadows, destroying with their hoofs the canals, the edges of the slopes, the level of the ground, all the work of many months. The dry wood was uselessly burning in the park. Through carelessness or mischief, someone had set the wood piles on fire. The trees, with the bark dried by the summer heat, were crackling on being licked by the flame.

The building was likewise occupied by a multitude of men under this same superintendent. The open windows showed a continual shifting through the rooms. Desnoyers heard great blows that re-echoed within his breast. Ay, his historic mansion! . . . The General was going to establish himself in it, after having examined on the banks of the Marne, the works of the pontoon builders, who had been constructing several military bridges for the troops. Don Marcelo's outraged sense of ownership forced him to speak. He feared that they would break the doors of the locked rooms—he would like to go for the keys in order to give them up to those in charge. The commissary would not listen to him but continued ignoring his existence. The lieutenant replied with cutting amiability:

"It is not necessary; do not trouble yourself!"

After this considerate remark, he started to rejoin his regiment but deemed it prudent before losing sight of Desnoyers to give him a little advice. He must remain quietly at the castle; outside, he might be taken for a spy, and he already knew how promptly the soldiers of the Emperor settled all such little matters.

He could not remain in the garden looking at his dwelling from any distance, because the Germans who were going and coming were diverting themselves by playing practical jokes upon him. They would march toward him in a straight line, as though they did not see him, and he would have to hurry out of their way to avoid being thrown down by their mechanical and rigid advance.

Finally he sought refuge in the lodge of the Keeper, whose good wife stared with astonishment at seeing him drop into a kitchen chair breathless and downcast, suddenly aged by losing the remarkable energy that had been the wonder of his advanced years.

"Ah, Master. . . . Poor Master!"

Of all the events attending the invasion, the most unbelievable for this poor woman was seeing her employer take refuge in her cottage.

"What is ever going to become of us!" she groaned.

Her husband was in constant demand by the invaders. His Excellency's assistants, installed in the basement apartments of the castle were incessantly calling him to tell them the whereabouts of things which they could not find.

From every trip, he would return humiliated, his eyes filled with tears. On his forehead was the black and blue mark of a blow, and his jacket was badly torn. These were souvenirs of a futile attempt at opposition, during his master's absence, to the German plundering of stables and castle rooms.

The millionaire felt himself linked by misfortune to these people, considered until then with indifference. He was very grateful for the loyalty of this sick and humble man, and the poor woman's interest in the castle as though it were her own, touched him greatly. The presence of their daughter brought Chichi to his mind. He had passed near her without noting the transformation in her, seeing her just the same as when, with her little dog trot, she had accompanied the Master's daughter on her rounds through the parks and grounds. Now she was a woman, slender and full grown, with the first feminine graces showing subtly in her fourteen-year-old figure. Her mother would not let her leave the lodge, fearing the soldiery which was invading every other spot with its overflowing current, filtering into all open places, breaking every obstacle which impeded their course.

Desnoyers broke his despairing silence to admit that he was feeling hungry. He was ashamed of this bodily want, but the emotions of the day, the executions seen so near, the danger still threatening, had awakened in him a nervous appetite. The fact that he was so impotent in the midst of his riches and unable to avail himself of anything on his estate but aggravated his necessity.

"Poor Master!" again exclaimed the faithful soul.

And the woman looked with astonishment at the millionaire devouring a bit of bread and a triangle of cheese, the only food that she could find in her humble dwelling. The certainty that he would not be able to find any other nourishment, no matter how much he might seek it, greatly sharpened his cravings. To have acquired an enormous fortune only to perish with hunger at the end of his existence! . . . The good wife, as though guessing his thoughts, sighed, raising her eyes beseechingly to heaven. Since the early morning hours, the world had completely changed its course. Ay, this war! . . .

The rest of the afternoon and a part of the night, the proprietor kept receiving news from the Keeper after his visits to the castle. The General and numerous officers were now occupying the rooms. Not a single door was locked, all having been opened with blows of the axe or gun. Many things had completely disappeared; the man did not know exactly how, but they had vanished—perhaps destroyed, or perhaps carried off by those who were coming and going. The chief with the banded sleeve was going from room to room examining everything, dictating in German to a soldier who was writing down his orders. Meanwhile the General and his staff were in the dining room drinking heavily, consulting the maps spread out on the floor, and ordering the Warden to go down into the vaults for the very best wines.

By nightfall, an onward movement was noticeable in the human tide that had been overflowing the fields as far as the eye could reach. Some bridges had been constructed across the Marne and the invasion had renewed its march, shouting enthusiastically. "Nach Paris!" Those left behind till the following day were to live in the ruined houses or the open air. Desnoyers heard songs. Under the splendor of the evening stars, the soldiers had grouped themselves in musical knots, chanting a sweet and solemn chorus of religious gravity. Above the trees was floating a red cloud, intensified by the dusk—a reflection of the still burning village. Afar off were bonfires of farms and homesteads, twinkling in the night with their blood-colored lights.

The bewildered proprietor of the castle finally fell asleep in a bed in the lodge, made mercifully unconscious by the heavy and stupefying slumber of exhaustion, without fright nor nightmare. He seemed to be falling, falling into a bottomless pit, and on awaking fancied that he had slept but a few minutes. The sun was turning the window shades to an orange hue, spattered with shadows of waving boughs and birds fluttering and twittering among the leaves. He shared their joy in the cool refreshing dawn of the summer day. It certainly was a fine morning—but whose dwelling was this? . . . He gazed dumbfounded at his bed and surroundings. Suddenly the reality assaulted his brain that had been so sweetly dulled by the first splendors of the day. Step by step, the host of emotions compressed into the preceding day, came climbing up the long stairway of his memory to the last black and red landing of the night before. And he had slept tranquilly surrounded by enemies, under the surveillance of an arbitrary power which might destroy him in one of its caprices!

When he went into the kitchen, the Warden gave him some news. The Germans were departing. The regiment encamped in the park had left at daybreak, and after them others, and still others. In the village there was still one regiment occupying the few houses yet standing and the ruins of the charred ones. The General had gone also with his numerous staff. There was nobody in the castle now but the head of a Reserve brigade whom his aide called "The Count," and a few officials.

Upon receiving this information, the proprietor ventured to leave the lodge. He saw his gardens destroyed, but still beautiful. The trees were still stately in spite of the damage done to their trunks. The birds were flying about excitedly, rejoicing to find themselves again in possession of the spaces so recently flooded by the human inundation.

Suddenly Desnoyers regretted having sallied forth. Five huge trucks were lined up near the moat before the castle bridge. Gangs of soldiers were coming out carrying on their shoulders enormous pieces of furniture, like peons conducting a moving. A bulky object wrapped in damask curtains—an excellent substitute for sacking—was being pushed by four men toward one of the drays. The owner suspected immediately what it must be. His bath! The famous tub of gold! . . . Then with an abrupt revulsion of feeling, he felt no grief at his loss. He now detested the ostentatious thing, attributing to it a fatal influence. On account of it he was here. But, ay! . . . the other furnishings piled up in the drays! . . . In that moment he suffered the extreme agony of misery and impotence. It was impossible for him to defend his property, to dispute with the head thief who was sacking his castle, tranquilly ignoring the very existence of the owner. "Robbers! thieves!" and he fled back to the lodge.

He passed the remainder of the morning with his elbow on the table, his head in his hands, the same as the day before, letting the hours grind slowly by, trying not to hear the rolling of the vehicles that were bearing away these credentials of his wealth.

Toward midday, the Keeper announced that an officer who had arrived a few hours before in an automobile was inquiring for him.

Responding to this summons, Desnoyers encountered outside the lodge, a captain arrayed like the others in sheathed and pointed helmet, in mustard-colored uniform, red leather boots, sword, revolver, field-glasses and geographic map hanging in a case from his belt. He appeared young; on his sleeve was the staff emblem.

"Do you know me? . . . I did not wish to pass through here without seeing you."

He spoke in Castilian, and Don Marcelo felt greater surprise at this than at the many things which he had been experiencing so painfully during the last twenty-four hours.

"You really do not know me?" queried the German, always in Spanish. "I am Otto. . . . Captain Otto von Hartrott."

The old man's mind went painfully down the staircase of memory, stopping this time at a far-distant landing. There he saw the old ranch, and his brother-in-law announcing the birth of his second son. "I shall give him Bismarck's name," Karl had said. Then, climbing back past many other platforms, Desnoyers saw himself in Berlin during his visit to the von Hartrott home where they were speaking proudly of Otto, almost as learned as the older brother, but devoting his talents entirely to martial matters. He was then a lieutenant and studying for admission to the General Staff. "Who knows but he may turn out to be another Moltke?" said the proud father . . . and the charming Chichi had thereupon promptly bestowed upon the warlike wonder a nickname, accepted through the family. From that time, Otto was Moltkecito (the baby Moltke) to his Parisian relatives.

Desnoyers was astounded by the transformation which had meanwhile taken place in the youth. This vigorous captain with the insolent air who might shoot him at any minute was the same urchin whom he had seen running around the ranch, the beardless Moltkecito who had been the butt of his daughter's ridicule. . . .

The soldier, meanwhile, was explaining his presence there. He belonged to another division. There were many . . . many! They were advancing rapidly, forming an extensive and solid wall from Verdun to Paris. His general had sent him to maintain the contact with the next division, but finding himself near the castle, he had wished to visit it. A family tie was not a mere word. He still remembered the days that he had spent at Villeblanche when the Hartrott family had paid a long visit to their relatives in France. The officials now occupying the edifice had detained him that he might lunch with them. One of them had casually mentioned that the owner of the castle was somewhere about although nobody knew exactly where. This had been a great surprise to Captain von

Hartrott who had tried to find him, regretting to see him taking refuge in the Warden's quarters.

"You must leave this hut; you are my uncle," he said haughtily. "Return to your castle where you belong. My comrades will be much pleased to make your acquaintance; they are very distinguished men."

He very much regretted whatever the old gentleman might have suffered. . . . He did not know exactly in what that suffering had consisted, but surmised that the first moments of the invasion had been cruel ones for him.

"But what else can you expect?" he repeated several times. "That is war."

At the same time he approved of his having remained on his property. They had special orders to seize the goods of the fugitives. Germany wished the inhabitants to remain in their dwellings as though nothing extraordinary had occurred. . . . Desnoyers protested. . . . "But if the invaders were shooting the innocent ones and burning their homes!" . . . His nephew prevented his saying more. He turned pale, an ashy hue spreading over his face; his eyes snapped and his face trembled like that of the lieutenant who had taken possession of the castle.

"You refer to the execution of the mayor and the others. My comrades have just been telling me about it; yet that castigation was very mild; they should have completely destroyed the entire village. They should have killed even the women and children. We've got to put an end to these sharpshooters."

His uncle looked at him in amazement. His Moltkecito was as formidable and ferocious as the others. . . . But the captain brought the conversation to an abrupt close by repeating the monstrous and everlasting excuse.

"Very horrible, but what else can you expect! . . . That is war."

He then inquired after his mother, rejoicing to learn that she was in the South. He had been uneasy at the idea of her remaining in Paris . . . especially with all those revolutions which had been breaking out there lately! . . . Desnoyers looked doubtful as if he could not have heard correctly. What revolutions were those? . . . But the officer, without further explanation, resumed his conversation about his family, taking it for granted that his relative would be impatient to learn the fate of his German kin.

They were all in magnificent state. Their illustrious father was president of various patriotic societies (since his years no longer permitted him to go to war) and was besides organizing future industrial enterprises to improve the conquered countries. His brother, "the Sage," was giving lectures about the nations that the imperial victory was bound to annex, censuring severely those whose ambitions were unpretending or weak. The remaining brothers were distinguishing themselves in the army, one of them having been presented with a medal at Lorraine. The two sisters, although somewhat depressed by the absence of their fiances, lieutenants of the Hussars, were employing their time in visiting the hospitals and begging God to chastise traitorous England.

Captain von Hartrott was slowly conducting his uncle toward the castle. The gray and unbending soldiers who, until then, had been ignoring the existence of Don Marcelo, looked at him with interest, now that he was in intimate conversation with a member of the General Staff. He perceived that these men were about to humanize themselves by casting aside temporarily their inexorable and aggressive automatonism.

Upon entering his mansion something in his heart contracted with an agonizing shudder. Everywhere he could see dreadful vacancies, which made him recall the objects which had formerly been there. Rectangular spots of stronger color announced the theft of furniture and paintings. With what despatch and system the gentleman of the armlet had been doing his work! . . . To the sadness that the cold and orderly spoliation caused was added his indignation as an economical man, gazing upon the slashed curtains, spotted rugs, broken crystal and porcelain—all the debris from a ruthless and unscrupulous occupation.

His nephew, divining his thoughts, could only offer the same old excuse— "What a mess! . . . But that is war!"

With Moltkecito, he did not have to subside into the respectful civilities of fear.

"That is NOT war!" he thundered bitterly. "It is an expedition of bandits. . . . Your comrades are nothing less than highwaymen."

Captain von Hartrott swelled up with a jerk. Separating himself from the complainant and looking fixedly at him, he spoke in a low voice, hissing with wrath. "Look here, uncle! It is a lucky thing for you that you have expressed yourself in Spanish, and those around you could not understand you. If you persist in such comments you will probably receive a bullet by way of an answer. The Emperor's officials permit no insults." And his threatening attitude demonstrated the facility with which he could forget his relationship if he should receive orders to proceed against Don Marcelo.

Thus silenced, the vanquished proprietor hung his head. What was he going to do? . . . The Captain now renewed his affability as though he had forgotten what he had just said. He wished to present him to his companions-at-arms. His Excellency, Count Meinbourg, the Major General, upon learning that he was a relative of the von Hartrotts, had done him the honor of inviting him to his table.

Invited into his own demesne, he finally reached the dining room, filled with men in mustard color and high boots. Instinctively, he made an inventory of the room. All in good order, nothing broken—walls, draperies and furniture still intact; but an appraising glance within the sideboard again caused a clutch at his heart. Two entire table services of silver, and another of old porcelain had disappeared without leaving the most insignificant of their pieces. He was obliged to respond gravely to the presentations which his nephew was making, and take the hand which the Count was extending with aristocratic languor. The adversary began considering him with benevolence, on learning that he was a millionaire from a distant land where riches were acquired very rapidly.

Soon he was seated as a stranger at his own table, eating from the same dishes that his family were accustomed to use, served by men with shaved heads, wearing coarse, striped aprons over their uniforms. That which he was eating was his, the wine was from his vaults; all that adorned the room he had bought: the trees whose boughs were waving outside the window also belonged to him. . . . And yet he felt as though he were in this place for the first time, with all the discomfort and diffidence of a total stranger. He ate because he was hungry, but the food and wines seemed to have come from another planet.

He continued looking with consternation at those occupying the places of his wife, children and the Lacours. . . .

They were speaking in German among themselves, but those having a limited knowledge of French frequently availed themselves of that language in order that their guest might understand them. Those who could only mumble a few words, repeated them to an accompaniment of amiable smiles. All were displaying an amicable desire to propitiate the owner of the castle.

"You are going to lunch with the barbarians," said the Count, offering him a seat at his side. "Aren't you afraid that we may eat you alive?"

The Germans burst into roars of laughter at the wit of His Excellency. They all took great pains to demonstrate by word and manner that barbarity was wrongly attributed to them by their enemies.

Don Marcelo looked from one to another. The fatigues of war, especially the forced march of the last days, were very apparent in their persons. Some were tall and slender with an angular slimness; others were stocky and corpulent with short neck and head sunk between the shoulders. These had lost much of their fat in a month's campaign, the wrinkled and flabby skin hanging in folds in various parts of their bodies. All had shaved heads, the same as the soldiers. Around the table shone two rows of cranial spheres, reddish or dark. Their ears stood out grotesquely, and their jaw bones were in strong relief owing to their thinness. Some had preserved the upright moustache in the style of the Emperor; the most of them were shaved or had a stubby tuft like a brush.

A golden bracelet glistened on the wrist of the Count, stretched on the table. He was the oldest of them all and the only one that kept his hair, of a frosty red, carefully combed and glistening with pomade. Although about fifty years old, he still maintained a youthful vigor cultivated by exercise. Wrinkled, bony and strong, he tried to dissimulate his uncouthness as a man of battle under a suave and indolent laziness. The officers treated him with the greatest respect. Hartrott told his uncle that the Count was a great artist, musician and poet. The Emperor was his friend; they had known each other from boyhood. Before the war, certain scandals concerning his private life had exiled him from Court—mere lampoons of the socialists and scandal-mongers. The Kaiser had always kept a secret affection for his former chum. Everybody remembered his dance, "The Caprices of Scheherazade," represented with the greatest luxury in Berlin through the endorsement of his powerful friend, William II. The Count had lived many years in the Orient. In fact, he was a great gentleman and an artist of exquisite sensibility as well as a soldier.

Since Desnoyers was now his guest, the Count could not permit him to remain silent, so he made an opportunity of bringing him into the conversation.

"Did you see any of the insurrections? . . . Did the troops have to kill many people? How about the assassination of Poincare? . . ."

He asked these questions in quick succession and Don Marcelo, bewildered by their absurdity, did not know how to reply. He believed that he must have fallen in with a feast of fools. Then he suspected that they were making fun of him. Uprisings? Assassinations of the President? . . .

Some gazed at him with pity because of his ignorance, others with suspicion, believing that he was merely pretending not to know of these events which had happened so near him.

His nephew insisted. "The daily papers in Germany have been full of accounts of these matters. Fifteen days ago, the people of Paris revolted against the Government, bombarding the Palais de l'Elysee, and assassinating the President. The army had to resort to the machine guns before order could be restored. . . . Everybody knows that."

But Desnoyers insisted that he did not know it, that nobody had seen such things. And as his words were received in an atmosphere of malicious doubt, he preferred to be silent. His Excellency, superior spirit, incapable of being associated with the popular credulity, here intervened to set matters straight. The report of the assassination was, perhaps, not certain; the German periodicals might have unconsciously exaggerated it. Just a few hours ago, the General of the Staff had told him of the flight of the French Government to Bordeaux, and the statement about the revolution in Paris and the firing of the French troops was indisputable. "The gentleman has seen it all without doubt, but does not wish to admit it." Desnoyers felt obliged to contradict this lordling, but his negative was not even listened to.

Paris! This name made all eyes glisten and everybody talkative. As soon as possible they wished to reach the Eiffel Tower, to enter victorious into the city, to receive their recompense for the privations and fatigues of a month's campaign. They were devotees of military glory, they considered war necessary to existence, and yet they were bewailing the hardship that it was imposing upon them. The Count exhaled the plaint of the craftsmaster.

"Oh, the havoc that this war has brought in my plans!" he sighed. "This winter they were going to bring out my dance in Paris!"

They all protested at his sadness; his work would surely be presented after the triumph, and the French would have to recognize it.

"It will not be the same thing," complained the Count. "I confess that I adore Paris. . . . What a pity that these people have never wished to be on familiar terms with us!" . . . And he relapsed into the silence of the unappreciated man.

Desnoyers suddenly recognized in one of the officers who was talking, with eyes bulging with covetousness, of the riches of Paris, the Chief Thief with the band on his arm. He it was who so methodically had sacked the castle. As though divining the old Frenchman's thought, the commissary began excusing himself.

"It is war, monsieur. . . ."

The same as the others! . . . War had to be paid with the treasures of the conquered. That was the new German system; the healthy return to the wars of ancient days; tributes imposed on the cities, and each house sacked separately. In this way, the enemy's resistance would be more effectually overcome and the war soon brought to a close. He ought not to be downcast over the appropriations, for his furnishings and ornaments would all be sold in Germany. After the French defeat, he could place a remonstrance claim with his government, petitioning it to indemnify his loss; his relatives in Berlin would support his demand.

Desnoyers listened in consternation to his counsels. What kind of mentality had these men, anyway? Were they insane, or were they trying to have some fun at his expense? . . .

When the lunch was at last ended, the officers arose and adjusted their swords for service. Captain von Hartrott rose, too; it was necessary for him to return to his general; he had already dedicated too much time to family expansion. His uncle accompanied him to the automobile where Moltkecito once more justified the ruin and plunder of the castle.

"It is war. . . . We have to be very ruthless that it may not last long. True kindness consists in being cruel, because then the terror-stricken enemy gives in sooner, and so the world suffers less."

Don Marcelo shrugged his shoulders before this sophistry. In the doorway, the captain gave some orders to a soldier who soon returned with a bit of chalk which had been used to number the lodging places. Von Hartrott wished to protect his uncle and began tracing on the wall near the door:—"Bitte, nicht plundern. Es sind freundliche Leute."

In response to the old man's repeated questions, he then translated the inscription. "It means, 'Please do not sack this house. Its occupants are kind people . . . friendly people.'"

Ah, no! . . . Desnoyers repelled this protection vehemently. He did not wish to be kind. He was silent because he could not be anything else. . . . But a friend of the invaders of his country! . . . No, NO, NO!

His nephew rubbed out part of the lettering, leaving the first words, "Bitte, nicht plundern." Then he repeated the scrawled request at the entrance of the park. He thought this notice advisable because His Excellency might go away and other officials might be installed in the castle. Von Hartrott had seen much and his smile seemed to imply that nothing could surprise him, no matter how outrageous it might be. But his relative continued scorning his protection, and laughing bitterly at the impromptu signboard. What more could they carry off? . . . Had they not already stolen the best?

"Good-bye, uncle! Soon we shall meet in Paris."

And the captain climbed into his automobile, extending a soft, cold hand that seemed to repel the old man with its flabbiness.

Upon returning to his castle, he saw a table and some chairs in the shadow of a group of trees. His Excellency was taking his coffee in the open air, and obliged him to take a seat beside him. Only three officers were keeping him company. . . . There was here a grand consumption of liquors from his wine cellars. They were talking together in German, and for an hour Don Marcelo remained there, anxious to go but never finding the opportune moment to leave his seat and disappear.

He employed his time in imagining the great stir among the troops hidden by the trees. Another division of the army was passing by with the incessant, deafening roar of the sea. An inexplicable phenomenon kept the luminous calm of the afternoon in a continuous state of vibration. A constant thundering sounded afar off as though an invisible storm were always approaching from beyond the blue horizon line.

The Count, noticing his evident interest in the noise, interrupted his German chat to explain.

"It is the cannon. A battle is going on. Soon we shall join in the dance."

The possibility of having to give up his quarters here, the most comfortable that he had found in all the campaign, put His Excellency in a bad humor.

"War," he sighed, "a glorious life, but dirty and deadening! In an entire month—to-day is the first that I have lived as a gentleman."

And as though attracted by the luxuries that he might shortly have to abandon, he rose and went toward the castle. Two of the Germans betook themselves toward the village, and Desnoyers remained with the other officer who was delightfully sampling his liquors. He was the chief of the battalion encamped in the village.

"This is a sad war, Monsieur!" he said in French.

Of all the inimical group, this man was the only one for whom Don Marcelo felt a vague attraction. "Although a German, he appears a good sort," meditated the old man, eyeing him carefully. In times of peace, he must have been stout, but now he showed the loose and flaccid exterior of one who has just lost much in weight. Desnoyers surmised that the man had formerly lived in tranquil and vulgar sensuousness, in a middle-class happiness suddenly cut short by war.

"What a life, Monsieur!" the officer rambled on. "May God punish well those who have provoked this catastrophe!"

The Frenchman was almost affected. This man represented the Germany that he had many times imagined, a sweet and tranquil Germany composed of burghers, a little heavy and slow perhaps, but atoning for their natural uncouthness by an innocent and poetic sentimentalism. This Blumhardt whom his companions called Bataillon-Kommandeur, was undoubtedly the good father of a large family. He fancied him walking with his wife and children under the lindens of a provincial square, all listening with religious unction to the melodies played by a military band. Then he saw him in the beer gardens with his friends, discussing metaphysical problems between business conversations. He was a man from old Germany, a character from a romance by Goethe. Perhaps the glory of the Empire had modified his existence, and instead of going to the beer gardens, he was now accustomed to frequent the officers' casino, while his family maintained a separate existence—separated from the civilians by the superciliousness of military caste; but at heart, he was always the good German, ready to weep copiously before an affecting family scene or a fragment of good music.

Commandant Blumhardt, meanwhile, was thinking of his family living in Cassel.

"There are eight children, Monsieur," he said with a visible effort to control emotion. "The two eldest are preparing to become officers. The youngest is starting school this year. . . . He is just so high."

And with his right hand he measured off the child's diminutive stature. He trembled with laughter and grief at recalling the little chap. Then he broke forth into eulogies about his wife—excellent manager of the home, a mother who was always modestly sacrificing herself for her children and husband. Ay, the sweet Augusta! . . . After twenty years of married life, he adored her as on the day he first saw her. In a pocket of his uniform, he was keeping all the letters that she had written him since the beginning of the campaign.

"Look at her, Monsieur. . . . There are my children."

From his breast pocket, he had drawn forth a silver medallion, adorned with the art of Munich, and touching a spring, he displayed the pictures of all the family—the Frau Kommandeur, of an austere and frigid beauty, imitating the air and coiffure of the Empress; the Frauleine Kommandeur, clad in white, with uplifted eyes as though they were singing a musical romance; and at the end, the children in the uniforms of the army schools or private institutions. And to think that he might lose these beloved beings if a bit of iron should hit him! . . . And he had to live far from them now that it was such fine weather for long walks in the country! . . .

"Sad war!" he again said. "May God punish the English!"

With a solicitude that Don Marcelo greatly appreciated, he in turn inquired about the Frenchman's family. He pitied him for having so few children, and smiled a little over the enthusiasm with which the old gentleman spoke of his daughter, saluting Fraulein Chichi as a witty sprite, and expressing great sympathy on learning that the only son was causing his parents great sorrow by his conduct.

Tender-hearted Commandant! . . . He was the first rational and human being that he had met in this hell of an invasion. "There are good people everywhere," he told himself. He hoped that this new acquaintance would not be moved from the castle; for if the Germans had to stay there, it would better be this man than the others.

An orderly came to summon Don Marcelo to the presence of His Excellency. After passing through the salons with closed eyes so as to avoid useless distress and wrath, he found the Count in his own bedroom. The doors had been forced open, the floors stripped of carpet and the window frames of curtains. Only the pieces of furniture broken in the first moments now occupied their former places. The sleeping rooms had been stripped more methodically, everything having been taken that was not required for immediate use. Because the General with his suite had been lodging there the night before, this apartment had escaped the arbitrary destruction.

The Count received him with the civility of a grandee who wishes to be attentive to his guests. He could not consent that HERR Desnoyers—a relative of a von Hartrott—whom he vaguely remembered having seen at Court, should be staying in the Keeper's lodge. He must return to his own room, occupying that bed, solemn as a catafalque with columns and plumes, which had had the honor, a few hours before, of serving as the resting-place of an illustrious General of the Empire.

"I myself prefer to sleep here," he added condescendingly. "This other habitation accords better with my tastes."

While saying this, he was entering Dona Luisa's rooms, admiring its Louis Quinze furniture of genuine value, with its dull golds and tapestries mellowed by time. It was one of the most successful purchases that Don Marcelo had made. The Count smiled with an artist's scorn as he recalled the man who had superintended the official sacking.

"What an ass! . . . To think that he left this behind, supposing that it was old and ugly!"

Then he looked the owner of the castle squarely in the face.

"Monsieur Desnoyers, I do not believe that I am committing any indiscretion, and even imagine that I am interpreting your desires when I inform you that I intend taking this set of furniture with me. It will serve as a souvenir of our acquaintance, a testimony to the friendship springing up between us. . . . If it remains here, it will run the risk of being destroyed. Warriors, of course, are not obliged to be artists. I will guard these excellent treasures in Germany where you may see them whenever you wish. We are all going to be one nation, you know. . . . My friend, the Emperor, is soon to be proclaimed sovereign of the French."

Desnoyers remained silent. How could he reply to that look of cruel irony, to the grimace with which the noble lord was underscoring his words? . . .

"When the war is ended, I will send you a gift from Berlin," he added in a patronizing tone.

The old collector could say nothing to that, either. He was looking at the vacant spots which many small pictures had left on the walls, paintings by famous masters of the XVIII century. The banded brigand must also have passed these by as too insignificant to carry off, but the smirk illuminating the Count's face revealed their ultimate destination.

He had carefully scrutinized the entire apartment—the adjoining bedroom, Chichi's, the bathroom, even the feminine robe-room of the family, which still contained some of the daughter's gowns. The warrior fondled with delight the fine silky folds of the materials, gloating over their cool softness.

This contact made him think of Paris, of the fashions, of the establishments of the great modistes. The rue de la Paix was the spot which he most admired in his visits to the enemy's city.

Don Marcelo noticed the strong mixture of perfumes which came from his hair, his moustache, his entire body. Various little jars from the dressing table were on the mantel.

"What a filthy thing war is!" exclaimed the German. "This morning I was at last able to take a bath after a week's abstinence; at noon I shall take another. By the way, my dear sir, these perfumes are good, but they are not elegant. When I have the pleasure of being presented to the ladies, I shall give them the addresses of my source of supply. . . . I use in my home essences from Turkey. I have many friends there. . . . At the close of the war, I will send a consignment to the family."

While speaking the Count's eyes had been fixed upon some photographs upon the table. Examining the portrait of Madame Desnoyers, he guessed that she must be Dona Luisa. He smiled before the bewitchingly mischievous face of Mademoiselle Chichi. Very enchanting; he specially admired her militant, boyish expression; but he scrutinized the photograph of Julio with special interest.

"Splendid type of youth," he murmured. "An interesting head, and artistic, too. He would create a great sensation in a fancy-dress ball. What a Persian prince he would make! . . . A white aigrette on his head, fastened with a great jewel, the breast bared, a black tunic with golden birds. . . ."

And he continued seeing in his mind's eye the heir of the Desnoyers arrayed in all the gorgeous raiment of an Oriental monarch. The proud father, because of the interest which his son was inspiring, began to feel a glimmer of sympathy with the man. A pity that he should select so unerringly and appropriate the choicest things in the castle!

Near the head of the bed, Don Marcelo saw lying upon a book of devotions forgotten by his wife, a medallion containing another photograph. It did not belong to his family, and the Count, following the direction of his eyes, wished to show it to him. The hands of this son of Mars trembled. . . . His disdainful haughtiness had suddenly disappeared. An official of the Hussars of Death was smiling from the case; his sharp profile with a beak curved like a bird of prey, was surmounted by a cap adorned with skull and cross-bones.

"My best friend," said the Count in tremulous tones. "The being that I love most in all the world. . . . And to think that at this moment he may be fighting, and they may kill him! . . . To think that I, too, may die!"

Desnoyers believed that he must be getting a glimpse into a romance of the nobleman's past. That Hussar was undoubtedly his natural son. His simplicity of mind could not conceive of anything else. Only a father's tenderness could so express itself . . . and he was almost touched by this tenderness.

Here the interview came to an end, the warrior turning his back as he left the room in order to hide his emotion. A few minutes after was heard on the floor below the sound of a grand piano which the Commissary had not been able to carry off, owing to the general's interposition. His voice was soon heard above the chords that he was playing. It was rather a lifeless baritone, but he managed to impart an impassioned tremolo to his romance. The listening old man was now really affected; he did not understand the words, but the tears came into his eyes. He thought of his family, of the sorrows and dangers about them and of the difficulties surrounding his return to them. . . . As though under the spell of the melody, little by little, he descended the stairs. What an artist's soul that haughty scoffer had! . . . At first sight, the Germans with their rough exterior and their discipline which made them commit the greatest atrocities, gave one a wrong impression. One had to live intimately with them to appreciate their true worth.

By the time the music had ceased, he had reached the castle bridge. A sub-officer was watching the graceful movements of the swans gliding double over the waters of the moat. He was a young Doctor of Laws who just now was serving as secretary to His Excellency—a university man mobilized by the war.

On speaking with Don Marcelo, he immediately revealed his academic training. The order for departure had surprised the professor in a private institute; he was just about to be married and all his plans had been upset.

"What a calamity, sir! . . . What an overturning for the world! . . . Yet many of us have foreseen that this catastrophe simply had to come. We have felt strongly that it might break out any day. Capital, accursed Capital is to blame."

The speaker was a Socialist. He did not hesitate to admit his co-operation in certain acts of his party that had brought persecutions and set-backs to his career. But the Social-Democracy was now being accepted by the Emperor and flattered by the most reactionary Junkers. All were now one. The deputies of his party were forming in the Reichstag the group most obedient to the government. . . . The only belief that it retained from its former creed, was its anathematization of Capital—responsible for the war.

Desnoyers ventured to disagree with this enemy who appeared of an amiable and tolerant character. "Did he not think that the real responsibility rested with German militarism? Had it not sought and prepared this conflict, by its arrogance preventing any settlement?"

The Socialist denied this roundly. His deputies were supporting the war and, therefore, must have good reason. Everything that he said showed an absolute submission to discipline—the eternal German discipline, blind and obedient, which was dominating even the most advanced parties. In vain the Frenchman repeated arguments and facts which everybody had read from the beginning of the war. His words simply slid over the calloused brains of this revolutionist, accustomed to delegating all his reasoning functions to others.

"Who can tell?" he finally said. "Perhaps we have made a mistake. But just at this moment all is confused; the premises which would enable us to draw exact conclusions are lacking. When the conflict ends, we shall know the truly guilty parties, and if they are ours we shall throw the responsibility upon them."

Desnoyers could hardly keep from laughing at his simplicity. To wait till the end of the war to know who was to blame! . . . And if the Empire should come out conqueror, what responsibility could the Socialists exact in the full pride of victory, they who always confined themselves to electoral battles, without the slightest attempt at rebellion?

"Whatever the cause may be," concluded the Socialist, "this war is very sad. How many dead! . . . I was at Charleroi. One has to see modern warfare close by. . . . We shall conquer; we are going to enter Paris, so they say, but many of our men must fall before obtaining the final victory."

And as though wishing to put these visions of death out of his mind, he resumed his diversion of watching the swans, offering them bits of bread so as to make them swing around in their slow and majestic course.

The Keeper and his family were continually crossing and recrossing the bridge. Seeing their master on such friendly terms with the invaders, they had lost some of the fear which had kept them shut up in their cottage. To the woman it seemed but natural that Don Marcelo's authority should be recognized by these people; the master is always the master. And as though she had received a part of this authority, she was entering the castle fearlessly, followed by her daughter, in order to put in order her master's sleeping room. They had decided to pass the night in rooms near his, that he might not feel so lonely among the Germans.

The two women were carrying bedding and mattresses from the lodge to the top floor. The Keeper was occupied in heating a second bath for His Excellency while his wife was bemoaning with gestures of despair the sacking of the castle. How many exquisite things had disappeared! . . . Desirous of saving the remainder, she besought her master to make complaints, as though he could prevent the individual and stealthy robberies. The orderlies and followers of the Count were pocketing everything they could lay their hands on, saying smilingly that they were souvenirs. Later on the woman approached Desnoyers with a mysterious air to impart a new revelation. She had seen a head officer force open the chiffoniers where her mistress was accustomed to keep her lingerie, and he was making up a package of the finest pieces, including a great quantity of blonde lace.

"That's the one, Master," she said soon after, pointing to a German who was writing in the garden, where an oblique ray of sunlight was filtering through the branches upon his table.

Don Marcelo recognized him with surprise. Commandant Blumhardt, too! . . . But immediately he excused the act. He supposed it was only natural that this official should want to take something away from the castle, since the Count had set the example. Besides, he took into account the quality of the objects which he was appropriating. They were not for himself; they were for the wife, for the daughters. . . . A good father of his family! For more than an hour now, he had been sitting before that table writing incessantly, conversing, pen in hand, with his Augusta and all the family in Cassel. Better that this good man should carry off his stuff than those other domineering officers with cutting voices and insolent stiffness.

Desnoyers noticed, too, that the writer raised his head every time that Georgette, the Warden's daughter, passed by, following her with his eyes. The poor father! . . . Undoubtedly he was comparing her with his two girls home in Germany, with all their thoughts on the war. He, too, was thinking of Chichi, fearing sometimes, that he might never see her again. In one of her trips from the castle to her home, Blumhardt called the child to him. She stopped before the table, timid and shrinking as though she felt a presentiment of danger, but making an effort to smile. The Prussian father meanwhile chatted with her, and patted her cheeks with his great paws—a sight which touched Desnoyers deeply. The memories of a pacific and virtuous life were rising above the horrors of war. Decidedly this one enemy was a good man, anyway.

Because of his conclusion, the millionaire smiled indulgently when the Commandant, leaving the table, came toward him—after delivering his letter and a bulky package to a soldier to take to the battalion post-office in the village.

"It is for my family," he explained. "I do not let a day pass without sending them a letter. Theirs are so precious to me! . . . I am also sending them a few remembrances."

Desnoyers was on the point of protesting. . . . But with a shrug of indifference, he concluded to keep silence as if he did not object. The Commandant continued talking of the sweet Augusta and their children while the invisible tempest kept on thundering beyond the serene twilight horizon. Each time the cannonading was more intense.

"The battle," continued Blumhardt. "Always a battle! . . . Surely it is the last and we are going to win. Within the week, we shall be entering Paris. . . . But how many will never see it! So many dead! . . . I understand that to-morrow we shall not be here. All the Reserves are to combine with the attack so as to overcome the last resistance. . . . If only I do not fall!" . . .

Thoughts of the possibility of death the following day contracted his forehead in a scowl of hatred. A deep, vertical line was parting his eyebrows. He frowned ferociously at Desnoyers as though making him responsible for his death and the trouble of his family. For a few moments Don Marcelo could hardly recognize this man, transformed by warlike passions, as the sweet-natured and friendly Blumhardt of a little while before.

The sun was beginning to set when a sub-officer, the one of the Social-Democracy, came running in search of the Commandant. Desnoyers could not understand what was the matter because they were speaking in German, but following the direction of the messenger's continual pointing, he saw beyond the iron gates a group of country people and some soldiers with guns. Blumhardt, after a brief reflection, started toward the group and Don Marcelo behind him.

Soon he saw a village lad in the charge of some Germans who were holding their bayonets to his breast. His face was colorless, with the whiteness of a wax candle. His shirt, blackened with soot, was so badly torn that it told of a hand-to-hand struggle. On one temple was a gash, bleeding badly. A short distance away was a woman with dishevelled hair, holding a baby, and surrounded by four children all covered with black grime as though coming from a coal mine.

The woman was pleading desperately, raising her hands appealingly, her sobs interrupting her story which she was uselessly trying to tell the soldiers, incapable of understanding her. The petty officer convoying the band spoke in German with the Commandant while the woman besought the intervention of Desnoyers. When she recognized the owner of the castle, she suddenly regained her serenity, believing that he could intercede for her.

That husky young boy was her son. They had all been hiding since the day before in the cellar of their burned house. Hunger and the danger of death from asphyxiation had forced them finally to venture forth. As soon as the Germans had seen her son, they had beaten him and were going to shoot him as they were shooting all the young men. They believed that the lad was twenty years old, the age of a soldier, and in order that he might not join the French army, they were going to kill him.

"It's a lie!" shrieked the mother. "He is not more than eighteen . . . not eighteen . . . a little less—he's only seventeen."

She turned to those who were following behind, in order to implore their testimony—sad women, equally dirty, their ragged garments smelling of fire, poverty and death. All assented, adding their outcries to those of the mother. Some even went so far as to say that the overgrown boy was only sixteen . . . fifteen! And to this feminine chorus was added the wailing of the little ones looking at their brother with eyes distended with terror.

The Commandant examined the prisoner while he listened to the official. An employee of the township had said carelessly that the child was about twenty, never dreaming that with this inaccuracy he was causing his death.

"It was a lie!" repeated the mother guessing instinctively what they were saying. "That man made a mistake. My boy is robust and, therefore, looks older than he is, but he is not twenty. . . . The gentleman from the castle who knows him can tell you so. Is it not so, Monsieur Desnoyers?"

Since, in her maternal desperation, she had appealed to his protection, Don Marcelo believed that he ought to intervene, and so he spoke to the Commandant. He knew this youth very well (he did not ever remember having seen him before) and believed that he really was under twenty.

"And even if he were of age," he added, "is that a crime to shoot a man for?"

Blumhardt did not reply. Since he had recovered his functions of command, he ignored absolutely Don Marcelo's existence. He was about to say something, to give an order, but hesitated. It might be better to consult His Excellency . . . and seeing that he was going toward the castle, Desnoyers marched by his side.

"Commandant, this cannot be," he commenced saying. "This lacks common sense. To shoot a man on the suspicion that he may be twenty years old!"

But the Commandant remained silent and continued on his way. As they crossed the bridge, they heard the sound of the piano—a good omen, Desnoyers thought. The aesthete who had so touched him with his impassioned voice, was going to say the saving word.

On entering the salon, he did not at first recognize His Excellency. He saw a man sitting at the piano wearing no clothing but a Japanese dressing gown—a woman's rose-colored kimono, embroidered with golden birds, belonging to Chichi. At any other time, he would have burst into roars of laughter at beholding this scrawny, bony warrior with the cruel eyes, with his brawny braceleted arms appearing through the loose sleeves. After taking his bath, the Count had delayed putting on his uniform, luxuriating in the silky contact of the feminine tunic so like his Oriental garments in Berlin. Blumhardt did not betray the slightest astonishment at the aspect of his general. In the customary attitude of military erectness, he spoke in his own language while the Count listened with a bored air, meanwhile passing his fingers idly over the keys.

A shaft of sunlight from a nearby window was enveloping the piano and musician in a halo of gold. Through the window, too, was wafting the poetry of the sunset—the rustling of the leaves, the hushed song of the birds and the hum of the insects whose transparent wings were glowing like sparks in the last rays of the sun. The General, annoyed that his dreaming melancholy should be interrupted by this inopportune visit, cut short the Commandant's story with a gesture of command and a word . . . one word only. He said no more. He took two puffs from a Turkish cigarette that was slowly scorching the wood of the piano, and again ran his hands over the ivory keys, catching up the broken threads of the vague and tender improvisation inspired by the gloaming.

"Thanks, Your Excellency," said the gratified Desnoyers, surmising his magnanimous response.

The Commandant had disappeared, nor could the Frenchman find him outside the castle. A soldier was pacing up and down near the iron gates in order to transmit commands, and the guards were pushing back with blows from their guns, a screaming group of women and tiny children. The entrance was entirely cleared! undoubtedly the crowds were returning to the village after the General's pardon. . . . Desnoyers was half way down the avenue when he heard a howling sound composed of many voices, a hair-raising shriek such as only womanly desperation can send forth. At the same time, the air was vibrating with snaps, the loud cracking sound that he knew from the day before. Shots! . . . He imagined that on the other side of the iron railing there were some writhing bodies struggling to escape from powerful arms, and others fleeing with bounds of fear. He saw running toward him a horror-stricken, sobbing woman with her hands to her head. It was the wife of the Keeper who a little while before had joined the desperate group of women.

"Oh, don't go on, Master," she called stopping his hurried step. "They have killed him. . . . They have just shot him."

Don Marcelo stood rooted to the ground. Shot! . . . and after the General's pardon! . . . Suddenly he ran back to the castle, hardly knowing what he was doing, and soon reached the salon. His Excellency was still at the piano humming in low tones, his eyes moistened by the poesy of his dreams. But the breathless old gentleman did not stop to listen.

"They have shot him, Your Excellency. . . . They have just killed him in spite of your order."

The smile which crossed the Count's face immediately informed him of his mistake.

"That is war, my dear sir," said the player, pausing for a moment. "War with its cruel necessities. . . . It is always expedient to destroy the enemy of to-morrow."

And with a pedantic air as though he were giving a lesson, he discoursed about the Orientals, great masters of the art of living. One of the personages most admired by him was a certain Sultan of the Turkish conquest who, with his own hands, had strangled the sons of the adversary. "Our foes do not come into the world on horseback and brandishing the lance," said that hero. "All are born as children, and it is advisable to wipe them from the face of the earth before they grow up."

Desnoyers listened without taking it in. One thought only was occupying his mind. . . . That man that he had supposed just, that sentimentalist so affected by his own singing, had, between two arpeggios, coldly given the order for death! . .

The Count made a gesture of impatience. He might retire now, and he counselled him to be more discreet in the future, avoiding mixing himself up in the affairs of the service. Then he turned his back, running his hands over the piano, and giving himself up to harmonious melancholy.

For Don Marcelo there now began an absurd life of the most extraordinary events, an experience which was going to last four days. In his life history, this period represented a long parenthesis of stupefaction, slashed by the most horrible visions.

Not wishing to meet these men again, he abandoned his own bedroom, taking refuge on the top floor in the servants' quarters, near the room selected by the Warden and his family. In vain the good woman kept offering him things to eat as the night came on—he had no appetite. He lay stretched out on the bed, preferring to be alone with his thoughts in the dark. When would this martyrdom ever come to an end? . . .

There came into his mind the recollection of a trip which he had made to London some years ago. In his imagination he again saw the British Museum and certain Assyrian bas-reliefs—relics of bestial humanity, which had filled him with terror. The warriors were represented as burning the towns; the prisoners were beheaded in heaps; the pacific countrymen were marching in lines with chains on their necks, forming strings of slaves. Until that moment he had never realized the advance which civilization had made through the centuries. Wars were still breaking out now and then, but they had been regulated by the march of progress. The life of the prisoner was now held sacred; the captured towns must be respected; there existed a complete code of international law to regulate how men should be killed and nations should combat, causing the least possible harm. . . . But now he had just seen the primitive realities of war. The same as that of thousands of years ago! The men with the helmets were proceeding in exactly the same way as those ferocious and perfumed satraps with blue mitre and curled beard. The adversary was shot although not carrying arms; the prisoner died of shot or blow from the gun; the civilian captives were sent in crowds to Germany like those of other centuries. Of what avail was all our so-called Progress? Where was our boasted civilization? . . .

He was awakened by the light of a candle in his eyes. The Warden's wife had come up again to see if he needed anything.

"Oh, what a night, Master! Just hear them yelling and singing! The bottles that they have emptied! . . . They are in the dining room. You better not see them. Now they are amusing themselves by breaking the furniture. Even the

Count is drunk; drunk, too, is that Commandant that you were talking with, and all the rest. . . . Some of them are dancing half-naked."

She evidently wished to keep quiet about certain details, but her love of talking got the better of her discretion. Some of the officers had dressed themselves up in the hats and gowns of her mistress and were dancing and shouting, imitating feminine seductiveness and affectations. . . . One of them had been greeted with roars of enthusiasm upon presenting himself with no other clothing than a "combination" of Mademoiselle Chichi's. Many were taking obscene delight in soiling the rugs and filling the sideboard drawers with indescribable filth, using the finest linens that they could lay their hands on.

Her master silenced her peremptorily. Why tell him such vile, disgusting things? . . .

"And we are obliged to wait on them!" wailed the woman. "They are beside themselves; they appear like different beings. The soldiers are saying that they are going to resume their march at daybreak. There is a great battle on, and they are going to win it; but it is necessary that everyone of them should fight in it. . . . My poor, sick husband just can't stand it any longer. So many humiliations . . . and my little girl . . . . My little girl!"

The child was her greatest anxiety. She had her well hidden away, but she was watching uneasily the goings and comings of some of these men maddened with alcohol. The most terrible of them all was that fat officer who had patted Georgette so paternally.

Apprehension for her daughter's safety made her hurry restlessly away, saying over and over:

"God has forgotten the world. . . . Ay, what is ever going to become of us!"

Don Marcelo was now tinglingly awake. Through the open window was blowing the clear night air. The cannonading was still going on, prolonging the conflict way into the night. Below the castle the soldiers were intoning a slow and melodious chant that sounded like a psalm. From the interior of the edifice rose the whoopings of brutal laughter, the crash of breaking furniture, and the mad chase of dissolute pursuit. When would this diabolical orgy ever wear itself down? . . . For a long time he was not at all sleepy, but was gradually losing consciousness of what was going on around him when he was roused with a start. Near him, on the same floor, a door had fallen with a crash, unable to resist a succession of formidable batterings. This was followed immediately by the screams of a woman, weeping, desperate supplications, the noise of a struggle, reeling steps, and the thud of bodies against the wall. He had a presentiment that it was Georgette shrieking and trying to defend herself. Before he could put his feet to the floor he heard a man's voice, which he was sure was the Keeper's; she was safe.

"Ah, you villain!" . . .

Then the outbreak of a second struggle . . . a shot . . . silence!

Rushing down the hallway that ended at the stairway Desnoyers saw lights, and many men who came trooping up the stairs, bounding over several steps at a time. He almost fell over a body from which escaped a groan of agony. At his feet lay the Warden, his chest moving like a pair of bellows, his eyes glassy and unnaturally distended, his mouth covered with blood. . . . Near him glistened a kitchen knife. Then he saw a man with a revolver in one hand, and holding shut with the other a broken door that someone was trying to open from within. Don Marcelo recognized him, in spite of his greenish pallor and wild look. It was Blumhardt—another Blumhardt with a bestial expression of terrifying ferocity and lust.

Don Marcelo could see clearly how it had all happened—the debauchee rushing through the castle in search of his prey, the anxious father in close pursuit, the cries of the girl, the unequal struggle between the consumptive with his emergency weapon and the warrior triumphant. The fury of his youth awoke in the old Frenchman, sweeping everything before it. What did it matter if he did die? . . .

"Ah, you villain!" he yelled, as the poor father had done.

And with clenched fists he marched up to the German, who smiled coldly and held his revolver to his eyes. He was just going to shoot him . . . but at that instant Desnoyers fell to the floor, knocked down by those who were leaping up the stairs. He received many blows, the heavy boots of the invaders hammering him with their heels. He felt a hot stream pouring over his face. Blood! . . . He did not know whether it was his own or that of the palpitating mortal slowly dying beside him. Then he found himself lifted from the floor by many hands which pushed him toward a man. It was His Excellency, with his uniform burst open and smelling of wine. Eyes and voice were both trembling.

"My dear sir," he stuttered, trying to recover this suave irony, "I warned you not to interfere in our affairs and you have not obeyed me. You may now take the consequences of your lack of discretion."

He gave an order, and the old man felt himself pushed downstairs to the cellars underneath the castle. Those conducting him were soldiers under the command of a petty officer whom he recognized as the Socialist. This young professor was the only one sober, but he maintained himself erect and unapproachable with the ferocity of discipline.

He put his prisoner into an arched vault without any breathing-place except a tiny window on a level with the floor. Many broken bottles and chests with some straw were all that was in the cave.

"You have insulted a head officer!" said the official roughly, "and they will probably shoot you to-morrow. Your only salvation lies in the continuance of the revels, in which case they may forget you."

As the door of this sub-cellar was broken, like all the others in the building, a pile of boxes and furniture was heaped in the entrance way.

Don Marcelo passed the rest of the night tormented with the cold—the only thing which worried him just then. He had abandoned all hope of life; even the images of his family seemed blotted from his memory. He worked in the dark in order to make himself more comfortable on the chests, burrowing down into the straw for the sake of its heat. When the morning breeze began to sift in through the little window he fell slowly into a heavy, overpowering sleep, like that of criminals condemned to death, or duellists before the fatal morning. He thought he heard shouts in German, the galloping of horses, a distant sound of tattoo and whistle such as the battalions of the invaders made with their fifes and drums. . . . Then he lost all consciousness of his surroundings.

On opening his eyes again a ray of sunlight, slipping through the window, was tracing a little golden square on the wall, giving a regal splendor to the hanging cobwebs. Somebody was removing the barricade before the door. A woman's voice, timid and distressed, was calling repeatedly:

"Master, are you here?"

He sprang up quickly, wishing to aid the worker outside, and pushing vigorously. He thought that the invaders must have left. In no other way could he imagine the Warden's wife daring to try to get him out of his cell.

"Yes, they have gone," she said. "Nobody is left in the castle."

As soon as he was able to get out Don Marcelo looked inquiringly at the woman with her bloodshot eyes, dishevelled hair and sorrow-drawn face. The night had weighed her down pitilessly with the pressure of many years. All the energy with which she had been working to free Desnoyers disappeared on seeing him again. "Oh, Master . . . Master," she moaned convulsively; and she flung herself into his arms, bursting into tears.

Don Marcelo did not need to ask anything further; he dreaded to know the truth. Nevertheless, he asked after her husband. Now that he was awake and free, he cherished the fleeting hope that what he had gone through the night before was but another of his nightmares. Perhaps the poor man was still living. . . .

"They killed him, Monsieur. That man who seemed so good murdered him. . . . And I don't know where his body is; nobody will tell me."

She had a suspicion that the corpse was in the fosse. The green and tranquil waters had closed mysteriously over this victim of the night. . . . Desnoyers suspected that another sorrow was troubling the mother still more, but he kept modestly silent. It was she who finally spoke, between outbursts of grief. . . . Georgette was now in the lodge. Horror-stricken and shuddering, she had fled there when the invaders had left the castle. They had kept her in their power until the last minute.

"Oh, Master, don't look at her. . . . She is trembling and sobbing at the thought that you may speak with her about what she has gone through. She is almost out of her mind. She longs to die! Ay, my little girl! . . . And is there no one who will punish these monsters?"

They had come up from the cellars and crossed the bridge, the woman looking fixedly into the silent waters. The dead body of a swan was floating upon them. Before their departure, while their horses were being saddled, two officers had amused themselves by chasing with revolver shots the birds swimming in the moat. The aquatic plants were spotted with blood; among the leaves were floating some tufts of limp white plumage like a bit of washing escaped from the hands of a laundress.

Don Marcelo and the woman exchanged a compassionate glance, and then looked pityingly at each other as the sunlight brought out more strongly their aging, wan appearance.

The passing of these people had destroyed everything. There was no food left in the castle except some crusts of dry bread forgotten in the kitchen. "And we have to live, Monsieur!" exclaimed the woman with reviving energy as she thought of her daughter's need. "We have to live, if only to see how God punishes them!" The old man shrugged his shoulders in despair; God? . . . But the woman was right; they had to live.

With the famished audacity of his early youth, when he was travelling over boundless tracts of land, driving his herds of cattle, he now rushed outside the park, hunting for some form of sustenance. He saw the valley, fair and green, basking in the sun; the groups of trees, the plots of yellowish soil with the hard spikes of stubble; the hedges in which the birds were singing—all the summer splendor of a countryside developed and cultivated during fifteen centuries by dozens and dozens of generations. And yet—here he was alone at the mercy of chance, likely to perish with hunger—more alone than when he was crossing the towering heights of the Andes—those irregular slopes of rocks and snow wrapped in endless silence, only broken from time to time by the flapping of the condor's wings. Nobody. . . . His gaze could not distinguish a single movable point—everything fixed, motionless, crystallized, as though contracted with fear before the peals of thunder which were still rumbling around the horizon.

He went on toward the village—a mass of black walls with a few houses still intact, and a roofless bell tower with its cross twisted by fire. Nobody in the streets sown with bottles, charred chunks of wood, and soot-covered rubbish. The dead bodies had disappeared, but a nauseating smell of decomposing and burned flesh assailed his nostrils. He saw a mound of earth where the shooting had taken place, and from it were protruding two feet and a hand. At his approach several black forms flew up into the air from a trench so shallow that the bodies within were exposed to view. A whirring of stiff wings beat the air above him, flying off with the croakings of wrath. He explored every nook and corner, even approaching the place where the troopers had erected their barricade. The carts were still by the roadside.

He then retraced his steps, calling out before the least injured houses, and putting his head through the doors and windows that were unobstructed or but half consumed. Was nobody left in Villeblanche? He descried among the ruins something advancing on all fours, a species of reptile that stopped its crawling with movements of hesitation and fear, ready to retreat or slip into its hole under the ruins. Suddenly the creature stopped and stood up. It was a man, an old man. Other human larvae were coming forth conjured by his shouts—poor beings who hours ago had given up the standing position which would have attracted the bullets of the enemy, and had been enviously imitating the lower organisms, squirming through the dirt as fast as they could scurry into the bosom of the earth. They were mostly women and children, all filthy and black, with snarled hair, the fierceness of animal appetite in their eyes—the faintness of the weak animal in their hanging jaws. They were all living hidden in the ruins of their homes. Fear had made them temporarily forget their hunger, but finding that the enemy had gone, they were suddenly assailed by all necessitous demands, intensified by hours of anguish.

Desnoyers felt as though he were surrounded by a tribe of brutalized and famished Indians like those he had often seen in his adventurous voyages. He had brought with him from Paris a quantity of gold pieces, and he pulled out a coin which glittered in the sun. Bread was needed, everything eatable was needed; he would pay without haggling.

The flash of gold aroused looks of enthusiasm and greediness, but this impression was short-lived, all eyes contemplating the yellow discs with indifference. Don Marcelo was himself convinced that the miraculous charm had lost its power. They all chanted a chorus of sorrow and horrors with slow and plaintive voice, as though they stood weeping before a bier: "Monsieur, they have killed my husband." . . . "Monsieur, my sons! Two of them are missing." . . . "Monsieur, they have taken all the men prisoners: they say it is to work the land in Germany." . . . "Monsieur, bread! . . . My little ones are dying of hunger!"

One woman was lamenting something worse than death. "My girl! . . . My poor girl!" Her look of hatred and wild desperation revealed the secret tragedy; her outcries and tears recalled that other mother who was sobbing in the same way up at the castle. In the depths of some cave, was lying the victim, half-dead with fatigue, shaken with a wild delirium in which she still saw the succession of brutal faces, inflamed with simian passion.

The miserable group, forming themselves into a circle around him, stretched out their hands beseechingly toward the man whom they knew to be so very rich. The women showed him the death-pallor on the faces of their scarcely breathing babies, their eyes glazed with starvation. "Bread! . . . bread!" they implored, as though he could work a miracle. He gave to one mother the gold piece that he had in his hand and distributed more to the others. They took them without looking at them, and continued their lament, "Bread! . . . Bread!" And he had gone to the village to make the same supplication! . . . He fled, recognizing the uselessness of his efforts.

CHAPTER VI

THE BANNER OF THE RED CROSS

Returning in desperation to his estate, Don Marcelo Desnoyers saw huge automobiles and men on horseback, forming a very long convoy and completely filling the road. They were all going in his direction. At the entrance to the park a band of Germans was putting up the wires for a telephone line. They had just been reconnoitering the rooms befouled with the night's saturnalia, and were ha-haing boisterously over Captain von Hartrott's inscription, "Bitte, nicht plundern." To them it seemed the acme of wit—truly Teutonic.

The convoy now invaded the park with its automobiles and trucks bearing a red cross. A war hospital was going to be established in the castle. The doctors were dressed in grayish green and armed the same as the officers; they also imitated their freezing hauteur and repellent unapproachableness. There came out of the drays hundreds of folding cots, which were placed in rows in the different rooms. The furniture that still remained was thrown out in a heap under the trees. Squads of soldiers were obeying with mechanical promptitude the brief and imperious orders. An odor of an apothecary shop, of concentrated drugs, now pervaded the quarters, mixed with the strong smell of the antiseptics with which they were sprinkling the walls in order to disinfect the filthy remains of the nocturnal orgy.

Then he saw women clad in white, buxom girls with blue eyes and flaxen hair. They were grave, bland, austere and implacable in appearance. Several times they pushed Desnoyers out of their way as if they did not see him. They looked like nuns, but with revolvers under their habits.

At midday other automobiles began to arrive, attracted by the enormous white flag with the red cross, which was now waving from the castle tower. They came from the division battling beyond the Marne. Their metal fittings were dented by projectiles, their wind-shields broken by star-shaped holes. From their interiors appeared men and more men; some on foot, others on canvas stretchers—faces pale and rubicund, profiles aquiline and snubby, red heads and skulls wrapped in white turbans stiff with blood; mouths that laughed with bravado and mouths that groaned with bluish lips; jaws supported with mummy-like bandages; giants in agony whose wounds were not apparent; shapeless forms ending in a head that talked and smoked; legs with hanging flesh that was dyeing the First Aid wrappings with their red moisture; arms that hung as inert as dead boughs; torn uniforms in which were conspicuous the tragic vacancies of absent members.

This avalanche of suffering was quickly distributed throughout the castle. In a few hours it was so completely filled that there was not a vacant bed—the last arrivals being laid in the shadow of the trees. The telephones were ringing incessantly; the surgeons in coarse aprons were going from one side to the other, working rapidly; human life was submitted to savage proceedings with roughness and celerity. Those who died under it simply left one more cot free for the others that kept on coming. Desnoyers saw bloody baskets filled with shapeless masses of flesh, strips of skin, broken bones, entire limbs. The orderlies were carrying these terrible remnants to the foot of the park in order to bury them in a little plot which had been Chichi's favorite reading nook.

Pairs of soldiers were carrying out objects wrapped in sheets which the owner recognized as his. These were the dead, and the park was soon converted into a cemetery. No longer was the little retreat large enough to hold the corpses and the severed remains from the operations. New grave trenches were being opened near by. The Germans armed with shovels were pressing into service a dozen of the farmer-prisoners to aid in unloading the dead. Now they were bringing them down by the cartload, dumping them in like the rubbish from some demolished building. Don Marcelo felt an abnormal delight in contemplating this increasing number of vanquished enemies, yet he grieved at the same time that this precipitation of intruders should be deposited forever on his property.

At nightfall, overwhelmed by so many emotions, he again suffered the torments of hunger. All day long he had eaten nothing but the crust of bread found in the kitchen by the Warden's wife. The rest he had left for her and her daughter. A distress as harrowing to him as his hunger was the sight of poor Georgette's shocked despondency. She was always trying to escape from his presence in an agony of shame.

"Don't let the Master see me!" she would cry, hiding her face. Since his presence seemed to recall more vividly the memory of her assaults, Desnoyers tried, while in the lodge, to avoid going near her.

Desperate with the gnawings of his empty stomach, he accosted several doctors who were speaking French, but all in vain. They would not listen to him, and when he repeated his petitions they pushed him roughly out of their way. . . . He was not going to perish with hunger in the midst of his riches! Those people were eating; the indifferent nurses had established themselves in his kitchen. . . . But the time passed on without encountering anybody who would take pity on this old man dragging himself weakly from one place to another, in the misery of an old age intensified by despair, and suffering in every part of the body, the results of the blows of the night before. He now knew the gnawings of a hunger far worse than that which he had suffered when journeying over the desert plains—a hunger among men, in a civilized country, wearing a belt filled with gold, surrounded with towers and castle halls which were his, but in the control of others who would not condescend to listen to him. And for this piteous ending of his life he had amassed millions and returned to Europe! . . . Ah, the irony of fate! . . .

He saw a doctor's assistant leaning up against a tree, about to devour a slab of bread and sausage. His envious eyes scrutinized this fellow, tall, thick-set, his jaws bristling with a great red beard. The trembling old man staggered up to him, begging for the food by signs and holding out a piece of money. The German's eyes glistened at the sight of the gold, and a beatific smile stretched his mouth from ear to ear.

"Ya," he responded, and grabbing the money, he handed over the food.

Don Marcelo commenced to swallow it with avidity. Never had he so appreciated the sheer ecstasy of eating as at that instant—in the midst of his gardens converted into a cemetery, before his despoiled castle where hundreds of human beings were groaning in agony. A grayish arm passed before his eyes; it belonged to the German, who had returned with two slices of bread and a bit of meat snatched from the kitchen. He repeated his smirking "Ya?" . . . and after his victim had secured it by means of another gold coin, he was able to take it to the two women hidden in the cottage.

During the night—a night of painful watching, cut with visions of horror, it seemed to him that the roar of the artillery was coming nearer. It was a scarcely perceptible difference, perhaps the effect of the silence of the night which always intensifies sound. The ambulances continued coming from the front, discharging their cargoes of riddled humanity and going back for more. Desnoyers surmised that his castle was but one of the many hospitals established in a line of more than eighty miles, and that on the other side, behind the French, were many similar ones in which the same activity was going on—the consignments of dying men succeeding each other with terrifying frequency. Many of the combatants were not even having the satisfaction of being taken from the battle field, but were lying groaning on the ground, burying their bleeding members in the dust or mud, and weltering in the ooze from their wounds. . . . And Don Marcelo, who a few hours before had been considering himself the unhappiest of mortals, now experienced a cruel joy in reflecting that so many thousands of vigorous men at the point of death could well envy him for his hale old age, and for the tranquillity with which he was reposing on that humble bed.

The next morning the orderly was waiting for him in the same place, holding out a napkin filled with eatables. Good red-bearded man, helpful and kind! . . . and he offered him the piece of gold.

"Nein," replied the fellow, with a broad, malicious grin. Two gleaming gold pieces appeared between Don Marcelo's fingers. Another leering "Nein" and a shake of the head. Ah, the robber! How he was taking advantage of his necessity! . . . And not until he had produced five gold coins was he able to secure the package.

He soon began to notice all around him a silent and sly conspiracy to get possession of his money. A giant in a sergeant's uniform put a shovel in his hand pushing him roughly forward. He soon found himself in a corner of the park that had been transformed into a graveyard, near the cart of cadavers; there he had to shovel dirt on his own ground in company with the indignant prisoners.

He averted his eyes so as not to look at the rigid and grotesque bodies piled above him at the edge of the pit, ready to be tumbled in. The ground was sending forth an insufferable odor, for decomposition had already set in in the nearby trenches. The persistence with which his overseers accosted him, and the crafty smile of the sergeant made him see through the deep-laid scheme. The red-beard must be at the bottom of all this. Putting his hand in his pocket he dropped the shovel with a look of interrogation. "Ya," replied the sergeant. After handing over the required sum, the tormented old man was permitted to stop grave-digging and wander around at his pleasure; he knew, however, what was probably in store for him—those men were going to submit him to a merciless exploitation.

Another day passed by, like its predecessor. In the morning of the following day his perceptions, sharpened by apprehension, made him conjecture that something extraordinary had occurred. The automobiles were arriving and departing with greater rapidity, and there was greater disorder and confusion among the executive force. The telephone was ringing with mad precipitation; and the wounded arrivals seemed more depressed. The day before they had been singing when taken from the vehicles, hiding their woe with laughter and bravado, all talking of the near victory and regretting that they would not be able to witness the triumphal entry into Paris. Now they were all very silent, with furrowed brows, thinking no longer about what was going on behind them, wondering only about their own fate.

Outside the park was the buzz of the approaching throng which was blackening the roads. The invasion was beginning again, but with a refluent movement. For hours at a time great strings of gray trucks went puffing by; then regiments of infantry, squadrons, rolling stock. They were marching very slowly with a deliberation that puzzled Desnoyers, who could not make out whether this recessional meant flight or change of position. The only thing that gave him any satisfaction was the stupefied and downcast appearance of the soldiers, the gloomy sulks of the officers. Nobody was shouting; they all appeared to have forgotten their "Nach Paris!" The greenish gray monster still had its armed head stretched across the other side of the Marne, but its tail was beginning to uncoil with uneasy wrigglings.

After night had settled down the troops were still continuing to fall back. The cannonading was certainly coming nearer. Some of the thunderous claps sounded so close that they made the glass tremble in the windows. A fugitive farmer, trying to find refuge in the park, gave Don Marcelo some news. The Germans were in full retreat. They had installed some of their batteries on the banks of the Marne in order to attempt a new resistance. . . . And the new arrival remained without attracting the attention of the invaders who, a few days before, would have shot him on the slightest suspicion.

The mechanical workings of discipline were evidently out of gear. Doctors and nurses were running from place to place, shouting orders and breaking out into a volley of curses every time a fresh ambulance load arrived. The drivers were commanded to take their patients on ahead to another hospital near the rear-guard. Orders had been received to evacuate the castle that very night.

In spite of this prohibition, one of the ambulances unloaded its relay of wounded men. So deplorable was their state that the doctors accepted them, judging it useless for them to continue their journey. They remained in the garden, lying on the same stretchers that they had occupied within the vehicle. By the light of the lanterns Desnoyers recognized one of the dying. It was the secretary to His Excellency, the Socialist professor who had shut him in the cellar vaults.

At the sight of the owner of the castle he smiled as though he had met a comrade. His was the only familiar face among all those people who were speaking his language. He was ghastly in hue, with sunken features and an impalpable glaze spreading over his eyes. He had no visible wounds, but from under the cloak spread over his abdomen his torn intestines exhaled a fatal warning. The presence of Don Marcelo made him guess where they had brought him, and little by little he co-ordinated his recollections. As though the old gentleman might be interested in the whereabouts of his comrades, he told him all he knew in a weak and strained voice. . . . Bad luck for their brigade! They had reached the front at a critical moment for the reserve troops. Commandant Blumhardt had died at the very first, a shell of '75 taking off his head. Dead, too, were all the officers who had lodged in the castle. His Excellency had had his jaw bone torn off by a fragment of shell. He had seen him on the ground, howling with pain, drawing a portrait from his breast and trying to kiss it with his broken mouth. He had himself been hit in the stomach by the same shell. He had lain forty-two hours on the field before he was picked up by the ambulance corps. . . .

And with the mania of the University man, whose hobby is to see everything reasoned out and logically explained, he added in that supreme moment, with the tenacity of those who die talking:

"Sad war, sir. . . . Many premises are lacking in order to decide who is the culpable party. . . . When the war is ended they will have to . . . will have to . . ." And he closed his eyes overcome by the effort. Desnoyers left the dead man, thinking to himself. Poor fellow! He was placing the hour of justice at the termination of the war, and meanwhile hundreds like him were dying, disappearing with all their scruples of ponderous and disciplined reasoning.

That night there was no sleep on the place. The walls of the lodge were creaking, the glass crashing and breaking, the two women in the adjoining room crying out nervously. The noise of the German fire was beginning to mingle with that of other explosives close at hand. He surmised that this was the smashing of the French projectiles which were coming in search of the enemy's artillery above the Marne.

For a few minutes his hopes revived as the possibility of victory flashed into his mind, but he was so depressed by his forlorn situation that such a hope evaporated as quickly as it had come. His own troops were advancing, but this advance did not, perhaps, represent more than a local gain. The line of battle was so extensive! . . . It was going to be as in 1870; the French would achieve partial victories, modified at the last moment by the strategy of the enemies until they were turned into complete defeat.

After midnight the cannonading ceased, but silence was by no means re-established. Automobiles were rolling around the lodge midst hoarse shouts of command. It must be the hospital convoy that was evacuating the castle. Then near daybreak the thudding of horses' hoofs and the wheels of chugging machines thundered through the gates, making the ground tremble. Half an hour afterwards sounded the tramp of multitudes moving at a quick pace, dying away in the depths of the park.

At dawn the old gentleman leaped from his bed, and the first thing he spied from the cottage window was the flag of the Red Cross still floating from the top of the castle. There were no more cots under the trees. On the bridge he met one of the doctors and several assistants. The hospital force had gone with all its transportable patients. There only remained in the castle, under the care of a company, those most gravely wounded. The Valkyries of the health department had also disappeared.

The red-bearded Shylock was among those left behind, and on seeing Don Marcelo afar off, he smiled and immediately vanished. A few minutes after he returned with full hands. Never before had he been so generous. Foreseeing pressing necessity, the hungry man put his hands in his pockets as usual, but was astonished to learn from the orderly's emphatic gestures that he did not wish any money.

"Nein. . . . Nein!"

What generosity was this! . . . The German persisted in his negatives. His enormous mouth expanded in an ingratiating grin as he laid his heavy paws on Marcelo's shoulders. He appeared like a good dog, a meek dog, fawning and licking the hands of the passer-by, coaxing to be taken along with him. "Franzosen. . . . Franzosen." He did not know how to say any more, but the Frenchman read in his words the desire to make him understand that he had always been in great sympathy with the French. Something very important was evidently transpiring—the ill-humored air of those left behind in the castle, and the sudden servility of this plowman in uniform, made it very apparent. . . .

Some distance beyond the castle he saw soldiers, many soldiers. A battalion of infantry had spread itself along the walls with trucks, draught horses and swift mounts. With their pikes the soldiers were making small openings in the mud walls, shaping them into a border of little pinnacles. Others were kneeling or sitting near the apertures, taking off their knapsacks in order that they might be less hampered. Afar off the cannon were booming, and in the intervals between their detonations could be heard the bursting of shrapnel, the bubbling of frying oil, the grinding of a coffee-mill, and the incessant crackling of rifle-fire. Fleecy clouds were floating over the fields, giving to near objects the indefinite lines of unreality. The sun was a faint spot seen between curtains of mist. The trees were weeping fog moisture from all the cracks in their bark.

A thunderclap rent the air so forcibly that it seemed very near the castle. Desnoyers trembled, believing that he had received a blow in the chest. The other men remained impassive with their customary indifference. A cannon had just been discharged but a few feet away from him, and not till then did he realize that two batteries had been installed in the park. The pieces of artillery were hidden under mounds of branches, the gunners having felled trees in order to mask their monsters more perfectly. He saw them arranging the last; with shovels, they were forming a border of earth, a foot in width, around each piece.

This border guarded the feet of the operators whose bodies were protected by steel shields on both sides of them. Then they raised a breastwork of trunks and boughs, leaving only the mouth of the cylindrical mortar visible.

By degrees Don Marcelo became accustomed to the firing which seemed to be creating a vacuum within his cranium. He ground his teeth and clenched his fists at every detonation, but stood stock-still with no desire to leave, dominated by the violence of the explosions, admiring the serenity of these men who were giving orders, erect and coolly, or moving like humble menials around their roaring metal beasts.

All his ideas seemed to have been snatched away by that first discharge of cannon. His brain was living in the present moment only. He turned his eyes insistently toward the white and red banner which was waving from the mansion.

"That is treachery," he thought, "a breach of faith."

Far away, on the other side of the Marne, the French artillery were belching forth their deadly fire. He could imagine their handiwork from the little yellowish clouds that were floating in the air, and the columns of smoke which were spouting forth at various points of the landscape where the German troops were hidden, forming a line which appeared to lose itself in infinity. An atmosphere of protection and respect seemed to be enveloping the castle.

The morning mists had dissolved; the sun was finally showing its bright and limpid light, lengthening the shadows of men and trees to fantastic dimensions. Hills and woods came forth from the haze, fresh and dripping after their morning bath. The entire valley was now completely exposed, and Desnoyers was surprised to see the river from the spot to which he had been rooted—the cannon having opened great windows in the woods that had hid it from view. What most astonished him in looking over this landscape, smiling and lovely in the morning light, was that nobody was to be seen—absolutely nobody. Mountain tops and forests were bellowing without anyone's being in evidence. There must be more than a hundred thousand men in the space swept by his piercing gaze, and yet not a human being was visible. The deadly boom of arms was causing the air to vibrate without leaving any optical trace. There was no other smoke but that of the explosions, the black spirals that were flinging their great shells to burst on the ground. These were rising on all sides, encircling the castle like a ring of giant tops, but not one of that orderly circle ventured to touch the edifice. Don Marcelo again stared at the Red Cross flag. "It is treachery!" he kept repeating; yet at the same time he was selfishly rejoicing in the base expedient, since it served to defend his property.

The battalion was at last completely installed the entire length of the wall, opposite the river. The soldiers, kneeling, were supporting their guns on the newly made turrets and grooves, and seemed satisfied with this rest after a night of battling retreat. They all appeared sleeping with their eyes open. Little by little they were letting themselves drop back on their heels, or seeking the support of their knapsacks. Snores were heard in the brief spaces between the artillery fire. The officials standing behind them were examining the country with their field glasses, or talking in knots. Some appeared disheartened, others furious at the backward flight that had been going on since the day before. The majority appeared calm, with the passivity of obedience. The battle front was immense; who could foresee the outcome? . . . There they were in full retreat, but in other places, perhaps, their comrades might be advancing with decided gains. Until the very last moment, no soldier knows certainly the fate of the struggle. What was most grieving this detachment was the fact that it was all the time getting further away from Paris.

Don Marcelo's eye was caught by a sparkling circle of glass, a monocle fixed upon him with aggressive insistence. A lank lieutenant with the corseted waist of the officers that he had seen in Berlin, a genuine Junker, was a few feet away, sword in hand behind his men, like a wrathful and glowering shepherd.

"What are you doing here?" he said gruffly.

Desnoyers explained that he was the owner of the castle. "French?" continued the lieutenant. "Yes, French." . . . The official scowled in hostile meditation, feeling the necessity of saying something against the enemy. The shouts and antics of his companions-at-arms put a summary end to his reflections. They were all staring upward, and the old man followed their gaze.

For an hour past, there had been streaking through the air frightful roarings enveloped in yellowish vapors, strips of cloud which seemed to contain wheels revolving with frenzied rotation. They were the projectiles of the heavy German artillery which, fired from various distances, threw their great shells over the castle. Certainly that could not be what was interesting the officials!

He half shut his eyes in order to see better, and finally near the edge of a cloud, he distinguished a species of mosquito flashing in the sunlight. Between brief intervals of silence, could be heard the distant, faint buzz announcing its presence. The officers nodded their heads. "Franzosen!" Desnoyers thought so, too. He could not believe that the enemy's two black crosses were between those wings. Instead he saw with his mind's eye, two tricolored rings like the circular spots which color the fluttering wings of butterflies.

This explained the agitation of the Germans. The French air-bird remained motionless for a few seconds over the castle, regardless of the white bubbles exploding underneath and around it. In vain the cannon nearest hurled their deadly fire. It wheeled rapidly, and returned to the place from which it came.

"It must have taken in the whole situation," thought the old Frenchman. "It has found them out; it knows what is going on here."

He guessed rightly that this information would swiftly change the course of events. Everything which had been happening in the early morning hours was going to sink into insignificance compared with what was coming now. He shuddered with fear, the irresistible fear of the unknown, and yet at the same time, he was filled with curiosity, impatience and nervous dread before a danger that threatened and would not stay its relentless course.

Outside the park, but a short distance from the mud wall, sounded a strident explosion like a stupendous blow from a gigantic axe—an axe as big as his castle. There began flying through the air entire treetops, trunks split in two, great chunks of earth with the vegetation still clinging, a rain of dirt that obscured the heavens. Some stones fell down from the wall. The Germans crouched but with no visible emotion. They knew what it meant; they had been expecting it as something inevitable after seeing the French aeroplane. The Red Cross flag could no longer deceive the enemy's artillery.

Don Marcelo had not time to recover from his surprise before there came a second explosion nearer the mud wall . . . a third inside the park. It seemed to him that he had been suddenly flung into another world from which he was seeing men and things across a fantastic atmosphere which roared and rocked and destroyed with the violence of its reverberations. He was stunned with the awfulness of it all, and yet he was not afraid. Until then, he had imagined fear in a very different form. He felt an agonizing vacuum in his stomach. He staggered violently all the time, as though some force were pushing him about, giving him first a blow on the chest, and then another on the back to straighten him up.

A strong smell of acids penetrated the atmosphere, making respiration very difficult, and filling his eyes with smarting tears. On the other hand, the uproar no longer disturbed him, it did not exist for him. He supposed it was still going on from the trembling air, the shaking of things around him, in the whirlwind which was bending men double but was not reacting within his body. He had lost the faculty of hearing; all the strength of his senses had concentrated themselves in looking. His eyes appeared to have acquired multiple facets like those of certain insects. He saw what was happening before, beside, behind him, simultaneously witnessing extraordinary things as though all the laws of life had been capriciously overthrown.

An official a few feet away suddenly took an inexplicable flight. He began to rise without losing his military rigidity, still helmeted, with furrowed brow, moustache blond and short, mustard-colored chest, and gloved hands still holding field-glasses and map—but there his individuality stopped. The lower extremities, in their grayish leggings remained on the ground, inanimate as reddening, empty moulds. The trunk, in its violent ascent, spread its contents abroad like a bursting rocket. Further on, some gunners, standing upright, were suddenly stretched full length, converted into a motionless row, bathed in blood.

The line of infantry was lying close to the ground. The men had huddled themselves together near the loopholes through which they aimed their guns, trying to make themselves less visible. Many had placed their knapsacks over their heads or at their backs to defend themselves from the flying bits of shell. If they moved at all, it was only to worm their way further into the earth, trying to hollow it out with their stomachs. Many of them had changed position with mysterious rapidity, now lying stretched on their backs as though asleep. One had his uniform torn open across the abdomen, showing between the rents of the cloth, slabs of flesh, blue and red that protruded and swelled up with a bubbling expansion. Another had his legs shot away, and was looking around with surprised eyes and a black mouth rounded into an effort to howl, but from which no sound ever came.

Desnoyers had lost all notion of time. He could not tell whether he had been rooted to that spot for many hours or for a single moment. The only thing that caused him anxiety was the persistent trembling of his legs which were refusing to sustain him. . . .

Something fell behind him. It was raining ruin. Turning his head, he saw his castle completely transformed. Half of the tower had just been carried off. The pieces of slate were scattered everywhere in tiny chips; the walls were crumbling; loose window frames were balancing on edge like fragments of stage scenery, and the old wood of the tower hood was beginning to burn like a torch.

The spectacle of this instantaneous change in his property impressed him more than the ravages of death, making him realize the Cyclopean power of the blind, avenging forces raging around him. The vital force that had been concentrated in his eyes, now spread to his feet . . . and he started to run without knowing whither, feeling the same necessity to hide himself as had those men enchained by discipline who were trying to flatten themselves into the earth in imitation of the reptile's pliant invisibility.

His instinct was pushing him toward the lodge, but half way up the avenue, he was stopped by another lot of astounding transformations. An unseen hand had just snatched away half of the cottage roof. The entire side wall doubled over, forming a cascade of bricks and dust. The interior rooms were now exposed to view like a theatrical setting—the kitchen where he had eaten, the upper floor with the room in which he descried his still unmade bed. The poor women! . . .

He turned around, running now toward the castle, trying to make the sub-cellar in which he had been fastened for the night; and when he finally found himself under those dusty cobwebs, he felt as though he were in the most luxurious salon, and he devoutly blessed the good workmanship of the castle builders.

The subterranean silence began gradually to bring back his sense of hearing. The cannonading of the Germans and the bursting of the French shells sounded from his retreat like a distant tempest. There came into his mind the eulogies which he had been accustomed to lavish upon the cannon of '75 without knowing anything about it except by hearsay. Now he had witnessed its effects. "It shoots TOO well!" he muttered. In a short time it would finish destroying his castle—he was finding such perfection excessive.

But he soon repented of these selfish lamentations. An idea, tenacious as remorse, had fastened itself in his brain. It now seemed to him that all he was passing through was an expiation for the great mistake of his youth. He had evaded the service of his country, and now he was enveloped in all the horrors of war, with the humiliation of a passive and defenseless being, without any of the soldier's satisfaction of being able to return the blows. He was going to die—he was sure of that—but a shameful death, unknown and inglorious. The ruins of his mansion were going to become his sepulchre. . . . And the certainty of dying there in the darkness, like a rat that sees the openings of his hole being closed up, made this refuge intolerable.

Above him the tornado was still raging. A peal like thunder boomed above his head, and then came the crash of a landslide. Another projectile must have fallen upon the building. He heard shrieks of agony, yells and precipitous steps on the floor above him. Perhaps the shell, in its blind fury, had blown to pieces many of the dying in the salons.

Fearing to remain buried in his retreat, he bounded up the cellar stairs two steps at a time. As he scudded across the first floor, he saw the sky through the shattered roofs. Along the edges were hanging sections of wood, fragments of swinging tile and furniture stopped halfway in its flight. Crossing the hall, he had to clamber over much rubbish. He stumbled over broken and twisted iron, parts of beds rained from the upper rooms into the mountain of debris in which he saw convulsed limbs and heard anguished voices that he could not understand.

He leaped as he ran, feeling the same longing for light and free air as those who rush from the hold to the deck of a shipwreck. While sheltered in the darkness more time had elapsed than he had supposed. The sun was now very high. He saw in the garden more corpses in tragic and grotesque postures. The wounded were doubled over with pain or lying on the ground or propping themselves against the trees in painful silence. Some had opened their knapsacks and drawn out their sanitary kits and were trying to care for their cuts. The infantry was now firing incessantly. The number of riflemen had increased. New bands of soldiers were entering the park—some with a sergeant at their head, others followed by an officer carrying a revolver at his breast as though guiding his men with it. This must be the infantry expelled from their position near the river which had come to reinforce the second line of defense. The mitrailleuses were adding their tac-tac to the cracks of the fusileers.

The hum of the invisible swarms was buzzing incessantly. Thousands of sticky horse-flies were droning around Desnoyers without his even seeing them. The bark of the trees was being stripped by unseen hands; the leaves were falling in torrents; the boughs were shaken by opposing forces, the stones on the ground were being crushed by a mysterious foot. All inanimate objects seemed to have acquired a fantastic life. The zinc spoons of the soldiers, the metallic parts of their outfit, the pails of the artillery were all clanking as though in an imperceptible hailstorm. He saw a cannon lying on its side with the wheels broken and turned over among many men who appeared asleep; he saw soldiers who stretched themselves out without a contraction, without a sound, as though overcome by sudden drowsiness. Others were howling and dragging themselves forward in a sitting position.

The old man felt an extreme sensation of heat. The pungent perfume of explosive drugs brought the tears to his eyes and clawed at his throat. At the same time he was chilly and felt his forehead freezing in a glacial sweat.

He had to leave the bridge. Several soldiers were passing bearing the wounded to the edifice in spite of the fact that it was falling in ruins. Suddenly he was sprinkled from head to foot, as if the earth had opened to make way for a waterspout. A shell had fallen into the moat, throwing up an enormous column of water, making the carp sleeping in the mud fly into fragments, breaking a part of the edges and grinding to powder the white balustrades with their great urns of flowers.

He started to run on with the blindness of terror, when he suddenly saw before him the same little round crystal, examining him coolly. It was the Junker, the officer of the monocle. . . . With the end of his revolver, the German pointed to two pails a short distance away, ordering Desnoyers to fill them from the lagoon and give the water to the men overcome by the sun. Although the imperious tone admitted of no reply, Don Marcelo tried, nevertheless, to resist. He received a blow from the revolver on his chest at the same time that the lieutenant slapped him in the face. The old man doubled over, longing to weep, longing to perish; but no tears came, nor did life escape from his body under this affront, as he wished. . . . With the two buckets in his hands, he found himself dipping up water from the canal, carrying it the length of the file, giving it to men who, each in his turn, dropped his gun to gulp the liquid with the avidity of panting beasts.

He was no longer afraid of the shrill shrieks of invisible bodies. His one great longing was to die. He was strongly convinced that he was going to die; his sufferings were too great; there was no longer any place in the world for him.

He had to pass by breaches opened in the wall by the bursting shells. There was no natural object to arrest the eye looking through these gaps. Hedges and groves had been swept away or blotted out by the fire of the artillery. He descried at the foot of the highway near his castle, several of the attacking columns which had crossed the Marne. The advancing forces were coming doggedly on, apparently unmoved by the steady, deadly fire of the Germans. Soon they were rushing forward with leaps and bounds, by companies, shielding themselves behind bits of upland in bends of the road, in order to send forth their blasts of death.

The old man was now fired with a desperate resolution;—since he had to die, let a French ball kill him! And he advanced very erect with his two pails among those men shooting, lying down. Then, with a sudden fear, he stood still hanging his head; a second thought had told him that the bullet which he might receive would be one danger less for the enemy. It would be better for them to kill the Germans . . . and he began to cherish the hope that he might get possession of some weapon from those dying around him, and fall upon that Junker who had struck him.

He was filling his pails for the third time, and murderously contemplating the lieutenant's back when something occurred so absurd and unnatural that it reminded him of the fantastic flash of the cinematograph;—the officer's head suddenly disappeared; two jets of blood spurted from his severed neck and his body collapsed like an empty sack.

At the same time, a cyclone was sweeping the length of the wall, tearing up groves, overturning cannon and carrying away people in a whirlwind as though they were dry leaves. He inferred that Death was now blowing from another direction. Until then, it had come from the front on the river side, battling with the enemy's line ensconced behind the walls. Now, with the swiftness of an atmospheric change, it was blustering from the depths of the park. A skillful manoeuver of the aggressors, the use of a distant road, a chance bend in the German line had enabled the French to collect their cannon in a new position, attacking the occupants of the castle with a flank movement.

It was a lucky thing for Don Marcelo that he had lingered a few moments on the bank of the fosse, sheltered by the bulk of the edifice. The fire of the hidden battery passed the length of the avenue, carrying off the living, destroying for a second time the dead, killing horses, breaking the wheels of vehicles and making the gun carriages fly through the air with the flames of a volcano in whose red and bluish depths black bodies were leaping. He saw hundreds of fallen men; he saw disembowelled horses trampling on their entrails. The death harvest was not being reaped in sheaves; the entire field was being mowed down with a single flash of the sickle. And as though the batteries opposite divined the catastrophe, they redoubled their fire, sending down a torrent of shells. They fell on all sides. Beyond the castle, at the end of the park, craters were opening in the woods, vomiting forth the entire trunks of trees. The projectiles were hurling from their pits the bodies interred the night before.

Those still alive were firing through the gaps in the walls. Then they sprang up with the greatest haste. Some grasped their bayonets, pale, with clamped lips and a mad glare in their eyes; others turned their backs, running toward the exit from the park, regardless of the shouts of their officers and the revolver shots sent after the fugitives.

All this occurred with dizzying rapidity, like a nightmare. On the other side of the wall came a murmur, swelling in volume, like that of the sea. Desnoyers heard shouts, and it seemed to him that some hoarse, discordant voices were singing the Marseillaise. The machine-guns were working with the swift steadiness of sewing machines. The attack was going to be opposed with furious resistance. The Germans, crazed with fury, shot and shot. In one of the breaches appeared a red kepis followed by legs of the same color trying to clamber over the ruins. But this vision was instantly blotted out by the sprinkling from the machine guns, making the invaders fall in great heaps on the other side of the wall. Don Marcelo never knew exactly how the change took place. Suddenly he saw the red trousers within the park. With irresistible bounds they were springing over the wall, slipping through the yawning gaps, and darting out from the depths of the woods by invisible paths. They were little soldiers, husky, panting, perspiring, with torn cloaks; and mingled with them, in the disorder of the charge, African marksmen with devilish eyes and foaming mouths, Zouaves in wide breeches and chasseurs in blue uniforms.

The German officers wanted to die. With upraised swords, after having exhausted the shots in their revolvers, they advanced upon their assailants followed by the soldiers who still obeyed them. There was a scuffle, a wild melee. To the trembling spectator, it seemed as though the world had fallen into profound silence. The yells of the combatants, the thud of colliding bodies, the clang of arms seemed as nothing after the cannon had quieted down. He saw men pierced through the middle by gun points whose reddened ends came out through their kidneys; muskets raining hammer-like blows, adversaries that grappled in hand-to-hand tussles, rolling over and over on the ground, trying to gain the advantage by kicks and bites.

The mustard-colored fronts had entirely disappeared, and he now saw only backs of that color fleeing toward the exit, filtering among the trees, falling midway in their flight when hit by the pursuing balls. Many of the invaders were unable to chase the fugitives because they were occupied in repelling with rude thrusts of their bayonets the bodies falling upon them in agonizing convulsions.

Don Marcelo suddenly found himself in the very thick of these mortal combats, jumping up and down like a child, waving his hands and shouting with all his might. When he came to himself again, he was hugging the grimy head of a young French officer who was looking at him in astonishment. He probably thought him crazy on receiving his kisses, on hearing his incoherent torrent of words. Emotionally exhausted, the worn old man continued to weep after the officer had freed himself with a jerk. . . . He needed to give vent to his feelings after so many days of anguished self-control. Vive la France! . . .

His beloved French were already within the park gates. They were running, bayonets in hand, in pursuit of the last remnants of the German battalion trying to escape toward the village. A group of horsemen passed along the road. They were dragoons coming to complete the rout. But their horses were fagged out; nothing but the fever of victory transmitted from man to beast had sustained their painful pace. One of the equestrians came to a stop near the entrance of the park, the famished horse eagerly devouring the herbage while his rider settled down in the saddle as though asleep. Desnoyers touched him on the hip in order to waken him, but he immediately rolled off on the opposite side. He was dead, with his entrails protruding from his body, but swept on with the others, he had been brought thus far on his steady steed.

Enormous tops of iron and smoke now began falling in the neighborhood. The German artillery was opening a retaliatory fire against its lost positions. The advance continued. There passed toward the North battalions, squadrons and batteries, worn, weary and grimy, covered with dust and mud, but kindled with an ardor that galvanized their flagging energy.

The French cannon began thundering on the village side. Bands of soldiers were exploring the castle and the nearest woods. From the ruined rooms, from the depths of the cellars, from the clumps of shrubbery in the park, from the stables and burned garage, came surging forth men dressed in greenish gray and pointed helmets. They all threw up their arms, extending their open hands:— "Kamarades . . . kamarades, non kaput." With the restlessness of remorse, they were in dread of immediate execution. They had suddenly lost all their haughtiness on finding that they no longer had any official powers and were free from discipline. Some of those who knew a little French, spoke of their wives and children, in order to soften the enemies that were threatening them with their bayonets. A brawny Teuton came up to Desnoyers and clapped him on the back. It was Redbeard. He pressed his heart and then pointed to the owner of the castle. "Franzosen . . . great friend of the Franzosen" . . . and he grinned ingratiatingly at his protector.

Don Marcelo remained at the castle until the following morning, and was astounded to see Georgette and her mother emerge unexpectedly from the depths of the ruined lodge. They were weeping at the sight of the French uniforms.

"It could not go on," sobbed the widow. "God does not die."

After a bad night among the ruins, the owner decided to leave Villeblanche. What was there for him to do now in the destroyed castle? . . . The presence of so many dead was racking his nerves. There were hundreds, there were thousands. The soldiers and the farmers were interring great heaps of them wherever he went, digging burial trenches close to the castle, in all the avenues of the park, in the garden paths, around the outbuildings. Even the depths of the circular lagoon were filled with corpses. How could he ever live again in that tragic community composed mostly of his enemies? . . . Farewell forever, castle of Villeblanche!

He turned his steps toward Paris, planning to get there the best way he could. He came upon corpses everywhere, but they were not all the gray-green uniform. Many of his countrymen had fallen in the gallant offensive. Many would still fall in the last throes of the battle that was going on behind them, agitating the horizon with its incessant uproar. Everywhere red pantaloons were sticking up out of the stubble, hobnailed boots glistening in upright position near the roadside, livid heads, amputated bodies, stray limbs—and, scattered through this funereal medley, red kepis and Oriental caps, helmets with tufts of horse hair, twisted swords, broken bayonets, guns and great mounds of cannon cartridges. Dead horses were strewing the plain with their swollen carcasses. Artillery wagons with their charred wood and bent iron frames revealed the tragic moment of the explosion. Rectangles of overturned earth marked the situation of the enemy's batteries before their retreat. Amidst the broken cannons and trucks were cones of carbonized material, the remains of men and horses burned by the Germans on the night before their withdrawal.

In spite of these barbarian holocausts corpses were every where in infinite numbers. There seemed to be no end to their number; it seemed as though the earth had expelled all the bodies that it had received since the beginning of the world. The sun was impassively flooding the fields of death with its waves of light. In its yellowish glow, the pieces of the bayonets, the metal plates, the fittings of the guns were sparkling like bits of crystal. The damp night, the rain, the rust of time had not yet modified with their corrosive action these relics of combat.

But decomposition had begun to set in. Graveyard odors were all along the road, increasing in intensity as Desnoyers plodded on toward Paris. Every half hour, the evidence of corruption became more pronounced—many of the dead on this side of the river having lain there for three or four days. Bands of crows, at the sound of his footsteps, rose up, lazily flapping their wings, but returning soon to blacken the earth, surfeited but not satisfied, having lost all fear of mankind.

From time to time, the sad pedestrian met living bands of men—platoons of cavalry, gendarmes, Zouaves and chasseurs encamped around the ruined farmsteads, exploring the country in pursuit of German fugitives. Don Marcelo had to explain his business there, showing the passport that Lacour had given him in order to make his trip on the military train. Only in this way, could he continue his journey. These soldiers—many of them slightly wounded—were still stimulated by victory. They were laughing, telling stories, and narrating the great dangers which they had escaped a few days before, always ending with, "We are going to kick them across the frontier!" . . .

Their indignation broke forth afresh as they looked around at the blasted towns—farms and single houses, all burned. Like skeletons of prehistoric beasts, many steel frames twisted by the flames were scattered over the plains. The brick chimneys of the factories were either levelled to the ground or, pierced with the round holes made by shells, were standing up like giant pastoral flutes forced into the earth.

Near the ruined villages, the women were removing the earth and trying to dig burial trenches, but their labor was almost useless because it required an immense force to inter so many dead. "We are all going to die after gaining the victory," mused the old man. "The plague is going to break out among us."

The water of the river must also be contaminated by this contagion; so when his thirst became intolerable he drank, in preference, from a nearby pond. . . . But, alas, on raising his head, he saw some greenish legs on the surface of the shallow water, the boots sunk in the muddy banks. The head of the German was in the depths of the pool.

He had been trudging on for several hours when he stopped before a ruined house which he believed that he recognized. Yes, it was the tavern where he had lunched a few days ago on his way to the castle. He forced his way in among the blackened walls where a persistent swarm of flies came buzzing around him. The smell of decomposing flesh attracted his attention; a leg which looked like a piece of charred cardboard was wedged in the ruins. Looking at it bitterly he seemed to hear again the old woman with her grandchildren clinging to her skirts—"Monsieur, why are the people fleeing? War only concerns the soldiers. We countryfolk have done no wrong to anybody, and we ought not to be afraid."

Half an hour later, on descending a hilly path, the traveller had the most unexpected of encounters. He saw there a taxicab, an automobile from Paris. The chauffeur was walking tranquilly around the vehicle as if it were at the cab stand, and he promptly entered into conversation with this gentleman who appeared to him as downcast and dirty as a tramp, with half of his livid face discolored from a blow. He had brought out here in his machine some Parisians who had wanted to see the battlefield; they were reporters; and he was waiting there to take them back at nightfall.

Don Marcelo buried his right hand in his pocket. Two hundred francs if the man would drive him to Paris. The chauffeur declined with the gravity of a man faithful to his obligations. . . . "Five hundred?" . . . and he showed his fist bulging with gold coins. The man's only response was a twirl of the handle which started the machine to snorting, and away they sped. There was not a battle in the neighborhood of Paris every day in the year! His other clients could just wait.

And settling back into the motor-car, Desnoyers saw the horrors of the battle field flying past at a dizzying speed and disappearing behind him. He was rolling toward human life . . . he was returning to civilization!

As they came into Paris, the nearly empty streets seemed to him to be crowded with people. Never had he seen the city so beautiful. He whirled through the avenue de l'Opera, whizzed past the place de la Concorde, and thought he must be dreaming as he realized the gigantic leap that he had taken within the hour. He compared all that was now around him with the sights on that plain of death but a few miles away. No; no, it was not possible. One of the extremes of this contrast must certainly be false!

The automobile was beginning to slow down; he must be now in the avenue Victor Hugo. . . . He couldn't wake up. Was that really his home? . . .

The majestic concierge, unable to understand his forlorn appearance, greeted him with amazed consternation. "Ah. Monsieur! . . . Where has Monsieur been?"
. . .

"In hell!" muttered Don Marcelo.

His wonderment continued when he found himself actually in his own apartment, going through its various rooms. He was somebody once more. The sight of the fruits of his riches and the enjoyment of home comforts restored his self-respect at the same time that the contrast recalled to his mind the recollection of all the humiliations and outrages that he had suffered. . . . Ah, the scoundrels! . . .

Two mornings later, the door bell rang. A visitor!

There came toward him a soldier—a little soldier of the infantry, timid, with his kepis in his hand, stuttering excuses in Spanish:—"I knew that you were here . . . I come to . . ."

That voice? . . . Dragging him from the dark hallway, Don Marcelo conducted him to the balcony. . . . How handsome he looked! . . . The kepis was red, but darkened with wear; the cloak, too large, was torn and darned; the great shoes had a strong smell of leather. Yet never had his son appeared to him so elegant, so distinguished-looking as now, fitted out in these rough ready-made clothes.

"You! . . . You! . . ."

The father embraced him convulsively, crying like a child, and trembling so that he could no longer stand.

He had always hoped that they would finally understand each other. His blood was coursing through the boy's veins; he was good, with no other defect than a certain obstinacy. He was excusing him now for all the past, blaming himself for a great part of it. He had been too hard.

"You a soldier!" he kept exclaiming over and over. "You defending my country, when it is not yours!" . . .

And he kissed him again, receding a few steps so as to get a better look at him. Decidedly he was more fascinating now in his grotesque uniform, than when he was so celebrated for his skill as a dancer and idolized by the women.

When the delighted father was finally able to control his emotion, his eyes, still filled with tears, glowed with a malignant light. A spasm of hatred furrowed his face.

"Go," he said simply. "You do not know what war is; I have just come from it; I have seen it close by. This is not a war like other wars, with rational enemies; it is a hunt of wild beasts. . . . Shoot without a scruple against them all. . . . Every one that you overcome, rids humanity of a dangerous menace."

He hesitated a few seconds, and then added with tragic calm:

"Perhaps you may encounter familiar faces. Family ties are not always formed to our tastes. Men of your blood are on the other side. If you see any one of them . . . do not hesitate. Shoot! He is your enemy. Kill him! . . . Kill him!"

PART III

CHAPTER I

AFTER THE MARNE

At the end of October, the Desnoyers family returned to Paris. Dona Luisa could no longer live in Biarritz, so far from her husband. In vain la Romantica discoursed on the dangers of a return. The Government was still in Bordeaux, the President of the Republic and the Ministry making only the most hurried apparitions in the Capital. The course of the war might change at any minute; that little affair of the Marne was but a momentary relief. . . . But the good senora, after having read Don Marcelo's letters, opposed an adamantine will to all contrary suggestions. Besides, she was thinking of her son, her Julio, now a soldier. . . . She believed that, by returning to Paris, she might in some ways be more in touch with him than at this seaside resort near the Spanish frontier.

Chichi also wished to return because Rene was now filling the greater part of her thoughts. Absence had shown her that she was really in love with him. Such a long time without seeing her little sugar soldier! . . . So the family abandoned their hotel life and returned to the avenue Victor Hugo.

Since the shock of the first September days, Paris had been gradually changing its aspect. The nearly two million inhabitants who had been living quietly in their homes without letting themselves be drawn into the panic, had accepted the victory with grave serenity. None of them could explain the exact course of the battle; they would learn all about it when it was entirely finished.

One September Sunday, at the hour when the Parisians are accustomed to take advantage of the lovely twilight, they had learned from the newspapers of the great triumph of the Allies and of the great danger which they had so narrowly escaped. The people were delighted, but did not, however, abandon their calm demeanor. Six weeks of war had radically changed the temperament of turbulent and impressionable Paris.

The victory was slowly restoring the Capital to its former aspect. A street that was practically deserted a few weeks before was now filled with transients. The shops were reopening. The neighbors accustomed to the conventional silence of their deserted apartment houses, again heard sounds of returning life in the homes above and below them.

Don Marcelo's satisfaction in welcoming his family home was considerably clouded by the presence of Dona Elena. She was Germany returning to the encounter, the enemy again established within his tents. Would he never be able to free himself from this bondage? . . . She was silent in her brother-in-law's presence because recent events had rather bewildered her. Her countenance was stamped with a wondering expression as though she were gazing at the upsetting of the most elemental physical laws. In reflective silence she was puzzling over the Marne enigma, unable to understand how it was that the Germans had not conquered the ground on which she was treading; and in order to explain this failure, she resorted to the most absurd suppositions.

One especially engrossing matter was increasing her sadness. Her sons. . . . What would become of her sons! Don Marcelo had never told her of his meeting with Captain von Hartrott. He was maintaining absolute silence about his sojourn at Villeblanche. He had no desire to recount his adventures at the battle of the Marne. What was the use of saddening his loved ones with such miseries? . . . He simply told Dona Luisa, who was alarmed about the possible fate of the castle, that they would not be able to go there for many years to come, because the hostilities had rendered it uninhabitable. A covering of zinc sheeting had been substituted for the ancient roof in order to prevent further injury from wind and rain to the wrecked interior. Later on, after peace had been declared, they would think about its renovation. Just now it had too many inhabitants. And all the ladies, including Dona Elena, shuddered in imagining the thousands of buried bodies forming their ghastly circle around the building. This vision made Frau von Hartrott again groan, "Ay, my sons!"

Finally, for humanity's sake, her brother-in-law set her mind at rest regarding the fate of one of them, the Captain von Hartrott. He was in perfect health at the beginning of the battle. He knew that this was so from a friend who had conversed with him . . . and he did not wish to talk further about him.

Dona Luisa was spending a part of each day in the churches, trying to quiet her uneasiness with prayer. These petitions were no longer vague and generous for the fate of millions of unknown men, for the victory of an entire people. With maternal self-centredness they were focussed on one single person—her son, who was a soldier like the others, and perhaps at this very moment was exposed to the greatest danger. The tears that he had cost her! . . . She had implored that he and his father might come to understand each other, and finally just as God was miraculously granting her supplication, Julio had taken himself off to the field of death.

Her entreaties never went alone to the throne of grace. Someone was praying near her, formulating identical requests. The tearful eyes of her sister were raised at the same time as hers to the figure of the crucified Savior. "Lord, save my son!" . . . When uttering these words, Dona Luisa always saw Julio as he looked in a pale photograph which he had sent his father from the trenches—with kepis and military cloak, a gun in his right hand, and his face shadowed by a growing beard. "O Lord have mercy upon us!" . . . and Dona Elena was at the same time contemplating a group of officers with helmets and reseda uniforms reinforced with leather pouches for the revolver, field glasses and maps, with sword-belt of the same material.

Oftentimes when Don Marcelo saw them setting forth together toward Saint Honore d'Eylau, he would wax very indignant.

"They are juggling with God. . . . This is most unreasonable! How could He grant such contrary petitions? . . . Ah, these women!"

And then, with that superstition which danger awakens, he began to fear that his sister-in-law might cause some grave disaster to his son. Divinity, fatigued with so many contradictory prayers was going to turn His back and not listen to any of them. Why did not this fatal woman take herself off? . . .

He felt as exasperated at her presence in his home as he had at the beginning of hostilities. Dona Luisa was still innocently repeating her sister's statements, submitting them to the superior criticism of her husband. In this way, Don Marcelo had learned that the victory of the Marne had never really happened; it was an invention of the allies. The German generals had deemed it prudent to retire through profound strategic foresight, deferring till a little later the conquest of Paris, and the French had done nothing but follow them over the ground which they had left free. That was all. She knew the opinions of military men of neutral countries; she had been talking in Biarritz with some people of unusual intelligence; she knew what the German papers were saying about it. Nobody over there believed that yarn about the Marne. The people did not even know that there had been such a battle.

"Your sister said that?" interrupted Desnoyers, pale with wrath and amazement.

But he could do nothing but keep on longing for the bodily transformation of this enemy planted under his roof. Ay, if she could only be changed into a man! If only the evil genius of her husband could but take her place for a brief half hour! . . .

"But the war still goes on," said Dona Luisa in artless perplexity. "The enemy is still in France. . . . What good did the battle of the Marne do?"

She accepted his explanations with intelligent noddings of the head, seeming to take them all in, and an hour afterwards would be repeating the same doubts.

She, nevertheless, began to evince a mute hostility toward her sister. Until now, she had been tolerating her enthusiasms in favor of her husband's country because she always considered family ties of more importance than the rivalries of nations. Just because Desnoyers happened to be a Frenchman and Karl a German, she was not going to quarrel with Elena. But suddenly this forbearance had vanished. Her son was now in danger. . . . Better that all the von Hartrotts should die than that Julio should receive the most insignificant wound! . . . She began to share the bellicose sentiments of her daughter, recognizing in her an exceptional talent for appraising events, and now desiring all of Chichi's dagger thrusts to be converted into reality.

Fortunately La Romantica took herself off before this antipathy crystallized. She was accustomed to pass the afternoons somewhere outside, and on her return would repeat the news gleaned from friends unknown to the rest of the family.

This made Don Marcelo wax very indignant because of the spies still hidden in Paris. What mysterious world was his sister-in-law frequenting? . . .

Suddenly she announced that she was leaving the following morning; she had obtained a passport to Switzerland, and from there she would go to Germany. It was high time for her to be returning to her own; she was most appreciative of the hospitality shown her by the family. . . . And Desnoyers bade her good-bye with aggressive irony. His regards to von Hartrott; he was hoping to pay him a visit in Berlin as soon as possible.

One morning Dona Luisa, instead of entering the neighboring church as usual, continued on to the rue de la Pompe, pleased at the thought of seeing the studio once more. It seemed to her that in this way she might put herself more closely in touch with her son. This would be a new pleasure, even greater than poring over his photograph or re-reading his last letter.

She was hoping to meet Argensola, the friend of good counsels, for she knew that he was still living in the studio. Twice he had come to see her by the service stairway as in the old days, but she had been out.

As she went up in the elevator, her heart was palpitating with pleasure and distress. It occurred to the good lady that the "foolish virgins" must have had feelings like this when for the first time they fell from the heights of virtue.

The tears came to her eyes when she beheld the room whose furnishings and pictures so vividly recalled the absent. Argensola hastened from the door at the end of the room, agitated, confused, and greeting her with expressions of welcome at the same time that he was putting sundry objects out of sight. A woman's sweater lying on the divan, he covered with a piece of Oriental drapery—a hat trimmed with flowers, he sent flying into a far-away corner. Dona Luisa fancied that she saw a bit of gauzy feminine negligee embroidered in pink, flitting past the window frame. Upon the divan were two big coffee cups and bits of toast evidently left from a double breakfast. These artists! . . . The same as her son! And she was moved to compassion over the bad life of Julio's counsellor.

"My honored Dona Luisa. . . . My DEAR Madame Desnoyers. . . ."

He was speaking in French and at the top of his voice, looking frantically at the door through which the white and rosy garments had flitted. He was trembling at the thought that his hidden companion, not understanding the situation, might in a jealous fit, compromise him by a sudden apparition.

Then he spoke to his unexpected guest about the soldier, exchanging news with her. Dona Luisa repeated almost word for word the paragraphs of his letters so frequently read. Argensola modestly refrained from displaying his; the two friends were accustomed to an epistolary style which would have made the good lady blush.

"A valiant man!" affirmed the Spaniard proudly, looking upon the deeds of his comrade as though they were his own. "A true hero! and I, Madame Desnoyers, know something about what that means. . . . His chiefs know how to appreciate him." . . .

Julio was a sergeant after having been only two months in the campaign. The captain of his company and the other officials of the regiment belonged to the fencing club in which he had had so many triumphs.

"What a career!" he enthused. "He is one of those who in youth reach the highest ranks, like the Generals of the Revolution. . . . And what wonders he has accomplished!"

The budding officer had merely referred in the most casual way to some of exploits, with the indifference of one accustomed to danger and expecting the same attitude from his comrades; but his chum exaggerated them, enlarging upon them as though they were the culminating events of the war. He had carried an order across an infernal fire, after three messengers, trying to accomplish the same feat, had fallen dead. He had been the first to attack many trenches and had saved many of his comrades by means of the blows from his bayonet and hand to hand encounters. Whenever his superior officers needed a reliable man, they invariably said, "Let Sergeant Desnoyers be called!"

He rattled off all this as though he had witnessed it, as if he had just come from the seat of war, making Dona Luisa tremble and pour forth tears of joy mingled with fear over the glories and dangers of her son. That Argensola certainly possessed the gift of affecting his hearers by the realism with which he told his stories!

In gratitude for these eulogies, she felt that she ought to show some interest in his affairs. . . . What had he been doing of late?

"I, Madame, have been where I ought to be. I have not budged from this spot. I have witnessed the siege of Paris."

In vain, his reason protested against the inexactitude of that word, "siege." Under the influence of his readings about the war of 1870, he had classed as a siege all those events which had developed near Paris during the course of the battle of the Marne.

He pointed modestly to a diploma in a gold frame hanging above the piano against a tricolored flag. It was one of the papers sold in the streets, a certificate of residence in the Capital during the week of danger. He had filled in the blanks with his name and description of his person; and at the foot were very conspicuous the signatures of two residents of the rue de la Pompe—a tavern-keeper, and a friend of the concierge. The district Commissary of Police, with stamp and seal, had guaranteed the respectability of these honorable witnesses. Nobody could remain in doubt, after such precautions, as to whether he had or had not witnessed the siege of Paris. He had such incredulous friends! . . .

In order to bring the scene more dramatically before his amiable listener, he recalled the most striking of his impressions for her special benefit. Once, in broad daylight, he had seen a flock of sheep in the boulevard near the Madeleine. Their tread had resounded through the deserted streets like echoes from the city of the dead. He was the only pedestrian on the sidewalks thronged with cats and dogs.

His military recollections excited him like tales of glory.

"I have seen the march of the soldiers from Morocco. . . . I have seen the Zouaves in automobiles!"

The very night that Julio had gone to Bordeaux, he had wandered around till sunrise, traversing half of Paris, from the Lion of Belfort, to the Gare de l'Est. Twenty thousand men, with all their campaign outfit, coming from Morocco, had disembarked at Marseilles and arrived at the Capital, making part of the trip by rail and the rest afoot. They had come to take part in the great battle then beginning. They were troops composed of Europeans and Africans. The vanguard, on entering through the Orleans gate, had swung into rhythmic pace, thus crossing half Paris toward the Gare de l'Est where the trains were waiting for them.

The people of Paris had seen squadrons from Tunis with theatrical uniforms, mounted on horses, nervous and fleet, Moors with yellow turbans, Senegalese with black faces and scarlet caps, colonial artillerymen, and light infantry from Africa. These were professional warriors, soldiers who in times of peace, led a life of continual fighting in the colonies—men with energetic profiles, bronzed faces and the eyes of beasts of prey. They had remained motionless in the streets for hours at a time, until room could be found for them in the military trains. . . . And Argensola had followed this armed, impassive mass of humanity from the boulevards, talking with the officials, and listening to the primitive cries of the African warriors who had never seen Paris, and who passed through it without curiosity, asking where the enemy was.

They had arrived in time to attack von Kluck on the banks of the Ourq, obliging him to fall back or be completely overwhelmed.

A fact which Argensola did not relate to his sympathetic guest was that his nocturnal excursion the entire length of this division of the army had been accompanied by the amiable damsel within, and two other friends—an enthusiastic and generous coterie, distributing flowers and kisses to the swarthy soldiers, and laughing at their consternation and gleaming white teeth.

Another day he had seen the most extraordinary of all the spectacles of the war. All the taxicabs, some two thousand vehicles, conveying battalions of Zouaves, eight men to a motor car, had gone rolling past him at full speed, bristling with guns and red caps. They had presented a most picturesque train in the boulevards, like a kind of interminable wedding procession. And these soldiers got out of the automobiles on the very edge of the battle field, opening fire the instant that they leaped from the steps. Gallieni had launched all the men who knew how to handle a gun against the extreme right of the adversary at the supreme moment when the most insignificant weight might tip the scales in favor of the victory which was hanging in the balance. The clerks and secretaries of the military offices, the orderlies of the government and the civil police, all had marched to give that final push, forming a mass of heterogenous colors.

And one Sunday afternoon when, with his three companions of the "siege" he was strolling with thousands of other Parisians through the Bois de Boulogne, he had learned from the extras that the combat which had developed so near to the city was turning into a great battle, a victory.

"I have seen much, Madame Desnoyers. . . . I can relate great events."

And she agreed with him. Of course Argensola had seen much! . . . And on taking her departure, she offered him all the assistance in her power. He was the friend of her son, and she was used to his petitions. Times had changed; Don Marcelo's generosity now knew no bounds . . . but the Bohemian interrupted her with a lordly gesture; he was living in luxury. Julio had made him his trustee. The draft from America had been honored by the bank as a deposit, and he had the use of the interest in accordance with the regulations of the moratorium. His friend was sending him regularly whatever money was needed for household expenses. Never had he been in such prosperous condition. War had its good side, too . . . but not wishing to break away from old customs, he announced that once more he would mount the service stairs in order to bear away a basket of bottles.

After her sister's departure, Dona Luisa went alone to the churches until Chichi in an outburst of devotional ardor, suddenly surprised her with the announcement:

"Mama, I am going with you!"

The new devotee was no longer agitating the household by her rollicking, boyish joy; she was no longer threatening the enemy with imaginary dagger thrusts. She was pale, and with dark circles under her eyes. Her head was drooping as though weighed down with a set of serious, entirely new thoughts on the other side of her forehead.

Dona Luisa observed her in the church with an almost indignant jealousy. Her headstrong child's eyes were moist, and she was praying as fervently as the mother . . . but it was surely not for her brother. Julio had passed to second place in her remembrance. Another man was now completely filling her thoughts.

The last of the Lacours was no longer a simple soldier, nor was he now in Paris. Upon her return from Biarritz, Chichi had listened anxiously to the reports from her little sugar soldier. Throbbing with eagerness, she wanted to know all about the dangers which he had been experiencing; and the young warrior "in the auxiliary service" told her of his restlessness in the office during the interminable days in which the troops were battling around Paris, hearing afar off the boom of the artillery. His father had wished to take him with him to Bordeaux, but the administrative confusion of the last hour had kept him in the capital.

He had done something more. On the day of the great crisis, when the acting governor had sent out all the available men in automobiles, he had, unasked, seized a gun and occupied a motor with others from his office. He had not seen anything more than smoke, burning houses, and wounded men. Not a single German had passed before his eyes, excepting a band of Uhlan prisoners, but for some hours he had been shooting on the edge of the road . . . and nothing more.

For a while, that was enough for Chichi. She felt very proud to be the betrothed of a hero of the Marne, even though his intervention had lasted but a few hours. In a few days, however, her enthusiasm became rather clouded.

It was becoming annoying to stroll through the streets with Rene, a simple soldier and in the auxiliary service, besides. . . . The women of the town, excited by the recollection of their men fighting at the front, or clad in mourning because of the death of some loved one, would look at them with aggressive insolence. The refinement and elegance of the Republican Prince seemed to irritate them. Several times, she overheard uncomplimentary words hurled against the "embusques."

The fact that her brother who was not French was in the thick of the fighting, made the Lacour situation still more intolerable. She had an "embusque" for a lover. How her friends would laugh at her! . . .

The senator's son soon read her thoughts and began to lose some of his smiling serenity. For three days he did not present himself at the Desnoyers' home, and they all supposed that he was detained by work at the office.

One morning as Chichi was going toward the Bois de Boulogne, escorted by one of the nut-brown maids, she noticed a soldier coming toward her. He was wearing a bright uniform of the new gray-blue, the "horizon blue" just adopted by the French army. The chin strap of his kepi was gilt, and on his sleeve there was a little strip of gold. His smile, his outstretched hands, the confidence with which he advanced toward her made her recognize him. Rene an officer! Her betrothed a sub-lieutenant!

"Yes, of course! I could do nothing else. . . . I had heard enough!"

Without his father's knowledge, and assisted by his friends, he had in a few days, wrought this wonderful transformation. As a graduate of the Ecole Centrale, he held the rank of a sub-lieutenant of the Reserve Artillery, and he had requested to be sent to the front. Good-bye to the auxiliary service! . . . Within two days, he was going to start for the war.

"You have done this!" exclaimed Chichi. "You have done this!"

Although very pale, she gazed fondly at him with her great eyes—eyes that seemed to devour him with admiration.

"Come here, my poor boy. . . . Come here, my sweet little soldier! . . . I owe you something."

And turning her back on the maid, she asked him to come with her round the corner. It was just the same there. The cross street was just as thronged as the avenue. But what did she care for the stare of the curious! Rapturously she flung her arms around his neck, blind and insensible to everything and everybody but him.

"There. . . . There!" And she planted on his face two vehement, sonorous, aggressive kisses.

Then, trembling and shuddering, she suddenly weakened, and fumbling for her handkerchief, broke down in desperate weeping.

CHAPTER II

IN THE STUDIO

Upon opening the studio door one afternoon, Argensola stood motionless with surprise, as though rooted to the ground.

An old gentleman was greeting him with an amiable smile.

"I am the father of Julio."

And he walked into the apartment with the confidence of a man entirely familiar with his surroundings.

By good luck, the artist was alone, and was not obliged to tear frantically from one end of the room to the other, hiding the traces of convivial company; but he was a little slow in regaining his self-control. He had heard so much about Don Marcelo and his bad temper, that he was very uncomfortable at this unexpected appearance in the studio. . . . What could the fearful man want?

His tranquillity was restored after a furtive, appraising glance. His friend's father had aged greatly since the beginning of the war. He no longer had that air of tenacity and ill-humor that had made him unapproachable. His eyes were sparkling with childish glee; his hands were trembling slightly, and his back was bent. Argensola, who had always dodged him in the street and had thrilled with fear when sneaking up the stairway in the avenue home, now felt a sudden confidence. The transformed old man was beaming on him like a comrade, and making excuses to justify his visit.

He had wished to see his son's home. Poor old man! He was drawn thither by the same attraction which leads the lover to lessen his solitude by haunting the places that his beloved has frequented. The letters from Julio were not enough; he needed to see his old abode, to be on familiar terms with the objects which had surrounded him, to breathe the same air, to chat with the young man who was his boon companion.

His fatherly glance now included Argensola. . . . "A very interesting fellow, that Argensola!" And as he thought this, he forgot completely that, without knowing him, he had been accustomed to refer to him as "shameless," just because he was sharing his son's prodigal life.

Desnoyers' glance roamed delightedly around the studio. He knew well these tapestries and furnishings, all the decorations of the former owner. He easily remembered everything that he had ever bought, in spite of the fact that they were so many. His eyes then sought the personal effects, everything that would call the absent occupant to mind; and he pored over the miserably executed paintings, the unfinished dabs which filled all the corners.

Were they all Julio's? . . . Many of the canvases belonged to Argensola, but affected by the old man's emotion, the artist displayed a marvellous generosity. Yes, everything was Julio's handiwork . . . and the father went from canvas to canvas, halting admiringly before the vaguest daubs as though he could almost detect signs of genius in their nebulous confusion.

"You think he has talent, really?" he asked in a tone that implored a favorable reply. "I always thought him very intelligent . . . a little of the diable, perhaps, but character changes with years. . . . Now he is an altogether different man."

And he almost wept at hearing the Spaniard, with his ready, enthusiastic speech, lauding the departed "diable," graphically setting forth the way in which his great genius was going to take the world when his turn should come.

The painter of souls finally worked himself up into feeling as much affected as the father, and began to admire this old Frenchman with a certain remorse, not wishing to remember how he had ranted against him not so very long ago. What injustice! . . .

Don Marcelo clasped his hand like an old comrade. All of his son's friends were his friends. He knew the life that young men lived. . . . If at any time, he should be in any difficulties, if he needed an allowance so as to keep on with his painting—there he was, anxious to help him! He then and there invited him to dine at his home that very night, and if he would care to come every evening, so much the better. He would eat a family dinner, entirely informal. War had brought about a great many changes, but he would always be as welcome to the intimacy of the hearth as though he were in his father's home.

Then he spoke of Spain, in order to place himself on a more congenial footing with the artist. He had never been there but once, and then only for a short time; but after the war, he was going to know it better. His father-in-law was a Spaniard, his wife had Spanish blood, and in his home the language of the family was always Castilian. Ah, Spain, the country with a noble past and illustrious men! . . .

Argensola had a strong suspicion that if he had been a native of any other land, the old gentleman would have praised it in the same way. All this affection was but a reflex of his love for his absent son, but it so pleased the impressionable fellow that he almost embraced Don Marcelo when he took his departure.

After that, his visits to the studio were very frequent. The artist was obliged to recommend his friends to take a good long walk after lunch, abstaining from reappearing in the rue de la Pompe until nightfall. Sometimes, however, Don Marcelo would unexpectedly present himself in the morning, and then the soulful impressionist would have to scurry from place to place, hiding here, concealing there, in order that his workroom should preserve its appearance of virtuous labor.

"Youth . . . youth!" the visitor would murmur with a smile of tolerance.

And he actually had to make an effort to recall the dignity of his years, in order not to ask Argensola to present him to the fair fugitives whose presence he suspected in the interior rooms. Perhaps they had been his boy's friends, too. They represented a part of his past, anyway, and that was enough to make him presume that they had great charms which made them interesting.

These surprises, with their upsetting consequences, finally made the painter rather regret this new friendship; and the invitations to dinner which he was constantly receiving bored him, too. He found the Desnoyers table most excellent, but too tedious—for the father and mother could talk of nothing but their absent son. Chichi scarcely looked at her brother's friend. Her attention was entirely concentrated on the war. The irregularity in the mails was exasperating her so that she began composing protests to the government whenever a few days passed by without bringing any letter from sub-Lieutenant Lacour.

Argensola excused himself on various pretexts from continuing to dine in the avenue Victor Hugo. It pleased him far more to haunt the cheap restaurants with his female flock. His host accepted his negatives with good-natured resignation.

"Not to-day, either?"

And in order to compensate for his guest's non-appearance, he would present himself at the studio earlier than ever on the day following.

It was an exquisite pleasure for the doting father to let the time slip by seated on the divan which still seemed to guard the very hollow made by Julio's body, gazing at the canvases covered with color by his brush, toasting his toes by the beat of a stove which roared so cosily in the profound, conventual silence. It certainly was an agreeable refuge, full of memories in the midst of monotonous Paris so saddened by the war that he could not meet a friend who was not preoccupied with his own troubles.

His former purchasing dissipations had now lost all charm for him. The Hotel Drouot no longer tempted him. At that time, the goods of German residents, seized by the government, were being auctioned off;—a felicitous retaliation for the enforced journey which the fittings of the castle of Villeblanche had taken on the road to Berlin; but the agents told him in vain of the few competitors which he would now meet. He no longer felt attracted by these extraordinary bargains. Why buy anything more? . . . Of what use was such useless stuff? Whenever he thought of the hard life of millions of men in the open field, he felt a longing to lead an ascetic life. He was beginning to hate the ostentatious splendors of his home on the avenue Victor Hugo. He now recalled without a regretful pang, the destruction of the castle. No, he was far better off there . . . and "there" was always the studio of Julio.

Argensola began to form the habit of working in the presence of Don Marcelo. He knew that the resolute soul abominated inactive people, so, under the contagious influence of dominant will-power, he began several new pieces. Desnoyers would follow with interest the motions of his brush and accept all the explanations of the soulful delineator. For himself, he always preferred the old masters, and in his bargains had acquired the work of many a dead artist; but the fact that Julio had thought as his partner did was now enough for the devotee of the antique and made him admit humbly all the Spaniard's superior theories.

The artist's laborious zeal was always of short duration. After a few moments, he always found that he preferred to rest on the divan and converse with his guest.

The first subject, of course, was the absentee. They would repeat fragments of the letters they had received, and would speak of the past with the most discreet allusions. The painter described Julio's life before the war as an existence dedicated completely to art. The father ignored the inexactitude of such words, and gratefully accepted the lie as a proof of friendship. Argensola was such a clever comrade, never, in his loftiest verbal flights, making the slightest reference to Madame Laurier.

The old gentleman was often thinking about her nowadays, for he had seen her in the street giving her arm to her husband, now recovered from his wounds. The illustrious Lacour had informed him with great satisfaction of their reconciliation. The engineer had lost but one eye. Now he was again at the head of his factory requisitioned by the government for the manufacture of shells. He was a Captain, and was wearing two decorations of honor. The senator did not know exactly how this unexpected agreement had come about. He had one day seen them coming home together, looking affectionately at each other, in complete oblivion of the past.

"Who remembers things that happened before the war," said the politic sage. "They and their friends have completely forgotten all about their divorce. Nowadays we are all living a new existence. . . . I believe that the two are happier than ever before."

Desnoyers had had a presentiment of this happiness when he saw them together. And the man of inflexible morality who was, the year before, anathematizing his son's behavior toward Laurier, considering it the most unpardonable of his adventures, now felt a certain indignation in seeing Marguerite devoted to her husband, and talking to him with such affectionate interest. This matrimonial felicity seemed to him like the basest ingratitude. A woman who had had such an influence over the life of Julio! . . . Could she thus easily forget her love? . . .

The two had passed on as though they did not recognize him. Perhaps Captain Laurier did not see very clearly, but she had looked at him frankly and then hastily averted her eyes so as to evade his greeting. . . . The old man felt sad over such indifference, not on his own account, but on his son's. Poor Julio! . . . The unbending parent, in complete mental immorality, found himself lamenting this indifference as something monstrous.

The war was the other topic of conversation during the afternoons passed in the studio. Argensola was not now stuffing his pockets with printed sheets as at the beginning of hostilities. A serene and resigned calm had succeeded the excitement of those first moments when the people were daily looking for miraculous interventions. All the periodicals were saying about the same thing. He was content with the official report, and he had learned to wait for that document without impatience, foreseeing that with but few exceptions, it would say the same thing as the day before.

The fever of the first months, with its illusions and optimisms, now appeared to Argensola somewhat chimerical. Those not actually engaged in the war were returning gradually to their habitual occupations. Life had recovered its regular rhythm. "One must live!" said the people, and the struggle for existence filled their thoughts with its immediate urgency. Those whose relatives were in the army, were still thinking of them, but their occupations were so blunting the edge of memory, that they were becoming accustomed to their absence, regarding the unusual as the normal condition. At first, the war made sleep out of the question, food impossible to swallow, and embittered every pleasure with its funereal pall. Now the shops were slowly opening, money was in circulation, and people were able to laugh; they talked of the great calamity, but only at certain hours, as something that was going to be long, very long and would exact great resignation to its inevitable fatalism.

"Humanity accustoms itself easily to trouble," said Argensola, "provided that the trouble lasts long enough. . . . In this lies our strength."

Don Marcelo was not in sympathy with the general resignation. The war was going to be much shorter than they were all imagining. His enthusiasm had settled on a speedy termination;—within the next three months, the next Spring probably; if peace were not declared in the Spring, it surely would be in the Summer.

A new talker took part in these conversations. Desnoyers had become acquainted with the Russian neighbor of whom Argensola had so frequently spoken. Since this odd personage had also known his son, that was enough to make Tchernoff arouse his interest.

In normal times, he would have kept him at a distance. The millionaire was a great believer in law and order. He abominated revolutionists, with the instinctive fear of all the rich who have built up a fortune and remember their humble beginnings. Tchernoff's socialism and nationality brought vividly to his mind a series of feverish images—bombs, daggers, stabbings, deserved expiations on the gallows, and exile to Siberia. No, he was not desirable as a friend. . . .

But now Don Marcelo was experiencing an abrupt reversal of his convictions regarding alien ideas. He had seen so much! . . . The revolting proceedings of the invasion, the unscrupulous methods of the German chiefs, the tranquillity with which their submarines were sinking boats filled with defenseless passengers, the deeds of the aviators who were hurling bombs upon unguarded cities, destroying women and children—all this was causing the events of revolutionary terrorism which, years ago, used to arouse his wrath, to sink into relative unimportance.

"And to think," he said "that we used to be as infuriated as though the world were coming to an end, just because someone threw a bomb at a grandee!"

Those titled victims had had certain reprehensible qualities which had justified their execution. They had died in consequence of acts which they undertook, knowing well what the punishment would be. They had brought retribution on themselves without trying to evade it, rarely taking any precautions. While the terrorists of this war! . . .

With the violence of his imperious character, the old conservative now swung to the opposite extreme.

"The true anarchists are yet on top," he said with an ironical laugh. "Those who terrified us formerly, all put together, were but a few miserable creatures. . . . In a few seconds, these of our day kill more innocent people than those others did in thirty years."

The gentleness of Tchernoff, his original ideas, his incoherencies of thought, bounding from reflection to word without any preparation, finally won Don Marcelo so completely over that he formed the habit of consulting him about all his doubts. His admiration made him, too, overlook the source of certain bottles with which Argensola sometimes treated his neighbor. He was delighted to have Tchernoff consume these souvenirs of the time when he was living at swords' points with his son.

After sampling the wine from the avenue Victor Hugo, the Russian would indulge in a visionary loquacity similar to that of the night when he evoked the fantastic cavalcade of the four horsemen of the Apocalypse.

What his new convert most admired was his facility for making things clear, and fixing them in the imagination. The battle of the Marne with its subsequent combats and the course of both armies were events easily explained. . . . If the French only had not been so fatigued after their triumph of the Marne! . . .

"But human powers," continued Tchernoff, "have their limits, and the French soldier, with all his enthusiasm, is a man like the rest. In the first place, the most rapid of marches from the East to the North, in order to resist the invasion of Belgium; then the combats; then the swift retreat that they might not be surrounded; finally a seven days' battle—and all this in a period of three weeks, no more. . . . In their moment of triumph, the victors lacked the legs to follow up their advantage, and they lacked the cavalry to pursue the fugitives. Their beasts were even more exhausted than the men. When those who were retreating found that they were being spurred on with lessening tenacity, they had stretched themselves, half-dead with fatigue, on the field, excavating the ground and forming a refuge for themselves. The French also flung themselves down, scraping the soil together so as not to lose what they had gained. . . . And in this way began the war of the trenches."

Then each line, with the intention of wrapping itself around that of the enemy, had gone on prolonging itself toward the Northeast, and from these successive stretchings had resulted the double course toward the sea—forming the greatest battle front ever known to history.

When Don Marcelo with optimistic enthusiasm announced the end of the war in the following Spring or Summer—in four months at the outside—the Russian shook his head.

"It will be long . . . very long. It is a new war, the genuine modern warfare. The Germans began hostilities in the old way as though they had observed nothing since 1870—a war of involved movements, of battles in the open field, the same as Moltke might have planned, imitating Napoleon. They were desirous of bringing it to a speedy conclusion, and were sure of triumph. Why employ new methods? . . . But the encounter of the Marne twisted their plans, making them shift from the aggressive to the defensive. They then brought into service all that the war staff had learned in the campaigns of the Japanese and Russians, beginning the war of the trenches, the subterranean struggle which is the logical outcome of the reach and number of shots of the modern armament. The conquest of half a mile of territory to-day stands for more than did the assault of a stone fortress a century ago. Neither side is going to make any headway for a long time. Perhaps they may never make a definite advance. The war is bound to be long and tedious, like the athletic conquests between opponents who are equally matched."

"But it will have to come to an end, sometime," interpolated Desnoyers.

"Undoubtedly, but who knows when? . . . And in what condition will they both be when it is all over?" . . .

He was counting upon a rapid finale when it was least expected, through the exhaustion of one of the contestants, carefully dissimulated until the last moment.

"Germany will be vanquished," he added with firm conviction. "I do not know when nor how, but she will fall logically. She failed in her master-stroke in not entering Paris and overcoming its opposition. All the trumps in her pack of cards were then played. She did not win, but continues playing the game because she holds many cards, and she will prolong it for a long time to come. . . . But what she could not do at first, she will never be able to do."

For Tchernoff, the final defeat did not mean the destruction of Germany nor the annihilation of the German people.

"Excessive patriotism irritates me," he pursued. "Hearing people form plans for the definite extinction of Germany seems to me like listening to the Pan-Germanists of Berlin when they talk of dividing up the continents."

Then he summed up his opinion.

"Imperialism will have to be crushed for the sake of the tranquillity of the world; the great war machine which menaces the peace of nations will have to be suppressed. Since 1870, we have all been living in dread of it. For forty years, the war has been averted, but in all that time, what apprehension!" . . .

What was most irritating Tchernoff was the moral lesson born of this situation which had ended by overwhelming the world—the glorification of power, the sanctification of success, the triumph of materialism, the respect for the accomplished fact, the mockery of the noblest sentiments as though they were merely sonorous and absurd phrases, the reversal of moral values . . . a philosophy of bandits which pretended to be the last word of progress, and was no more than a return to despotism, violence, and the barbarity of the most primitive epochs of history.

While he was longing for the suppression of the representatives of this tendency, he would not, therefore, demand the extermination of the German people.

"This nation has great merits jumbled with bad conditions inherited from a not far-distant, barbarous past. It possesses the genius of organization and work, and is able to lend great service to humanity. . . . But first it is necessary to give it a douche—the douche of downfall. The Germans are mad with pride and their madness threatens the security of the world. When those who have poisoned them with the illusion of universal hegemony have disappeared, when misfortune has freshened their imagination and transformed them into a community of humans, neither superior nor inferior to the rest of mankind, they will become a tolerant people, useful . . . and who knows but they may even prove sympathetic!"

According to Tchernoff, there was not in existence to-day a more dangerous nation. Its political organization was converting it into a warrior horde, educated by kicks and submitted to continual humiliations in order that the willpower which always resists discipline might be completely nullified.

"It is a nation where all receive blows and desire to give them to those lower down. The kick that the Kaiser gives is transmitted from back to back down to the lowest rung of the social ladder. The blows begin in the school and are continued in the barracks, forming part of the education. The apprenticeship of the Prussian Crown Princes has always consisted in receiving fisticuffs and cowhidings from their progenitor, the king. The Kaiser beats his children, the officer his soldiers, the father his wife and children, the schoolmaster his pupils, and when the superior is not able to give blows, he subjects those under him to the torment of moral insult."

On this account, when they abandoned their ordinary avocations, taking up arms in order to fall upon another human group, they did so with implacable ferocity.

"Each one of them," continued the Russian, "carries on his back the marks of kicks, and when his turn comes, he seeks consolation in passing them on to the unhappy creatures whom war puts into his power. This nation of war-lords, as they love to call themselves, aspires to lordship, but outside of the country. Within it, are the ones who least appreciate human dignity and, therefore, long vehemently to spread their dominant will over the face of the earth, passing from lackeys to lords."

Suddenly Don Marcelo stopped going with such frequency to the studio. He was now haunting the home and office of the senator, because this friend had upset his tranquillity. Lacour had been much depressed since the heir to the family glory had broken through the protecting paternal net in order to go to war.

One night, while dining with the Desnoyers family, an idea popped into his head which filled him with delight. "Would you like to see your son?" He needed to see Rene and had begun negotiating for a permit from headquarters which would allow him to visit the front. His son belonged to the same army division as Julio; perhaps their camps were rather far apart, but an automobile makes many revolutions before it reaches the end of its journey.

It was not necessary to say more. Desnoyers instantly felt the most overmastering desire to see his boy, since, for so many months, he had had to content himself with reading his letters and studying the snap shot which one of his comrades had made of his soldier son.

From that time on, he besieged the senator as though he were a political supporter desiring an office. He visited him in the mornings in his home, invited him to dinner every evening, and hunted him down in the salons of the Luxembourg. Before the first word of greeting could be exchanged, his eyes were formulating the same interrogation. . . . "When will you get that permit?"

The great man could only reply by lamenting the indifference of the military department toward the civilian element; it always had been inimical toward parliamentarism.

"Besides, Joffre is showing himself most unapproachable; he does not encourage the curious. . . . To-morrow I will see the President."

A few days later, he arrived at the house in the avenue Victor Hugo, with an expression of radiant satisfaction that filled Don Marcelo with joy.

"It has come?"

"It has come. . . . We start the day after to-morrow."

Desnoyers went the following afternoon to the studio in the rue de la Pompe.

"I am going to-morrow!"

The artist was very eager to accompany him. Would it not be possible for him to go, too, as secretary to the senator? . . . Don Marcelo smiled benevolently. The authorization was only for Lacour and one companion. He was the one who was going to pose as secretary, valet or utility man to his future relative-in-law.

At the end of the afternoon, he left the studio, accompanied to the elevator by the lamentations of Argensola. To think that he could not join that expedition! . . . He believed that he had lost the opportunity to paint his masterpiece.

Just outside of his home, he met Tchernoff. Don Marcelo was in high good humor. The certainty that he was soon going to see his son filled him with boyish good spirits. He almost embraced the Russian in spite of his slovenly aspect, his tragic beard and his enormous hat which made every one turn to look after him.

At the end of the avenue, the Arc de Triomphe stood forth against a sky crimsoned by the sunset. A red cloud was floating around the monument, reflected on its whiteness with purpling palpitations.

Desnoyers recalled the four horsemen, and all that Argensola had told him before presenting him to the Russian.

"Blood!" shouted jubilantly. "All the sky seems to be blood-red. . . . It is the apocalyptic beast who has received his death-wound. Soon we shall see him die."

Tchernoff smiled, too, but his was a melancholy smile.

"No; the beast does not die. It is the eternal companion of man. It hides, spouting blood, forty . . . sixty . . . a hundred years, but eventually it reappears. All that we can hope is that its wound may be long and deep, that it may remain hidden so long that the generation that now remembers it may never see it again."

CHAPTER III

WAR

Don Marcelo was climbing up a mountain covered with woods.

The forest presented a tragic desolation. A silent tempest had installed itself therein, placing everything in violent unnatural positions. Not a single tree still preserved its upright form and abundant foliage as in the days of peace. The groups of pines recalled the columns of ruined temples. Some were still standing erect, but without their crowns, like shafts that might have lost their capitals; others were pierced like the mouthpiece of a flute, or like pillars struck by a thunderbolt. Some had splintery threads hanging around their cuts like used toothpicks.

A sinister force of destruction had been raging among these beeches, spruce and oaks. Great tangles of their cut boughs were cluttering the ground, as though a band of gigantic woodcutters had just passed by. The trunks had been severed a little distance from the ground with a clean and glistening stroke, as though with a single blow of the axe. Around the disinterred roots were quantities of stones mixed with sod, stones that had been sleeping in the recesses of the earth and had been brought to the surface by explosions.

At intervals—gleaming among the trees or blocking the roadway with an importunity which required some zigzagging—was a series of pools, all alike, of regular geometrical circles. To Desnoyers, they seemed like sunken basins for the use of the invisible Titans who had been hewing the forest. Their great depth extended to their very edges. A swimmer might dive into these lagoons without ever touching bottom. Their water was greenish, still water—rain water with a scum of vegetation perforated by the respiratory bubbles of the little organisms coming to life in its vitals.

Bordering the hilly pathway through the pines, were many mounds with crosses of wood—tombs of French soldiers topped with little tricolored flags. Upon these moss-covered graves were the old kepis of the gunners. The ferocious wood-chopper, in destroying this woods, had also blindly demolished many of the ants swarming around the trunks.

Don Marcelo was wearing leggings, a broad hat, and on his shoulders, a fine poncho arranged like a shawl—garments which recalled his far-distant life on the ranch. Behind him came Lacour trying to preserve his senatorial dignity in spite of his gasps and puffs of fatigue. He also was wearing high boots and a soft hat, but he had kept to his solemn frock-coat in order not to abandon entirely his parliamentary uniform. Before them marched two captains as guides.

They were on a mountain occupied by the French artillery, and were climbing to the top where were hidden cannons and cannons, forming a line some miles in length. The German artillery had caused the woodland ruin around the visitors, in their return of the French fire. The circular pools were the hollows dug by the German shells in the limy, non-porous soil which preserved all the runnels of rain.

The visiting party had left their automobile at the foot of the mountain. One of the officers, a former artilleryman, explained this precaution to them. It was necessary to climb this roadway very cautiously. They were within reach of the enemy, and an automobile might attract the attention of their gunners.

"A little fatiguing, this climb," he continued. "Courage, Senator Lacour! . . . We are almost there."

They began to meet artillerymen, many of them not in uniform but wearing the military kepis. They looked like workmen from a metal factory, foundrymen with jackets and pantaloons of corduroy. Their arms were bare, and some had put on wooden shoes in order to get over the mud with greater security. They were former iron laborers, mobilized into the artillery reserves. Their sergeants had been factory overseers, and many of them officials, engineers and proprietors of big workshops.

Suddenly the excursionists stumbled upon the iron inmates of the woods. When these spoke, the earth trembled, the air shuddered, and the native inhabitants of the forest, the crows, rabbits, butterflies and ants, fled in terrified flight, trying to hide themselves from the fearful convulsion which seemed to be bringing the world to an end. Just at present, the bellowing monsters were silent, so that they came upon them unexpectedly. Something was sticking up out of the greenery like a gray beam; at other times, this apparition would emerge from a conglomeration of dry trunks. Around this obstacle was cleared ground occupied by men who lived, slept and worked about this huge manufactory on wheels.

The senator, who had written verse in his youth and composed oratorical poetry when dedicating various monuments in his district, saw in these solitary men on the mountain side, blackened by the sun and smoke, with naked breasts and bare arms, a species of priests dedicated to the service of a fatal divinity that was receiving from their hands offerings of enormous explosive capsules, hurling them forth in thunderclaps.

Hidden under the branches, in order to escape the observation of the enemy's birdmen, the French cannon were scattered among the hills and hollows of the highland range. In this herd of steel, there were enormous pieces with wheels reinforced by metal plates, somewhat like the farming engines which Desnoyers had used on his ranch for plowing. Like smaller beasts, more agile and playful in their incessant yelping, the groups of '75 were mingled with the terrific monsters.

The two captains had received from the general of their division orders to show Senator Lacour minutely the workings of the artillery, and Lacour was accepting their observations with corresponding gravity while his eyes roved from side to side in the hope of recognizing his son. The interesting thing for him was to see Rene . . . but recollecting the official pretext of his journey, he followed submissively from cannon to cannon, listening patiently to all explanations.

The operators next showed him the servants of these pieces, great oval cylinders extracted from subterranean storehouses called shelters. These storage places were deep burrows, oblique wells reinforced with sacks of stones and wood. They served as a refuge to those off duty, and kept the munitions away from the enemy's shell. An artilleryman exhibited two pouches of white cloth, joined together and very full. They looked like a double sausage and were the charge for one of the large cannons. The open packet showed some rose-colored leaves, and the senator greatly admired this dainty paste which looked like an article for the dressing table instead of one of the most terrible explosives of modern warfare.

"I am sure," said Lacour, "that if I had found one of these delicate packets on the street, I should have thought that it had been dropped from some lady's vanity bag, or by some careless clerk from a perfumery shop . . . anything but an explosive! And with this trifle that looks as if it were made for the lips, it is possible to blow up an edifice!" . . .

As they continued their visit of investigation, they came upon a partially destroyed round tower in the highest part of the mountain. This was the most dangerous post. From it, an officer was examining the enemy's line in order to gauge the correctness of the aim of the gunners. While his comrades were under the ground or hidden by the branches, he was fulfilling his mission from this visible point.

A short distance from the tower a subterranean passageway opened before their eyes. They descended through its murky recesses until they found the various rooms excavated in the ground. One side of the mountain cut in points formed its exterior facade. Narrow little windows, cut in the stone, gave light and air to these quarters.

An old commandant in charge of the section came out to meet them. Desnoyers thought that he must be the floorwalker of some big department store in Paris. His manners were so exquisite and his voice so suave that he seemed to be imploring pardon at every word, or addressing a group of ladies, offering them goods of the latest novelty. But this impression only lasted a moment. This soldier with gray hair and near-sighted glasses who, in the midst of war, was retaining his customary manner of a building director receiving his clients, showed on moving his arms, some bandages and surgical dressings within his sleeves, He was wounded in both wrists by the explosion of a shell, but he was, nevertheless, sticking to his post.

"A devil of a honey-tongued, syrupy gentleman!" mused Don Marcelo. "Yet he is undoubtedly an exceptional person!"

By this time, they had entered into the main office, a vast room which received its light through a horizontal window about ten feet wide and only a palm and a half high, reminding one of the open space between the slats of a Venetian blind. Below it was a pine table filled with papers and surrounded by stools. When occupying one of these seats, one's eyes could sweep the entire plain. On the walls were electric apparatus, acoustic tubes and telephones—many telephones.

The Commandant sorted and piled up the papers, offering the stools with drawing-room punctilio.

"Here, Senator Lacour."

Desnoyers, humble attendant, took a seat at his side. The Commandant now appeared to be the manager of a theatre, preparing to exhibit an extraordinary show. He spread upon the table an enormous paper which reproduced all the features of the plain extended before them—roads, towns, fields, heights and valleys. Upon this map was a triangular group of red lines in the form of an open fan; the vertex represented the place where they were, and the broad part of the triangle was the limit of the horizon which they were sweeping with their eyes.

"We are going to fire at that grove," said the artilleryman, pointing to one end of the map. "There it is," he continued, designating a little dark line. "Take your glasses."

But before they could adjust the binoculars, the Commandant placed a new paper on top of the map. It was an enormous and somewhat hazy photograph upon whose plan appeared a fan of red lines like the other one.

"Our aviators," explained the gunner courteously, "have taken this morning some views of the enemy's positions. This is an enlargement from our photographic laboratory. . . . According to this information, there are two German regiments encamped in that wood."

Don Marcelo saw on the print the spot of woods, and within it white lines which represented roads, and groups of little squares which were blocks of houses in a village. He believed he must be in an aeroplane contemplating the earth from a height of three thousand feet. Then he raised the glasses to his eyes, following the direction of one of the red lines, and saw enlarged in the circle of the glass a black bar, somewhat like a heavy line of ink—the grove, the refuge of the foe.

"Whenever you say, Senator Lacour, we will begin," said the Commandant, reaching the topmost notch of his courtesy. "Are you ready?"

Desnoyers smiled slightly. For what was his illustrious friend to make himself ready? What difference could it possibly make to a mere spectator, much interested in the novelty of the show? . . .

There sounded behind them numberless bells, gongs that called and gongs that answered. The acoustic tubes seemed to swell out with the gallop of words. The electric wire filled the silence of the room with the palpitations of its mysterious life. The bland Chief was no longer occupied with his guests. They conjectured that he was behind them, his mouth at the telephone, conversing with various officials some distance off. Yet the urbane and well-spoken hero was not abandoning for one moment his candied courtesy.

"Will you be kind enough to tell me when you are ready to begin?" they heard him saying to a distant officer. "I shall be much pleased to transmit the order."

Don Marcelo felt a slight nervous tremor near one of his legs; it was Lecour, on the qui vive over the approaching novelty. They were going to begin firing; something was going to happen that he had never seen before. The cannons were above their heads; the roughly vaulted roof was going to tremble like the deck of a ship when they shot over it. The room with its acoustic tubes and its vibrations from the telephones was like the bridge of a vessel at the moment of clearing for action. The noise that it was going to make! . . . A few seconds flitted by that to them seemed unusually long . . . and then suddenly a sound like a distant peal of thunder which appeared to come from the clouds. Desnoyers no longer felt the nervous twitter against his knee. The senator seemed surprised; his expression seemed to say, "And is that all?" . . . The heaps of earth above them had deadened the report, so that the discharge of the great machine seemed no more than the blow of a club upon a mattress. Far more impressive was the scream of the projectile sounding at a great height but displacing the air with such violence that its waves reached even to the window.

It went flying . . . flying, its roar lessening. Some time passed before they noticed its effects, and the two friends began to believe that it must have been lost in space. "It will not strike . . . it will not strike," they were thinking. Suddenly there surged up on the horizon, exactly in the spot indicated over the blur of the woods, a tremendous column of smoke, a whirling tower of black vapor followed by a volcanic explosion.

"How dreadful it must be to be there!" said the senator.

He and Desnoyers were experiencing a sensation of animal joy, a selfish hilarity in seeing themselves in such a safe place several yards underground.

"The Germans are going to reply at any moment," said Don Marcelo to his friend.

The senator was of the same opinion. Undoubtedly they would retaliate, carrying on an artillery duel.

All of the French batteries had opened fire. The mountain was thundering, the shell whining, the horizon, still tranquil, was bristling with black, spiral columns. The two realized more and more how snug they were in this retreat, like a box at the theatre.

Someone touched Lacour on the shoulder. It was one of the captains who was conducting them through the front.

"We are going above," he said simply. "You must see close by how our cannons are working. The sight will be well worth the trouble."

Above? . . . The illustrious man was as perplexed, as astonished as though he had suggested an interplanetary trip. Above, when the enemy was going to reply from one minute to another? . . .

The captain explained that sub-Lieutenant Lacour was perhaps awaiting his father. By telephone they had advised his battery stationed a little further on; it would be necessary to go now in order to see him. So they again climbed up to the light through the mouth of the tunnel. The senator then drew himself up, majestically erect.

"They are going to fire at us," said a voice in his interior, "The foe is going to reply."

But he adjusted his coat like a tragic mantle and advanced at a circumspect and solemn pace. If those military men, adversaries of parliamentarism, fancied that they were going to laugh up their sleeve at the timidity of a civilian, he would show them their mistake!

Desnoyers could not but admire the resolution with which the great man made his exit from the shelter, exactly as if he were going to march against the foe.

At a little distance, the atmosphere was rent into tumultuous waves, making their legs tremble, their ears hum, and their necks feel as though they had just been struck. They both thought that the Germans had begun to return the fire, but it was the French who were shooting. A feathery stream of vapor came up out of the woods a dozen yards away, dissolving instantly. One of the largest pieces, hidden in the nearby thicket, had just been discharged. The captains continued their explanations without stopping their journey. It was necessary to pass directly in front of the spitting monster, in spite of the violence of its reports, so as not to venture out into the open woods near the watch tower. They were expecting from one second to another now, the response from their neighbors across the way. The guide accompanying Don Marcelo congratulated him on the fearlessness with which he was enduring the cannonading.

"My friend is well acquainted with it," remarked the senator proudly. "He was in the battle of the Marne."

The two soldiers evidently thought this very strange, considering Desnoyers' advanced age. To what section had he belonged? In what capacity had he served? . . .

"Merely as a victim," was the modest reply.

An officer came running toward them from the tower side, across the cleared space. He waved his kepi several times that they might see him better. Lacour trembled for him. The enemy might descry him; he was simply making a target of himself by cutting across that open space in order to reach them the sooner. . . . And he trembled still more as he came nearer. . . . It was Rene!

His hands returned with some astonishment the strong, muscular grasp. He noticed that the outlines of his son's face were more pronounced, and darkened with the tan of camp life. An air of resolution, of confidence in his own powers, appeared to emanate from his person. Six months of intense life had transformed him. He was the same but broader-chested and more stalwart. The gentle and sweet features of his mother were lost under the virile mask. . . . Lacour recognized with pride that he now resembled himself.

After greetings had been exchanged, Rene paid more attention to Don Marcelo than to his father, because he reminded him of Chichi. He inquired after her, wishing to know all the details of her life, in spite of their ardent and constant correspondence.

The senator, meanwhile, still under the influence of his recent emotion, had adopted a somewhat oratorical air toward his son. He forthwith improvised a fragment of discourse in honor of that soldier of the Republic bearing the glorious name of Lacour, deeming this an opportune time to make known to these professional soldiers the lofty lineage of his family.

"Do your duty, my son. The Lacours inherit warrior traditions. Remember our ancestor, the Deputy of the Convention who covered himself with glory in the defense of Mayence!"

While he was discoursing, they had started forward, doubling a point of the greenwood in order to get behind the cannons.

Here the racket was less violent. The great engines, after each discharge, were letting escape through the rear chambers little clouds of smoke like those from a pipe. The sergeants were dictating numbers, communicated in a low voice by another gunner who had a telephone receiver at his ear. The workmen around the cannon were obeying silently. They would touch a little wheel and the monster would raise its grey snout, moving it from side to side with the intelligent expression and agility of an elephant's trunk. At the foot of the nearest piece, stood the operator, rod in hand, and with impassive face. He must be deaf, yet his facial inertia was stamped with a certain authority. For him, life was no more than a series of shots and detonations. He knew his importance. He was the servant of the tempest, the guardian of the thunderbolt.

"Fire!" shouted the sergeant.

And the thunder broke forth in fury. Everything appeared to be trembling, but the two visitors were by this time so accustomed to the din that the present uproar seemed but a secondary affair.

Lacour was about to take up the thread of his discourse about his glorious forefather in the convention when something interfered.

"They are firing," said the man at the telephone simply.

The two officers repeated to the senator this news from the watch tower. Had he not said that the enemy was going to fire? . . . Obeying a sane instinct of preservation, and pushed at the same time by his son, he found himself in the refuge of the battery. He certainly did not wish to hide himself in this cave, so he remained near the entrance, with a curiosity which got the best of his disquietude.

He felt the approach of the invisible projectile, in spite of the roar of the neighboring cannon. He perceived with rare sensibility its passage through the air, above the other closer and more powerful sounds. It was a squealing howl that was swelling in intensity, that was opening out as it advanced, filling all space. Soon it ceased to be a shriek, becoming a rude roar formed by divers collisions and frictions, like the descent of an electric tram through a hillside road, or the course of a train which passes through a station without stopping.

He saw it approach in the form of a cloud, bulging as though it were going to explode over the battery. Without knowing just how it happened, the senator suddenly found himself in the bottom of the shelter, his hands in cold contact with a heap of steel cylinders lined up like bottles. They were projectiles.

"If a German shell," he thought, "should explode above this burrow . . . what a frightful blowing up!" . . .

But he calmed himself by reflecting on the solidity of the arched vault with its beams and sacks of earth several yards thick. Suddenly he was in absolute darkness. Another had sought refuge in the shelter, obstructing the light with his body; perhaps his friend Desnoyers.

A year passed by while his watch was registering a single second, then a century at the same rate . . . and finally the awaited thunder burst forth, making the refuge vibrate, but with a kind of dull elasticity, as though it were made of rubber. In spite of its thud, the explosion wrought horrible damage. Other minor explosions, playful and whistling, followed behind the first. In his imagination, Lacour saw the cataclysm—a writhing serpent, vomiting sparks and smoke, a species of Wagnerian monster that upon striking the ground was disgorging thousands of fiery little snakes, that were covering the earth with their deadly contortions. . . . The shell must have burst nearby, perhaps in the very square occupied by this battery.

He came out of the shelter, expecting to encounter a sickening display of dismembered bodies, and he saw his son smiling, smoking a cigar and talking with Desnoyers. . . . That was a mere nothing! The gunners were tranquilly finishing the charging of a huge piece. They had raised their eyes for a moment as the enemy's shell went screaming by, and then had continued their work.

"It must have fallen about three hundred yards away," said Rene cheerfully.

The senator, impressionable soul, felt suddenly filled with heroic confidence. It was not worth while to bother about his personal safety when other men— just like him, only differently dressed—were not paying the slightest attention to the danger.

And as the other projectiles soared over his head to lose themselves in the woods with the explosions of a volcano, he remained by his son's side, with no other sign of tension than a slight trembling of the knees. It seemed to him now that it was only the French missiles—because they were on his side—that were hitting the bull's eye. The others must be going up in the air and losing themselves in useless noise. Of just such illusions is valor often compounded! . . . "And is that all?" his eyes seemed to be asking.

He now recalled rather shamefacedly his retreat to the shelter; he was beginning to feel that he could live in the open, the same as Rene.

The German missiles were getting considerably more frequent. They were no longer lost in the wood, and their detonations were sounding nearer and nearer. The two officials exchanged glances. They were responsible for the safety of their distinguished charge.

"Now they are warming up," said one of them.

Rene, as though reading their thoughts, prepared to go. "Good-bye, father!" They were needing him in his battery. The senator tried to resist; he wished to prolong the interview, but found that he was hitting against something hard and inflexible that repelled all his influence. A senator amounted to very little with people accustomed to discipline. "Farewell, my boy! . . . All success to you! . . . Remember who you are!"

The father wept as he embraced his son, lamenting the brevity of the interview, and thinking of the dangers awaiting him.

When Rene had disappeared, the captains again recommended their departure. It was getting late; they ought to reach a certain cantonment before nightfall. So they went down the hill in the shelter of a cut in the mountain, seeing the enemy's shells flying high above them.

In a hollow, they came upon several groups of the famed seventy-fives spread about through the woods, hidden by piles of underbrush, like snapping dogs, howling and sticking up their gray muzzles. The great cannon were roaring only at intervals, while the steel pack of hounds were yelping incessantly without the slightest break in their noisy wrath—like the endless tearing of a piece of cloth. The pieces were many, the volleys dizzying, and the shots uniting in one prolonged shriek, as a series of dots unite to form a single line.

The chiefs, stimulated by the din, were giving their orders in yells, and waving their arms from behind the pieces. The cannon were sliding over the motionless gun carriages, advancing and receding like automatic pistols. Each charge dropped an empty shell, and introduced a fresh one into the smoking chamber.

Behind the battery, the air was racking in furious waves. With every shot, Lacour and his companion received a blow on the breast, the violent contact with an invisible hand, pushing them backward and forward. They had to adjust their breathing to the rhythm of the concussions. During the hundredth part of a second, between the passing of one aerial wave and the advance of the next, their chests felt the agony of vacuum. Desnoyers admired the baying of those gray dogs. He knew well their bite, extending across many kilometres. Now they were fresh and at home in their own kennels.

To Lacour it seemed as though the rows of cannon were chanting a measure, monotonous and fiercely impassioned that must be the martial hymn of the humanity of prehistoric times. This music of dry, deafening, delirious notes was awakening in the two what is sleeping in the depths of every soul— the savagery of a remote ancestry. The air was hot with acrid odors, pungent and brutishly intoxicating. The perfumes from the explosions were penetrating to the brain through the mouth, the eyes and the ears.

They began to be infected with the same ardor as the directors, shouting and swinging their arms in the midst of the thundering. The empty capsules were mounting up in thick layers behind the cannon. Fire! . . . always, fire!

"We must sprinkle them well," yelled the chiefs. "We must give a good soaking to the groves where the Boches are hidden."

So the mouths of '75 rained without interruption, inundating the remote thickets with their shells.

Inflamed by this deadly activity, frenzied by the destructive celerity, dominated by the dizzying sway of the ruby leaves, Lacour and Desnoyers found themselves waving their hats, leaping from one side to another as though they were dancing the sacred dance of death, and shouting with mouths dry from the acrid vapor of the powder. . . . "Hurrah! . . . Hurrah!"

The automobile rode all the afternoon long, stopping only when it met long files of convoys. It traversed uncultivated fields with skeletons of dwellings, and ran through burned towns which were no more than a succession of blackened facades.

"Now it is your turn," said the senator to Desnoyers. "We are going to see your son."

At nightfall, they ran across groups of infantry, soldiers with long beards and blue uniforms discolored by the inclemency of the weather. They were returning from the intrenchments, carrying over the hump of their knapsacks, spades, picks and other implements for removing the ground, that had acquired the importance of arms of combat. They were covered with mud from head to foot. All looked old in full youth. Their joy at returning to the cantonment after a week in the trenches, made them fill the silence of the plain with songs in time to the tramp of their nailed boots. Through the violet twilight drifted the winged strophes of the Marseillaise, or the heroic affirmations of the Chant du Depart.

"They are the soldiers of the Revolution," exclaimed Lacour with enthusiasm. "France has returned to 1792."

The two captains established their charges for the night in a half-ruined town where one of their divisions had its headquarters, and then took their leave. Others would act as their escort the following morning.

The two friends were lodging in the Hotel de la Siren, an old inn with its front gnawed by shell-fire. The proprietor showed them with pride a window broken in the form of a crater. This window had made the old tavern sign—a woman of iron with the tail of a fish—sink into insignificance. As Desnoyers was occupying the room next to the one that had received the mark of the shell, the inn-keeper was anxious to point it out to them before they went to bed.

Everything was broken—walls, floor, roof. The furniture, a pile of splinters in the corner; the flowered wall paper, a fringe of tatters hanging from the walls. Through an enormous hole they could see the stars and feel the chill of the night. The owner stated that this destruction was not the work of the Germans, but was caused by a projectile from one of the seventy-fives when repelling the invaders from the village. And he beamed on the ruin with patriotic pride, repeating:

"There's a sample of French marksmanship for you! How do you like the workings of the seventy-fives? . . . What do you think of that now? . . ."

In spite of the fatigue of the journey, Don Marcelo slept badly, excited by the thought that his son was not far away.

An hour before daybreak, they left the village, in an automobile, guided by another official. On both sides of the road, they saw camps and camps. They left behind the parks of munitions, passed the third line of troops, and then the second. Thousands and thousands of men were bivouacking there in the open, improvising as best they could their habitations. These human ant-hills seemed vaguely to recall, with the variety of uniforms and races, some of the mighty invasions of history; but it was not a nation en marche. The exodus of people takes with it the women and children. Here there were nothing but men, men everywhere.

All kinds of housing ever used by humanity were here utilized, these military assemblages beginning with the cave. Caverns and quarries were serving as barracks. Some low huts recalled the American ranch; others, high and conical, were facsimiles of the gurbi of Africa. Many of the soldiers had come from the colonies; some had been living as business men in the new world, and upon having to provide a house more stable than the canvas tent, had recalled the architecture of the tribes with which they had had dealings. In this conglomerate of combatants, there were also Moors, blacks and Asiatics who were accustomed to live outside the cities and had acquired in the open a physical superiority which made them more masterful than the civilized peoples.

Near the river beds was flapping white clothing hung out to dry. Rows of men with bared breasts were out in the morning freshness, leaning over the streams, washing themselves with noisy ablutions followed by vigorous rubbings. . . . On a bridge was a soldier writing, utilizing a parapet as a table. . . . The cooks were moving around their savory kettles, and a warm exhalation of morning soup was mixed with the resinous perfume of the trees and the smell of the damp earth.

Long, low barracks of wood and zinc served the cavalry and artillery for their animals and stores. In the open air, the soldiers were currying and shoeing the glossy, plump horses which the trench-war was maintaining in placid obesity.

"If they had only been like that at the battle of the Marne!" sighed Desnoyers to his friend.

Now the cavalry was leading an existence of interminable rest. The troopers were fighting on foot, and finding it necessary to exercise their steeds to keep them from getting sick with their full mangers.

There were spread over the fields several aeroplanes, like great, gray dragon flies, poised for the flight. Many of the men were grouped around them. The farmers, transformed into soldiers, were watching with great admiration their comrade charged with the management of these machines. They looked upon him as one of the wizards so venerated and feared in all the countryside.

Don Marcelo was struck by the general transformation in the French uniforms. All were now clad in gray-blue, from head to foot. The trousers of bright scarlet cloth, the red kepis which he had hailed with such joy in the expedition of the Marne, no longer existed. All the men passing along the roads were soldiers. All the vehicles, even the ox-carts, were guided by military men.

Suddenly the automobile stopped before some ruined houses blackened by fire.

"Here we are," announced the official. "Now we shall have to walk a little."

The senator and his friend started along the highway.

"Not that way, no!" the guide turned to say grimly. "That road is bad for the health. We must keep out of the currents of air."

He further explained that the Germans had their cannon and intrenchments at the end of this highroad which sloped suddenly and again appeared as a white ribbon on the horizon line between two rows of trees and burned houses. The pale morning light with its hazy mist was sheltering them from the enemy's fire.

On a sunny day, the arrival of their automobile would have been saluted with a shell. "That is war," he concluded. "One is always near to death without seeing it."

The two recalled the warning of the general with whom they had dined the day before: "Be very careful! The war of the trenches is treacherous."

In the sweep of plains unrolled before them, not a man was visible. It seemed like a country Sunday, when the farmers are in their homes, and the land scene lying in silent meditation. Some shapeless objects could be seen in the fields, like agricultural implements deserted for a day of rest. Perhaps they were broken automobiles, or artillery carriages destroyed by the force of their volleys.

"This way," said the officer who had added four soldiers to the party to carry the various bags and packages which Desnoyers had brought out on the roof of the automobile.

They proceeded in a single file the length of a wall of blackened bricks, down a steep hill. After a few steps the surface of the ground was about to their knees; further on, up to their waists, and thus they disappeared within the earth, seeing above their heads, only a narrow strip of sky. They were now under the open field, having left behind them the mass of ruins that hid the entrance of the road. They were advancing in an absurd way, as though they scorned direct lines—in zig-zags, in curves, in angles. Other pathways, no less complicated, branched off from this ditch which was the central avenue of an immense subterranean cavity. They walked . . . and walked . . . and walked. A quarter of an hour went by, a half, an entire hour. Lacour and his friend thought longingly of the roadways flanked with trees, of their tramp in the open air where they could see the sky and meadows. They were not going twenty steps in the same direction. The official marching ahead was every moment vanishing around a new bend. Those who were coming behind were panting and talking unseen, having to quicken their steps in order not to lose sight of the party. Every now and then they had to halt in order to unite and count the little band, to make sure that no one had been lost in a transverse gallery. The ground was exceedingly slippery, in some places almost liquid mud, white and caustic like the drip from the scaffolding of a house in the course of construction.

The thump of their footsteps, and the friction of their shoulders, brought down chunks of earth and smooth stones from the sides. Little by little they climbed through the main artery of this underground body and the veins connected with it. Again they were near the surface where it required but little effort to see the blue above the earth-works. But here the fields were uncultivated, surrounded with wire fences, yet with the same appearance of Sabbath calm. Knowing by sad experience, what curiosity oftentimes cost, the official would not permit them to linger here. "Keep right ahead! Forward march!"

For an hour and a half the party kept doggedly on until the senior members became greatly bewildered and fatigued by their serpentine meanderings. They could no longer tell whether they were advancing or receding, the sudden steeps and the continual turning bringing on an attack of vertigo.

"Have we much further to go?" asked the senator.

"There!" responded the guide pointing to some heaps of earth above them. "There" was a bell tower surrounded by a few charred houses that could be seen a long ways off—the remains of a hamlet which had been taken and retaken by both sides.

By going in a direct line on the surface they would have compassed this distance in half an hour. To the angles of the underground road, arranged to impede the advance of an enemy, there had been added the obstacles of campaign fortification, tunnels cut with wire lattice work, large hanging cages of wire which, on falling, could block the passage and enable the defenders to open fire across their gratings.

They began to meet soldiers with packs and pails of water who were soon lost in the tortuous cross roads. Some, seated on piles of wood, were smiling as they read a little periodical published in the trenches.

The soldiers stepped aside to make way for the visiting procession, bearded and curious faces peeping out of the alleyways. Afar off sounded a crackling of short snaps as though at the end of the winding lanes were a shooting lodge where a group of sportsmen were killing pigeons.

The morning was still cloudy and cold. In spite of the humid atmosphere, a buzzing like that of a horsefly, hummed several times above the two visitors.

"Bullets!" said their conductor laconically.

Desnoyers meanwhile had lowered his head a little, he knew perfectly well that insectivorous sound. The senator walked on more briskly, temporarily forgetting his weariness.

They came to a halt before a lieutenant-colonel who received them like an engineer exhibiting his workshops, like a naval officer showing off the batteries and turrets of his battleships. He was the Chief of the battalion occupying this section of the trenches. Don Marcelo studied him with special interest, knowing that his son was under his orders.

To the two friends, these subterranean fortifications bore a certain resemblance to the lower parts of a vessel. They passed from trench to trench of the last line, the oldest—dark galleries into which penetrated streaks of light across the loopholes and broad, low windows of the mitrailleuse. The long line of defense formed a tunnel cut by short, open spaces. They had to go stumbling from light to darkness, and from darkness to light with a visual suddenness very fatiguing to the eyes. The ground was higher in the open spaces. There were wooden benches placed against the sides so that the observers could put out the head or examine the landscape by means of the periscope. The enclosed space answered both for batteries and sleeping quarters.

As the enemy had been repelled and more ground had been gained, the combatants who had been living all winter in these first quarters, had tried to make themselves more comfortable. Over the trenches in the open air, they had laid beams from the ruined houses; over the beams, planks, doors and windows, and on top of the wood, layers of sacks of earth. These sacks were covered by a top of fertile soil from which sprouted grass and herbs, giving the roofs of the trenches, an appearance of pastoral placidity. The temporary arches could thus resist the shock of the abuses which went ploughing into the earth without causing any special damage. When an explosion was pounding too noisily and weakening the structure, the troglodytes would swarm out in the night like watchful ants, and skilfully readjust the roof of their primitive dwellings.

Everything appeared clean with that simple and rather clumsy cleanliness exercised by men living far from women and thrown upon their own resources. The galleries were something like the cloisters of a monastery, the corridors of a prison, and the middle sections of a ship. Their floors were a half yard lower than that of the open spaces which joined the trenches together. In order that the officers might avoid so many ups and downs, some planks had been laid, forming a sort of scaffolding from doorway to doorway.

Upon the approach of their Chief, the soldiers formed themselves in line, their heads being on a level with the waist of those passing over the planks. Desnoyers ran his eye hungrily over the file of men. Where could Julio be? . . .

He noticed the individual contour of the different redoubts. They all seemed to have been constructed in about the same way, but their occupants had modified them with their special personal decorations. The exteriors were always cut with loopholes in which there were guns pointed toward the enemy, and windows for the mitrailleuses. The watchers near these openings were looking over the lonely landscape like quartermasters surveying the sea from the bridge. Within were the armories and the sleeping rooms—three rows of berths made with planks like the beds of seamen. The desire for artistic ornamentation which even the simplest souls always feel, had led to the embellishment of the underground dwellings. Each soldier had a private museum made with prints from the papers and colored postcards. Photographs of soubrettes and dancers with their painted mouths smiled from the shiny cardboard, enlivening the chaste aspect of the redoubt.

Don Marcelo was growing more and more impatient at seeing so many hundreds of men, but no Julio. The senator, complying with his imploring glance, spoke a few words to the chief preceding him with an aspect of great deference. The official had at first to think very hard to recall Julio to mind, but he soon remembered the exploits of Sergeant Desnoyers. "An excellent soldier," he said. "He will be sent for immediately, Senator Lacour. . . . He is on duty now with his section in the first line trenches."

The father, in his anxiety to see him, proposed that they betake themselves to that advanced site, but his petition made the Chief and the others smile. Those open trenches within a hundred or fifty yards from the enemy, with no other defence but barbed wire and sacks of earth, were not for the visits of civilians. They were always filled with mud; the visitors would have to crawl around exposed to bullets and under the dropping chunks of earth loosened by the shells. None but the combatants could get around in these outposts.

"It is always dangerous there," said the Chief. "There is always random shooting. . . . Just listen to the firing!"

Desnoyers indeed perceived a distant crackling that he had not noted before, and he felt an added anguish at the thought that his son must be in the thick of it. Realization of the dangers to which he must be daily exposed, now stood forth in high relief. What if he should die in the intervening moments, before he could see him? . . .

Time dragged by with desperate sluggishness for Don Marcelo. It seemed to him that the messenger who had been despatched for him would never arrive. He paid scarcely any attention to the affairs which the Chief was so courteously showing them—the caverns which served the soldiers as toilet rooms and bathrooms of most primitive arrangement, the cave with the sign, "Cafe de la Victoire," another in fanciful lettering, "Theatre." . . . Lacour was taking a lively interest in all this, lauding the French gaiety which laughs and sings in the presence of danger, while his friend continued brooding about Julio. When would he ever see him?

They stopped near one of the embrasures of a machine-gun position stationing themselves at the recommendations of the soldiers, on both sides of the horizontal opening, keeping their bodies well back, but putting their heads far enough forward to look out with one eye. They saw a very deep excavation and the opposite edge of ground. A short distance away were several rows of X's of wood united by barbed wire, forming a compact fence. About three hundred feet further on, was a second wire fence. There reigned a profound silence here, a silence of absolute loneliness as though the world was asleep.

"There are the trenches of the Boches," said the Commandant, in a low tone.

"Where?" asked the senator, making an effort to see.

The Chief pointed to the second wire fence which Lacour and his friend had supposed belonged to the French. It was the German intrenchment line.

"We are only a hundred yards away from them," he continued, "but for some time they have not been attacking from this side."

The visitors were greatly moved at learning that the foe was such a short distance off, hidden in the ground in a mysterious invisibility which made it all the more terrible. What if they should pop out now with their saw-edged bayonets, fire-breathing liquids and asphyxiating bombs to assault this stronghold! . . .

From this window they could observe more clearly the intensity of the firing on the outer line. The shots appeared to be coming nearer. The Commandant brusquely ordered them to leave their observatory, fearing that the fire might become general. The soldiers, with their customary promptitude, without receiving any orders, approached their guns which were in horizontal position, pointing through the loopholes.

Again the visitors walked in single file, going down into cavernous spaces that had been the old wine-cellars of former houses. The officers had taken up their abode in these dens, utilizing all the residue of the ruins. A street door on two wooden horses served as a table; the ceilings and walls were covered with cretonnes from the Paris warehouses; photographs of women and children adorned the side wall between the nickeled glitter of telegraphic and telephonic instruments.

Desnoyers saw above one door an ivory crucifix, yellowed with years, probably with centuries, transmitted from generation to generation, that must have witnessed many agonies of soul. In another den he noticed in a conspicuous place, a horseshoe with seven holes. Religious creeds were spreading their wings very widely in this atmosphere of danger and death, and yet at the same time, the most grotesque superstitions were acquiring new values without any one laughing at them.

Upon leaving one of the cells, in the middle of an open space, the yearning father met his son. He knew that it must be Julio by the Chief's gesture and because the smiling soldier was coming toward him, holding out his hands; but this time his paternal instinct which he had heretofore considered an infallible thing, had given him no warning. How could he recognize Julio in that sergeant whose feet were two cakes of moist earth, whose faded cloak was a mass of tatters covered with mud, even up to the shoulders, smelling of damp wool and leather? . . . After the first embrace, he drew back his head in order to get a good look at him without letting go of him. His olive pallor had turned to a bronze tone. He was growing a beard, a beard black and curly, which reminded Don Marcelo of his father-in-law. The centaur, Madariaga, had certainly come to life in this warrior hardened by camping in the open air. At first, the father grieved over his dirty and tired aspect, but a second glance made him sure that he was now far more handsome and interesting than in his days of society glory.

"What do you need? . . . What do you want?"

His voice was trembling with tenderness. He was speaking to the tanned and robust combatant in the same tone that he was wont to use twenty years ago when, holding the child by the hand, he had halted before the preserve cupboards of Buenos Aires.

"Would you like money? . . ."

He had brought a large sum with him to give to his son, but the soldier gave a shrug of indifference as though he had offered him a plaything. He had never been so rich as at this moment; he had a lot of money in Paris and he didn't know what to do with it—he didn't need anything.

"Send me some cigars . . . for me and my comrades."

He was constantly receiving from his mother great baskets full of choice goodies, tobacco and clothing. But he never kept anything; all was passed on to his fellow-warriors, sons of poor families or alone in the world. His munificence had spread from his intimates to the company, and from that to the entire battalion. Don Marcelo divined his great popularity in the glances and smiles of the soldiers passing near them. He was the generous son of a millionaire, and this popularity seemed to include even him when the news went around that the father of Sergeant Desnoyers had arrived—a potentate who possessed fabulous wealth on the other side of the sea.

"I guessed that you would want cigars," chuckled the old man.

And his gaze sought the bags brought from the automobile through the windings of the underground road.

All of the son's valorous deeds, extolled and magnified by Argensola, now came trooping into his mind. He had the original hero before his very eyes.

"Are you content, satisfied? . . . You do not repent of your decision?"

"Yes, I am content, father . . . very content."

Julio spoke without boasting, modestly. His life was very hard, but just like that of millions of other men. In his section of a few dozens of soldiers there were many superior to him in intelligence, in studiousness, in character; but they were all courageously undergoing the test, experiencing the satisfaction of duty fulfilled. The common danger was helping to develop the noblest virtues of these men. Never, in times of peace, had he known such comradeship. What magnificent sacrifices he had witnessed!

"When all this is over, men will be better . . . more generous. Those who survive will do great things."

Yes, of course, he was content. For the first time in his life he was tasting the delights of knowing that he was a useful being, that he was good for something, that his passing through the world would not be fruitless. He recalled with pity that Desnoyers who had not known how to occupy his empty life, and had filled it with every kind of frivolity. Now he had obligations that were taxing all his powers; he was collaborating in the formation of a future. He was a man at last!

"I am content," he repeated with conviction.

His father believed him, yet he fancied that, in a corner of that frank glance, he detected something sorrowful, a memory of a past which perhaps often forced its way among his present emotions. There flitted through his mind the lovely figure of Madame Laurier. Her charm was, doubtless, still haunting his son. And to think that he could not bring her here! . . . The austere father of the preceding year contemplated himself with astonishment as he caught himself formulating this immoral regret.

They passed a quarter of an hour without loosening hands, looking into each other's eyes. Julio asked after his mother and Chichi. He frequently received letters from them, but that was not enough for his curiosity. He laughed heartily at hearing of Argensola's amplified and abundant life. These interesting bits of news came from a world not much more than sixty miles distant in a direct line . . . but so far, so very far away!

Suddenly the father noticed that his boy was listening with less attention. His senses, sharpened by a life of alarms and ambushed attacks, appeared to be withdrawing itself from the company, attracted by the firing. Those were no longer scattered shots; they had combined into a continual crackling.

The senator, who had left father and son together that they might talk more freely, now reappeared.

"We are dismissed from here, my friend," he announced. "We have no luck in our visits."

Soldiers were no longer passing to and fro. All had hastened to their posts, like the crew of a ship which clears for action. While Julio was taking up the rifle which he had left against the wall, a bit of dust whirled above his father's head and a little hole appeared in the ground.

"Quick, get out of here!" he said pushing Don Marcelo.

Then, in the shelter of a covered trench, came the nervous, very brief farewell. "Good-bye, father," a kiss, and he was gone. He had to return as quickly as possible to the side of his men.

The firing had become general all along the line. The soldiers were shooting serenely, as though fulfilling an ordinary function. It was a combat that took place every day without anybody's knowing exactly who started it—in consequence of the two armies being installed face to face, and such a short distance apart. . . . The Chief of the battalion was also obliged to desert his guests, fearing a counter-attack.

Again the officer charged with their safe conduct put himself at the head of the file, and they began to retrace their steps through the slippery maze. Desnoyers was tramping sullenly on, angry at the intervention of the enemy which had cut short his happiness.

Before his inward gaze fluttered the vision of Julio with his black, curly beard which to him was the greatest novelty of the trip. He heard again his grave voice, that of a man who has taken up life from a new viewpoint.

"I am content, father . . . I am content."

The firing, growing constantly more distant, gave the father great uneasiness. Then he felt an instinctive faith, absurd, very firm. He saw his son beautiful and immortal as a god. He had a conviction that he would come out safe and sound from all dangers. That others should die was but natural, but Julio! . . .

As they got further and further away from the soldier boy, Hope appeared to be singing in his ears; and as an echo of his pleasing musings, the father kept repeating mentally:

"No one will kill him. My heart which never deceives me, tells me so. . . . No one will kill him!"

CHAPTER IV

"NO ONE WILL KILL HIM"

Four months later, Don Marcelo's confidence received a rude shock. Julio was wounded. But at the same time that Lacour bought him this news, lamentably delayed, he tranquilized him with the result of his investigations in the war ministry. Sergeant Desnoyers was now a sub-lieutenant, his wound was almost healed and, thanks to the wire-pulling of the senator, he was coming to pass a fortnight with his family while convalescing.

"An exceptionally brave fellow," concluded the influential man. "I have read what his chiefs say about him. At the head of his platoon, he attacked a German company; he killed the captain with his own hand; he did I don't know how many more brave things besides. . . . They have presented him with the military medal and have made him an officer. . . . A regular hero!"

And the rapidly aging father, weeping with emotion, but with increasing enthusiasm, shook his head and trembled. He repented now of his momentary lack of faith when the first news of his wounded boy reached him. How absurd! . . . No one would kill Julio; his heart told him so.

Soon after, he saw him coming home amid the cries and delighted exclamations of the women. Poor Dona Luisa wept as she embraced him, hanging on his neck with sobs of emotion. Chichi contemplated him with grave reflection, putting half of her mind on the recent arrival while the rest flew far away in search of the other warrior. The dusky, South American maids fought each other for the opening in the curtains, peering through the crack with the gaze of an antelope.

The father admired the little scrap of gold on the sleeve of the gray cloak, with the skirts buttoning behind, examining afterwards the dark blue cap with its low brim, adopted by the French for the war in the trenches. The traditional kepi had disappeared. A suitable visor, like that of the men in the Spanish infantry, now shadowed Julio's face. Don Marcelo noted, too, the short and well-cared-for beard, very different from the one he had seen in the trenches. The boy was coming home, groomed and polished from his recent stay in the hospital.

"Isn't it true that he looks like me?" queried the old man proudly.

Dona Luisa responded with the inconsequence that mothers always show in matters of resemblance.

"He has always been the living image of you!"

Having made sure that he was well and happy, the entire family suddenly felt a certain disquietude. They wished to examine his wound so as to convince themselves that he was completely out of danger.

"Oh, it's nothing at all," protested the sub-lieutenant. "A bullet wound in the shoulder. The doctor feared at first that I might lose my left arm, but it has healed well and it isn't worth while to think any more about it."

Chichi's appraising glance swept Julio from head to foot; taking in all the details of his military elegance. His cloak was worn thin and dirty; the leggings were spatter-dashed with mud; he smelled of leather, sweaty cloth and strong tobacco; but on one wrist he was wearing a watch, and on the other, his identity medal fastened with a gold chain. She had always admired her brother for his natural good taste, so she stowed away all these little details in her memory in order to pass them on to Rene. Then she surprised her mother with a demand for a loan that she might send a little gift to her artilleryman.

Don Marcelo gloated over the fifteen days of satisfaction ahead of him. Sub-lieutenant Desnoyers found it impossible to go out alone, for his father was always pacing up and down the reception hall before the military cap which was shedding modest splendor and glory upon the hat rack. Scarcely had Julio put it on his head before his sire appeared, also with hat and cane, ready to sally forth.

"Will you permit me to accompany you? . . . I will not bother you."

This would be said so humbly, with such an evident desire to have his request granted, that his son had not the heart to refuse him. In order to take a walk with Argensola, he had to scurry down the back stairs, or resort to other schoolboy tricks.

Never had the elder Desnoyers promenaded the streets of Paris with such solid satisfaction as by the side of this muscular youth in his gloriously worn cloak, on whose breast were glistening his two decorations—the cross of war and the military medal. He was a hero, and this hero was his son. He accepted as homage to them both the sympathetic glances of the public in the street cars and subways. The interest with which the women regarded the fine-looking youth tickled him immensely. All the other military men that they met, no matter how many bands and crosses they displayed, appeared to the doting father mere embusques, unworthy of comparison with his Julio. . . . The wounded men who got out of the coaches by the aid of staffs and crutches inspired him with the greatest pity. Poor fellows! . . . They did not bear the charmed life of his son. Nobody could kill him; and when, by chance, he had received a wound, the scars had immediately disappeared without detriment to his handsome person.

Sometimes, especially at night, Desnoyers senior would show an unexpected magnanimity, letting Julio fare forth alone. Since before the war, his son had led a life filled with triumphant love-affairs, what might he not achieve now with the added prestige of a distinguished officer! . . .

Passing through his room on his way to bed, the father imagined the hero in the charming company of some aristocratic lady. None but a feminine celebrity was worthy of him; his paternal pride could accept nothing less. . . . And it never occurred to him that Julio might be with Argensola in a music-hall or in a moving-picture show, enjoying the simple and monotonous diversions of a Paris sobered by war, with the homely tastes of a sub-lieutenant whose amorous conquests were no more than the renewal of some old friendships.

One evening as Don Marcelo was accompanying his son down the Champs Elysees, he started at recognizing a lady approaching from the opposite direction. It was Madame Laurier. . . . Would she recognize Julio? He noted that the youth turned pale and began looking at the other people with feigned interest. She continued straight ahead, erect, unseeing. The old gentleman was almost irritated at such coldness. To pass by his son without feeling his presence instinctively! Ah, these women! . . . He turned his head involuntarily to look after her, but had to avert his inquisitive glance immediately. He had surprised Marguerite motionless behind them, pallid with surprise, and fixing her gaze earnestly on the soldier who was separating himself from her. Don Marcelo read in her eyes admiration, love, all of the past that was suddenly surging up in her memory. Poor woman! . . . He felt for her a paternal affection as though she were the wife of Julio. His friend Lacour had again spoken to him about the Lauriers. He knew that Marguerite was going to become a mother, and the old man, without taking into account the reconciliation nor the passage of time, felt as much moved at the thought of this approaching maternity as though the child were going to be Julio's.

Meanwhile Julio was marching right on, without turning his head, without being conscious of the burning gaze fixed upon him, colorless, but humming a tune to hide his emotion. He always believed that Marguerite had passed near him without recognizing him, since his father did not betray her.

One of Don Marcelo's pet occupations was to make his son tell about the encounter in which he had been hurt. No visitor ever came to see the sub-lieutenant but the father always made the same petition.

"Tell us how you were wounded. . . . Explain how you killed that German captain."

Julio tried to excuse himself with visible annoyance. He was already surfeited with his own history. To please his father, he had related the facts to the senator, to Argensola and to Tchernoff in his studio, and to other family friends. . . . He simply could not do it again.

So the father began the narration on his own account, giving the relief and details of the deed as though seen with his own eyes. . . .

He had to take possession of the ruins of a sugar refinery in front of the trench. The Germans had been expelled by the French cannon. A reconnoitring survey under the charge of a trusty man was then necessary. And the heads, as usual, had selected Sergeant Desnoyers.

At daybreak, the platoon had advanced stealthily without encountering any difficulty. The soldiers scattered among the ruins. Julio then went on alone, examining the positions of the enemy; on turning around a corner of the wall, he had the most unexpected of encounters. A German captain was standing in front of him. They had almost bumped into each other. They looked into each other's eyes with more suspense than hate, yet at the same time, they were trying instinctively to kill each other, each one trying to get the advantage by his swiftness. The captain had dropped the map that he was carrying. His right hand sought his revolver, trying to draw it from its case without once taking his eyes off his enemy. Then he had to give this up as useless—it was too late. With his eyes distended by the proximity of death, he kept his gaze fixed upon the Frenchman who had raised his gun to his face. A shot, from a barrel almost touching him . . . and the German fell dead.

Not till then did the victor notice the captain's orderly who was but a few steps behind. He shot Desnoyers, wounding him in the shoulder. The French hurried to the spot, killing the corporal. Then there was a sharp cross-fire with the enemy's company which had halted a little ways off while their commander was exploring the ground. Julio, in spite of his wound, continued at the head of his section, defending the factory against superior forces until supports arrived, and the land remained definitely in the power of the French.

"Wasn't that about the way of it?" Don Marcelo would always wind up.

The son assented, desirous that his annoyance with the persistent story should come to an end as soon as possible. Yes, that was the way of it. But what the father didn't know, what Julio would never tell, was the discovery that he had made after killing the captain.

The two men, during the interminable second in which they had confronted each other, had showed in their eyes something more than the surprise of an encounter, and the wish to overcome the other. Desnoyers knew that man. The captain knew him, too. He guessed it from his expression. . . . But self-preservation was more insistent than recollection and prevented them both from co-ordinating their thoughts.

Desnoyers had fired with the certainty that he was killing someone that he knew. Afterwards, while directing the defense of the position and guarding against the approach of reinforcements, he had a suspicion that the enemy whose corpse was lying a few feet away might possibly be a member of the von Hartrott family. No, he looked much older than his cousins, yet younger than his Uncle Karl who at his age, would be no mere captain of infantry.

When, weakened by the loss of blood, they were about to carry him to the trenches, the sergeant expressed a wish to see again the body of his victim. His doubt continued before the face blanched by death. The wide-open eyes still seemed to retain their startled expression. The man had undoubtedly recognized him. His face was familiar. Who was he? . . . Suddenly in his mind's eye, Julio saw the heaving ocean, a great steamer, a tall, blonde woman looking at him with half-closed eyes of invitation, a corpulent, moustached man making speeches in the style of the Kaiser. "Rest in peace, Captain Erckmann!" . . . Thus culminated in a corner of France the discussions started at table in mid-ocean.

He excused himself mentally as though he were in the presence of the sweet Bertha. He had had to kill, in order not to be killed. Such is war. He tried to console himself by thinking that Erckmann, perhaps, had failed to identify him, without realizing that his slayer was the shipmate of the summer. . . . And he kept carefully hidden in the depths of his memory this encounter arranged by Fate. He did not even tell Argensola who knew of the incidents of the trans-atlantic passage.

When he least expected it, Don Marcelo found himself at the end of that delightful and proud existence which his son's presence had brought him. The fortnight had flown by so swiftly! The sub-lieutenant had returned to his post, and all the family, after this period of reality, had had to fall back on the fond illusions of hope, watching again for the arrival of his letters, making conjectures about the silence of the absent one, sending him packet after packet of everything that the market was offering for the soldiery—for the most part, useless and absurd things.

The mother became very despondent. Julio's visit home but made her feel his absence with greater intensity. Seeing him, hearing those tales of death that her husband was so fond of repeating, made her realize all the more clearly the dangers constantly surrounding her son. Fatality appeared to be warning her with funereal presentiments.

"They are going to kill him," she kept saying to Desnoyers. "That wound was a forewarning from heaven."

When passing through the streets, she trembled with emotion at sight of the invalid soldiers. The convalescents of energetic appearance, filled her with the greatest pity. They made her think of a certain trip with her husband to San Sebastian where a bull fight had made her cry out with indignation and compassion, pitying the fate of the poor, gored horses. With entrails hanging, they were taken to the corrals, and submitted to a hurried adjustment in order that they might return to the arena stimulated by a false energy. Again and again they were reduced to this makeshift cobbling until finally a fatal goring finished them. . . . These recently cured men continually brought to her mind those poor beasts. Some had been wounded three times since the beginning of the war, and were returning surgically patched together and re-galvanized to take another chance in the lottery of Fate, always in the expectation of the supreme blow. . . . Ay, her son!

Desnoyers waxed very indignant over his wife's low spirits, retorting:

"But I tell you that Nobody will kill Julio! . . . He is my son. In my youth I, too, passed through great dangers. They wounded me, too, in the wars in the other world, and nevertheless, here I am at a ripe old age."

Events seemed to reinforce his blind faith. Calamities were raining around the family and saddening his relatives, yet not one grazed the intrepid sub-lieutenant who was persisting in his daring deeds with the heroic nerve of a musketeer.

Dona Luisa received a letter from Germany. Her sister wrote from Berlin, transmitting her letters through the kindness of a South American in Switzerland. This time, the good lady wept for some one besides her son; she wept for Elena and the enemies. In Germany there were mothers, too, and she put the sentiment of maternity above all patriotic differences.

Poor Frau von Hartrott! Her letter written a month before, had contained nothing but death notices and words of despair. Captain Otto was dead. Dead, too, was one of his younger brothers. The fact that the latter had fallen in a territory dominated by their nation, at least gave the mother the sad comfort of being able to weep near his grave. But the Captain was buried on French soil, nobody knew where, and she would never be able to find his remains, mingled with hundreds of others. A third son was wounded in Poland. Her two daughters had lost their promised lovers, and the sight of their silent grief, was intensifying the mother's suffering. Von Hartrott continued presiding over patriotic societies and making plans of expansion after the near victory, but he had aged greatly in the last few months. The "sage" was the only one still holding his own. The family afflictions were aggravating the ferocity of Professor Julius von Hartrott. He was calculating, in a book he was writing, the hundreds of thousands of millions that Germany must exact after her triumph, and the various nations that she would have to annex to the Fatherland.

Dona Luisa imagined that in the avenue Victor Hugo, she could hear the mother's tears falling in her home in Berlin. "You will understand, Luisa, my despair. . . . We were all so happy! May God punish those who have brought such sorrow on the world! The Emperor is innocent. His adversaries are to blame for it all . . ."

Don Marcelo was silent about the letter in his wife's presence. He pitied Elena for her losses, so he overlooked her political connections. He was touched, too, at Dona Luisa's distress about Otto. She had been his godmother and Desnoyers his godfather. That was so—Don Marcelo had forgotten all about it; and the fact recalled to his mental vision the placid life of the ranch, and the play of the blonde children that he had petted behind their grandfather's back, before Julio was born. For many years, he had lavished great affection on these youngsters, when dismayed at Julio's delayed arrival. He was really affected at thinking of what must be Karl's despair.

But then, as soon as he was alone, a selfish coldness would blot out this compassion. War was war, and the Germans had sought it. France had to defend herself, and the more enemies fell the better. . . . The only soldier who interested him now was Julio. And his faith in the destiny of his son made him feel a brutal joy, a paternal satisfaction almost amounting to ferocity.

"No one will kill HIM! . . . My heart tells me so."

A nearer trouble shook his peace of mind. When he returned to his home one evening, he found Dona Luisa with a terrified aspect holding her hands to her head.

"The daughter, Marcelo . . . our daughter!"

Chichi was stretched out on a sofa in the salon, pale, with an olive tinge, looking fixedly ahead of her as if she could see somebody in the empty air. She was not crying, but a slight palpitation was making her swollen eyes tremble spasmodically.

"I want to see him," she was saying hoarsely. "I must see him!"

The father conjectured that something terrible must have happened to Lacour's son. That was the only thing that could make Chichi show such desperation. His wife was telling him the sad news. Rene was wounded, very seriously wounded. A shell had exploded over his battery, killing many of his comrades. The young officer had been dragged out from a mountain of dead, one hand was gone, he had injuries in the legs, chest and head.

"I've got to see him!" reiterated Chichi.

And Don Marcelo had to concentrate all his efforts in making his daughter give up this dolorous insistence which made her exact an immediate journey to the front, trampling down all obstacles, in order to reach her wounded lover.

The senator finally convinced her of the uselessness of it all. She would simply have to wait; he, the father, had to be patient. He was negotiating for Rene to be transferred to a hospital in Paris.

The great man moved Desnoyers to pity. He was making such heroic efforts to preserve the stoic serenity of ancient days by recalling his glorious ancestors and all the illustrious figures of the Roman Republic. But these oratorical illusions had suddenly fallen flat, and his old friend surprised him weeping more than once. An only child, and he might have to lose him! . . . Chichi's dumb woe made him feel even greater commiseration. Her grief was without tears or faintings. Her sallow face, the feverish brilliancy of her eyes, and the rigidity that made her move like an automaton were the only signs of her emotion. She was living with her thoughts far away, with no knowledge of what was going on around her.

When the patient arrived in Paris, his father and fiancee were transfigured. They were going to see him, and that was enough to make them imagine that he was already recuperated.

Chichi hastened to the hospital with her mother and the senator. Then she went alone and insisted on remaining there, on living at the wounded man's side, waging war on all regulations and clashing with Sisters of Charity, trained nurses, and all who roused in her the hatred of rivalry. Soon realizing that all her violence accomplished nothing, she humiliated herself and became suddenly very submissive, trying with her wiles, to win the women over one by one. Finally, she was permitted to spend the greater part of the day with Rene.

When Desnoyers first saw the wounded artilleryman in bed, he had to make a great effort to keep the tears back. . . . Ay, his son, too, might be brought to this sad pass! . . . The man looked to him like an Egyptian mummy, because of his complete envelopment in tight bandage wrappings. The sharp hulls of the shell had fairly riddled him. There could only be seen a pair of sweet eyes and a blond bit of moustache sticking up between white bands. The poor fellow was trying to smile at Chichi, who was hovering around him with a certain authority as though she were in her own home.

Two months rolled by. Rene was better, almost well. His betrothed had never doubted his recovery from the moment that they permitted her to remain with him.

"No one that I love, ever dies," she asserted with a ring of her father's self-confidence. "As if I would ever permit the Boches to leave me without a husband!"

She had her little sugar soldier back again, but, oh, in what a lamentable state! . . . Never had Don Marcelo realized the de-personalizing horrors of war as when he saw entering his home this convalescent whom he had known months before—elegant and slender, with a delicate and somewhat feminine beauty. His face was now furrowed by a network of scars that had transformed it into a purplish arabesque. Within his body were hidden many such. His left hand had disappeared with a part of the forearm, the empty sleeve hanging over the remainder. The other hand was supported on a cane, a necessary aid in order to be able to move a leg that would never recover its elasticity.

But Chichi was content. She surveyed her dear little soldier with more enthusiasm than ever—a little deformed, perhaps, but very interesting. With her mother, she accompanied the convalescent in his constitutionals through the Bois de Boulogne. When, in crossing a street, automobilists or coachmen failed to stop their vehicles in order to give the invalid the right of way, her eyes shot lightning shafts, as she thundered, "Shameless embusques!" . . . She was now feeling the same fiery resentment as those women of former days who used to insult her Rene when he was well and happy. She trembled with satisfaction and pride when returning the greetings of her friends. Her eloquent eyes seemed to be saying, "Yes, he is my betrothed . . . a hero!" She was constantly arranging the war cross on his blouse of "horizon blue," taking pains to place it as conspicuously as possible. She also spent much time in prolonging the life of his shabby uniform—always the same one, the old one which he was wearing when wounded. A new one would give him the officery look of the soldiers who never left Paris.

As he grew stronger, Rene vainly tried to emancipate himself from her dominant supervision. It was simply useless to try to walk with more celerity or freedom.

"Lean on me!"

And he had to take his fiancee's arm. All her plans for the future were based on the devotion with which she was going to protect her husband, on the solicitude that she was going to dedicate to his crippled condition.

"My poor, dear invalid," she would murmur lovingly. "So ugly and so helpless those blackguards have left you! . . . But luckily you have me, and I adore you! . . . It makes no difference to me that one of your hands is gone. I will care for you; you shall be my little son. You will just see, after we are married, how elegant and stylish I am going to keep you. But don't you dare to look at any of the other women! The very first moment that you do, my precious little invalid, I'll leave you alone in your helplessness!"

Desnoyers and the senator were also concerned about their future, but in a very definite way. They must be married as soon as possible. What was the use of waiting? . . . The war was no longer an obstacle. They would be married as quietly as possible. This was no time for wedding pomp.

So Rene Lacour remained permanently in the house on the avenida Victor Hugo, after the nuptial ceremony witnessed by a dozen people.

Don Marcelo had had dreams of other things for his daughter—a grand wedding to which the daily papers would devote much space, a son-in-law with a brilliant future . . . but ay, this war! Everybody was having his fondest hopes dashed to pieces every few hours.

He took what comfort he could out of the situation. What more did they want? Chichi was happy—with a rollicking and selfish happiness which took no interest in anything but her own love-affairs. The Desnoyers business returns could not be improved upon;—after the first crisis had passed, the necessities of the belligerents had begun utilizing the output of his ranches, and never before had meat brought such high prices. Money was flowing in with greater volume than formerly, while the expenses were diminishing. . . . Julio was in daily danger of death, but the old ranchman was buoyed up by his conviction that his son led a charmed life—no harm could touch him. His chief preoccupation, therefore, was to keep himself tranquil, avoiding all emotional storms. He had been reading with considerable alarm of the frequency with which well-known persons, politicians, artists and writers, were dying in Paris. War was not doing all its killing at the front; its shocks were falling like arrows over the land, causing the fall of the weak, the crushed and the exhausted who, in normal times, would probably have lived to a far greater age.

"Attention, Marcelo!" he said to himself with grim humor. "Keep cool now! . . . You must avoid Friend Tchernoff's four horsemen, you know!"

He spent an afternoon in the studio going over the war news in the papers. The French had begun an offensive in Champagne with great advances and many prisoners.

Desnoyers could not but think of the loss of life that this must represent. Julio's fate, however, gave him no uneasiness, for his son was not in that part of the front. But yesterday he had received a letter from him, dated the week before; they all took about that length of time to reach him. Sub-lieutenant Desnoyers was as blithe and reckless as ever. They were going to promote him again—he was among those proposed for the Legion d'Honneur. These facts intensified Don Marcelo's vision of himself as the father of a general as young as those of the revolution; and as he contemplated the daubs and sketches around him, he marvelled at the extraordinary way in which the war had twisted his son's career.

On his way home, he passed Marguerite Laurier dressed in mourning. The senator had told him a few days before that her brother, the artilleryman, had just been killed at Verdun.

"How many are falling!" he said mournfully to himself. "How hard it will be for his poor mother!"

But he smiled immediately after at the thought of those to be born. Never before had the people been so occupied in accelerating their reproduction. Even Madame Laurier now showed with pride the very visible curves of her approaching maternity, and Desnoyers noted sympathetically the vital volume apparent beneath her long mourning veil. Again he thought of Julio, without taking into account the flight of time. He felt as interested in the little newcomer as though he were in some way related to it, and he promised himself to aid generously the Laurier baby if he ever had the opportunity.

On entering his house, he was met in the hall by Dona Luisa, who told him that Lacour was waiting for him.

"Very good!" he responded gaily. "Let us see what our illustrious father-in-law has to say."

His good wife was uneasy. She had felt alarmed without knowing exactly why at the senator's solemn appearance; with that feminine instinct which perforates all masculine precautions, she surmised some hidden mission. She had noticed, too, that Rene and his father were talking together in a low tone, with repressed emotion.

Moved by an irresistible impulse, she hovered near the closed door, hoping to hear something definite. Her wait was not long.

Suddenly a cry . . . a groan . . . the groan that can come only from a body from which all vitality is escaping.

And Dona Luisa rushed in just in time to support her husband as he was falling to the floor.

The senator was excusing himself confusedly to the walls, the furniture, and turning his back in his agitation on the dismayed Rene, the only one who could have listened to him.

"He did not let me finish. . . . He guessed from the very first word. . . ."

Hearing the outcry, Chichi hastened in in time to see her father slipping from his wife's arms to the sofa, and from there to the floor, with glassy, staring eyes, and foaming at the mouth.

From the luxurious rooms came forth the world-old cry, always the same from the humblest home to the highest and loneliest:—

"Oh, Julio! . . . Oh, my son, my son! . . ."

CHAPTER V

THE BURIAL FIELDS

The automobile was going slowly forward under the colorless sky of a winter morning.

In the distance, the earth's surface seemed trembling with white, fluttering things resembling a band of butterflies poised on the furrows. On one of the fields the swarm was of great size, on others, it was broken into small groups.

As the machine approached these white butterflies, they seemed to be taking on other colors. One wing was turning blue, another flesh-colored. . . . They were little flags, by the hundreds, by the thousands which palpitated night and day, in the mild, sunny, morning breeze, in the damp drip of the dull mornings, in the biting cold of the interminable nights. The rains had washed and re-washed them, stealing away the most of their color. Some of the borders of the restless little strips were mildewed by the dampness while others were scorched by the sun, like insects which have just grazed the flames.

In the midst of the fluttering flags could be seen the black crosses of wood. On these were hanging dark kepis, red caps, and helmets topped with tufts of horsehair, slowly disintegrating and weeping atmospheric tears at every point.

"How many are dead!" sighed Don Marcelo's voice from the automobile.

And Rene, who was seated in front of him, sadly nodded his head. Dona Luisa was looking at the mournful plain while her lips trembled slightly in constant prayer. Chichi turned her great eyes in astonishment from one side to the other. She appeared larger, more capable in spite of the pallor which blanched her olive skin.

The two ladies were dressed in deepest mourning. The father, too, was in mourning, huddled down in the seat in a crushed attitude, his legs carefully covered with the great fur rugs. Rene was wearing his campaign uniform under his storm coat. In spite of his injuries, he had not wished to retire from the army. He had been transferred to a technical office till the termination of the war.

The Desnoyers family were on the way to carry out their long-cherished hope.

Upon recovering consciousness after the fatal news, the father had concentrated all his will power in one petition.

"I must see him. . . . Oh, my son! . . . My son!"

Vain were the senator's efforts to show him the impossibility of such a journey. The fighting was still going on in the zone where Julio had fallen. Later on, perhaps, it might be possible to visit it. "I want to see it!" persisted the broken-hearted old man. It was necessary for him to see his son's grave before dying himself, and Lacour had to requisition all his powers, for four long months formulating requests and overcoming much opposition, in order that Don Marcelo might be permitted to make the trip.

Finally a military automobile came one morning for the entire Desnoyers family. The senator could not accompany them. Rumors of an approaching change in the cabinet were floating about, and he felt obliged to show himself in the senate in case the Republic should again wish to avail itself of his unappreciated services.

They passed the night in a provincial city where there was a military post, and Rene collected considerable information from officers who had witnessed the great combat. With his map before him, he followed the explanations until he thought he could recognize the very plot of ground which Julio's regiment had occupied.

The following morning they renewed their expedition. A soldier who had taken part in the battle acted as their guide, seated beside the chauffeur. From time to time, Rene consulted the map spread out on his knees, and asked questions of the soldier whose regiment had fought very close to that of Desnoyers', but he could not remember exactly the ground which they had gone over so many months before. The landscape had undergone many transformations and had presented a very different appearance when covered with men. Its deserted aspect bewildered him . . . and the motor had to go very slowly, veering to the north of the line of graves, following the central highway, level and white, entering crossroads and winding through ditches muddied with deep pools through which they splashed with great bounds and jar on the springs. At times, they drove across fields from one plot of crosses to another, their pneumatic tires crushing flat from the furrows opened by the plowman.

Tombs . . . tombs on all sides! The white locusts of death were swarming over the entire countryside. There was no corner free from their quivering wings. The recently plowed earth, the yellowing roads, the dark woodland, everything was pulsating in weariless undulation. The soil seemed to be clamoring, and its words were the vibrations of the restless little flags. And the thousands of cries, endlessly repeated across the days and nights, were intoning in rhythmic chant the terrible onslaught which this earth had witnessed and from which it still felt tragic shudderings.

"Dead . . . dead," murmured Chichi, following the rows of crosses incessantly slipping past the sides of the automobile.

"O Lord, for them! . . . for their mothers," moaned Dona Luisa, renewing her prayers.

Here had taken place the fiercest part of the battle—the fight in the old way, man to man outside of the trenches, with bayonets, with guns, with fists, with teeth.

The guide who was beginning to get his bearings was pointing out the various points on the desolate horizon. There were the African sharpshooters; further on, the chasseurs. The very large groups of graves were where the light infantry had charged with their bayonets on the sides of the road.

The automobile came to a stop. Rene climbed out after the soldier in order to examine the inscriptions on a few of the crosses. Perhaps these might have belonged to the regiment they were seeking. Chichi also alighted mechanically with the irresistible desire of aiding her husband.

Each grave contained several men. The number of bodies within could be told by the mouldering kepis or rusting helmets hanging on the arms of the cross; the number of the regiments could still be deciphered between the rows of ants crawling over the caps. The wreaths with which affection had adorned some of the sepulchres were blackened and stripped of their leaves. On some of the crucifixes, the names of the dead were still clear, but others were beginning to fade out and soon would be entirely illegible.

"What a horrible death! . . . What glory!" thought Chichi sadly.

Not even the names of the greater part of these vigorous men cut down in the strength of their youth were going to survive! Nothing would remain but the memory which would from time to time overwhelm some old countrywoman driving her cow along the French highway, murmuring between her sobs. "My little one! . . . I wonder where they buried my little one!" Or, perhaps, it would live in the heart of the village woman clad in mourning who did not know how to solve the problem of existence; or in the minds of the children going to school in black blouses and saying with ferocious energy—"When I grow up I am going to kill the Boches to avenge my father's death!"

And Dona Luisa, motionless in her seat, followed with her eyes Chichi's course among the graves, while returning to her interrupted prayer—"Lord, for the mothers without sons . . . for the little ones without fathers! . . . May thy wrath not be turned against us, and may thy smile shine upon us once more!"

Her husband, shrunken in his seat, was also looking over the funereal fields, but his eyes were fixed most tenaciously on some mounds without wreaths or flags, simple crosses with a little board bearing the briefest inscription. These were the German bodies which seemed to have a page to themselves in the Book of Death. On one side, the innumerable French tombs with inscriptions as small as possible, simple numbers—one, two, three dead. On the other, in each of the spacious, unadorned sepulchres, great quantities of soldiers, with a number of terrifying terseness. Fences of wooden strips, narrow and wide, surrounded these latter ditches filled to the top with bodies. The earth was as bleached as though covered with snow or saltpetre. This was the lime returning to mix with the land. The crosses raised above these huge mounds bore each an inscription stating that it contained Germans, and then a number—200 . . . 300 . . . 400.

Such appalling figures obliged Desnoyers to exert his imagination. It was not easy to evoke with exactitude the vision of three hundred carcasses in helmets, boots and cloaks, in all the revolting aspects of death, piled in rows as though they were bricks, locked forever in the depths of a great trench. . . . And this funereal alignment was repeated at intervals all over the great immensity of the plain!

The mere sight of them filled Don Marcelo with a kind of savage joy, as his mourning fatherhood tasted the fleeting consolation of vengeance. Julio had died, and he was going to die, too, not having strength to survive his bitter woe;

but how many hundreds of the enemy wasting in these awful trenches were also leaving in the world loved beings who would remember them as he was remembering his son! . . .

He imagined them as they must have been before the death call sounded, as he had seen them in the advance around his castle.

Some of them, the most prominent and terrifying, probably still showed on their faces the theatrical cicatrices of their university duels. They were the soldiers who carried books in their knapsacks, and after the fusillade of a lot of country folk, or the sacking and burning of a hamlet, devoted themselves to reading the poets and philosophers by the glare of the blaze which they had kindled. They were bloated with science as with the puffiness of a toad, proud of their pedantic and all-sufficient intellectuality. Sons of sophistry and grandsons of cant, they had considered themselves capable of proving the greatest absurdities by the mental capers to which they had accustomed their acrobatic intellects.

They had employed the favorite method of the thesis, antithesis and synthesis in order to demonstrate that Germany ought to be the Mistress of the World; that Belgium was guilty of her own ruin because she had defended herself; that true happiness consisted in having all humanity dominated by Prussia; that the supreme idea of existence consisted in a clean stable and a full manger; that Liberty and Justice were nothing more than illusions of the romanticism of the French; that every deed accomplished became virtuous from the moment it triumphed, and that Right was simply a derivative of Might. These metaphysical athletes with guns and sabres were accustomed to consider themselves the paladins of a crusade of civilization. They wished the blond type to triumph definitely over the brunette; they wished to enslave the worthless man of the South, consigning him forever to a world regulated by "the salt of the earth," "the aristocracy of humanity." Everything on the page of history that had amounted to anything was German. The ancient Greeks had been of Germanic origin; German, too, the great artists of the Italian Renaissance. The men of the Mediterranean countries, with the inherent badness of their extraction, had falsified history. . . .

"That's the best place for you. . . You are better where you are buried, you pitiless pedants!" thought Desnoyers, recalling his conversations with his friend, the Russian.

What a shame that there were not here, too, all the Herr Professors of the German universities—those wise men so unquestionably skilful in altering the trademarks of intellectual products and changing the terminology of things! Those men with flowing beards and gold-rimmed spectacles, pacific rabbits of the laboratory and the professor's chair that had been preparing the ground for the present war with their sophistries and their unblushing effrontery! Their guilt was far greater than that of the Herr Lieutenant of the tight corset and the gleaming monocle, who in his thirst for strife and slaughter was simply and logically working out the professional charts.

While the German soldier of the lower classes was plundering what he could and drunkenly shooting whatever crossed his path, the warrior student was reading by the camp glow, Hegel and Nietzsche. He was too enlightened to execute with his own hands these acts of "historical justice," but he, with the professors, was rousing all the bad instincts of the Teutonic beast and giving them a varnish of scientific justification.

"Lie there, in your sepulchre, you intellectual scourge!" continued Desnoyers mentally.

The fierce Moors, the negroes of infantile intelligence, the sullen Hindus, appeared to him more deserving of respect than all the ermine-bordered togas parading haughtily and aggressively through the cloisters of the German universities. What peacefulness for the world if their wearers should disappear forever! He preferred the simple and primitive barbarity of the savage to the refined, deliberate and merciless barbarity of the greedy sage;—it did less harm and was not so hypocritical.

For this reason, the only ones in the enemy's ranks who awakened his commiseration were the lowly and unlettered dead interred beneath the sod. They had been peasants, factory hands, business clerks, German gluttons of measureless (intestinal) capacity, who had seen in the war an opportunity for satisfying their appetites, for beating somebody and ordering them about after having passed their lives in their country, obeying and receiving kicks.

The history of their country was nothing more than a series of raids—like the Indian forays, in order to plunder the property of those who lived in the mild Mediterranean climes. The Herr Professors had proved to their countrymen that such sacking incursions were indispensable to the highest civilization, and that the German was marching onward with the enthusiasm of a good father sacrificing himself in order to secure bread for his family.

Hundreds of thousands of letters, written by their relatives with tremulous hands, were following the great Germanic horde across the invaded countries. Desnoyers had overheard the reading of some of these, at nightfall before his ruined castle. These were some of the messages found in the pockets of the imprisoned or dead:—"Don't show any pity for the red pantaloons. Kill WHOMEVER YOU CAN, and show no mercy even to the little ones." . . . "We would thank you for the shoes, but the girl cannot get them on. Those French have such ridiculously small feet!" . . . "Try to get hold of a piano.". . . "I would very much like a good watch." . . . "Our neighbor, the Captain, has sent his wife a necklace of pearls. . . . And you send only such insignificant things!"

The virtuous German had been advancing heroically with the double desire of enlarging his country and of making valuable gifts to his offspring. "Deutschland uber alles!" But their most cherished illusions had fallen into the burial ditch in company with thousands of comrades-at-arms fed on the same dreams.

Desnoyers could imagine the impatience on the other side of the Rhine, the pitiful women who were waiting and waiting. The lists of the dead had, perhaps, overlooked the missing ones; and the letters kept coming and coming to the

German lines, many of them never reaching their destination. "Why don't you answer! Perhaps you are not writing so as to give us a great surprise. Don't forget the necklace! Send us a piano. A carved china cabinet for the dining room would please us greatly. The French have so many beautiful things!" . . .

The bare cross rose stark and motionless above the lime-blanched land. Near it the little flags were fluttering their wings, moving from side to side like a head shaking out a smiling, ironical protest—No! . . . No!

The automobile continued on its painful way. The guide was now pointing to a distant group of graves. That was undoubtedly the place where the regiment had been fighting. So the vehicle left the main road, sinking its wheels in the soft earth, having to make wide detours in order to avoid the mounds scattered about so capriciously by the casualties of the combat.

Almost all of the fields were ploughed. The work of the farmer extended from tomb to tomb, making them more prominent as the morning sun forced its way through the enshrouding mists.

Nature, blind, unfeeling and silent, ignoring individual existence and taking to her bosom with equal indifference, a poor little animal or a million corpses, was beginning to smile under the late winter suns.

The fountains were still crusted with their beards of ice; the earth snapped as the feet weighed down its hidden crystals; the trees, black and sleeping, were still retaining the coat of metallic green in which the winter had clothed them; from the depths of the earth still issued an acute, deadly chill, like that of burned-out planets. . . . But Spring had already girded herself with flowers in her palace in the tropics, and was saddling with green her trusty steed, neighing with impatience. Soon they would race through the fields, driving before them in disordered flight the black goblins of winter, and leaving in their wake green growing things and tender, subtle perfumes. The wayside greenery, robing itself in tiny buds, was already heralding their arrival. The birds were venturing forth from their retreats in order to wing their way among the crows croaking wrathfully above the closed tombs. The landscape was beginning to smile in the sunlight with the artless, deceptive smile of a child who looks candidly around while his pockets are stuffed with stolen goodies.

The husbandmen had ploughed the fields and filled the furrows with seed. Men might go on killing each other as much as they liked; the soil had no concern with their hatreds, and on that account, did not propose to alter its course. As every year, the metal cutter had opened its usual lines, obliterating with its ridges the traces of man and beast, undismayed and with stubborn diligence filling up the tunnels which the bombs had made.

Sometimes the ploughshare had struck against an obstacle underground . . . an unknown, unburied man; but the cultivator had continued on its way without pity. Every now and then, it was stopped by less yielding obstructions, projectiles which had sunk into the ground intact. The rustic had dug up these instruments of death which occasionally had exploded their delayed charge in his hands.

But the man of the soil knows no fear when in search of sustenance, and so was doggedly continuing his rectilinear advance, swerving only before the visible tombs; there the furrows had curved mercifully, making little islands of the mounds surmounted by crosses and flags. The seeds of future bread were preparing to extend their tentacles like devil fish among those who, but a short time before, were animated by such monstrous ambition. Life was about to renew itself once more.

The automobile came to a standstill. The guide was running about among the crosses, stooping over in order to examine their weather-stained inscriptions.

"Here we are!"

He had found above one grave the number of the regiment.

Chichi and her husband promptly dismounted again. Then Dona Luisa, with sad resolution, biting her lips to keep the tears back. Then the three devoted themselves to assisting the father who had thrown off his fur lap-robe. Poor Desnoyers! On touching the ground, he swayed back and forth, moving forward with the greatest effort, lifting his feet with difficulty, and sinking his staff in the hollows.

"Lean on me, my poor dear," said the old wife, offering her arm.

The masterful head of the family could no longer take a single step without their aid.

Then began their slow, painful pilgrimage among the graves.

The guide was still exploring the spot bristling with crosses, spelling out the names, and hesitating before the faded lettering. Rene was doing the same on the other side of the road. Chichi went on alone, the wind whirling her black veil around her, and making the little curls escape from under her mourning hat every time she leaned over to decipher a name. Her daintily shod feet sunk deep into the ruts, and she had to gather her skirts about her in order to move more comfortably—revealing thus at every step evidences of the joy of living, of hidden beauty, of consummated love following her course through this land of death and desolation.

In the distance sounded feebly her father's voice:

"Not yet?"

The two elders were growing impatient, anxious to find their son's resting place as soon as possible.

A half hour thus dragged by without any result—always unfamiliar names, anonymous crosses or the numbers of other regiments. Don Marcelo was no longer able to stand. Their passage across the irregularities of the soft earth had been torment for him. He was beginning to despair. . . . Ay, they would never find Julio's remains! The parents, too, had been scrutinizing the plots nearest them, bending sadly before cross after cross. They stopped before a long, narrow hillock, and read the name. . . . No, he was not there, either; and they continued desperately along the painful path of alternate hopes and disappointments.

It was Chichi who notified them with a cry, "Here. . . . Here it is!" The old folks tried to run, almost falling at every step. All the family were soon grouped around a heap of earth in the vague outline of a bier, and beginning to be covered with herbage. At the head was a cross with letters cut in deep with the point of a knife, the kind deed of some of his comrades-at-arms— "DESNOYERS." . . . Then in military abbreviations, the rank, regiment and company.

A long silence. Dona Luisa had knelt instantly, with her eyes fixed on the cross—those great, bloodshot eyes that could no longer weep. Till then, tears had been constantly in her eyes, but now they deserted her as though overcome by the immensity of a grief incapable of expressing itself in the usual ways.

The father was staring at the rustic grave in dumb amazement. His son was there, there forever! . . . and he would never see him again! He imagined him sleeping unshrouded below, in direct contact with the earth, just as Death had surprised him in his miserable and heroic old uniform. He recalled the exquisite care which the lad had always given his body—the long bath, the massage, the invigorating exercise of boxing and fencing, the cold shower, the elegant and subtle perfume . . . all that he might come to this! . . . that he might be interred just where he had fallen in his tracks, like a wornout beast of burden!

The bereaved father wished to transfer his son immediately from the official burial fields, but he could not do it yet. As soon as possible it should be done, and he would erect for him a mausoleum fit for a king. . . . And what good would that do? He would merely be changing the location of a mass of bones, but his body, his physical semblance—all that had contributed to the charm of his personality would be mixed with the earth. The son of the rich Desnoyers would have become an inseparable part of a poor field in Champagne. Ah, the pity of it all! And for this, had he worked so hard and so long to accumulate his millions? . . .

He could never know how Julio's death had happened. Nobody could tell him his last words. He was ignorant as to whether his end had been instantaneous, overwhelming—his idol going out of the world with his usual gay smile on his lips, or whether he had endured long hours of agony abandoned in the field, writhing like a reptile or passing through phases of hellish torment before collapsing in merciful oblivion. He was also ignorant of just how much was beneath this mound—whether an entire body discreetly touched by the hand of Death, or an assemblage of shapeless remnants from the devastating hurricane of steel! . . . And he would never see him again! And that Julio who had been filling his thoughts would become simply a memory, a name that would live while his parents lived, fading away, little by little, after they had disappeared! . . .

He was startled to hear a moan, a sob. . . . Then he recognized dully that they were his own, that he had been accompanying his reflections with groans of grief.

His wife was still at his feet, kneeling, alone with her heartbreak, fixing her dry eyes on the cross with a gaze of hypnotic tenacity. . . . There was her son near her knees, lying stretched out as she had so often watched him when sleeping in his cradle! . . . The father's sobs were wringing her heart, too, but with an unbearable depression, without his wrathful exasperation. And she would never see him again! . . . Could it be possible! . . .

Chichi's presence interrupted the despairing thoughts of her parents. She had run to the automobile, and was returning with an armful of flowers. She hung a wreath on the cross and placed a great spray of blossoms at the foot. Then she scattered a shower of petals over the entire surface of the grave, sadly, intensely, as though performing a religious rite, accompanying the offering with her outspoken thoughts—"For you who so loved life for its beauties and pleasures! . . . for you who knew so well how to make yourself beloved!" . . . And as her tears fell, her affectionate memories were as full of admiration as of grief. Had she not been his sister, she would have liked to have been his beloved.

And having exhausted the rain of flower-petals, she wandered away so as not to disturb the lamentations of her parents.

Before the uselessness of his bitter plaints, Don Marcelo's former dominant character had come to life, raging against destiny.

He looked at the horizon where so often he had imagined the adversary to be, and clenched his fists in a paroxysm of fury. His disordered mind believed that it saw the Beast, the Nemesis of humanity. And how much longer would the evil be allowed to go unpunished? . . .

There was no justice; the world was ruled by blind chance;—all lies, mere words of consolation in order that mankind might exist unterrified by the hopeless abandon in which it lived!

It appeared to him that from afar was echoing the gallop of the four Apocalyptic horsemen, riding rough-shod over all his fellow-creatures. He saw the strong and brutal giant with the sword of War, the archer with his repulsive smile, shooting his pestilential arrows, the bald-headed miser with the scales of Famine, the hard-riding spectre with the scythe of Death. He recognized them as only divinities, familiar and terrible-which had made their presence felt by mankind. All the rest was a dream. The four horsemen were the reality. . . .

Suddenly, by the mysterious process of telepathy, he seemed to read the thoughts of the one grieving at his feet.

The mother, impelled by her own sorrow, was thinking of that of others. She, too, was looking toward the distant horizon. There she seemed to see a procession of the enemy, grieving in the same way as were her family. She saw Elena with her daughters going in and out among the burial grounds, seeking a loved one, falling on their knees before a cross. Ay, this mournful satisfaction, she could never know completely! It would be forever impossible for her to pass to the opposite side in search of the other grave, for, even after some time had passed by, she could never find it. The beloved body of Otto would have disappeared forever in one of the nameless pits which they had just passed.

"O Lord, why did we ever come to these lands? Why did we not continue living in the land where we were born?" . . .

Desnoyers, too, uniting his thoughts with hers, was seeing again the pampas, the immense green plains of the ranch where he had become acquainted with his wife. Again he could hear the tread of the herds. He recalled Madariaga on tranquil nights proclaiming, under the splendor of the stars, the joys of peace, the sacred brotherhood of these people of most diverse extraction, united by labor, abundance and the lack of political ambition.

And as his thoughts swung back to the lost son he, too, exclaimed with his wife, "Oh, why did we ever come? . . ." He, too, with the solidarity of grief, began to sympathize with those on the other side of the battle front. They were suffering just as he was; they had lost their sons. Human grief is the same everywhere.

But then he revolted against his commiseration. Karl had been an advocate of this war. He was among those who had looked upon war as the perfect state for mankind, who had prepared it with their provocations. It was just that War should devour his sons; he ought not to bewail their loss. . . . But he who had always loved Peace! He who had only one son, only one! . . . and now he was losing him forever! . . .

He was going to die; he was sure that he was going to die. . . . Only a few months of life were left in him. And his pitiful, devoted companion kneeling at his feet, she, too, would soon pass away. She could not long survive the blow which they had just received. There was nothing further for them to do; nobody needed them any longer.

Their daughter was thinking only of herself, of founding a separate home interest—with the hard instinct of independence which separates children from their parents in order that humanity may continue its work of renovation.

Julio was the only one who would have prolonged the family, passing on the name. The Desnoyers had died; his daughter's children would be Lacour. . . . All was ended.

Don Marcelo even felt a certain satisfaction in thinking of his approaching death. More than anything else, he wished to pass out of the world. He no longer had any curiosity as to the end of this war in which he had been so interested. Whatever the end might be, it would be sure to turn out badly. Although the Beast might be mutilated, it would again come forth years afterward, as the eternal curse of mankind. . . . For him the only important thing now was that the war had robbed him of his son. All was gloomy, all was black. The world was going to its ruin. . . . He was going to rest.

Chichi had clambered up on the hillock which contained, perhaps, more than their dead. With furrowed brow, she was contemplating the plain. Graves . . . graves everywhere! The recollection of Julio had already passed to second place in her mind. She could not bring him back, no matter how much she might weep.

This vision of the fields of death made her think all the more of the living. As her eyes roved from side to side, she tried, with her hands, to keep down the whirling of her wind-tossed skirts. Rene was standing at the foot of the knoll, and several times after a sweeping glance at the numberless mounds around them, she looked thoughtfully at him, as though trying to establish a relationship between her husband and those below. And he had exposed his life in combats just as these men had done! . . .

"And you, my poor darling," she continued aloud. "At this very moment you, too, might be lying here under a heap of earth with a wooden cross at your head, just like these poor unfortunates!"

The sub-lieutenant smiled sadly. Yes, it was so.

"Come here; climb up here!" said Chichi impetuously. "I want to give you something!"

As soon as he approached her, she flung her arms around his neck, pressed him against the warm softness of her breast, exhaling a perfume of life and love, and kissed him passionately without a thought of her brother, without seeing her aged parents grieving below them and longing to die. . . . And her skirts, freed by the breeze, molded her figure in the superb sweep of the curves of a Grecian vase.

Printed in the United States
PP3286400002B